The Grey Man
-Vignettes-

JL Curtis

All rights reserved. No part of this publication may be reproduced, distributed or transmitted in any form or by any means, including photocopying, recording, or other electronic or mechanical methods, without the prior written permission of the publisher, except in the case of brief quotations embodied in critical reviews and certain other noncommercial uses permitted by copyright law. For permission requests, contact the author, addressed "Attention: Permissions Coordinator," at the address below:

Oldnfo@gmail.com

Author's Note: This is a work of fiction. Names, characters, places, and incidents are a product of the author's imagination. Locales and public names are sometimes used for atmospheric purposes. Any resemblance to actual people, living or dead, or to businesses, companies, events, institutions, or locales is completely coincidental.

Available from Amazon.com in Kindle format or soft cover book, BN.com in Nook format. Printed by CreateSpace.

The Grey Man/ JL Curtis. -- 1st ed.
ISBN-13: 978-1495411311

ISBN-10: 1495411311

DEDICATION

Dedicated to the Officers, Men and Women of the United States Military, and those who serve in Law Enforcement, Fire and EMS professions.

Greater love hath no man than this, that a man lay down his life for his friends..

—John 15:13 KJV

Contents

Prolog 2

1 Texas— Thirty Years Later 5

2 Another Day at the Office 11

3 Road Trip 21

4 Quantico 30

5 WV Six Months Later 43

6 Night Shoot 54

7 The Competition 65

8 The Party 75

9 The Challenge Coin 81

10 Guess Who 86

11 Visitors 93

12 Fandango 105

13 Practice 117

14 Riding the Range 124

15 On Patrol 128

16 Shots Fired	138
17 The Aftermath	151
18 The Morning After	163
19 Unexpected Twist	172
20 Planes and Trucks	184
21 The Raid	196
22 Now What	214
23 Heads Up	220
24 Lawyer Up	227
25 JAG	237
26 No He Didn't	247
27 Recovery	254
28 On The Range	261
29 Together Again	273
30 Thailand Here We Come	287
31 The Hunt Is On	298
32 The Chase	309
33 Bingo	320

34 Homeward Bound 328

35 The Reception 340

36 Winding Down..350

Epilog 356

ACKNOWLEDGMENTS

Thanks to Dawn, Bob, Joe, Tina, Bill, Jean, Ian, Rita, Kelly 1, Kelly 2, Johnny, Tom 1, Tom 2, Earl, Steph, Rick and Brigid for all your alpha and beta reads.

Special thanks to my editor Cara Lockwood.

Cover art by Tina Garceau

Prolog

Vietnam 1968, Central Highlands, LZ Dragon

Sitting on an landing zone carved out of the jungle about ten kilometers from the Ho Chi Min trail, Staff Sergeant Cronin and ten Montegnard[1] irregulars waited patiently for a resupply so they could continue their spying mission on the trail. Suddenly one of the Yards pointed off to the east, and Cronin dimly saw what could be a helicopter flitting over the jungle.

Shortly thereafter, over the sound of a Huey helicopter climbing to their altitude, the AN/GRC-9 broke squelch, "Smoke."

Cronin pulled a yellow smoke from his web gear, checked it, pulled the pin and threw it into the clearing hacked out of the jungle. He picked up the mike and said, "Yellow."

"Copy yellow, inbound."

The helicopter barely cleared the trees as it flared into a hover and descended into the clearing. As soon as it touched down, the crew chief and gunners started throwing ammo cans and supplies out of both doors as a small Green Beret hopped nimbly down from the helo.

Cronin ran in under the blades. "Dammit, Billy, I said to send a medic!"

Staff Sergeant Moore grabbed Cronin and dragged him out from under the blades, "I'm a medic as a

---

[1] Montegnard is the term for the mountain dwellers in Vietnam, common use was 'Yard. Language spoken is the Degar dialect.

secondary and I needed to talk you without anybody listening," he shouted over the noise of the helicopter.

John leaned in and yelled back, "Did you at least bring another Angry Nine? That POS is on its last legs. And I hope you brought meds. Need 'em bad.

Harrington's daughter pulled through, and I don't want her to relapse..."

The crew finished throwing supplies out and the Huey lifted off immediately. The gunner waved as they rolled to clear the trees and disappeared.

Billy said, "Yeah, two of the damn things. Listen, we've got a problem. The new NVA colonel in charge of this section of the trail is actually doing shit, so you need to move. I've got forty-eight hours on the deck, and then they are picking me back up either here or at X-ray. So let's get humping."

John and Billy ran back into the clearing; John directed the Montagnards to load up. The Yards got the ammo and most of the supplies. John and Billy each picked up a radio , a box of medical supplies, and they hit the trail back to the village. Four hours later they trudged back in, and the village elder welcomed Billy as a shaman. After a couple of hours treating the various ills of the tribe, they finally got a few minutes in the long house in relative privacy.

John said, "The Elder has already decided to move, this place is dead for them and he's been getting nervous about how close the strikes are hitting. I got blown ass over teakettle day before yesterday at the OP, and if I hadn't been behind a boulder, I'd be dead."

Billy asked, "You catch anything? How are you

feeling?"

"Yeah, a little shrapnel in the arm. Other than dysentery, malaria, and shitting through a screen door I'm fine."

In the dimly lit long house, Billy cleaned and bandaged the wound as best he could, and slipped John a packet of meds and iodine tabs for the water. They racked out for a few hours and the next morning more people showed up. Billy treated them while John and the Elder met with the males in the tribe.

The decision was made to move about two hours east and north, which put them two ridges further away from the trail, and on fresh land. Billy finished an intel dump to John, got information in return, and took the film John handed him. Billy grabbed a camera from his pack and documented the ville. He got John, the Elder, the men and a few of the children in another picture standing in front of the long house.

Packing his Alice pack, he and John shook hands and with a few quiet words, Billy and a security team humped it for the LZ.

1 Texas— Thirty Years Later

Cronin Ranch

John got up from the rocking chair and stood on the front steps of the ranch house, swirled the dregs of coffee in his cup and threw it off the porch. Rex trotted back up the steps and sat at the door waiting to be let in, but John just stood there bouncing the coffee cup in his hand. *Thirty five years. That's how long I've been doing this*, John thought, t*hirty five years of ups and downs running this ranch. And I've lost a step, hell three or four steps.*

Jack, this should've been yours, he thought, looking out over the land. *You were born forty-three years ago today, and would've taken over for me by now.* His son should've been here, but he'd been taken, along with his wife, many years ago. Amy, John's wife, had died not too long after, of cancer and what John thought was a broken heart.

He thought as he always did that his family sure had seen more than its fair share of death.

Pulling the door open, John walked back into the house with Rex at his side. In the kitchen, John pulled the coffee pot out and refilled his cup as Juanita came in the back door; he glanced at her and was rewarded with a smile. "Good morning, Senor John," she said.

"Morning, Juanita. Is your other half awake this morning or is he sleeping in again?"

Juanita laughed. "You know he was up with the sun,

and checking on the horses. Of course Toby was up too, so they have been prowling around the horses, the barn and the corrals since all hours. I know he was worried about that fence on the backside of the corral after that last rain, so they are probably down there now."

The old man nodded. "Plotting ways to spend more of my money I'm sure." But he defused his words with a grin.

"Well, you aren't as young as you used to be, Senor, and there are things that need to be done that require plain old manual labor," Juanita chided.

He replied, "I'll have you know I'm only sixty-three, I can work just as hard as they can! Hell, I grew up doing ranch work."

Jesse, his granddaughter, tousled and yawning, came through the kitchen door.

Can't believe she's a grown woman, John thought.

He remembered when she was just five, chasing fireflies through the backyard at dusk. Had it been so many years since then?

Jack, you would've been proud of your girl. Strong and smart as a whip, that one. His son and his daughter-in-law had been killed when Jesse was so little. She hardly had memories of them. John had raised Jesse as his own, but even he didn't know how he'd managed it. John had no business raising a girl all by himself. *Amy, I wish you were here to see her.*

"What's got you so grumpy this morning, Papa?" She picked up a cup and poured herself a cup of coffee.

Making a show of looking at his watch, the old man said, "Well, look who finally decided to grace us with her presence!"

Jesse stuck out her tongue at the old man. "You know damn well I pulled a reserve shift last night. We ended up with a van with the two smugglers with two keys of grass and a pistol in the bag down on I-ten. Before it was over, that ended up involving DPS, the Rangers and who the hell else I don't know. I didn't clear the station until sometime after two AM, and I didn't get home until almost three."

The old man just nodded, refilled his coffee cup and headed out the back door. Juanita and Jesse both went to the kitchen window and watched him walking toward the back corral. At right at six feet tall, and around one hundred-eighty pounds, other than the grey hair and moustache, the old man didn't look sixty-three. The women presented quite a contrast too. Juanita at forty-plus was a short plump Hispanic woman, always smiling and seeing the humor in life; Jesse at twenty-three was tall and girl-next-door-pretty, with shoulder length brown hair that she was always flipping out of her face. As a deputy in Pecos County, she was quiet and reserved most of the time, especially around people she didn't know.

Watching the old man walk away, Jesse reached over and hugged Juanita. "What's got Papa so upset this morning?"

"I don't know. Francisco said he saw him just sitting on the porch this morning, lost in thought. That is not like him at all, I wonder if he's worried about you pulling those reserve sheriff patrols in the middle of the night by yourself."

"I dunno, since he's the one that helped me get into the Sheriff's Department to start with," Jesse replied. "I'm more worried about getting secretarial spread from those hours in the seat than anything else!" She smiled ruefully and patted her hips.

Juanita looked at Jesse. "That is not what causes the spread, it's babies. And you're getting to be an old maid; all the old biddies are talking about how you don't do anything but work at the test track, and patrols and work here on the ranch. All the boys you've dated never lasted more than six months, and they wonder why."

"They're boring that's why! All they want is to get me in bed, and make a lot of promises, and all that crap. And the ones around here all know about the ranch, so I think they're looking at getting a piece of that action when Papa dies," Jesse said.

"What about all those engineers you work with?" Juanita asked.

Jesse laughed ruefully. "All they know is their damn computers and spreadsheets, and the young ones are all too busy sucking up to the program managers. The drivers all see me as arm candy, or a quick piece of ass, since most of them are flown in just to do the tire testing."

"All you work with are spreadsheets too, so what is wrong with that? You need a nice long girl's vacation Jesse, what about the girls you went to school with? Can't y'all get together and go somewhere nice?"

"Most of them are married with kids now, so that's not an option. Besides, I like the quiet life of an accountant and when Papa dies, I'll have to take over the ranch. I know that, and I want to make sure I do that with the right person. And I damn well better know accounting to keep track of everything on this ranch!"

Juanita shook her head and turned away. "I need to get breakfast started. You want anything special this morning?"

"Can we have pancakes? I haven't had pancakes in forever and I love the ones you make!" Jesse said.

Juanita smiled. "Pancakes it is. Now go get presentable."

Jesse disappeared with a smile as Juanita prepared breakfast for everyone. After everything was ready, Juanita stepped out back she rang the triangle calling the men in, as Jesse now freshly out of the shower and ready for the day came back into the kitchen. She took the place settings out of the cabinets and set the table for everyone, poured juice and was setting coffee cups at each place as the old man, Francisco and Toby trooped into the kitchen.

Francisco gave Juanita a quick hug and a peck on the cheek, and smiled at Jesse as he sat down. Toby sat quickly and smiled shyly at Jesse, "Morning, Miss Jesse."

"Morning Toby, morning Francisco. Has the old grouch put y'all to work already?" Jesse asked.

Francisco laughed. "Everyday, all day; such a slave driver he is."

The old man sat at the head of the table saying, "Dammit, you trying to stir up trouble with the hired help again?" But he couldn't keep a straight face, and everyone laughed.

After breakfast, Jesse and the old man went into the office to do the weekend updates on the ranch books and Jesse asked, "Papa, what's got you in such a snit this morning?"

"Nothing, just life in general."

Jesse opened up the spreadsheet and started making entries from the receipts stacked in the inbox on the desk, not saying anything.

Finally, the old man looked over at Jesse, "Why do you still call me Papa?"

Taken by surprise, Jesse stopped typing and thought for a moment, "What else would I call you? I know you're not my daddy, but you've raised me, and been my Papa since I was a little girl. I'm not going to call you grandpa, or even worse, Mr. Cronin, so what *am* I supposed to call you?"

The old man shrugged, "Well, I hear kids calling their dads Pops, or their names. I do have a first name you know. Calling me Papa makes you sound like you're twelve years old."

Turning around Jesse looked at the old man, "I can't call you John, that's just not right. I'm not going to insult you by calling you Pops either! I could always call you captain, I guess. Would that be better?"

Frustrated the old man shook his head. "Jesse we're all that's left of the family. Maybe it's just old age, but I can't help but wonder what is going to happen when I'm gone. Hell, I never should have lived through half the shit I did, and I worry about you patrolling by yourself. I'm almost sorry I ever got you involved with the department."

"Papa, don't even start that! I did that because I *wanted* to, not because you pushed me into it! I saw enough shit in college to ensure I want to be able to protect myself, and by default other women if it comes to that. You're going to be here a long time yet, and I'm not planning on going anywhere anyway." Getting up Jesse went over and put her arms around the old man, "Besides I love harassing you and causing hate and discontent, you know that."

Returning her hug he said, "Let's just say this is not one of my better days and let it go at that."

"Deal." Sitting back down Jesse asked, "Any other receipts or things I need to get in the book?"

Two hours later, books caught up and both of them in a better mood, they went out and watched Toby working with a new colt. For someone who had never been around horses until he came to Texas three years ago, Toby was amazing with them. He was a Montagnard and given his upbringing, would have been more likely to eat the horse than train it. At just over five feet tall, he looked more like a young child than an adult, but he was in his element.

2 Another Day at the Office

The old man grumped into the sheriff's office Monday morning, flopped in a chair across from the sheriff and glared down at his coffee cup.

"Okay, John, what's got your balls in an uproar?" the sheriff asked.

"I'm worried about Jesse. We're seeing more and more drugs coming through here on I-ten and I-twenty, and I don't want her ending up on a damn kill list for the cartel. One of us in this family is enough. We don't need the crap they've got going over in Arizona, and I talked to Bucky last night and at least three or four troopers are getting protection since they got named."

The sheriff leaned back. "Well, I can't promise she won't ever get caught up in that. Not honestly anyway. But you know I'll do my damnest to keep her and all the other deputies off paperwork that gets sent anywhere out of the department. The troopers took credit for the stop she initiated the other night, and I didn't fight it."

The old man looked intently at the sheriff. "Why, especially when we would have gotten credit for a vehicle confiscation, and at least a few bucks back from the state?"

The sheriff shrugged. "It would be peanuts, it's another damn Ford van, and the last one I think we got a hundred twenty dollars out of that one. Besides, it would cost us damn near that much to do the paperwork."

The old man nodded. "Good point, and it's not like we don't have enough damn confiscated vehicles sitting in impound now. I'm not asking for special consideration for Jesse, but… well…"

"John, I know you, I know Jesse. Believe me, I understand. Did Bucky say anything about that new bunch that's pushing stuff up this way? That offshoot of the Zetas?"

The old man leaned forward. "Not really, all they've been able to get out of their contacts, is that 'somebody,' person or persons unknown has been allowed to set up another route, probably coming up through Big Bend, since that area is wild as hell. I wouldn't be surprised if they are using mules and coming up through Coahuila on the eastern side of the Sierra Madres. If they are trucking it up, it's on highway sixty-seven and they're walking it across somewhere around Ojinaga. There are way too many places to cross, and nowhere near the coverage to actually monitor that section of the border."

The sheriff got up and walked to the Texas map hanging on the wall. "So this takes pressure off Laredo and McAllen?"

The old man said, "That's what Bucky is thinking, since they've been hammering them pretty well lately. I'll quit bothering you. I've got paperwork to do to finish that investigation on the robbery out at the truck stop."

The sheriff chuckled. "Ah yes, we also serve who file paperwork don't we."

The old man shook his head and left the office. Wandering the halls rather than going back to finish the report, he stopped by intake and flipped through the intake photos of the arrestees from the weekend. It looked like the usual suspects, until he got to the last two pictures.

Calling the sergeant over he asked, "Willie, where did these two come from?"

The sergeant spun the folder around, "Oh those are the two that were arrested for the kilo of grass on

Saturday night. I think Jesse was in on that one. We're waiting to transfer them to state custody later today."

"No wants or warrants, I take it?"

"Nothing, Captain, or at least nothing under the names we have on them," the sergeant said.

Tapping one of the pictures, the old man said, "Can you shoot that one to my email, Roberto Hernandez? He looks familiar for some reason."

"It'll be there by the time you get to your desk, Captain," the sergeant replied.

The old man swung by the kitchen, refilled his coffee cup and went back to the office. Settling into the chair, he called up the email and looked once again at the picture, and the attached documentation. The name for some reason didn't match the face in his mind, but he couldn't tease it out. Playing a hunch, he forwarded the email to Bucky's DEA account down at Laredo. Picking up the phone, he tried Bucky's office, but it went to voice mail, so he left a message asking for a callback.

Restlessly moving around the building, the old man kept thinking he was missing something. There was something about Hernandez that just wasn't right, but he couldn't tease the thought out. *Damn age striking again*, he thought

Two hours later, he still hadn't figured it out when an email popped in from Bucky and his phone rang. Punching the speaker, he growled, "Cronin."

Bucky's voice came from the speaker, "Good morning grumpy, what the hell are you doing sending me a picture of Iggy?"

"Iggy? Ah shit, *that* was what was wrong! I thought we killed that sumbitch years ago in that gunfight down in Guadalajara," the old man exclaimed.

"Nah, we got lead in him, but never did find a body, and he showed back up again about ten years ago. He's a mid-level mule and crew boss, or was, for the Zetas," Bucky replied. "What did y'all get him with?"

The old man looked through the papers on the screen, "Apparently, not much. He was in a van where the driver was busted for a key of grass."

A hacking noise came over the speaker, and the old man realized Bucky was laughing. Bucky ran down and said, "You missed something John, that sumbitch never shows his face outside ol' Mexico unless he's got a major deal going down. You must be slipping in your old age."

The old man rocked back in the chair thinking, "Hell, Bucky, I didn't even get involved. This was a routine traffic stop Saturday night. Guess I better go investigate this one a bit more."

Bucky said, "Yeah, I'll send you some particulars in a few, but I'd bet he was up to something."

The old man hung up, and looking at his watch, called Jesse, asking her to come to the sheriff's office at lunch. When she asked why, he said he'd discuss it when she got there.

Walking down to dispatch, he asked Lisa, "Where is Roberts patrolling today, and do you know if he's got Roscoe with him?"

Checking her notes, Lisa answered, "Captain, he's in sector four and Roscoe is in the back; you need him?"

Nodding, the old man said, "Yeah, ask him to come on by the station as soon as he can and I need he and Roscoe to check a vehicle." He leaned on the desk as Lisa sent the alert and deputy Roberts came back with an ETA of fifteen minutes. The old man headed back to the sheriff's office and stuck his head in. "Sheriff, looks like we got a problem or maybe more than one on our hands."

Annoyed, the sheriff asked, "What *now*?"

"Oh nothing much, just a mid-level drug crew boss sitting in the tank, and a possibility we've got a major drug bust missed…"

"You're shitting me, right? Please tell me you're… You're not are you? Gahdammit John, what the hell is going on?

"Sheriff, I don't know, but I'm in the process of finding out. This is from Jesse and the trooper's bust Saturday night. The mid-level guy is really named Ignacio Hernandez, but the paperwork and DL said Roberto Hernandez, and obviously came back clean, so I'm betting no prints got run. Bucky said Iggy doesn't stick his head out of Mexico unless he's running something, so the question is what. I'm betting it's going to be more than just a key of grass. I've got Roberts and Roscoe on the way in, and I'm going to go over the van with a fine toothed comb, I've also got Jesse coming at lunch to try to get the rest of the story out of her."

Disgusted the sheriff banged down his coffee cup, "Do it, and let me know if we screwed the pooch *before* I call the troopers in."

"Will do, sheriff," the old man said as he headed back down the hall.

The old man got the keys to the van from the evidence locker and made it to the back door of the station as Jesse pulled in closely followed by the deputy and Roscoe. As he waited for Roberts to unload Roscoe, he asked Jesse, "Did y'all run a dog against the vehicle during the stop or after it got back here?"

"Nope, we smelled marijuana smoke ourselves on the initial stop, and the trooper pulled them out. I guarded them while he searched the van and found the kilo of marijuana in the driver's bag sitting by the driver's seat.… Why?" Jesse asked.

Grimacing the old man answered, "Well, your clean passenger is in fact a drug mule and smuggling crew leader, and we may have a major drug bust that we almost missed."

Stunned, Jesse just looked at the old man. "Papa? What…"

The old man just held up his hand, turning to the deputy he said, "Roberts would you please take Roscoe to that white van and see if he alerts please?"

Roberts nodded and walked Roscoe over to the van, commanding Roscoe to search, he walked Roscoe around the van, but the dog didn't like approaching it, and started pawing his nose and sneezing. Coming back the deputy was shaking his head, "Captain, I've never seen him act like that. It's like he *wanted* to alert, but something was bothering him real bad. What do you want me to do now?"

"Put Roscoe back in the car, get your gloves and we're gonna do a search of this van." Turning to Jesse he said, "If you can, I'd like you to help and you might learn something here."

Jesse wasn't happy, but agreed. Going back to her car, she opened the trunk and got a set of gloves out of her duty bag as the old man grabbed a couple of other deputies that were standing outside the back door. The old man decided to make this a teaching experience for all of them and unlocked the van, popped the hood release and started walking them around the vehicle. He also got inside and pulled the engine cover from the cab, showed them what to look for and proceeded around the van. He found a piece of cardboard and got on the ground and slid under the vehicle, checking the undercarriage and talking everyone through what he was doing. Still not finding anything, he opened the back of the van to be confronted by a load of flat screen TVs that were new in the box. Turning to Jesse he asked, "Where did they say they were going?"

"They said they were delivering these to a new hotel

being built in New Orleans. But now that I think about it, I know I didn't follow up on that. I don't know if the trooper did or not," she said.

"Okay. Guys, lets pull enough of these TVs out to see the floor of the van," the old man directed. He counted off forty-five TVs as they pulled them out.

After that was done, he inspected the van's floor to make sure there wasn't a false floor, again talking the others through what he was doing. Looking at the TVs again, he asked Jesse to go get the scale out of the women's bathroom, and asked Deputy Roberts to go get Roscoe again. Taking one boxed TV and placing it well clear of the van, he had Roberts work Roscoe against the box, with the same results.

Jesse came back with the scale and the old man set it on the pad. They set a TV on the scales and the old man started chuckling, "Anybody see a problem here?"

Jesse and the three deputies all shook their heads, and the old man picked up another TV box and set it on the scale. Now laughing out loud he said, "Oh, you sneaky bastards."

Mystified, Jesse asked, "What Papa? What are we missing?"

The old man shook his head, "Look at the weight."

Jesse read off the scale, "It says thirty-four and a half pounds. So?"

Deputy Roberts finally caught on and looked at the box itself, "Captain it says thirty pounds."

"Bingo, what weighs four point four pounds more or less?"

All of them mumbled two kilos at about the same time. "Exactly, I'm betting we're going to find two kilos of something in these boxes or inside the TVs themselves. Go get the tool kit and let's see what we've got."

As one of the deputies went for the tool kit, the old

man was shifting the box to figure out the least damaging way to get into it. The bottom seam had both staples and tape, so he cut the tape around the box and eased the TV out of the box. Checking the Styrofoam, he set it to the side, took the plastic off the TV, opened the parts box, and finally started taking the back off the TV. Roberts jumped in and helped, and the old man eased the TV apart. He leaned down and sniffed; nodding to himself, he called to the others, "Okay, take a look at tell me what you see."

Jesse looked in and said, "Dammit, I screwed up didn't I, Papa?"

The other deputies all looked in and reacted in various ways, but it was Roberts who finally said, "Two damn kilos *in* the damn TV? Captain, what sent you down that track?"

The old man smiled. "Well, Roscoe's reaction made me wonder if something was hidden and covered up by something that the dog wouldn't like. When the truck came up clean, the TVs were the next option and the weight gave it away. Now that we've got the TV apart, you can catch a whiff of capsicum. That would tear a dog's nose up, and Roscoe was probably getting a little scent of the cocaine, but more capsicum than anything else. Jesse would you go ask the sheriff to step out here please?"

Jesse nodded and walked to the door mumbling to herself. The old man pulled out his phone and called Bucky, leaving him a message that there was an estimated ninety kilos of probable cocaine in the van.

The sheriff came out, took one look and said, "Damn John, you've lived up to your reputation one more time. Did you call Bucky already?"

The old man nodded and watched as Roberts tested the cocaine in one bag. It turned the compound a deep blue, indicating almost pure cocaine. Jesse just shook her head, "Papa, I need to get back to work, can we talk when I get home?"

"Yep, and don't feel bad, you're not to blame for this, it got taken away from you," he said.

Jesse spent the afternoon in a funk over the missed drugs, while the old man and deputies tore apart TVs and collected the ninety kilos of cocaine. Bucky showed up late in the afternoon with two other DEA agents, and they took control of the cocaine, the driver, and 'Iggy' Hernandez. The old man got Bucky off to the side, and asked him to keep Jesse's name out of the reports, and just let the trooper have all the credit. The sheriff agreed, and also told Bucky the troopers were going to take credit for "directing" the search for the drugs too.

***

Jesse was still in a funk at dinner, and nothing the old man could say seem to bring her out of it. She finally said, "Papa, I made a big mistake by not following procedures. You've taught me better; and I want to know, what could have happened out there?"

The old man set his coffee cup down. "Well, the worst case is they could have blown you away. I think the trooper showing up might have diffused the situation to some extent, but you were lucky. Take that as a warning, and remember to always wear your vest to start with."

Jesse just stared at the old man then said, "Is this the kind of stuff you used to do? Is that where you learned all the stuff about smuggling?"

Picking the cup back up, the old man rolled it between his hands. "Jesse, a lot of what I learned about smuggling was during my time with DEA, but a good bit was working the old back roads in this county and the border for years. A lot of it is getting a feeling for people and their actions, and I can't teach you that. The mechanics yes, but it's always evolving. Call it an undeclared war, call it what you want; the bottom line is we're trying to stop the drugs, they are trying to move the drugs. We don't always win, and neither do they."

"Is that why you co-wrote that article I read about smuggling?" Jesse asked curiously.

"Yeah, I'm trying to pass on some of the hard earned knowledge. Hopefully without all the hate and discontent I went through to get that knowledge. I'm leaving in the morning, and I'll be back by the weekend, okay?" he asked.

Jesse nodded, "Okay, I'm on Saturday day shift, and maybe I need to stay there for a while until I get some more training."

The old man leaned forward. "No, you need to get back on that horse, if you don't go back on nights and make stops, you just need to quit now. Understand? You *know* what to do and how, this was one case. You can't let it get to you, okay?"

Jesse got up and took her plate to the sink, then came and hugged the old man. "Yes, Papa. I won't let it get to me. I'm *not* getting up at zero dark thirty to see you off, so have fun on your trip."

The old man hugged her back, and gave her a peck on the cheek. Jesse headed off to bed, while John and Francisco did the dishes to give Juanita a break.

3 Road Trip

John looked up as Juanita slid a plate on the counter in front of him.

"The sheriff called and he'll be here in thirty minutes to pick you up John, so eat," she said. "I know they don't feed you worth a damn on those airplanes."

John took the plate and coffee to the table. "Thanks Juanita, I didn't mean for you to get up and fix me breakfast, but I appreciate it."

"*De nada*. Francisco was already up since he wanted to check on that cow in the barn, he's afraid she's breech with that calf, and he's trying to make sure he's got everything he needs when she drops it," Juanita replied.

John sighed. "Yeah, this is not the best time for me to be leaving, but I'm stuck with being on this panel with Sergi and Antonio and it's been scheduled for four months so there is no way to get out of it."

John finished the plate and took it to the sink, rinsed it and shoved it in the dishwasher. "Well, if anything comes up, you know how to access the operating accounts to get what you need, and keep an eye on Rex will you?"

Juanita harrumphed. "John how many damn years have we worked for you? Of course we can do what we need, and I think that damn dog has *no* idea who he belongs to. Everybody and their damn brother feeds him, or lets him out, or lets him in."

Francisco limped into the kitchen in time to catch the last of Juanita's rant. "Thanks a bunch John, spin her up and leave *me* to deal with it why don't ya," he said with a smile as he grabbed a cup and poured coffee.

"Hip bothering you again Francisco?" John asked.

"Ah, damn weather change is kicking my hip, shoulder, ass, you name it; it'll quit sometime." Francisco slipped into a chair as Rex came over and laid his head in Francisco's lap. Petting the dog without thinking, Francisco added, "You're gone a week right? Do you need me to pick you up at Midland?"

"Nah, I'm going to make the sheriff—" John was interrupted by the sound of a car horn. "Helluva watch dog there, Rex." He glanced at the dog. "I'm going to make him come get me."

Rex sighed, and followed the old man out of the kitchen as he went into the living room and picked up his suitcase and briefcase. Carrying his gear, he walked down to the sheriff's SUV, opened the back door and dumped his bags in the back seat.

Juanita handed him a thermos of coffee as he got in the truck.

The sheriff leaned over and said with a smile, "Thank you, Juanita. I'll say it 'cause I know this grumpy old bastard won't! And tell that hubby of yours to stop by and pick up the renewal of his reserve deputy commission."

"I'll do that, sheriff, thank you."

"It's Jose. You've known me long *enough* to call me that, and known me long before I was sheriff, just like grumpy here has."

That prompted Jose to think back over the last twenty-odd years, first as a young deputy who was scared to death of John as a training officer, then as a co-worker and now as the sheriff. *Hell, I'm still scared of him,* Jose thought. John was rich and didn't need to work, and spent weeks sometimes months on strange, sometimes secretive trips. He flew around as a "consultant" to different law enforcement agencies. *Damn, his Spanish is better than mine, and I'm a damn native!* Jose thought. *I know he talks with Toby in Toby's native language, I wonder how many languages he does speak.* Shaking his head, he put the thermos of coffee where they could both reach it as John, nodding to Juanita, climbed into the truck and slammed the door, buckling his seatbelt as he slumped back in the seat.

"God, you *are* grumpy this morning aren't you John? What's got your tits in a ringer?" Jose said as he turned on to 18 South.

"If you really want to know, I don't like the timing of this trip. Too much stuff going on here, especially that last bust Jesse was involved in. Honestly, I don't feel like I'm really qualified to sit on this damn panel. I know a bit about smuggling but I'm *not* a damn expert, and I wish they'd never published that damn paper we wrote," John answered.

Jose laughed. "You don't realize how good you really are. How many busts did you have when you were with DEA? Both ships *and* trucks, and how many coyotes have you caught on ten and twenty while helping out DPS? Or the smugglers you and Antonio got when you went over there? And how many years of working with the Marshals, on both personnel and drug smuggling? Hell, how much did you teach my old fat ass when I was a young rookie?"

The old man had to smile at that. "Not a damn lot, you were too lazy! And anybody who runs for office just to get outta work needs their heads checked!"

Settling back they chatted through the hour plus trip up to the Midland/Odessa airport, where the sheriff pulled into the drop off lane. Stopping the truck, he reached into the back seat and handed John a folder, "Here are your 'orders' if you will, permission to carry your piece, and

PO's to pay for the hotel in Virginia, but if they won't take them, use the credit card."

Looking at John he asked, "You *did* bring a suit didn't you? I know you hate like hell to wear anything other than those ratty ass old Dickies, but you DO have a reputation to uphold ya know."

Grabbing his bags, the old man grinned. "Suit, I don't need no stinkin suit! What they see is what they get; hell they're going to think I'm some kinda redneck cowboy, so why not live up to that image? Of course I've got a damn suit Jose, and shirts and ties, and I'm even wearing my barbecue rig, happy now?"

Jose just shook his head. "Fly safe John, and I'll pick you up Friday afternoon at five."
Putting the truck in gear, the sheriff looked over, waved and then drove off.

With a wave, the old man opened walked into the airport. He checked his bag and looked around until he found the on duty police officer, showing him the travel authorization and the officer got him through security with a minimum of hassle although TSA did want to search his briefcase.

Five hours and one lousy airline meal later, he landed at Washington National, grabbed his bag and headed for the rental car agency. Picking up the rental car, he looked at the map and figured out what he *thought* was the best way to get out to Dulles to pick up Sergi and Antonio. Looking at the time, he realized he was going to be right in the middle of rush hour, so he just gritted his teeth and hit the road.

An hour later, he finally made it to Dulles and pulled up in front of the arrivals level. He remembered from his previous trip to Italy that they had come out at the west end of the terminal, so he pulled in front of the police car and parked.

Getting out, he walked over to two airport police and pulled his jacket back far enough for them to see the badge. "I need to pick up a couple of LEOs coming in from overseas. Is this the best place to get them?"

The older of the two nodded saying, "Sure, you know if they are coming in on the same flight?"

The old man nodded, pulled out his wheel book, the little flip top notebook that went everywhere with him, a habit that was as ingrained as putting on his pants or his gun. He read the flight number from the appropriate page, and the officer called on his radio and confirmed the flight had landed about thirty minutes earlier saying, "They should be clearing customs in about fifteen minutes, if they haven't already. Leave your car here. Go in that first door and straight down to the main floor; that is where the international passengers come out, and you should be able to find them with no problem."

After about ten minutes, he saw Sergi and Antonio coming out together. He waved at them, and he couldn't help but laugh, since they truly resembled Mutt and Jeff.

Sergi stood at least six-foot-five, was blonde, blue-eyed and in great physical shape, looking like a movie star or model; Antonio, on the other hand, was only about five-foot-six, with grey hair going in all directions, a soup-strainer moustache, rolly polly like a beach ball and looked like he'd been sleeping in his clothes for a week.

After a round of handshakes, back-slapping and John threatening to shoot Antonio if he tried to kiss him, they trooped out to the parking lot. The older officer was still standing there, obviously keeping an eye on their car. John got the trunk open and looking over at the officer, realized he was curious as to who was who.

John motioned him over. "Sergi, Tony, this officer was nice enough to let me park here to retrieve y'all, so introduce yourselves and we can head to Quantico and dinner."

Sergi came to attention, shook the officer's hand and introduced himself. "Sergi Laine, Keskusrikospoliisi or NBI, our equivalent of your FBI. Thank you for letting the Cowboy park here!"

Tony strolled over, sticking out his hand and said, "Antonio Russo, Carabinieri, Direzione Anti Droga, our anti-drug task force. And, yes, thank you for not arresting the Cowboy. *He* has to drive because we are too scared to!"

The officer took the men's hands, shook his head and then just waved them on. Sergi and Tony finished grabbing knives and other assorted things out of their bags, and closed the trunk. As usual, Sergi grabbed the front seat and just as typically Tony bitched at him about it. On the drive in, they caught up with each other, and Tony pushed the idea of grabbing Italian food, as this would probably be the only chance they had, since they had to return to Filomena in Georgetown.

Grumbling, John finally got down into Georgetown, and couldn't find parking anywhere close, so ended up in a public lot. John decided to lock his hat in the trunk rather than call any additional attention to him or them.

Just like the last time, Tony broke into Italian walking in the restaurant, and disappeared into the kitchen while Sergi and the old man were escorted to a private table. A few minutes later Tony reappeared, and pronounced that he had taken care of everything.

Sergi just rolled his eyes, and John just shook his head. "Dammit, Tony. I told you *last* time we would split the bill, I know this place is expensive and you aren't made of money; Angela does get most of what you make and you spend the rest on the kids!"

During dinner, they chatted over how to handle the panel during the seminar, deciding whom would take the lead on the various sections and who would lead the discussions. They decided to wait until they were at the conference center tomorrow to get a look at how things would be set up. By the time "only" a five course dinner was over, it was dark and being a Monday night, not that many folks were out.

Walking back to the car, John realized something didn't feel right, and looking quickly at both Sergi and Tony he realized they had picked up the vibe also. John said quietly, ".45 on my right hip."

Sergi responded, "Knife only. I have right."

Tony chimed in, "Knife and baton, I have the left."

Rounding the corner at the parking lot, John realized the lights were out in the lot, either broken or just out. Behind him he heard a scuff of feet, and bouncing of a ball.

Turning, he realized they didn't have any place to go, trapped between a building and a large truck parked on the street, unless they backed into the parking lot, but he had no idea who or what was in there. Cussing himself, he decided to see what was going to happen here and now, rather than later. All three of them stopped and turned around as John motioned for the young guys with the basketball to go on by, but they didn't; stopping and blocking the sidewalk, the one on his right continued to bounce the basketball, while the one on his left turned and looked quickly over his back.

The one in the center, obviously the leader spoke softly, "Ol' man, you needs to give us yo' money, an' yo' watches right now fore we hurts y'all."

Sergi, bless his heart, rattled off an answer in Finnish that did nothing but confuse the punks, and the leader said, "Get 'em, quiet like."

Tony answered in Italian with a querulous response, and once again confused the punks. They started to move in and John held out a hand. "Wait, I'll give you my wallet and watch, just let my friends go," and started fumbling with his watch band.

Hearing the snick of a blade opening on the right, and a pop on the left, he assumed both Sergi and Tony were ready to act as necessary. The one facing Sergi suddenly threw the basketball at him, and started to rush. Sergi caught the ball and a hissing noise sliced through the night, momentarily stopping the rush. "Oh, it looks like your ball has a leak. I'm sorry for that!"

Using the distraction, John drew his .45 and pulled his tac light from his pocket with his off hand as he dropped into a combat crouch. The punk on the left realized what happened seconds too late and yelped, "Bro, he got a gun!" His eyes widening and half blinded, as he reached for John's arm; he didn't see Tony's hand move as Tony cracked him across the wrist with the ASP baton, and the punk dropped to his knees in pain.

Sergi dropped the now deflated basketball off the end of his knife seemingly ignoring the three punks and asked, "Well, do we shoot them, cut them or just beat them, Cowboy?"

The old man was still in a combat stance, light in the leader's eyes and the punk's arms were now at shoulder level and he was wavering between offensive and defensive posture.

"Well, if we shoot 'em, it's gonna take all damn night to do the paperwork, but it *would* take em off the streets permanently."

Tony said in a thick Italian accent, as he waved his knife in a comedic parody of fighting. "I want to cut them; I haven't had any fun since I left Sicily!"

"But that looks like a police car coming now, we could cut them and give them to the police right?"

The three punks broke and ran at that point, and

John, Sergi and Tony retreated to their car and slumped in their seats, letting the adrenalin drain off. Sergi folded his knife and John, seeing it out of the corner of his eye asked, "How BIG is that damn thing?"

Sergi flipped it open and chuckled. "Cowboy, do you not recognize the knife you gave me for Christmas a few years ago? It's a Creekit M-16? I *like* this knife. It fits my hand well!"

Shaking his head, John looked down at the floorboard of the car. "What's that Tony?

"Oh, I thought since they left their basketball, it would be a good challenge for some folks to see if they might get prints off it. Did I do wrong? Should I have returned it?"
John just threw up his hands as both Tony and Sergi laughed.

While the old man navigated the freeways down to the Garrisonville exit, Tony and Sergi brought each other up to speed on their respective activities since they'd seen each other, and they all discussed the family status and bemoaned how much money it cost to feed the families and cars and animals. They finally got to the hotel late, at nearly eleven. They checked in and agreed to meet in the lobby at 0600 and go find breakfast from there.

4 Quantico

After a breakfast at Waffle House, they rolled out to the back gate at Quantico and onto the FBI's portion of the base. Pulling into the parking lot in front of the complex, Antonio shuddered. "I still have nightmares about this place. It is no wonder I couldn't sleep last night!"

Sergi just grunted and the old man laughed. "Hey we're back as the pros from Dover now, so we don't have to play their games. And the reason you had nightmares was all that damn food!"

Getting out of the car, they stopped momentarily to look at those faded brick buildings, each dealing with their own memories of the place. Automatically, they all slipped on and straightened their suit coats, and the old man put on his cowboy hat. As they walked up the walkway to the entry, a familiar figure stepped out.

"John Cronin, you old bastard, I wondered if that was really you! I see that it is, and you're as ugly as ever," SAC[2] Miller said with a smile, as he extended his hand. The old man proceeded to fold the SAC into a bear hug and pounded him on the back. "Milty, who the hell let you up here? Goddamn, it's been, what, twenty years? These are my co-authors, Sergi and Tony!"

Handshakes and introductions followed.
"Hell, John, I'm so old they put my tired ass out to pasture and this is the pasture," the SAC said. "I'm the lead instructor and for my sins, the damn coordinator for

---

[2] Special Agent in Charge

this cluster fuck we've got this week. C'mon, we'll get some coffee and I brought donuts for all you cops!"

Leading them into the building and the theater, they caught up with each other and discussed the plan for the seminars and their panel. Since they weren't on until eleven, they could either attend the first panels or come back. They decided since they'd already come out, and there was really nothing to do at the hotel, they would sit in on the earlier portion of the seminar.

Sergi and Tony wandered off, talking with a few of the early arrivals as the Miller pulled the old man to the side. "Just to give you a heads up," the SAC said, "Klopstein is going to be here, and he's been writing a lot of memos on how flawed your paper is, so be prepared. Also, I'm pulling you guys out after lunch, we've got another meeting y'all have to attend. Don't say anything to anybody else about that. I'll come get you when we need to leave."

"Klopstein?" the old man replied. "I thought that bastard got fired! How the hell did he get his nose back under the tent?"

Shaking his head, the SAC said. "Oh, he wangled a position at Columbia in their Criminal Justice program," he said. "BS'ed his way into a department chair in Forensics and Analysis. You know about his whole model and simulation spiel, right? Well, he's managed to keep pushing that shit down here and the head shed keeps giving him money to expand it into a real study."

"Can I just shoot the bastard and be done with it Milty? I never could stand that sumbitch when he was trying to BS us in the forensics classes down here back in the day." Miller laughed. "Hey, any chance we can sneak over to the range? I still owe you a chance to get your money back from our last little competition," the old man said with a grin.

Tony came back over and borrowed the keys to the car, saying he'd be back in a couple of minutes. As Tony came back with a laundry bag in his hand, Sergi wandered up from the front of the theater. When he saw Tony he started laughing. "Mr. SAC, we have a little challenge for you, if you please. We would like to know if your great lab here can get fingerprints for us."

The old man shook his head. "Milty, we had a bit of a set to last night, and they left a bit of evidence behind. Not sure how you want to handle this or if you even do."

The SAC held out his hand and Tony passed him the laundry bag, opening it and seeing the basketball he looked at the three of them with a quizzical expression. "Evidence? Are there bodies to go with this, or is this it?"

After a humorous retelling of the events of the previous night, the SAC chuckled with them and said he'd see what he could do, and knew just the person at Metro DC to pass the info to if they came up with anything.

He glanced at his watch. "Well, time to get this show on the road, if you guys want to go or hide in the back feel free, I doubt you'll need to be back before ten-thirty."

Shaking hands all around, they broke up; the old man decided to stay and see what the other presenters were going to say, and Tony and Sergi decided to go visit the museum and stretch their legs.

After the first presenter and panel, the old man snuck out the back and wandered around the buildings, letting the memories wash over him. It was hard to believe it had been almost thirty years since he'd last been here and that was for ten long weeks. Homesick, damn near ready to leave after the second week, but determined to stick it out after Amy chewed his ass... But the folks he'd met had opened his eyes to the world-wide fraternity of good cops.

And the classes got him interested and back in the books, especially the forensics classes, which focused on how to correctly collect evidence and pursue investigations. That had opened up a whole new world for the young deputy back then, and taken him down the road that had now brought him back here. As the Chief Investigator for the Sheriff's Office, he'd worked with so many different departments over the years and managed to put some truly bad guys behind bars, and a couple in the ground too. But his fascination with smuggling started right here, well that and the two years with the DEA in South America and the raids on labs and smuggling operations.

He realized he was standing in front of the old forensics classroom and there were still exhibits outside the door, but he didn't recognize a single one of them. He wondered what had happened to the old ones, and figured they were in some storage unit somewhere on the compound. Hell, they'd had stuff from Dillinger here when he'd gone through. Looking at his watch, he decided to head back and make sure he was ready for the panel discussion that was to come.

At 10:45, the seminar stopped for a fifteen minute break and the SAC came out the back. Seeing the old man, Sergi and Tony he motioned them over and told them, "Okay, you guys are up, and I'll introduce you then we'll give you about fifteen minutes to give your open and then open the floor for questions, y'all got that?"

They nodded and followed the SAC back down to the stage, and he showed them the computer controls and gave them each their mikes and had them each do sound checks.

As the last stragglers wandered back to their seats,

he tapped the mike on the podium and started the introductions. "Okay, ladies and gentlemen, the next panel is on smuggling of both drugs and personnel via both sea and land. I'll let the three presenters introduce themselves and give a quick overview of their paper and then we'll open the floor for questions." With that, he waved to the old man to start.

Stepping to the center of the stage the old man began. "Morning folks, I'm Captain John Cronin, Pecos County Texas Sheriff's Department chief investigator. The paper we co-wrote is based on a small sample of smuggling operations the three of us have directly participated in either individually or together in Europe so this will be a micro view of a much larger picture, but in our case we have complete documentation and photos and video in many cases. I'm a graduate of the NA back in 1983, and investigator since 1984. My co-hosts are Sergi and Antonio." Waving at Sergi, he walked behind the table and sat down.

Sergi walked to the center of the stage and introduced himself. "Sergi Laine, Keskusrikospoliisi or NBI, our equivalent of your FBI. I am a graduate of this National Academy in 1986 and I am a field operations person specializing in smuggling into Finland. Approximately eight of the examples are from my borders."

Tony got up next. "Antonio Russo, Carabinieri, Direzione Anti Droga, our anti-drug task force," Tony said. " I, too, am a graduate, 1988 and I am specialist in drug smuggling with a minor specialty in slave smuggling out of Africa. Four of the events are ones that we performed as part of Interpol operations and two of the events are joint smuggling events that both the Cowboy…" He paused as he smiled at the old man. "…and the big Finn…" He waved to Sergi. "And I ended up working as a team during 1996. The first event was originally thought to be a simple cigarette smuggling case from Corsica but turned out to be a cartel operation from Columbia and Mexico via the Bahamas and the United States to smuggle both marijuana and cocaine into Europe disguised as a standard cigarette smuggling operation.

"The second operation was from a lead from that led to a much larger organization smuggling slaves out of Ghana on coastal freighters to the Mediterranean and drugs and slaves being transshipped to other ships and to both Macedonia and the Baltic regions."

Pacing the stage, Tony looked out at the audience, and waved at Sergi. "Sergi was brought in through Interpol and was instrumental in getting us assistance from the Baltic nations to allow a focal follow on the ship of interest to its final rendezvous with small boats off Hanku, Finland and the final end point of Helsinki; while the Cowboy and I picked up the trucks and small boats used to deliver the product and slaves into Albania, Yugoslavia, and finally ending in Skopje, Macedonia. Since then, Sergi and I have cooperated through Interpol on six other cases."

The old man got up and gave a précis of the article, delving into the similarities observed in the way the smugglers set up their vehicles and/or ships. He also talked to the apparent international spread of very similar plans for adding concealment and spaces which they believed were probably based on the cartels' reach into international crime. Sergi and Tony both discussed specific cases they had each worked on. Finally, they opened the floor to questions, most of which revolved around key points for determining whether there were compartments and cues to look for.

Then Professor Klopstein strutted to the microphone, rattling papers and adjusting his glasses and ostentatiously clearing his throat, he glanced out around the audience. "I am Professor Klopstein from Columbia University, head of the Criminal Justice Forensics Department and based on my twenty years of research in this area, and my modeling which is used by a number of organizations world-wide, I find that your entire premise is flawed because your sample size is not statistically significant, I find no definition of the so called 'slavery' you claim to have observed, and I can help but notice that you killed nine, *let me repeat*, nine people in these two so-called coordinated takedowns. My question to you captain—or should I call you 'Cowboy?' –is what was your justification for all these people being killed without arrest or trial?"

Rustling his papers again, he stood in the aisle awaiting a response.

The old man started to get up, but Tony put out his hand. "I will handle this if you don't mind, sir."

Walking to the front of the stage, Tony went from happy-go-lucky to deadly serious. Even Klopstein took a step backward. "Signor professore, if I may call you that, you have insulted all of us with your comment, and you are lucky we are not in Italy, because I would personally take you out in the street and whip you. But I will deign to answer your pathetic little question."

Putting his hands behind his back, Tony paced slowly from one side of the stage to the other. "Remember this distance please: I will refer to it later. Now to your first point, we stated both here and in the paper this was a limited sample and we were very specific about that. There was no attempt to place this in any larger context than that of a limited look at drug smuggling *specifically* coming in from South America, and slave smuggling from Ghana. As for the definition of slavery, you should really keep up with the INTERPOL definitions professore, you are sadly uninformed in reality. Secondly, for a so called world-wide presence, we looked at your pathetic little model and summarily recommended not adopting it because you had nothing in the model that actually supports any law enforcement agency other than a US federal agency."

Walking back across the stage, he stopped at the edge. "Please dim the lights up here and down in front if you would please." As the lights dimmed, he paced slowly to the center of the stage, stopped, put his hands behind his back and bowed his head for a minute.

Klopstein started back to his seat, but Tony yelled, "NO, YOU STAY RIGHT THERE. You want answers? I give you answers."

Klopstein froze in place, as Tony walked back to the side of the stage. "Signor John, or Cowboy and I call him that in honor, as you so derisively called him killed four people in the first operation for two reasons. You see, I was the lead boarder when we did a covert boarding of the first ship. It was a little darker than you see here. We used two Zodiacs with five people in each, one driver and four boarders. I was first up the rope to the starboard stern of the vessel. It was about seven feet up that boarding rope. As soon as I got on deck, I crouched until I was sure Cowboy was almost on deck and I started moving forward." Tony walked quickly to the center of the stage. "I was shot by at least three smugglers at this point, actually shot multiple times in the vest, but one shot hit me in the side of the head and I dropped immediately."

Murmurs and one "ouch" were heard from the audience as Klopstein glared at Tony.

Pacing to the far side of the stage, he continued. "Cowboy was barely aboard when they shot me. He took out his pistol and shot all three of the smugglers with head shots from this distance, in less light than we have now. He took five rounds to the vest, and one shot in the left bicep. He then rushed forward and charged the bridge. As he was coming up the ladder, a fourth smuggler tried to shoot him off the ladder. Cowboy put him down also with a head shot."

Stalking back to center stage, Tony again put his hands behind is back. "Cowboy then captured the captain and the bridge, forcing them to kill all power on the ship and putting it adrift in the Adriatic while the rest of the team boarded. These smugglers did not go easily, and in fact we killed eight just in this boarding alone. I was medically evacuated by a helicopter, so you might ask how I know this. I know this from my team, who followed Cowboy and completed the takedown. And I have no doubt, nor do any of the men there that night that Cowboy saved my life. Lights, please."

As the lights came back up, Tony walked back to the table and leaned on it rubbing his hands. "Sergi and the Cowboy finished my job in Skopje, and only *two* smugglers were shot there when they first shot at us."

Walking back to the front of the stage, Tony looked down at Klopstein and asked softly, "Have *you* ever been in the field 'professore'?"

Klopstein flushed. "No," he blustered. "My work does not require me to go in the field. I rely on the 'proper' documentation from field agents for my work."

Laugher was heard from the audience and Klopstein glared at those close to him.

"You don't remember me do you?"

"No, why should I? Klopstein asked in puzzlement."

"Professore, or should I say Analyst Klopstein, does the name SNC Technologies bring anything to mind? 1988 in Hogan's Alley?"

Klopstein visible recoiled at that, turned pale and sat

in the first seat he could find.

Tony looked out at the audience, which was riveted now. "In 1988 as a student here, I among others was invited to participate in a new training technology called Simunitions today. That is the reduced power and reduced velocity polymer rounds used for force on force training. Analyst Klopstein here, who used to be employed by the FBI in that capacity here, decided that he needed to participate in the exercise to quote, get a feel unquote for how operations are handled. He was placed on the hostage guard side of the exercise to get an understanding of how fast a takedown had to take place to save the hostages. When he was hit for the first and ONLY time with a Simunition, he dropped his weapon and ran screaming to the corner and collapsed, yelling for us to not shoot him anymore."

Dead silence fell on the audience. "Are there any more questions?" Tony asked. The audience sat very still. Professor Klopstein had flushed beet red, his eyes fixed on his shoes. "No? Thank you."

The SAC stepped to the podium and thanked them for the presentation and called a lunch break for all.

As the old man, Sergi and Tony walked off the stage, Miller met them at the bottom of the steps. At the same time a young Thai policeman approached them diffidently and then gave the traditional bow and hands together gesture to the old man, "Sawasdee krup."

The old man returned the gesture and greeting, and the young Thai continued, "Sir, Pan Wattanapanit asked to be remembered to you and hopes that you and your family are well."

The old man stood there for a second or two, and then looked sharply at the young Thai policeman. "You mean Joe? What is that bastard up to these days?"

A bit taken aback by the response and not sure how

to answer, he said, "Sir, Pan Wattanapanit is the director of the Central Investigation Bureau now, and my superior."

The old man started laughing, to everyone's surprise. He shook his head. "Joe or I guess 'Cho' as you say it was my roommate here, and talk about a homesick sumbitch, and lousy card player, but smart as a whip and all whang leather tough and damn that little shit could drink! And he loved Kentucky sour mash! That Joe?"

"Yes sir," the young Thai said smiling, "He still loves it and requested that I bring him some Blanton's home. He said he will never forget that gift."

Turning to the others, the old man said, "On the tenth and twentieth anniversaries of our graduations, I've sent him bottles of Blanton's and all I get back is that damn Sang Thip." Turning back to the young Thai he smiled. "And you are?"

The young Thai bowed slightly. "My name is Som Anuwat honored Sir. Here, I go by Sam."

Returning the bow, the old man said, "Thank you, Sam, and pleased to meet you. Please see me tomorrow and I will make sure you have another bottle or two to deliver to that old souse…"

Bowing, the young Thai nodded and left. Miller just shook his head. "Okay guys, we need to make a little road trip here, so if y'all will join me, we're outta here." Sergi and Tony just looked at each other, but the old man nodded.

"Let's go, I need to eat something though, Milty."

Laughing, he just led them out to his car. "Y'all are going over to the Marine side, and give another brief and Q and A with a few military folks. This one is going to be NATO Secret, and you're all cleared to that level."

After crossing through the gate, the SAC turned again. "McDonalds?" They all laughed and agreed, so they did the drive through and proceeded over to the Marine Corps Combat Developments building.

After clearing the front desk, Miller told them he would be back to get them in an hour. They were escorted to a secure conference room by a young Marine captain, and offered coffee. Shortly thereafter, the room began to fill with various very fit young men in civilian clothes, and one older Coast Guard Captain. The old captain did a double take, then walked over to them. Sticking out his hand he introduced himself, saying to the old man, "Captain Jeff Carson, you don't remember me do you?"

Shaking his hand, he said, "No, Captain, I can't say that I do, John Cronin by the way. Should I remember you?"

The captain laughed. "Probably not. The last time I saw you, you were playing at being a second class petty officer and that was in 1979, remember? And hopping on and off a Cutter down off Columbia in the middle of the night?"

Slapping his head, the old man grinned. "LTJG Carson, how you've changed! My God that was *years* ago! I see you've stuck it out, and done pretty well since I know they don't make a lot of Coastie Captains!" Looking over at Tony and Sergi, he quickly related the tale of his dropping in on the Coasties in the middle of the night as a DEA agent to do a takedown on a particular mother ship off Columbia.

A Marine colonel entered and the room came to attention. Motioning the three to the front, he introduced them in a very truncated fashion and said, "Gentlemen, these folks have been there and done it, you've all received copies of the paper they wrote and now is your chance to ask any questions and get any details you think are pertinent. Captains, these young men are from a variety of military organizations and are here for special operations joint training using new technology in a program called Visit, Boarding, Search and Seizure or as we know it VBSS. This is not your generation's version of it, and we are doing our best to standardize this across services and countries so that we can operate effectively not only with each other, but from a variety of platforms. Gentlemen, you have one hour."

An hour and a half later, John, Sergi and Tony thought they had been through the wringer.

SAC Miller picked them up and took them back to the theater, and pulled the old man off to the side, handing him a flyer. "John, I know you're still a shooter, and this is right up your alley if you're not too old. It's a little competition over in West Virginia in about six months. If you want to take a break, this would be a good one to go do, and you'll be against the best around. Trust me."

The old man looked at the flyer and folded it neatly and put it in his pocket. "Thanks, Milty, maybe this will be my last one. Speaking of which, are we gonna go shoot or not?"

"Not this trip, John, but Becky wanted to invite y'all to come to dinner tonight at six thirty if that works for y'all."

Shaking hands with him, the old man replied, "We'll be there with bells on."

Back at the hotel the old man pulled the flyer from his pocket, read it and thoughtfully tapping it, decided this would be an opportunity to get Jesse out of Texas for a few days and let her see some real snipers at work. And maybe this would be his final fling in that arena.

5 WV Six Months Later

The young deputy guarding the parking lot didn't quite know what to make of the old Suburban driving past the gate: it had a Texas plate and was dirty as hell and the old man in a grey work shirt driving was probably lost. He decided he'd be polite if nothing else and get the old truck out of the way.

Not even thinking about it, the deputy let his hand rest on the butt of his pistol as the truck pulled up next to him. "Afternoon, sir, can I help you?"

The grizzled, gray-haired old man behind the wheel cocked his head and said, "Yep, you can point me to where the competitors park, son."

"Sir, you *do* know this is a restricted competition don't you? It's limited to military and law enforcement only?" The deputy said politely, as he casually scanned the truck, and suddenly realized there was a good looking young girl sitting in the passenger's seat.

"Yes, I do son, and I'm deputy sheriff out in Texas. That's why I'm here. Now where can we park?"

Chagrined, the deputy replied, "Oh, well, park over there next to the fence and the check in is in the clubhouse up to the right", now looking at the young girl and realizing she was wearing what looked like a full sized revolver on her belt. She just looked back at him and smiled as the old man drove off.

As he rolled the truck across the parking lot, the old man chuckled and glanced at Jesse sitting next to him. "Dammit, I knew this was a bad idea to bring you. This ain't going to be fun, and it's gonna be nothing but trouble."

Jesse rolled her eyes, shook her head and looked over. "Well, Grandpa, who *else* could you bring? I know how to spot for you, I'm in better shape than anybody else in this truck; and for damn sure nobody else was going to put up with riding with you for three days in this beat up old truck! And all I've heard is how I need to get out of Texas and see the big world, and yada, yada." She rolled up her window. "Besides, I can out shoot everybody but you anyway."

"I know, honey, but this is still a man's game, like it or not. And they're *not* going to like you messing with their egos when we start shooting."

He rolled the truck against the fence, looked around and liked what he saw. This was a really nice range, and it looked like there would be some climbing, probably some running, and the longest ranges would be about 7-800 yards. It was one helluva lot greener than West Texas, and he just hoped the light and shadows wouldn't be a big problem, since they were used to open shooting. Getting out and stretching, the old man stamped his feet into his boots, shrugged into a light jacket to cover the 1911 riding on his hip, and patted his badge to ensure it was still sitting on his belt.

The old man looked around casually, noting the positions of the range, the hills, and where people were moving in the parking lot. He shook his head, looking at the greenery and hills brought back memories he'd rather forget, but this was really not about him, not now.

Jesse was doing the same thing on the other side of the truck, and making sure her Colt Python was covered and she reached back into the truck to grab her badge off the seat where it had fallen.

The deputy watched from a distance and saw the badge flashes as they walked to the back of the truck, shook his head and went back to watching the entrance.

"Got your creds?"

"Yes, Papa, I've got my creds. Do you have *yours*?" Jesse asked, sticking out her tongue. "And yes, I'm covered. And I need to pee, and I'm hungry. Does that answer the rest of your questions?" With that she turned and walked to the back of the truck checking the rear doors.

Shaking his head, the old man locked the truck, rolled his shoulders and walked after Jesse. Still wondering if he'd done the right thing, or if he really should have even tried this. At sixty-three, there was a chance in hell of him not embarrassing himself and her. But he figured this would be the last chance to do something like this, and yes she was a damn fine shot, a good spotter, and she needed to see a bigger part of the world than just the West Texas scrub oaks and mesquite. And the assholes that worked at the tire test track out off 103 with her. *She didn't need the job, but she liked having her 'own' money; and being a reserve deputy was just Jesse's way of paying back to the community. I guess she takes after me with that.*

Jesse looked around. "You know, Papa, I don't think I've ever seen this much *green* in one spot! Everything has been green the last two hundred miles, and these hills look like they're worn down nubs of what they once were. I'd hate like hell to try to chase a cow through this, much less a bad guy!"

The old man chuckled and didn't say anything as they walked up to the old white clubhouse; he was mentally cataloging the players. Seeing a number of police cars: Suburbans, Explorers, Excursions, and a couple of vans with military tags his hopes were realized, the *good* shooters were here. Opening the door for Jesse, she slid in and to the left, he did the same to the right. It was like a hundred other clubhouses: one big room, a kitchen to the left with a coffee pot going on the counter, a hint of wood smoke from the fireplace that centered the back wall, various animal heads hanging on the wall and down a hallway off to the left, the bathrooms.

As he scanned the room, it was readily apparent there were some serious competitors here, and every damn one of them was at least twenty years younger than he was.

Jesse interrupted his recriminations. "Pa, I'm going to the little girl's room, I'm pretty sure I can find you when I come back," she joked. She'd noticed they were the only two folks in the room not wearing tactical clothes.

Jesse walked off, drawing stares from most of the men in the room as she crossed to the rest rooms. The old man shook his head, knowing she was putting on a show, and walked up to the line at the registration table. The shooters in the room looked from Jesse to the old man, then looked again, as they realized there was something about this old man dressed all in grey work clothes and a beat-up old cowboy hat that said this was not an old man to fool with.

He finally got to the front of the line, and the harried gent behind the table looked up. "Can I help you?" he asked.

"Yep, here to check in for the competition, John Cronin, shooter; Jesse Cronin, spotter. Pecos County, Texas," the old man said laying his credentials on the table so the registrar could see them.

Scanning down his list, the registrar checked off their names, reached behind him and grabbed a packet out of a box and slid it across the table. "Sighting in, doping and safety checks on range one for the next couple of hours. Maximum one hour on the line. Be back here at five pm for COF safety brief. There's a night shoot tonight and starting at oh seven thirty tomorrow there's a couple of presentations prior to the competition if you're interested. Y'all are team twenty-three."

"Thanks, what's the altitude here?"

"Twelve hundred, but the density altitude will vary depending on the weather, figure around thirteen hundred for the match."

The old man turned and scanned the room, looking for Jesse. Not seeing her, he walked over to the coffee pot, dropped fifty cents in the can, got a Styrofoam cup, poured himself a cup, and headed for the door. Jesse came out of the rest room area, and met him at the door.

"Are we in?" she asked, opening the door and holding it for the old man.

As they walked back toward the truck, he said, "Yep, but I don't think they know you're my spotter yet." He chuckled. "We can go sight in in thirty minutes, and this is about a thousand feet lower than where we are, so we've got maybe an inch of difference, but it's quite a bit cooler up here. Let's go get the guns and go check the zeros and see if we've got any problem."

Back at the truck, the old man unlocked the rear doors, reached in and flipped the blanket aside, revealing two gun cases and two ammo cans. Popping the lid on his ammo can, he reached in and grabbed one of the plastic cases, opened it and took out five rounds. Dropping them in his pocket, he turned to Jesse, "How many rounds to you want?"

Cocking her head, Jesse thought for a minute. "I guess five, since I don't think we've bounced them around and screwed up the scope alignments." Reaching in she slid her gun case out of the truck, and took the rounds he handed to her.

After re-locking the truck, they trudged back up the

parking lot to the side of the clubhouse and walked through the gate down to the line, finally seeing range one all the way at the right end of the ranges.

The Range Officer met them at the line, and confirming their event number said they could take any station they wanted. The old man wandered down to the very end of the range, and picked a station that didn't have any tables, since he figured there wouldn't be any nice benches to shoot off of the next couple of days.

Using the bench at the back of the station, he and Jesse uncased their rifles, and Jesse took the old Baush and Lomb 7 X 50 binoculars out of their case and wiped the lenses down with her shirt tail.

It all reminded the old man of when Jesse was about eleven or twelve and he'd let her shoot a 30-30 for the first time. They'd shot at one hundred yards, and he'd shown her how to use the binocs to check the hits. She'd been a little thing in pigtails, boots and blue jeans with her shirt-tail hanging out, and she'd done the same exact thing. She'd hung on his every word about shooting, and pretty much everything else back then, but now she was an adult with her own life. Shooting was about the only time they really connected like they'd done back then.

Shaking his head, the old man walked back down to the RO[3] and found out they would be going cold range in about five minutes, and he was free to grab any of the various types of targets stacked on the RO's table to use for sighting in. He picked up a couple of the gridded orange sighter targets and with temps in the low sixties and 1300 feet of altitude; he mentally ran the numbers and figured that he would be within ½ inch or less of his point of aim at 100 yards.

When the RO called cold range, he grabbed a stapler

---

[3] Range Officer

off the back bench and walked down range to post the targets. He got a chance to look at the other ranges, and see if there were any wind or potential wind tunnels that he couldn't see from the line. After putting the targets up, he stood for a minute looking back at the line and what the terrain was behind the range, noting the hills and the one valley they'd driven up to get here.

When he got back to the line, Jesse was talking with two military shooters and smiling so he just went on by and sat down at the back bench. He reached into his pocket and pulled out his earplugs and reached over and picked up his glasses from the gun case.

When the RO called the line hot, Jesse immediately excused herself put on her eye and ear protection and came back to him. "Are we both shooting or just you, Papa?"

"Let's carry both rifles to the line, and if I didn't beat the gun up, I should be good to go in a couple of rounds, then you can check your zero, too," the old man said as he grabbed his rifle out of the rack and patted his shirt pocket to make sure he had the five rounds in there.

Jesse looped the binoculars over her head, grabbed her rifle and followed the old man up to the line. He dropped to his knees, opened the bolt on the rifle and loaded three rounds into the magazine, and then got into the sling. Jesse laid her rifle down making sure the chamber flag was in it and the action was facing up. She laid down and propped herself up on her elbows and adjusted the binoculars to focus on the targets.

The old man dropped down into the prone position, snugged the rifle down and looked over at Jesse. "You ready?"

"Yes, Papa, right target, no wind, center sighter," Jesse replied.

"Sure," he said, throwing the bolt closed and shifting

to put his natural point of aim on the target.

"Target."

"Send it," Jesse said.

The boom of the rifle seemed to relax the old man, now he was in his element. Working the bolt without ever coming out of the hold, he waited for Jesse's call.

"Dead on windage, two and a half high Papa," Jesse repeated.

"One more, target."

"Send it."

Another boom, and he was on the bolt even as the recoil ended.

"Still dead on windage, two and a half high touching the first one Papa, where are you holding?" Jesse asked.

"Dead center, both shots; one more and I'm done. Target," the old man said.

"Send it," Jessie replied.

Boom. "Last round." As he opened the bolt, inserted the chamber flag and shrugged out of the sling.

Jesse passed over the binoculars and he quickly scanned his target, and smiled a little bit. The shots weren't all through the same hole, but they were a nice little cloverleaf with all three rounds touching.

Settling in on the other target he asked, "What's your zero, girl?"

"Uhf... Ah, 200, Papa, so if this is 100 I should print three inches high," Jessie said as she pushed three rounds through the loading gate of the Winchester. Levering a round into the rifle, she wiggled into a position she liked and said, "Target."

"Send it, Jesse." The crack of the rifle and the hole in the target were almost simultaneous.

"Three and a quarter high quarter left, give me one more," the old man rattled off.

"Target."

"Send it."

Crack. Jesse looked over as the old man concentrated on the binoculars, finally rolling off and looking at Jesse. "Give me one click right, and let's see if that is it," the old man suggested.

Jesse reached up, put in one click right windage and got back into position, "Target."

"Send it," the old man replied.

Crack. "Okay, that was dead on windage, elevation looks good. You want any more shots?"

"If that was on, why screw with success? Papa, let's just leave it where it is," Jesse retorted. Rolling over and levering the spent case out, she inserted the chamber flag and picked up her spent cases. The old man, doing the same, got up slowly and rolled his shoulders. He reached down and picked up both rifles, and the RO called cold range so Jesse went down range to pick up the targets. When he turned around, the same two gents were standing there watching them.

The older of the two waited until the rifles were back in the rack and stuck out his hand. "First Sergeant Matt Carter Sir and this is Sergeant Aaron Miller. We're out of the school house at Quantico and former Two MEF[4]."

The old man shook hand with both and said, "John Cronin, and my granddaughter Jesse. We're out of Texas."

"Mr. Cronin, I've gotta ask, what are you shooting?" Matt asked.

The old man smiled and said, "Well it's a mongrel, it started life as a Winchester model 70, and I added a Schneider-bull barrel, and did my own bedding job and it's running an old US Optics SN-9 up top. And it's a 30-

---

[4] Marine Expeditionary Force

06 too. The action is about sixty-years-old, the rest of the rifle dates to the late 80s early 90s. And Jesse is shooting my 94 Winchester 30-30, and it's got a Redfield up top. Nothing fancy, just comfortable old guns."

Just then Jesse walked back up with the targets. Handing the targets to the old man, she smiled at the two Marines. "Hi, guys, y'all bored or what?"

Sergeant Miller, looking at the targets whistled and asked. "Well, I was just wondering who your spotter was, but now I know. But I can't figure out how she can spot for you since this is supposed to be a military and law enforcement only shoot?"

The old man just shook his head and said, "Jesse, show the man."

Jesse grinned and pulled out her credentials, and flipped them open. "I've been spotting for Papa for about as long as I can remember, and yes, I really am a Deputy Sheriff, and yes, I do carry a gun, and yes, I am a girl, too."

The young sergeant just goggled at the credentials, and Matt shook his head, smiling.

Once Jesse was back from the targets, the RO strolled over and said, "Okay, if y'all are done sighting in, you can restow your rifles. After the barbecue late this afternoon and COF[5] brief, we're going to do a bonus shoot in low light if you're interested. It's not required, but folks seem to like the challenge."

The old man nodded and finished stowing the rifle in the case. Jesse cased her rifle and they carried them back to the truck in a companionable silence.

Aaron looked at Matt as they walked back into the clubhouse, Matt just shook his head saying, "Don't mention a word of what we saw out there, I think some

---

[5] Course Of Fire

folks are in for a bigger surprise than they think."

"I won't, but she is a real cutie!"

"Down, sergeant, we're here to shoot not chase skirts; besides, she'd probably kick your ass."

"Maybe, but in her case, I think I'd like it!"

Laughing they headed back to the clubhouse, as Aaron glanced back over his shoulder one more time at Jesse.

6 Night Shoot

At five, all the competitors gathered in the clubhouse to hear the course of fire layout for the competition the next day. Since most of the teams had shot together either at this match or others, there was the usual babble of noise, backslapping and insults flying back and forth. The old man hit the coffee pot again and he and Jesse slipped into the back row of chairs and sat quietly, just watching the interplay.

An older man walked to the front of the room and banged on the table for attention. "All right gentlemen, shaddap, siddown and let's get this show on the road. I'm Kyle Edwards and I'm the RO for this little get together and I want to get all this info out now and make sure y'all don't have any questions. Everyone here is either military or law enforcement, so if you're carrying that is not a problem. The entire COF will be considered a hot range the entire time. However, if you exhibit unsafe behavior, you will be DQ[6]'ed immediately and without recourse. All RSOs[7] will be open carrying, will be in red shirts, and will be positioned at each station."

Walking to the front row, he handed a stack of papers to the first man on the row. "Take one and pass 'em down; here's the layout of the course, it's a seven klick course, fifteen stages, starting and ending here at the range."

---

[6] Disqualified
[7] Range Safety Officer

Walking back to the table, he clicked the computer and the COF popped up on the back wall. "First and last stages are on the range here. Total target count is forty seven, with shot opportunities for both shooter and spotter depending on how you want to run your teams," Kyle said as he paced back and forth. "In addition to the RSOs, there will be two scoring persons at each position. They will be in white event shirts and *will not*, lemme say that again, *will not* reveal your scores on any stage. That's what your spotter is for."

"When you come to the line tomorrow, you must have everything you will need to complete the entire COF, including weapons, the round count you need or want to carry, water, batteries or anything else. The first stage here will be a cold bore shot at 100 yards for each member of the team. You will then proceed onto the course out the left exit from the firing line. You will be responsible for navigation to each stage, and once there you will get specific engagement parameters from the RSO at that point. There will probably be a few spectators at some of the stages. Now I'll tell ya, this first stage is the *only* stage that is an exact range, so it's shooter beware, and ya better know your equipment. Lasers are approved, since everybody and their brothers have one now, and the scoring is as follows."

Picking up a paper off the table and clicking the computer to the next slide, Kyle read, "Anything less than three hundred yards will have a one half MOA[8] ten slash X ring, and four more one half MOA rings outside those. Maximum score is ten points, going down by two points per ring. Over three hundred yards, will have a one MOA ten slash X ring, and four more one MOA rings outside of those. If the spotter is shooting, those sizes are doubled.

---

[8] Minute Of Angle- 1.047" at 100 yards

If you get movers or swingers, they will have a one MOA X ring and a two MOA ten ring, and those will also be doubled if the spotter takes those shots. The final standings will be based on a combination of time to complete the course and scoring for the shots."

The old man and Jesse looked over the COF paper that had finally made it to the back row. It was set up with compass courses and distances from stage to stage, overlayed on a topo map of the area, but no specific information on each stage. Tracing the route with his finger the old man chuckled. "Well, we're not gonna win this one honey, it's up down and around, with some pretty steep climbs just prior to the stages, so we're gonna get beat on the time. But maybe we can outshoot a few of these young bucks."

Smiling, Kyle looked out over the room. "Now we *did* bring y'all's favorite stage back from last year."

And was interrupted by groans, and grumbling including one, "Fucking *dots,* , gahdam," from the shooters.

Kyle laughed. "Yes, sir, it's the dots again, stage seven, on top of the ridge, and you'll draw for colors. Now those are all one MOA targets, but you gotta get ten of them out of each target."

Jesse leaned over to the old man. "Dots, Papa?"

"I don't know, Jesse, but I'm guessing it's not going to be a fun stage. Probably something like a dot torture target, but colored dots and something else thrown in. And if it's on top of a ridge, wind's going to play a part."

Tracing the route again, he laughed softly. "Damn that is almost a vertical climb to get to stage seven. *That* is gonna hurt."

Concern wrinkled Jesse's brow. "Papa, are you going to be okay doing these? I mean this is a lot of walking, climbing and all, and you're not exactly young anymore."

"Hell, Jesse, this is no worse than a typical day on the ranch, and I'm not in that bad a shape. This is all about heart rate, breath control, and knowing when to take a shot. We're not going to win, but I don't believe we'll be last either."

Kyle held up a card and waved it at the room. "Here is your time card, you will be required to keep this with you at all times tomorrow, and here's how we will run this. On command, you will punch the clock to start stage one, do your shots and proceed to the next stage. At each stage you will clock out and hand your card to the RSO. He or she will brief you on the engagement and when you have received the brief, you will clock back in and shoot the stage, then proceed. If, as has happened before, we have more than one team on a stage at the same time, you will not be put back on the clock until the previous team has completed the stage, so the time waiting will not be held against you. Remember, it's cumulative time and score, so if you forget to clock out at each stage, you'll be adding time that could cost ya."

Kyle leaned against the table and looked out over the teams. "Now, one last thing before the barbecue: we're going to do a low light night shoot starting at 1900 as a bonus shoot, so participation is NOT mandatory, but we'll have some fun with it. The other thing is show time is 0800 tomorrow morning for check–in and breakfast; and we will have two presentations that you are welcome to attend on optics and long range shooting, and new technology rifles and bullets and their impact on long range shooting. These are being sponsored by American Snipers dot org, and y'all might find them informative. Now the food's out back, go eat!"

At that point, the room erupted into noise and movement as folks headed for the doors to get in line for the BBQ. The old man and Jesse hung back, and didn't take part in any of the byplay going on. Matt walked over, and Jesse asked, "What is the dot thing he was talking about?"

Matt shuddered. "It's fuc..er... damn diabolical that's what it is. It's about 100 dots on a board, but they are NOT all circles, they are various shapes, but all of 'em have dots *in* them. And the colors are mixed all over the board, you get up there, draw a color and then each of you will have to hit five dots to clear the stage. There is no ammo limit, but you *do* have to hit all ten to clear the stage successfully. Last year some folks ran out of ammo trying to clean that stage, and basically DQ'ed themselves, but they were allowed to finish. Last year it was about a hundred ten yards, so just enough off that people were dropping shots low."

"So, one minute of angle at one hundred-ish yards is roughly one inch, and you're expected to hit five of five each?"

"Yep," Matt replied. "First thing is range the target and then go high or low from there. I've got incremental dope for twenty-five yard intervals all the way out to a thousand yards, since I screwed that one up last year."

Jesse turned to the old man. "Papa, we don't have anything but a hundred yard dope! What are we going to do?"

Grinning at her and Matt, he said slyly, "Why, we'll have to improvise, adapt and overcome."

Matt burst out laughing and just pointed a finger at the old man. "You got me with that one!"

Chatting quietly with the two Marines they moved through the line and picked up plates of BBQ, the old man jerked his head, and he and Jesse went back to the truck, unlocking the tailgate, they sat on it and ate the BBQ and fixins. After they'd finished, he looked at

Jesse. "Well, do you want to try this night shoot, hon? Or do you want to blow it off and go back and get some sleep?"

"Papa, I don't care, but if we 'need' bonus points, I'm all for it, and shooting tonight would give us an idea of what they might do to us on the stages."

"Good point, but let's reserve judgment until we see what they've got up their sleeves."

Getting up, Jesse grabbed the plates and headed back to the clubhouse, asking over her shoulder, "Coffee?" The old man just nodded.

After a restroom break, Jesse hit the coffee pot, getting two cups and putting their fifty cents in the can. As she was turning away, Kyle smiled and held out his hand. "Miss, I'd just like to welcome you to this shoot, and I'm gonna apologize ahead of time for the language you're gonna hear the next couple of days. I'm kinda surprised y'all came all the way from Texas for this, but you won't get the long distance award, cause that's going to the team from England."

Jesse smiled. "Well, I'm a ranch girl, so I'm pretty sure I've heard all that before, and I've probably *used* most of them at one time or another. Papa decided he wanted to do one last shoot, so this is kinda his swan song, so to speak. And before you ask, no he's not my real papa, he's my grandpa; but he raised me from the time I was seven after my parents were killed. So I call him Papa, since he's really the only papa I've known most of my life."

Aaron wandered over asking, "Any problems?"

Jesse smiled, "I don't think so. Are there any problems Mr. RO?"

Kyle, a smile plastered on his face said, "Well, this is law enforcement or military only, so I'm not sure you can legally participate."

Aaron started to defend Jesse, but she just held up her hand, "So you're questioning my ability since this all about the old boys club huh? Well, here are my creds, and yes I really *am* a deputy sheriff in Texas, albeit a reserve, but I do forty hours a month of patrol or operations."

Kyle handed the credentials back, abashed, "Well, I never doubted your creds, but some of the old farts around here were questioning how old you were, and whether you really were law enforcement. I'll straighten them out now."

Jesse just looked at Kyle. "I'm twenty-three, I went through the academy at twenty one, and was immediately brought on as a reserve when I graduated. You gotta understand, our county is forty-seven-hundred-square miles, and a population of a tad over fifteen-thousand folks and the total Sheriff's department only has twenty full-time officers on patrol. DPS has eleven, and we have *one* game warden. When you figure a four to one ratio, that means any given time there are a total of five Sheriff's department and one DPS on patrol in the entire county, so a bunch of us reserves are almost always available as backup or to take a call if it's close to our place. Otherwise, it could take twenty or twenty five minutes for an officer to get from one side of the county to the other, and that's running balls out since it's almost sixty miles across the county."

Kyle didn't reply. "Any 'other' questions Mr. RO?" asked Jesse.

Kyle just shook his head. "No, ma'am, not a one. Somehow I think you're going to surprise some folks tomorrow."

Aaron was still bristling when Kyle walked off. "That asshole…"

Jesse smiled. "Just drop it. I'm used to it, but thanks

for stepping up to defend me."

Jesse carried the coffee back to the truck and handed one of the cups to the old man. They sat and drank the coffee as others started filtering into the parking lot and getting gun cases from the various vehicles. Jesse looked over. "Well, Papa?"

Throwing the rest of the coffee on the ground the old man got up, rolled his shoulders and said, "Let's go see if we can do this, hon."

They grabbed the rifle cases, and Jesse threw the binoculars and range finder into her shoulder bag, and they walked back up to the range. It looked like every team was there, and there were rifles of every possible configuration sitting on the benches. They added theirs to the end of the bench, and filtered to the back of the group.

"Y'all hear me?" Kyle asked over the range PA as he tapped his finger on the mic. "Okay, you'll be shooting in order of team entry. Here's the scenario, you're responding to a call, and have to stop short of the scene. The caller states there are four unknowns with guns, and his wife and daughter are being held hostage by two of them, the others have fired at him from out of the darkness. They are holding them just over the berm. You've got to cover fifty yards, with two unknowns holding two hostages at something estimated at around one hundred yard range. There are two other unknowns somewhere in that fifty yard stretch that you can engage with either pistol or rifle, your choice.

The old man and Jesse both looked at the situation, realizing the only light between the benches and where the targets would be was one pole light on the opposite side of the range about fifty yards out. The rest of the range was in darkness, and without much of a moon, it was going to be interesting.

"If you're not on the line, please remain behind the

back bench, and feel free to sit in the bleachers. Oh yeah, and we will not post the times for tonight's shoot until the dinner tomorrow night, in case we need them for tie breakers."

Team after team rolled through the scenario until it was the old man and Jesse's turn. They picked up their rifles and walked over to the car sitting on the line. The old man looked at Jesse. "You've got the left. I'll take the right, two yard offset going down range. Looks like most of the pop-ups are showing between thirty and forty yards out but lets be ready just in case." Jesse nodded.

The RSO introduced himself. "Hi, I'm Paul and I'll be your RO for this run. If you want to load your rifles please don't put a round in the chamber. Place them in the trunk so you can get to them quickly, and set whatever else you need where you can get to it. Eyes and ears ahead of time, go strap into the seats, and when you're ready, I'll hit the timer. In two to four seconds you'll get the beep, and then it's on you. I'll be following you to catch the rounds fired, and record your total time. Please don't muzzle me or each other as you go down range. Any questions?"

The old man and Jesse looked at each other and shook their heads. Walking around the car they got in and buckled up. Paul stepped to the window. "Shooters ready?"

In the stands, Matt and Aaron both reached for their watches, ready to hit the timers. They knew from timing their runs, and most of the others, they were in pretty good shape, and were confident they'd both gotten at least ten rings, if not x's on the targets and they had cleared the poppers fairly quickly.

The old man nodded, Paul hit the timer, and three seconds later the beep sounded. They both cleared the car. Jesse pulled the trunk open and grabbed her shoulder bag, threw it over her shoulder and picked up her rifle as the old man cleared the back of the car. He grabbed his rifle and they started jogging down range with Paul following.

Jesse offset to the left to keep from muzzling the old man and scanned ahead and left. There definitely wasn't a lot of light and after about thirty-five yards she began to get nervous about when the unknowns were going to show. Suddenly, the poppers erupted from the ground ahead to the left and right of the line. Both Jesse and the old man drew and fired without breaking stride. The boom of the .45 and crack of the .357 sounded almost simultaneously.

Re-holstering on the run, they continued jogging to the shooter box. Both went prone, the old man scanning for the targets and calling, "Two up left one is a tighter shot, target is right. I'll take it; you take the right one, target is left."

"Left target 109 yards, right target 118 yards," Jesse responded. "Going to the gun. Up, on the right, Papa."

"On three- One, two, three..." Two cracks sounded almost simultaneously again, and John hit the timer.

In the stands, Matt and Aaron hit their timers on their watches, and just looked at each other. They had just been trounced by almost ten seconds.

"Damn, how'd they do that, Matt?" Aaron asked.

Shaking his head Matt replied, "Well, they didn't have to stop and fumble with the holsters like we did, and they didn't waste any time. They just went out and got it done."

The RO stepped up to the old man and Jesse. "Unload and show clear on the rifles please, keep your pistols holstered, flashlight coming on," Paul said. The old man and Jesse got up, unloaded and showed clear chambers to John.

The scorer putted by on his ATV as the old man and Jesse walked back to the line. Paul was looking at his timer and shaking his head. Of all the teams he'd RSO'ed tonight, this team was the fastest at 32.2 seconds by at least a ten- second margin. Now the question was how good were the shots they took? As they walked back, Paul took a can of white spray paint out of a pant pocket, and went to the poppers to spray the hit. Jesse looked at the old man's popper, "Head shot? Or was that an accident Papa?" She grinned.

The old man smiled. "Of course. Am I going to see a body shot on yours?"

"Nah. Right eye, Papa."

They walked to the other popper, and sure enough Jesse's shot was close enough to be called a right-eye shot. Paul just shook his head and sprayed the target. They walked back to the line in silence, and thanked Paul for RO'ing for them. They went straight to the truck, put the rifles away and headed to the hotel.

Paul was surprised they didn't ask about their scores, but then again, they weren't the normal team, either. He went over to the scoring table, showed the lady the timer, and she whistled. Paul cocked his head and looked at her. "What was that for, Merle?"

"Well, they're second fastest, and based on their shots, they're actually leading. How good were the hits on the poppers?"

"Merle, they were jogging, and I don't think either one even broke stride, two head shots, and they just kept on trucking. How good were the shots?"

"X and a ten ring, Paul."

"Damn, and she's shooting a lever gun, Merle! Tomorrow should be interesting!"

7 The Competition

The next morning, after breakfast and the lectures, the old man and Jesse grabbed coffees and headed to the truck. Knowing they'd drawn 6th place in the starting sequence, they would have an hour of prep time and a chance for the jitters to take hold. The old men turned to Jesse. "Well, are you ready for this? We've got an hour, so I'm thinking about a nap…"

Jesse just looked at him, surprised. "What do you mean a nap?"

"Well, all that snoring last night…"

"I *do not* snore, thank you very much!"

The old man chuckled, and Jesse realized she'd been had yet again, and finally shook her head and started laughing.

They turned to their guns, rechecking to make sure they were ready to run, and loading small backpacks with full water bladders, ammunition for both pistols and rifles, energy bars, and compasses, in addition to little medical blow out kits. Jesse also loaded the binoculars into the old man's pack and the laser range finder into her backpack after putting new batteries into it. They both checked their EDC[9] lights and knives in the pants pockets, and the old man slipped five rounds into his shirt pocket. He patted the other shirt pocket to make sure he had his wheel book safely tucked away.

They picked up their rifles and packs and walked back to the line. Laying their rifles on the end of a bench,

---

[9] Every Day Carry

they stacked their packs underneath the table. As they walked back to the stands, Jesse stopped and pulled a hair tie out of her pocket as they looked at all the rifles lying on the benches; putting her hair in a ponytail, she reset her cap and shook her head to make sure everything was where she wanted it. Matt and Aaron walked up and set their rifles down as Jesse and the old man walked by. Jesse stopped and asked Matt what his rifle was, he replied, "Well, this is the standard Marine Corps sniper rifle, it is an M-40A5 in .308, McMillan stock, Remington short action, Premier 3 by15 Tactical on top and a Surefire suppressor hanging off the front. It's magazine fed, 10 round Badger magazine modification."

Aaron jumped in. "Mine's an M-4 carbine with a TA-31 RCO AGOG[10] scope on top, and I'm shooting 62 grain Gold Medal Match ammo."

Jesse smiled at Aaron, and asked Matt, "Why the wrap on the silen...er, suppressor?"

"It keeps the heat from coming off the suppressor after multiple rounds." Matt pointed to other rifles setting on the benches, "See, about half of the rifles here have suppressors, and most of them have the wraps."

"So those with the muzzle brakes are going to be a lot louder, right?" Jesse asked.

"Oh yeah, and don't ever stand to the side of one of them, always get as directly behind one as you can," Aaron said and laughed. "I learned *that* the hard way downrange when we were doing some vehicle interdiction."

Jesse grinned and walked over to the old man who was lounging on the bleachers with his hat pulled down over his face. She plopped down next to him saying, "Papa, there are way too many nice rifles sitting out here.

---

[10] Advanced Combat Optical Gunsight

I'm almost embarrassed by that old gun of mine."

"Just remember, the gun you know is better than any pretty gun Jesse," the old man said. "And it's our turn next, so let's go gear up."

The old man got up, gave Jesse a hand, and walked to the bench. Picking up his pack, he took out his eyes and ears and set them on the bench. He shrugged the pack on, settled it and picked up his rifle. Jesse did the same and no words were needed. Methodically, he pulled out the earbuds, wet them and seated them comfortably in his ears, then pulled on his shooting glasses. The last thing was to make sure his ball cap was where he wanted it. Looking over at Jesse he asked, "You ready, hon?"

"Let's do this, Papa. We ain't getting any younger."

Picking up their rifles, they walked down to the end of the firing line, and met Kyle, the RO there. He gave them a timecard, gave them the first scenario for the cold bore shot and had them load and make ready. The old man scanned the range, and noted blue tarps blocking the view of the right side of the range and a set of scaffolding set up. He and Jesse loaded their rifles. Once they'd done so, he asked if they were ready, they nodded and the beep started them on the way.

Jogging to the line, they stepped into the shooter's box, went to prone, and confirmed targets.
"Papa, I've got the left target, ready any time."

"I'm on the right, in three; one, two, three…"
The two shots sounded almost as one, and they safed the rifles, got up and jogged slowly off the range.

"Okay, hon, steady slow jog here," the old man said, looking down at his compass to get a good heading and looking at the trail. It was scuffed by military boots, so everything was matching up.

Eight minutes later, they got to the first stage, clocked out and got the scenario, which was four targets spread across the hillside. Clocking in, they dropped down in the shooters box and Jesse started calling ranges. "Far left—75 yards, left center—125 yards, right center—225 yards, far right—256 yards; do you want me to take the two left?" She said as she reached for her rifle.

"Yep, left two are yours. I have the right two, engaging now." *Boom...*

Jesse shot the seventy-five yard target, the old man shot the far right target as Jesse jacked another shell into the Winchester, and shot the one hundred twenty-five yard target. Safing the rifles, they got up and took a heading to the next stage.

Stage after stage, either at a fast walk or slow jog, they proceeded around the course until they got to stage seven. Twice, they were passed by teams that had started behind them, but the old man just kept to a steady pace. At stage seven, they were caught by a third team at the clock, so the old man let them go ahead. Jesse was a little miffed. "Why did you do that, Papa? *We* were here first!"

Dropping down onto a convenient boulder, and patting the space next to him, he responded, "Think about it, Jesse. We get our breath back, get a break off the clock, and get our heart rates down. Let those boys get up there, shoot and move on. Betcha we do better than they do!"

Listening, he heard fifteen shots, before the team scrambled down from the shooting box. Jesse drew a card, and the RSO told them their color was blue, clock in and go.

The old man clocked them back in, and they scrambled up the bank the fifteen feet to the shooting box. Going prone the old man called, "Range check! You take the blue dots. I'll take the blue shapes."

Jesse got a quick range on the board. "One hundred and eleven yards Papa, looks like fifteen knots of wind, dead crosswind from the right."

"Aim point is bottom of the dot for elevation, right edge of dot for wind Jesse, there are five dots, you get em, I'm on the five shapes." *Boom*...

Jesse alternated shots with the old man, and had to take one extra shot as the wind shifted and she dropped one shot just to the right of the dot, "Cleared mine, Papa."

"Confirmed, safe and let's go," the old man said as he levered himself up off the ground.

"Jesse, something tells me it's about to start getting harder, this has been too easy to this point," the old man commented as they trudged further up the ridge line.

Getting to stage eight proved him prophetic, as they had to shoot from under a barricade with about six inches of clearance. Jesse grumbled in protest, as she had to get down in the dirt to get good ranges, and take one shot with dirt in her hair and dirt blowing back in her face after the shot. The old man just ticked along, not saying much, just shooting the calls.

As they headed to the next stage, the old man remembered how Jesse hated to get dirty while she was shooting. But had no problems as a kid or even now about getting down and dirty when it was time to brand calves or when either the cows or horses were foaling. Odd little quirks, but that was Jesse being raised without a woman in the house for years, he thought with a smile.

At stage ten, they finally got some long range targets, and also got their first significant angle shots. "Papa far target is 778, looks like fifteen degrees down, go up twenty-two MOA, wind is about fifteen knots, and it's about 135 degrees to us slightly helping so I'd say hold low and four MOA right." Jesse advised as she dropped the rangefinder down.

"Got it, glass and check my hit," the old man responded.

Jesse pushed the laser out of the way, got on the binoculars and gazed through them. She called, "On it."

"Target."

"Send it." *Boom.*

"Hit."

"Adjust right, second target, 525, ten degrees down, come down ten MOA, wind is 120 degrees, hold is five MOA right."

"Target."

"Send it." *Boom.*

"Hit"

"Adjust right, third target, 438, ten degrees down, come down four MOA, wind is 100 degrees, hold is six MOA right."

"Target."

"Send it." *Boom.*

"Hit"

"Last target."

"Okay, safe and let's roll," the old man said, getting slowly to his feet. Hunching and rolling his shoulders, he reslung his rifle and looked at Jesse. "How you holding up?"

"I'm okay, Papa, but we're about to get passed again." She glanced at him as he rolled his shoulder and winced. "Is your shoulder bothering you again?"
"A little, hon, but I'll survive. Don't worry about them passing us. Just concentrate on *us* getting through this."

At stage twelve, they had to shoot from the kneeling position to actually get clear shots at the target, and the old man noticed a couple of bullet tracks through the weeds, so he knew someone had tried to shoot that set prone.

On stage thirteen, Jesse burst out laughing when they got to there and saw a door and window standing there. The RSO told them they both had to shoot, one offhand through the door and one kneeling through the window. The old man had Jesse take the short target through the window using it as a rest, and he used the doorframe as a rest for his shot. Both hit and moved on to stage fourteen, which turned out to be a mover, the first one they'd seen in the competition.

The mover was a steel silhouette cycling back and forth at about the pace of a walking man, between the ends of a tar paper 'wall' that was angled away from the shooters. The mover could only be shot while visible through the windows in the tar paper. The windows ranged at 75, 85 and 95 yards from the shooting position.

Three shots were required, and three "windows" were available in the tar paper wall. The old man took the first shot through the first window, Jesse shot through the second window and the old man cleared the target in the second window as well.

Trotting back into the range an hour and a half after they left, they were directed to the right side of the range, where a clock was sitting next to some scaffolding. Kyle was there and took the card from Jesse after she punched in. "Last stage: you have a school bus hostage situation, one shooter on the bus and moving around. He has a blue hat on and is surrounded by children and is threatening to shoot them in the next five minutes. You have to climb the ladder to get a shot, and the powers that be want him taken out before the five minutes are up. Ready?"

The old man nodded and Kyle punched the time card in. "Go!"

Jesse immediately started scrambling up the ladder while the old man groaned. At the first landing Jesse stopped momentarily. "Can't see everything from here, going up to the top."

The old man continued climbing, shaking his head and thinking to himself that this heart rate was going to be through the roof by the time they both go to the top of the scaffolding. "Go, I'll get there in a minute."

Jesse got to the top of the scaffolding, flopped down, and pulled the range finder out of her backpack. As the old man got to the top, she yelled, "One hundred thirty-eight yards, wind is ten knots quartering left to right." She reached for the binoculars from the old man's backpack to start looking for the target.

"Got it, Jesse, get on your gun, 'cause we've only shot forty-five targets, so there might be two on this one."

Jesse stopped, and shook her head, then picked up her rifle and set up on the target, rolling the scope back to a 2x. "Looks like random timing on pop-ups in the windows Papa, first three windows left haven't seen a blue hat yet."

"M'kay, keep watching and tell me if it's the same figures that come up every time. I'll take the two back windows." Settling the scope on the bar between the last two windows gave the old man enough coverage to see both of them. A small head popped up in the last window, and he moved over to the next to the last window figuring that would probably be where the target showed.

Suddenly, it was there for about two seconds, but he wasn't ready for the shot with a small child being held in front of the target. Wiggling down one more time he called, "Got the target fourth window back, hostage child in front, tight shot. I'll take it if I get it again."

Jesse didn't answer, just kept watching the front windows. It seemed like it was taking forever for the targets to pop back up.

Boom! The old man had taken the shot and Jesse jumped a little bit, not expecting it.

Suddenly, there was a swinger at the front of the bus, Jesse sighted in, saw the gun on the target and took the shot. Crack! "Swinger at the front, Papa, I think I got him."

"Okay, unload and safe the guns and let's get down from here," the old grumbled.

Jesse repacked her bag, threw it over her shoulder and followed the old man down the ladders back to the ground. Kyle was standing there when they stepped up. "Unload and show clear on the rifles please. Y'all made it in the five minute window and y'all are completed."

The old man and Jesse both showed their rifles were empty and the old man grinned. "That was a tricky little set up there, with that swinger coming out. I can't help but wonder how many have gotten it, and how many missed it."

Kyle just smiled. "Well, let's just say you're one of the few who may have gotten it. Y'all can unload and either come back here and watch shooters come in, or go grab some lunch inside, or go back to the hotel and catch some down time. We're not posting any scores here. Those will be posted tonight at the restaurant after we award the various teams. Don't forget, six PM for the feed."

Walking back to the line, they stowed their rifles in the cases and carried them back to the truck. The old man opened the tailgate and they shoved the rifles into the back and covered them back up with the blanket. The old man sat down on the tailgate and reached over giving Jesse a hug. "You done good, girl. I'm proud of ya for hanging in there today, and I hope you've at least had a little fun out here."

Jesse hugged him back and laid her head on his shoulder. "Papa, I wouldn't have missed this for the world. It's been an education and then some. Thank you, but I stink, I'm dirty, and I'm hungry. So let's go eat then I want to go back and take a nice long hot bath!"

The old man just shook his head and chuckled, "Women…"

Getting up, they walked back to the clubhouse, grabbed some lunch and headed back to the hotel. Jesse got her long hot bath, and the old man got a nap in.

8 The Party

Pulling up at the restaurant just before six, the old man saw the same deputy directing traffic in the parking lot. The deputy held up his hand and walked over to the truck as the old man rolled the window down. "Sir, y'all drive around back, there's parking for y'all there and you can go right in the back to the room that's reserved for you."

Jesse smiled at the deputy as the old man grunted and pulled around to the back. Getting out of the truck, they met Matt and Aaron walking from their truck. Both of them were in khakis and red polo's with the Marine emblem. Jesse smiled. "Geez guys, I didn't realize it was 'formal' tonight."

Matt chuckled and Aaron blushed. Matt drawled, "Ma'am, us Marines are *always* formal."
Everyone laughed at that, and Aaron held the door for the four of them to enter. Jesse went left through the door, the old man to the right. Matt entered and stepped to the side as well, asking,"Mr. Cronin, why do you do that every time you walk through a door? I know we're trained to do that in our MOUT[11] training, but I don't normally do that back here."

The old man glanced around the room. "Well, Matt the only two times I've ever been shot that counted were both coming through doors, so I kinda have an aversion to standing there being a good target!"

"Twice that counted?"

---

[11] Mobile Operations on Urban Training

"Yep, once in Nam, and once in a bar in Fort Stockton. Decided not to be a target anymore; sides, it's harder'n hell to hit a moving target."

"That counted, Mr. Cronin?"

"Well, the others weren't serious, they were just dings," the old man said as he turned away.

Matt just shook his head and followed the others into the meeting room. They were some of the last to enter, and finally found an open table at the back of the room. The old man took a seat facing the door with Jesse on his left. Aaron and Matt took the two chairs facing the stage and left the last two open. At the head table Kyle was once again standing in front of the microphone scanning the room. He seemed satisfied with the crowd, and bent to the microphone. "Okay folks, buffet style for dinner, and the bar is open, but it's a cash bar. Y'all eat and then we'll give out the awards. Enjoy!"

A waitress came around as the crowd surged to the buffet, so the four of them stayed seated and ordered tea and took their time getting up. Finally, the line got short enough to make it worth their while to get up and get in line. Going through they piled their plates high, and headed back to their table.

Jesse picked through her plate. "This barbecue sauce is sure different than what I'm used to, and I didn't see any brisket at all. But it's not bad."

Matt, having grown up in Western Virginia, proceeded to give Jesse and the old man a history lesson on barbecue and the infighting between Virginia, North and South Carolina and Eastern and Western variations within each state that had both Jesse and the old man rolling laughing. Aaron just chuckled and refused to comment, since he had grown up around Boston, and didn't "do" barbecue until he'd joined the Marines; but he watched Jesse any time he thought he could get away with it. The old man picked up on it, and noticed that Jesse wasn't ignoring Aaron's attention either. He leaned back and decided to let nature take its course.

Finally, Kyle got back up from the head table and picked up the microphone while two assistants went over and unveiled two whiteboards standing off to the side of the room.

"Awright, let's get this show on the road. We're gonna start with third place and work up to first for LEOs then military; then then we'll hold the drawings for the prizes. Applause is fine. Boos are fine. No cussing the winners allowed. We've got ladies present."

Merle chimed in with a cackle, "Who you calling a lady you old fart?"

Over the laughter, Kyle responded, "Well, *excepting* you, Merle, there are a few ladies here…"

More laughter erupts and Merle just waved to Kyle, conceding the point to him.

"Third place, law enforcement, is… Jacksonville PD! Y'all come on up!" Kyle started clapping and the crowd joined in as the two officers from Jacksonville came forward. Kyle presented them their plaque and various cameras flash as the three pose for pictures. Kyle pointed off to the side of the stage and the JPD officers stepped to the side.

"Second place, law enforcement is Tulsa PD, come on up!" The Tulsa officers came forward, receive their plaques with more pictures, they move over to the side and the four shake hands as they juggle their plaques.

"And in first place, Broward County Sheriff's Department with a net score of 460 and a time of fifty-one minutes, give em a big round of applause!" Kyle led the applause and once the two officers got to the stage, presented them their plaque; gathering all the awardees, they posed for more pictures and shook hands all around to applause and various good natured catcalls from the audience.

Kyle walked back to the microphone and started on the military placing, "Okay folks, for *this* group please do not take pictures, as these folks are still going in harm's way and we don't want, nor do they want, their pictures out there. Now having said that, in third place are the Marines out of Quantico! Come on up fellows!"

Matt and Aaron looked at each other and got up and headed to the stage, as they were walking up, Jesse let out a wolf whistle that got everybody around their table laughing, and Aaron turning various shades of red.

Once on stage, Kyle covered the mic and whispered a question to Matt, then turned back to the microphone. "Folks, our Marines are First Sergeant Matt Carter and Sergeant Aaron Miller from the Weapons Battalion at MCB[12] Quantico. They are both instructors in the Scout Sniper course and former Scout Snipers in the Second Marine Expeditionary Force. And Aaron tells me they are known as 'Hogs.' Let's give them a big round of applause and again, no pictures please. And their score is 459 and forty-six minutes!"

Matt and Aaron shook hands with Kyle and walked back to the table as the applause continued along with a few good-natured jibes from the other services. The old man leaned over and shook both Matt and Aaron's hands saying, "Congrats, guys. Y'all had some pretty round competition to overcome there, and that's *damn* good shooting."

Jesse chimed in, "And pretty damn good running too!" Sticking her tongue out at Aaron, who promptly blushed.

Kyle started up again, "And in second place we have

---

[12] Marine Corps Base

the Navy SEALS, come on up gents!"

As the SEALS made their way to the stage, Kyle again muffled the microphone and spoke to the SEALS. Shaking his head, he came back to the mic, "Um... Mr. 'Smith' and Mr. 'Jones' here scored 460 and forty-three minutes! Let's give them a hand."

Laughter, applause and catcalls for "Smith and Jones" continued as the two SEALS returned to their seats.

Kyle waved at everyone to be quiet and said, "And the first place team are our friends from across the pond, the Brits! Y'all, er... I guess I better use proper English, you *gents* please come up to receive your plaques."

Applause and a standing ovation happened as the two Brits walked to the stage. One of the Brits leaned over a whispered in Kyle's ear, and Kyle started laughing.

Still chuckling, Kyle stepped back to the mic. "Um, Mr. 'Jones' and Mr. 'Smith' wanted to remind me they are the original owners of those names, going back well before this upstart country ever got started, and they are proud to be the 'Artists' from Albany. Their scores were 462 and forty minutes, and yes, they *ran* the entire course!"

Kyle presented them with the first place plaque as more applause and laughter ensued. "Okay folks, that's it for the presentations, we'll do the drawings in a bit."

Matt and Aaron got up and walked over to congratulate the other military shooters along with the law enforcement winners, and received the good-natured ribbing from the other military shooters in the room. The old man and Jesse stayed at the table and waved down a waitress for more coffee, as they watched the folks circulate.

Matt wandered over to the whiteboard and checked out the scoring, and was amazed to see that the old man and Jesse had matched the best shooters with a score of 462 points! Merle walked up and Matt turned to her, "Thanks for all the work you did on the scoring ma'am, and we do appreciate it!" Pointing to the scores, Matt said, "Did you see the scores for the deputies?"

Merle laughed. "Yep, all you young bucks might be faster, but that old man can shoot, and the girl is pretty damn good, too! Comes down to it, I wouldn't want him on my bad side, cause I don't think he'd hesitate to shoot. I watched them on the dots, and they didn't miss but a single shot; and that girl got right back on it, no muss, no fuss. Oh, and I noticed your buddy has been sniffing around the girl pretty heavy," she said with a grin.

Matt smiled. "Yeah, but I doubt that will go anywhere, because she's smarter than both of us, and I'm pretty sure the old man isn't going to let any of us get close to Jesse. He knows better."

Matt headed back to the table when Kyle announced they were about to start the drawings for the prizes.

9 The Challenge Coin

Throwing the last of the tickets on the table in disgust, Aaron looked at Matt and the rest of the table and said, "Well, I guess we got snookered again. Sometimes I think that is my typical luck, and it seems like it's rubbed off on everybody else tonight."

Matt laughed. "Well, we're not going home empty handed, Aaron, and I think the colonel will be pretty happy with this, considering our competition this weekend. I don't think we could legally have won anything anyway."

The old man, Jesse, Matt and Aaron sat in a companionable silence, sipping coffee and nibbling on the deserts and cookies. Watching the other shooters, wives and girlfriends circulating between tables and admiring the various plaques the different teams had won and the winners of the raffles admiring their prizes.

A small crowd gathered looking at the scores, and more than a few glances came their way. The SAS and the SEAL team were off in a corner by themselves and raucous laughter was heard every few minutes. Jesse looked at the plaque Matt and Aaron had won as the third place military team and decided to eat one more cookie.

"Oh damn, here comes the grunt again," Matt moaned.

The old man looked across the table with a quizzical expression. "What's the problem?"

"This damn Army sergeant keeps trying to catch us without our coins, sir. Aaron you've got yours right?" Matt shook his head and started digging in his wallet for his as Aaron went for his breast pocket.

Jesse, not understanding what was happening looked over and asked, "What coins are y'all talking about?"

The old man reached into his shirt and pulling out a pouch that was around his neck on a leather thong. He pulled an old silver coin from it and palmed it in his right hand. "Just wait and see, Jesse," he said, an evil grin on his face.

The Army Sergeant weaved up to the table and slapped his hand down on the table, calling out, "Coin check you misguided children! 101st, put up or buy up boys!" Removing his hand, he revealed a coin lying on the table.

Matt and Aaron both slapped their hands down on the table, saying in unison, "Two MEF." And showed their coins.

The Army Sergeant looked over at the Cronin. "Do you even know what we're talking about, old man?"

He raised his hand to the table top, gently laid it on the table and said, "DOL, Fifth Group. You know what we drink." And showed the old silver coin in his palm.

The Army sergeant turned pale and quickly put his coin back in his pocket, saying, "Yes, sir. Be right back, sir," as he turned away and headed for the bar.

Jesse, now totally confused, looked at Matt and Aaron, who were also uncertain at this point. The old man smiled, if it could be called that. "Papa, what in the hell is going on?"

"Well, he stepped on his dick is what just happened, Jesse; he didn't think there would be any chance of running across one of us here, and he got caught out. I hope y'all like brandy."

Jesse asked, "What do you mean one of 'us,' Papa, and what's DOL?"

Matt chimed in then. "I've never seen him do that

either, what did you show him sir or was it what you said?"

Grinning, the old man spun the coin in his hand and passed it to Jesse, reaching under his shirt and taking off the pouch that had held the coin. "There are a few of us old farts around that go back to the early days when Fifth Group was the main Special Forces group in Vietnam." Pointing at the coin he added, "All of the old farts like me got silver coins presented by the General in country, and we all had these elephant hide pouches made for them. We all wore them around our necks, and vowed never to be without them. DOL is De Oppresso Liber, Latin for to free from oppression and the motto of Special Forces."

As Jesse looked at both sides of the coin and passed it to Matt, she shook her head and just looked at the old man. "Why is *this* the first time I'm finding this out Papa? And what's this about drinking? I've never seen you take a drink in my life at least that I can remember."

"Honey, there are a *lot* of things you don't know, and I hope to God you never find out. That was a different life and a different time from today."

At that point, a very subdued Army Sergeant returned to the table with four shots and quietly asked, "Sir if there is nothing else, may I be excused?"

The old man just nodded. He gestured to the others and each picked up the shots, and he toasted, "De oppresso liber" as they downed their shots. Jesse shivered and wondered what she had gotten into, and realized she didn't really like brandy.

Matt realized the old man they were sitting with was one of the real warriors, and at least for him, things began to fall into place. The attitude, the old but well-cared for rifle, the shooting ability, and his watchfulness all snapped into place and he decided he truly did not want to get on the wrong side of this man. And he decided that this old man had put more than a few in the ground over the years.

He also wondered if Aaron had picked up on it, or was too enthralled by Jesse to be aware of the bigger picture.

The old man turned to Jesse. "You about ready girl? We got miles to go tomorrow and I ain't gettin' any younger."

Jesse just shook her head. "Well, Papa, I guess since 'you' need your sleep I guess we better get you to bed."

Aaron looked like he was going to say something, but stopped when Matt gave him the quiet hand signal. Matt noticed the old man smiling, and he guessed he caught it. The old man got up and so did Matt, Aaron and Jesse.

Fishing in his wallet, the old man passed Matt and Aaron cards. "Matt, Aaron, it was a pleasure to meet y'all, and I wish you the best in your careers; and if you ever get to West Texas, give me a call. I'll treat y'all to some good barbecue on me."

Aaron reached across and shook the old man's hand, and Jesse walked around the table to give both Matt and Aaron hugs, and a peck on the cheek for Aaron, who promptly started turning red again.

Matt took the card and shook hands with the old man. "Mr. Cronin, if I ever get out that way I will, and thanks for letting us join you. I couldn't help but notice that you've never even checked your scores. Do you know how well y'all did?"

"Nope, and I really don't care. This trip was just for fun and to get outta Texas for a bit, and let Jesse see a different part of the country," the old man replied.

Jesse looked at Matt asking, "Did you go look? And if you did, how'd we shoot? Papa never tells me anything."

Matt, looking at both Jesse and the old man responded, "Well sir, y'all out shot everybody but the SAS and you tied them at 462 of a possible 470 points. AND you did that without really modern guns, or scopes or spotting scopes. If y'all had been a bit faster, you would have won the law enforcement side hands down, and probably beaten most of the military folks."

Jesse and Aaron both looked at Matt in incredulity, but the old man just smiled. Jesse hit the old man on the shoulder. "Dammit Papa, why didn't you tell me we did that good?"

"Cause I don't care, hon. This is all for fun, so it don't make a damn how good we did. And I knew coming in I was too old to run that far that fast. But I wanted you to see that *you* can compete with the boys, and you don't have a damn thing to be apologetic for. Now let's go."

The old man and Jesse slipped out the back door, as quietly as they'd come.

10 Guess Who

Six months later, back in Texas...
   The old man came in the house and let the screen door bang shut, as he did, Jesse called from the kitchen, "Is that you, Papa?"
   Walking into the kitchen, he responded, "Who else would it be at five thirty in the morning? And if you took your damn dog out yourself, *I* wouldn't have to do it!"
   Juanita and Francisco laughed as Rex padded in behind the old man and came over and laid his head on Francisco's lap for a scratching.
   Jesse reached for the coffee pot and poured a cup of black coffee and sat it on the table next to the orange juice. "Thank you, Papa, and I've got some news," Jesse said with a grin.
   "Yeah, Aaron got orders and he's going to be here Friday, right? Umm, Juanita could I have some of your delicious Huevos Rancheros please?" the old man grinned as he sat down at the table.
   Juanita smiled and asked, "Anybody want anything different? Francisco, Jesse? Rex, out of the kitchen!"
   As the dog slunk out of the kitchen, Jesse shook her head and looked over at the old man with a stunned expression, "How did you know? He only emailed me an hour ago! Is it alright if he stays here?"
   The old man rocked back in his chair, "Well, *you* are not the only one that has friends in low places and I'm guessing it'll be okay. We can ask Juanita to open up the mother-in-law suite for him." He leaned back sipping his coffee, ostensibly ignoring Jesse with a little grin on his

face.

"Papa?"

Grinning, he turned to Jesse. "Matt called last night, he's on orders too, he's going to Pendleton to take charge of the range out there and be the senior enlisted instructor. He said Aaron is now a staff sergeant and will be going to MARSOC[13] at Pendleton, and then to the Marine First Special Operations Battalion after he completes training. They are driving out at the same time, and he'd asked if he could visit too."

"This Friday, John?" Juanita asked as she finished preparing four plates of eggs done Huevos Ranchero style.

"Do I need to get more food?"

"Well, they *are* Marines, Juanita, and at least one of them has already landed on somebody at the table, so yeah, we're probably going to need more food. Speaking of which, Francisco are the Ramos brothers still doing the rolling BBQ setup?"

As Jesse blushed and opened her mouth to retort, Francisco laughingly replied, "Sure I think so, you want me to check? Do you want them to get a beef and do the prep?"

The old man laughed. "Nah, I think it's about time that old brindle steer meets his maker, and I'll check with Grissom today to see if he's still got that half hog in the freezer. I figure we can do a little barbecue for a few folks, and maybe a little Tex-Mex if Juanita and the ladies are willing to do the fixins. You think you and Toby can wrangle the steer outta the Mesquite?"

Juanita served the plates and took a seat at the far end of the table as Francisco thought out what would be needed. "Sure, I think he's still up on the North 40. If we

---

[13] Marine Special Operations Command

can't get him out with the horses, I'll go in there and drop him. Then we can go get him with the truck and trailer or take the tractor up there and just drag his ass outta there."

"That should work okay, Francisco, and you know Juanita, the more I think about it, I think we'll just throw the Marines in the bunk house, it's not like they don't know how to live in cramped quarters!" The old man snuck a look at Jesse as he said it, and watched her trying to figure out how to respond.

Jesse just kept her head down and kept eating, so the old man decided to have a little fun. "At least this time, he's coming here rather than you inventing reasons you had to fly to the East coast Jesse, and I figure feeding them is the cheaper alternative."

Jesse wailed, "Papa *that's* not nice, and I *did* have good reasons to go, they sent me to that…"

All the others were laughing and the old man answered, "Sure you did, hon. But all of a sudden you're awful damn sensitive about it, and I haven't seen that idiot Frank sniffing around lately."

Francisco snorted into his coffee and Juanita had a coughing spell trying to cover her laughter; as Jesse, injured pride and all snipped, "Well, I decided Frank was not what I wanted to spend, ah hell, I give up. I'm going to work, which sector are you in today, Papa?" She picked up her plate, rinsed it in the sink and dropped it in the dishwasher, filling a to-go cup with coffee as she headed toward the door.

The old man replied, "I'm in sector three, so don't get in any trouble today, cause I would hate to haul your butt to jail, and tell that speed demon Rick that if I catch him screwing around I *will* put his ass in jail."

Kissing the old man on the cheek Jesse smirked. "Yes, Papa, I'll tell him." Dodging his attempt to swat her on the butt as she went by, she patted Rex as he snuck back into the kitchen and took his accustomed place at side of the old man's chair.

The old man got up and took his dishes to the sink, rinsed them and put them in the dishwasher, picked up the coffee pot and tipped it toward Francisco, who nodded and held out his cup, as Juanita waved it off. The old man poured him a cup, then one for himself as the screen door slammed, and they heard Jesse start her car and pull out of the driveway.

Juanita turned to face the old man as he leaned back against the sink. "Okay, John, what is going on?" asked Juanita. "Marines? Where is this coming from?"

Taking a sip of coffee, the old man thought for a second. "Well, you remember when we went back East to that sniper shoot?

"We drove back and shot against a bunch of military and LEOs in West Virginia. We met a couple of pretty sharp Marines from Quantico and the young one took a shine to Jesse. That's why she's made a couple of trips to the East Coast. Granted some of it was business, but mostly to see Aaron. I didn't think much about it till Frank stopped coming around."

"Okay, John, where do you really want to put them?" Juanita asked grabbing a pad and pencil. "You've got one bedroom here, and two in the old house, and then there is the bunkhouse. But I wouldn't want to put them in there with Toby, he's such a slob."

"The window units both work in the old house, so that's where I'd put them," Francisco said. "But if Jesse and this Aaron are 'friendly,' well that is going to complicate things."

The old man grinned. "Yeah, you're probably right, why don't we put Matt in here and Aaron in the old house, that way I don't have to listen to a bunch of noise, or react to a situation that I really ain't worrying about if you know what I mean. Hell, Jesse is of age, and knows her own business."

Francisco laughed and Juanita just shook her head saying, "*You* are a dirty old man John, but if that is what you want? So how many people do you want to invite?"

"Oh, I guess the usual suspects, and I'm assuming you'll invite your usual suspects so we'll be feeding what, fifty? Plus kids? And do you feel up to doing the Tex-Mex?" the old man asked.

Poking Francisco, Juanita replied, "Well, since this old man never takes me anywhere, I'll get the girls together and we'll put on a good feed for them and I'll get to have a girls day too!"

Mumbling under his breath, Francisco got up and rinsed his dishes and headed to the door. "I never take you because you *never* want to go, and unlike the rest of y'all, I have work to do. This ranch doesn't run itself. Stay safe today, John."

The old man nodded and then turned to Juanita. "Take whatever you need out of the operating account and I'll leave the menu in your capable hands. I gotta get to work too, since I'm down south today."

Juanita nodded as the old man went into the living room, picked up his gun belt and slung it around his hips, grabbed the radio out of the charger and put on his cowboy hat. Rex looked up hopefully and whined, but the old man gave him the stay command, and walked out the door.

At lunch, the old man gave Grissom a call and determined there was a half a hog available, and passed that along to Francisco. He also talked to the sheriff and switched his Friday patrol to sector four, figuring he'd have to go meet Matt and Aaron in Pecos and lead them back in rather than trying to give them directions on the back roads and farm roads in West Texas.

Back at the ranch, Francisco and Toby saddled up a couple of horses and rode up to the North 40, which was really a 160-acre section. They didn't see the old brindle steer, and split up to try to bust him out of the mesquite and creek bottom. Francisco, knowing steers and this particular one was a nasty one, decided to keep Toby out of trouble if he could. Toby was twenty, and becoming a pretty good hand, but he had a lot to learn about Longhorns and especially the cranky ones. He also loved to charge into things, sometimes getting himself in binds that took a bit to get out of, but this time that 'bind' could get him dead before Francisco could get there. After about three hours, Francisco called on the personal radio, "Toby, you seen anything yet?"

"No see, boss," Toby replied. " I working North to South on far side high ground but over by the bottoms, I not seeing him, see most the rest of the beeves but no him. How damn hell can something grande disappear?"

Francisco chuckled. "'Cause he's an old mossy back and he probably has a hidey hole in the bottoms that we just haven't found. Come on down to the big rock on the west side of the creek and we'll eat lunch and figure out what to do next."

"On way, boss!"

After sandwiches and bottles of water, Francisco decided to just run the creek out and see if the steer would show up. After about fifteen minutes, they found him on Francisco's side of the creek and moved him down to a corral at the back of the ranch house. Francisco called the Ramos brothers and set up for them to come out Friday and start the barbecue of the steer and the hog.

Meanwhile, Juanita had been on the phone to various friends and had come up with plenty of folks to help prepare the food, and meet Jesse's new beau. Most of her friends thought it was a shame she hadn't already married and had children, thinking she was going to be a spinster daughter. As Juanita was shopping for ingredients she reflected on how lucky she and Francisco were: making good money and having a nice house to live in, even if they didn't own it, but that was made up for by working for Senor John and Jesse. She worried that if Jesse *did* marry this Marine she would leave the ranch and then what would happen, but that was a thought for another time, not for now.

11 Visitors

Hanging up the cell, the old man called in, "Dispatch, car six. I'm heading up to the truck stop in Monahans to pick up my visitors, be out of the county about an hour ETR is fifteen hundred."

The female dispatcher came back. "Roger Car six, y'all going to come by here? I could use a good man, you know."

Chuckling the old man responded, "Dispatch, we'll see, but one of them is already taken."

His cell rang, and he picked it up to see the sheriff was calling. "Yeah, sheriff?"

Sheriff Rodriguez rustling paper paused. "John, do you want to go off early today? I can push Hart up to cover four for the rest of the day since he's just driving in circles over in sector six, and DPS has two cars working I-10 over there."

Cocking his head, the old man thought for a minute. "Nah, it's been quiet up here all day too, other than that idiot oil tanker driver that I wrote up this morning. I might stop at the house for a few to get them settled and introduce them to Francisco and Juanita, but I'll stay till the end of shift."

"Okay, sounds good, John. What time do the festivities start tomorrow? I know Betsy is helping with the fixings, but she never told me what time *I* was supposed to show up."

The old man smiled. "Well, you're welcome anytime, but the food is going to start about three or four. I've asked Jose Ramos to make up some cuts to take to the department for both the deputies and the fire rescue folks about five and I think Juanita is planning on feeding them better than she's feeding us."

Sighing, the sheriff replied, "Like I need to eat any big meals. But this is one feed I've never passed up. Call if you need more time John."

"Will do, Jose." Hanging up the cell, the old man eased down on the accelerator and headed up 18 to Monahans. He wondered what this weekend would bring, and hoped things didn't blow up, but he would be glad to see Matt, and even Aaron, too. But he would give Aaron a ration of crap, just to see what he was made of. Twenty minutes later he pulled into the truck stop at Monahans and spied two dirty SUVs sitting off to the side of the gas pumps with Virginia license plates. Looking closer he saw that both SUVs had Marine Corps stickers on the back glass, so he pulled in right behind them.

Getting out and stretching, he looked around but didn't see either Matt or Aaron, so he wandered into the coffee shop.

The waitress came over and asked if he'd like a cup of coffee, so the old man agreed and dropped a couple of dollars on the counter. Behind him he heard a quiet, "Oh damn." Turning around, he saw Matt and Aaron just coming out of the bathroom.

Matt walked over and started apologizing. "Sorry, sir, I didn't figure you'd get here that quickly, so I was trying to be ready."

The old man just stuck out his hand and laughed. "No biggie Matt, I know about hitting the bathroom, trust me!" He reached over and shook Aaron's hand too, and the waitress handed him his coffee. "Y'all need anything for the road? We've got about a thirty-minute drive from here."

A chorus of no sirs came back, so they headed for

the door. As they walked toward the vehicles, he noticed Matt heading toward the Chevy SUV, so he turned to Aaron, "Don't tell me you're driving a damn Ford! I don't allow Fords on my property; you can leave that POS here, and ride with Matt."

Aaron just looked at the old man with a stunned expression until he realized the old man was smiling and Matt was laughing. He finally responded, "Damn, I heard y'all were pretty parochial about trucks down here, but I didn't realize it was *that* bad, sir. Although I did notice as we got further south and west the more trucks and fewer cars were in dealerships."

"Yep, people have been disowned for buying a different brand down here, and that can go for generations. And you can bet every damn one of them has a least a rifle in it, if not a shotgun and a pistol or two. Y'all both have VA carry, right?"

Matt nodded and Aaron said, "Virginia and Florida both, sir."

"Okay, strange as it may seem, concealed is legal with either of those, but open carry is *not* legal any time you're off the ranch. We normally open carry when we're on the range, but remember off the property *concealed*."

A chorus of "yes, sirs" again, and the old man smiled. "Okay, we're going to follow 18 South for a while then out into the boonies a bit, 'bout 30 minutes. If something comes up and I have to haul ass, just continue to Ft. Stockton and call Jesse, and she can come get y'all. Okay, let's go."

Getting back in the car, the old man led Matt and Aaron back down 18 then back to the ranch. As they pulled into the yard, the Ramos brothers were finishing stripping out the hide of the old brindle steer hanging over the corral gate to the right of the driveway and the smell of barbecue was wafting over the yard.

Matt and Aaron got out and looked around in amazement. They were standing in front of the big house, with a porch that looked like it went all the way around the house. Off to the right was a smaller house that looked like it was really made out of logs, and further still stood barns and sheds all with tin roofs and most looking like they had been there a while. Off to the left, the west, they saw a row of cedar trees and a few oaks that seemed to lean to the east. More trees could be seen behind another log building and behind that a newer small house with more trees. Other than the driveway, everything was fenced and Matt remembered they'd crossed a cattle guard coming into the driveway.

The old man walked up to the house and an older Hispanic couple came out, along with a damn big German Shepherd, which bounded down the steps to the old man, then growled at Matt and Aaron.

Grabbing the dog's collar the old man said, "Friends, Rex, friends! You guys stick your hands out palms down and let him sniff 'em. This is Francisco, my ranch foreman, and Juanita his wife who takes care of all of us!"

Laughter and handshakes went around, and the old man bowed out to go back to work. Juanita took one look at the Marines and invited them into the house, putting glasses of iced tea in front of them. "You are Matthew and you are Aaron," she said, pointing at both men. "I have seen pictures of you. For you Matthew, you will be sleeping in the back bedroom here. Aaron, you will be in the guest house out back, and Francisco will show you where to put your bags. I have placed clean sheets on the beds and you have fresh towels and soap and shampoo on your beds. Supper will be at seven PM, breakfast at five thirty AM, and *no* eating the desserts! Those are for tomorrow. Any questions?"

Matt looked at her with a smile. "Yes, ma'am. One question, were you ever in the Marines? Because you sure sound like a drill instructor!"

Juanita playfully slapped Matt on the arm. "Maybe I should be, twenty years of taking care of lazy men around here and trying to keep this place clean. Maybe I need some Marines here to show these lazy bums how to clean up after themselves."

Francisco just rolled his eyes, earning a glare from Juanita. "Just ignore her. She's all bark and no bite just like Rex. Come, I will show you where to put your bags."

As they walked through the house, both Matt and Aaron looked around at the old but comfortable furniture, obvious antiques, and when Matt was shown the bedroom he would be sleeping in commented on the Winchester hanging in the deer antler rack by the bed, "Is that thing loaded?"

Francisco told him, "Of course it's loaded, and it's an 1886 in 45-70 and there are spare rounds in the night stand, top drawer. All the guns you see in this house and the others are always loaded for safety in case they are needed."

Aaron chimed in, "Always loaded for safety in case they are needed? What does that mean, sir?"

Francisco shrugged. "This is a ranch, senor, in west Texas, and one never knows when you will need a gun to hand."

He led them out the back hallway to the old house. "According to John, this is the original house built here in the 1870s and it is on part of the original ranch section of land his five times great grandfather settled after the Civil War. At one point, they had almost twenty thousand acres of ranch and farm land in this area," he said as he gestured to the old house. "Yes, those are bullet holes in the door, and around the windows. The house was attacked a few times over the years by Indians and rustlers. But they have continued to upgrade the house over the generations, and Senor John's dad was the last family member born in this house. He built the new house in the 1940s. It does have air conditioners in the windows, and it has running water, although that is in the addition on the back of the house. The kitchen no longer works, but the bathroom does, including the shower, and the sink in the kitchen has running water."

Opening the door, Matt and Aaron both stopped cold. It was like walking into a museum except it was real and Aaron would be staying here. Francisco opened the middle door on the right, and pointed out the light switches, and said, "Before you ask, yes that is also loaded, and also a .44-40, but that one is an 1873 Winchester and spare rounds are in the nightstand. Feel free to look around, I must go back to work now. John and Jesse should be here in about an hour."

Matt and Aaron unloaded their bags into their respective rooms and wandered around a bit, realizing they were literally seeing a family history in the furniture, the pictures on the walls, and the furnishings. Just looking at the houses, the set up and watching the Ramos brothers starting to cook both the steer and the half hog in a huge smoker they had pulled in behind their truck made them wonder what they'd walked into. Aaron was looking around like a pole axed steer, mumbling that Jesse had never said anything about any of this, just said she lived on a little old farm.

After they looked around a bit inside, the smell of barbecue convinced them to go outside and over to where Jose and his crew were working and Jose explained they don't use all hickory or mesquite, but put both apple and cherry woods into the mix also, and they would be cooking until the next afternoon before all the food was ready. They'd set up chairs, a picnic table, and had a little portable TV running on the table as they dusted the steer and hog with rubs. He also explained they wouldn't actually put any sauce onto either set of meats until the last half hour, and he and Matt got in a long discussion over types of barbecue. Aaron wandered over to the steer hide and poked at it, trying to imagine what it would be used for.

Half an hour later, they were sitting in the kitchen enjoying another glass of iced tea when they heard two cars pull into the driveway and shut off, two doors slammed and then the screen door. Matt looked at Aaron and noticed that Aaron had suddenly gotten very tense, and chuckled to himself.

He looked back and Jesse was standing in the door, suddenly as shy as Aaron seemed to be, until she got a push in the back from the old man. "If you're gonna kiss him, go kiss him; don't stand there like a love sick calf, girl."

Juanita laughed and that broke the spell. Jesse walked over to Aaron put a hand on his shoulder and kissed him on the cheek saying, "Hi, I'm glad you made it okay. Hi Matt, welcome."

Aaron reached up and put his hand over Jesse's and just looked at her.

The old man laughed. "Okay, y'all can go somewhere private and catch up, meantime I'm going to get a cup of coffee and talk with Matt."

Blushing, Jesse grabbed Aaron's hand and dragged him out the back door. They all laughed as they noticed the back of Aaron's neck was red, too.

Juanita yelled after them, "Catfish in an hour, don't be late!"

The old man grabbed a cup of coffee and led Matt into the library slash office. As he eased himself into his favorite rocker, he looked up at Matt, waved his hand about the room and said, "I'm sure you have a few questions don't ya Matt?"

Matt walked over to the book lined cases and looked at one shelf that had a few pictures and trinkets sitting on it. "Well, sir, it does seem you're not just an old country boy sheriff's deputy. And judging by the number of oil wells I've seen, and the size of this place, I think y'all are doing pretty well and have been here a *long* time!"

The old man sighed. "Well, Matt, short story is our family settled here in the 1870s, managed to get a pretty good piece of land out here 'bout 20,000 acres, lost some of it to keep the family fed, and we're down to about 3300 acres, give or take. Luckily nobody ever sold off the mineral rights, since this is actually the Permian basin, which is one of the largest oil fields in the US. But more specifically we're sitting on what's called the Delaware basin and Sheffield channel which connects to the Midland and Val Verde basins. The first field in Pecos County was the Yates field down in the Southeast corner of the county, round about 1926, and grandpa told me he hit oil a couple of times in the 30s trying to get water, which is actually more precious out here than oil by the way. But that was the Depression and he couldn't get anybody to come get it since he never sold or leased any mineral rights to anybody. It wasn't till World War II that they came looking up in this part of the county for oil and grandpa finally got some wells drilled down about eight thousand feet. We've done pretty well since, and manage to keep the place up, money in the bank, and we run a few head of Longhorns up on the north section."

"Is that what you referred to as the North 40?" Matt asked.

"Yep, but it's actually a full section, so it's really 640 acres."

Meanwhile, Jesse and Aaron walked down the path behind the house. Once they were out of sight of the houses and Jose and his crew, Aaron stopped and pulled Jesse into his arms and they kissed for a long time. Jesse laid her head on Aaron's chest.

"I've missed you Jesse, and there seems to be a few things you didn't tell me," he said, sweeping the property with one arm. "This is a helluva lot more than a little farm isn't it?"

Jesse leaned back in his arms, then glared over toward the trees. "Toby, you come out of there right now!"

Abashed, Toby came out of the brush, walked over and said, "Miss Jesse, just making sure he okay. No want bad guys here."

"Toby, Aaron is not a bad guy, he's my boyfriend. Aaron, this is Toby, he's the ranch hand that works for Papa and Francisco. Now the two of you shake hands, and Toby, you disappear, got it?"

Smiling and bobbing his head, Toby shook Aaron's hand and replied, "Yes, Miss Jesse, I go work with horses now. You ride Buttercup tomorrow?"

"Maybe Toby," she said, shooing him away.

Puzzled, Aaron looked after Toby, "What kind of Indian is he? Or is he? That didn't sound like…"

Putting her arms back around Aaron, Jesse answered, "He's a Montangard, Papa's friend's son who is here to try to make a life for himself outside his culture since they have way too many males. He's three years younger than me, but he knows horses and animals like nobody I've ever seen. And before you go there, yes I *do* have a horse named Buttercup. *Do not* go there, understand?"

Laughing Aaron kissed the top of Jesse's head, "Yes, dear."

"Now you're learning," she said, grabbing Aaron's hand as they walked down to the corral. Jesse introduced Aaron to Buttercup and the other horses, joking that if he wanted to hang around, he'd have to learn to ride and be able to keep up with her.

Back in the house, Matt pointed to a picture sitting in the back of the shelf. "Is that you sir, when you were in the Army?"

The old man got up and walked over to the shelf, taking out the picture and the piece of bracelet lying there, he bowed his head for a minute, and then looked at Matt. "Yeah, that's me as a staff sergeant, and that's a picture of the Degar village I lived in and worked out of for almost a year west of Pleiku. Of the people in that picture, I think maybe six are still alive."

"Degar?"

"Yards, Montagnards or hill people as they were known. Actually that ville was part of the Jarai tribe or family, if you will. I was there until early '68 before I got rotated out. We were sitting on the South end of the Ho Chi Min trail, and our job was to provide a tripwire for major movements and interdict if there were small movements. Those people were fantastic fighters, and they got fucked so bad, not only by their own government, but by us, and it still pisses me off. They were left behind to die when the US pulled out. A few have been relocated to North Carolina, maybe three thousand total; but they've got problems adapting here too. Actually my 'ranch hand' Toby, well, he's a Degar." Pointing to a young girl in the picture he continued, "His mother, I found out she and a couple of others made it out; I helped them out a little bit quite a few years ago, and actually brought them out here for a while. Toby, that's what we call him because we can't pronounce his real name, he fell in love with the horses and animals, but his momma couldn't handle the environment out here, and she went back to North Carolina. About two years ago, I got a call from her, wondering if I'd take Toby and put him to work. Since he's part white, he's pretty much an outcast to the tribe, and he still loves horses. Hell, he's doing all the breaking of the horses for us and a couple of other folks."

Shaking his head, he put the picture back on the shelf. Bouncing the piece of bracelet in his palm, he commented, "This is the last bracelet they made for me, and I wore it for about three years until I was directed to take it off. It's elephant hair, so it'll never wear out for all practical purposes. That was kinda a clue to folks where you were or had been too. I went back the last time in 71-72 as an advisor, hell there wasn't much to advise… Most of the ARVN were on the run or just going home, and we got the shit shot out of us a few times. I came home from that and did a couple of other short detachments in various places and got out in '75 after my dad died."

Matt pointed to the plaques shoved in the back of the shelf. "Those are quite a collection. Are they from the dets?"

The old man sat back down, grabbed his coffee and drained it. "Nah, I joined the sheriff's department here in '76, since we'd sold off the cows and there wasn't much to do here. I did a two-year second to the DEA and in '83 the department sent me to the FBI National Academy, that's the picture with the NA on it. The rest are from some things I've gotten for being loaned out here and there. I kinda know a little bit about smuggling."

Matt and the old man compared notes on the differences between the Army and Marines and combat in

Vietnam versus Afghanistan and Iraq. By the time dinner was called, they'd established a mutual respect that crossed both the age and service boundaries.

After dinner, Matt pleading a full stomach and being tired from the drive, headed for a shower and bed. The old man and Francisco helped Juanita clean up the kitchen and wash the dishes that didn't fit in the dishwasher; and Francisco and Juanita headed over to their house. Jesse and Aaron had disappeared, and the old man just smiled. He ruffled Rex's head and walked back into the office and worked a few emails before going to bed.

12 Fandango

The next morning everyone made it to breakfast, although Jesse and Aaron looked strangely tired and blushed a lot, much to the amusement of everyone else. After breakfast Juanita handed out assignments, freely drafting Matt and Aaron into the working parties necessary to set up for the hundred or more people that were expected.

With Francisco driving the tractor and trailer, tables and chairs were brought out of storage, washed down and set up between the old house and new house. The old man was summarily sent to the store for coolers full of ice, Matt and Aaron drafted into helping the arriving ladies unload various trunks, back seats, and generally carrying things that needed hauled.

The ladies took the measure of Aaron and numerous comments in Spanish and English flew around the kitchen and the yard as the ladies bustled around setting up the tables, serving and cooking areas.

Francisco, Matt and Aaron strung lights plugging them in and replacing the bulbs that had blown out and did a general cleanup of the area.

Aaron was almost to the point of a permanent blush until Jesse rescued him and Matt and sent them to the store for heavy-duty plates, silverware, packages of napkins and drink cups. After driving the horses all into the corral and securing the gate, Toby brought the tractor over and mowed about a third of the pasture and picked up the hay.

After Matt and Aaron returned, Francisco drafted them to help drive stakes to mark parking areas in the field and to help take the gate off the hinges and set it to the side of the cattle guard. Their next assignment was to move all the ladies cars over to the pasture, which became rather interesting, since most of the ladies were nowhere near as tall as Matt or Aaron, and hilarity ensued when Aaron tried to drive a Miata to the pasture without moving the seat back.

The old man finally returned with the ice and the sheriff in tow. Once the ice had been distributed, the men were finally allowed to go out on the front porch with a pitcher of iced tea.

After introducing everyone, the old man plopped down in one of the rockers. "*Now*, I remember why we don't do this very often. God, what a pain in the ass!"

Matt just shook his head saying, "Damn, Juanita could get a job tomorrow as a sergeant major in the Marine Corps, that lady has her act together!"

Aaron chimed in, "Hell, I think she could *teach* some of the sergeant majors I've seen some things. And I really wish I knew Spanish so I could figure out what they were saying."

The old man and sheriff both chuckled, and the sheriff replied, "No, son, you really don't. Those ladies in there are all basically farm girls, so they cut straight to the meat or bone depending. But it does look like they approve of you, so you're *really* in trouble now. They'll be planning the wedding before the night's over."

Aaron looked like he'd been hit with a two by four , while everyone else laughed. "Wedding, what damn wedding!?! I… er…"

More laughter ensued with the old man adding, "Well, you're a helluva lot better than the last one she was seeing. And most of those biddies in there think Jesse should be married with kids by now. So, all I can say is I hope to hell your intentions are honorable, otherwise they'll gut you like a fish, and hang your hide over the corral fence!"

Matt looked over at Aaron. "You're on your own now, buddy. I'm outta this one!"

Aaron was saved by Jesse walking out with a new pitcher of iced tea and the decree that the men needed to clean up and get presentable, but the bathrooms in the main house were off limits, since the women needed to freshen up and they'd laid claim to them. The men could use the bathroom in the old house, and step on it, people would start showing up in an hour.

Grumbling and claiming the homeowner's right, the old man went in grabbed his clothes and a towel and headed to the old house. Matt and Aaron decided to wear khakis and their red Marine polo shirts, figuring in for a penny, in for a pound. Francisco disappeared to his house, and left the sheriff sitting on the porch when Jesse returned to pick up the pitchers.

Jesse plopped into a chair sighing. "My feet are killing me already, and we haven't even started dancing yet."

The sheriff laughed. "Well, Jesse, y'all decided to do this, not us so you're getting no sympathy from me. And you do remember you're on the schedule for a patrol shift tomorrow don't you?"

"Oh shit... I forgot all about that. Ummm, if I take the shift can Aaron ride along? I mean it should be fairly quiet."

The sheriff rocked back in the chair and looked at Jesse. "If I say yes, you still have to do the patrol and you will have to pay attention. Can you do that?"

"Yes sir, I will. It's not like Aaron doesn't know about patrolling, I mean... he's done it in combat, so I don't think there will be a problem."

"Okay, but come see me before you go out

tomorrow. Holmes is out sick with a stomach bug, so I'll be in the office tomorrow."

Forty-five minutes later, the men were all back on the front porch, when Juanita came out and inspected them and brought a round of Shiners for them. "Y'all cleanup pretty good, and here's your reward, y'all get one now and one with dinner, no more just in case anybody gets stupid."
Aaron picked up the bottle and looked at it curiously, "Shiner Bock?"
The old man laughed. "It's a Texas beer, and about the only damn thing you'll see around here. We don't go in for those fancy beers, much less that import crap like Corona."

A chorus of "Yes, sirs" were followed by the old man's toast. "Once more into the breach dear friends, and absent comrades!" They all touched bottles and sipped appreciatively.

Shortly thereafter, cars started arriving and Francisco and Toby managed the parking as the old man played host. Matt and Aaron did their best to stay out of the way and help out where they could, ferrying food from the kitchen and coolers from the barn for the drinks. Finally, the old man and Jesse walked to the front of the tables. "Well, I think about everybody that's coming is here, so let's have a quick prayer and get to eating."

Everyone bowed their heads, and Jesse said a short prayer thanking God for his guidance. The line moved quickly as the Ramos brothers filled plates with the barbecue of folks' choice, and they moved to the next table with all the trimmings. Matt and Jesse hung back and waited for the old man, Francisco and Toby. Juanita came over, flushed and smiling and looked over the crowd. "I think we done good boss, what say you?"

"Yep, y'all done good, and Jose, thanks for coming

out and putting the barbecue on for us! Remember we need to set aside some plates for the folks on duty, and having said that, I'm *hungry*, let's eat!"

Jose nodded. "We've already prepped twenty-five plates and set them aside, we did twelve beef, twelve of pork, and one veggie so that should make 'em happy."

Juanita chimed in, "We'll load the trimmings on later, and the sheriff says he'll take them in when he leaves, so we've got a couple of hours. Now go, I'm hungry too!"

The old man told Matt to try both the beef and pork, so both Matt and Aaron took a little of each. There were barbecue beans and refried beans, potato salad, fresh-cut French fries, salad, tortillas, rice, fresh jalapenos, pickles and white bread to choose from. Jesse laughed as Aaron tried to figure out how to fit everything on one plate, telling him, "You can come back you know, it's not like there isn't going to be anything left."

Aaron ducked his head, blushed and let Jesse lead him over to a table on the side of the area where a number of younger folks sat. Toby had saved them two places together so they put the food down and Aaron went for drinks. Jesse introduced Aaron to everyone and after the "hi's" and "howareya's" were done, everybody got serious about eating. Aaron was amazed at the different taste and said so to Jesse, who just laughed. "Well, this is real Texas barbecue, not like that stuff we got in West Virginia. And they just don't know how to do real good brisket back there."

Matt sat with the old man, Francisco and Juanita and the sheriff. He realized this was really the first time he'd seen the old man even close to relaxed, but he was still sitting where he could see the doors and the drive into the yard. Matt wondered if the old man was carrying, and it hit Matt that he was probably the only one at the table that *wasn't* carrying. He'd noticed even Juanita with her apron on, probably either had a pistol in the pocket or behind it.

And she wasn't the only one, probably most of the people at the other tables were carrying too! Remembering the guns in the gunracks of the trucks in the field, there were some serious shooters in this bunch. Matt just shook his head in amazement, definitely *not* the kind of crowd he was used to seeing.

It also seemed most of the people were at least bi-lingual as the conversations flowed freely between Spanish and English depending on what was being said. The other thing he realized was all these folks were equals, regardless of their heritage. Definitely not what the media reported, but then again he reminded himself that he knew better than to listen to and believe the media after what they'd done to the Corps. He also noticed there were some pretty Spanish ladies here in their blouses and colorful skirts.

After finishing his plate, he turned to the old man. "Okay, I'll admit this is some damn good barbecue, and I don't think I've ever had better brisket anywhere. And I'll admit this is better than most of the Carolina barbecue, too."

The old man laughed. "Accepted, and now for the dessert. I'll explain what we've got over there."

Getting up and moving between tables, the old man greeted folks and introduced Matt as they went. Finally arriving at the dessert table, he pointed out the flan, tres leches, churros, chili-chocolate cake; blackberry, peach, and apple cobblers, and cakes and pies. At the end of the table were churns of home-made ice cream in at least three different flavors.

"Choose your poison, Marine, there's more where this came from," he said with a smile.

Matt groaned. "*Now,* you tell me all this is here, if I'd known this, I wouldn't have gone back for a second helping on the barbecue."

As they made their choices, Jesse dragged Aaron over to the patio and suddenly the music got cranked up to a 'dancing' level. Folks started getting up and moving toward the patio as Jesse and Aaron stood off to the side apparently disagreeing over something. Matt pointed, "Oops, looks like the first fight is in progress, and I'm betting it's over dancing. I don't think I've ever seen Aaron on a dance floor anywhere."

The old man chuckled. "Can't say I blame him, but Jesse's a dancing fool. Just watch! She'll embarrass him to the point he'll get up there. "God Bless Texas" by Alan Jackson came on and the line dancing was on. Some of the Hispanic folks disappeared to their cars and Matt asked, "Are they leaving?"

"Nah," the old man replied. "They're after their instruments. We'll have a pretty good little Mariachi band here in a bit. Once that happens, they'll alternate back and forth for a few hours or until I throw 'em all out."

Jesse was up leading the line dance and teasing Aaron anytime she came close. Matt and the old man sat back and just watched and enjoyed it. Getting up to get another cup of coffee, Matt stood by the table for a few minutes and realized there was a woman standing near him. He nodded to her. She smiled and walked over. "Hello, my name is Felicia and I've been keeping an eye on ya, you don't dance?"

Matt realized she was a very attractive lady and probably close to his age, mid- 30s, and not wearing a ring. He looked out at the dance floor and answered, "I'm Matt, and, well, I don't know how to line dance, and I'm not much good for anything but slow dancing. I'm one of those WASPs with no rhythm…"

Felicia cocked her head. "WASP? What is that?"

Matt chuckled. "Sorry, White Anglo-Saxon Protestant, it means I'm a lousy dancer. Besides I've got big feet."

Felicia looked up at Matt and said, "Well, you *are* a big man, and I think a hard man, but inside I think you've got a big heart. Of course, there's always the saying about the size of a man's feet….", she said with a small smile. "

Matt wasn't sure how to respond, so he excused himself, grabbed a second cup of coffee and headed back to the table with the old man. Handing him a cup, he looked back to see Felicia step onto the dance floor by herself and slot seamlessly into the line dance. The old man leaned over. "Why didn't you dance with her?"

Matt shrugged. "Hell, I'm too damn big and clumsy for dancing. Besides, she's just a little bitty thing!"

The old man just laughed.

A few minutes later the stereo went down and the Mexicans tuned up for a few minutes, and then swung into a salsa beat. The dancers changed out, some sitting and others jumping up to dance. Jesse was grabbed by a young Mexican and they swung into an excellent salsa that showed they'd danced together before. Aaron got disgusted and walked back over to the table and sat down. "I don't believe this, not a single damn song I can actually dance to, and I'm not about to make a fool out of myself!"

Finally Jesse came over, smiling and laughing, wiping her face with a napkin as she plopped next to Aaron. "They're going to play a slow dance in a couple of songs, and I want to dance with you, okay?"

Aaron nodded and perked up a little bit.

"Hon, I'm not trying to embarrass you but I like to

dance, and besides it's *good* exercise!"

Two songs later, as Jesse and Aaron got up, Matt also got up and walked over to Felicia. Holding out his hand he said, "I'm willing to try this if you are."

Felicia laughed, put her hand in Matts and led him to the dance floor as she whispered to him, "My, such a smooth talker you are." When they got on the floor, Matt realized how little Felicia really was; she barely came up to his shoulder, and felt light as a feather. Still trying to figure out what she meant by her comment and in an attempt to be polite he asked, "Are you from here too? I guess you know we're just here for a couple of days."

Felicia looked up at him smiling. "Originally, I was, but now I live in California and work as a translator for Customs and Border Patrol. I just happened to be back on vacation and got to come along tonight. I remember Senor John from when I was a little girl, my padre worked for him during roundups."

Matt's heart did a little flip, but he was afraid to ask where in California she lived. The dance ended way too soon for Matt, and he escorted her back to the table she was sharing with family. Thanking her for the dance, he grabbed another cup of coffee and headed back to their table. Francisco and Juanita were just sitting down and taking a break, too. Juanita glanced over at Matt. "Thank you for dancing with Felicia, her mother was afraid no one would dance with her."

"Why? She's a good dancer, and a pretty lady!"

Juanita answered, "Well, she doesn't live here anymore, and she's now a widow; her husband died a year ago in a construction accident. So any man she dances with here would be in trouble with his wife or family, especially if they danced with her because they feel sorry for her. I was afraid I was going to have to ask John to dance with her!"

"Well, I didn't mind it," he said. "And I don't think she did either."

Francisco broke in, "Matt, I think she lives not too far from where you are going to be stationed. I think Encinitas, Escondido, something like that."

The old man just sat drinking coffee and watching the dancers, he noticed that Jesse had finally convinced Aaron to try some line dances, and they were both laughing. They made a good couple.

At six-feet-plus Aaron topped Jesse's height by four or five inches, and he obviously loved her. Couldn't ask for much more, whether he realized it or not. Glancing over at Matt, the old man thought he and Felicia were an interesting pair: Matt looked like a Viking berserker, holding Felicia like she was a little Spanish doll and he was going to break her; that got him chuckling.

Jesse turned the stereo down and all four of them came over. Jesse turned to Matt and Aaron. "Eduardo and Rosa are going to do the Hat Dance, and that will be the last dance. They're married and actually professional dancers, but tonight it's for fun! Since I don't think y'all know the history, it's pretty much the representative dance of Mexico now, and represents the courtship of a man and a woman, with the woman first rejecting the man's advances, and then eventually accepting them. Now, Rosa is wearing the most traditional outfit is called the China Poblana: the blouse and skirt combination is named after a woman from India who came to Mexico on a ship in the early 19th century. Why China? I dunno. But the Asian dress was adapted in the State of Puebla, with the skirt now heavily embroidered. The traditional outfit for men is that of the charro, generally heavily decorated in silver trim; and Eduardo's using the traditional real silver Conchos that have been in his family for years."

After the dance, everyone started packing up and picking up, and the old man bid everyone a good evening and thanked them for coming. The ladies quickly and efficiently fixed the twenty-five plates for the sheriff to take back to the station, and everything else went into the fridges or freezers based on Juanita's direction. By midnight, everything was pretty much done, with the exception of the tables, and the old man gave Jose Ramos a check for his help and profuse thanks for doing the cooking.

Juanita finished cleaning the kitchen and poured one more cup of coffee as everyone filtered off to bed. Sitting down, she realized it had been a long day. Thinking back, Juanita remembered her first days here, not knowing if Francisco was going to live or not; then being offered a place to live and a new life. She had first thought that it was just out of pity, but now she knew it was really a partnership.

When Amy died, she'd become the de facto mother to Jesse. She'd been worried about Jesse and her finding a good man, but now after meeting Aaron and watching him for a couple of days, she was feeling a lot better. Both Matt and Aaron were a lot like John, the depth of character proven on the battlefield didn't show unless you knew what you were looking for; but both of them had it in spades. Aaron was almost as quiet as John, and it was funny to watch him try to figure out situations. She thought he probably hadn't had any siblings and probably wasn't real good at personal interactions.

And Jesse liked to poke him, but she was doing it both because she's truly in love and because she was testing him. *Just like I did with Francisco those many years ago in Guadalajara,* Juanita thought. *Yes, I think they've made the commitment, even if neither of them realizes it just yet.*

Finishing her coffee, Juanita made her way quietly out the door to her and Francisco's little house deciding all the work had been worth it after all.

13 Practice

Breakfast Sunday morning was done and on the table before Matt and Aaron made it out of bed and to the kitchen; both of them felt the night's exercise. When they came in they were laughed at by everyone else, and they both noticed that everyone wore shirts, pants and boots and pistols this morning. They helped themselves to the bacon, eggs, biscuits and sausage, along with coffee and orange juice before sitting down.

Sipping his coffee Matt asked, "Is there something I'm missing? Did somebody forget to tell us something last night?"

Juanita laughed. "But of course, today is training day. Every Sunday morning we go shoot for practice."

Aaron looked over a Jesse. "Where is this? Or is this something else you didn't tell me about?"

Jesse stuck her tongue out at Aaron. "Well, we are going to go shoot, you can stay here and be lazy; and honestly, I never even thought about it. So there…"

The old man looked over at Matt. "We have a little course we run. Then, shoot some steels, then do some rifle work. It was Francisco's turn to set targets this morning, so it'll be fairly easy; when Juanita does it, you're gonna have to work for it!"

"A course?"

"Yeah, the range is down in the creek bottom behind the corrals about fifty yards, so we put some targets on the trail, just for practice purposes, then when you get down to the bottom, we've got some steels at various ranges and the calliope. Francisco will bring down a couple of rifles so we can work them too. Speaking of which, you guys have eyes and ears?"

"A calliope? Yep, eyes and ears sir." Aaron nodded around a mouthful of biscuit.

And everybody except Matt and Aaron burst out laughing. "You'll have to see it first," Jesse said. "Then it will make sense."

After breakfast, Matt and Aaron changed into utilities and boots and both dug out thigh holsters for their Glocks as well as their eye and ear protection.

Trooping down to the back corral, they sat at the picnic table just behind the corral gate as Francisco gave everyone a safety brief and told them how many targets were set up. Today, it was nine targets, and he said the calliope was on and set at five seconds. The old man told Matt to follow him and for Aaron to follow Jesse to see the set up, and explained that one person ran it at a time, then came back and patched their targets; when they were back at the bench, the next person went.

The old man got up and motioned to Matt saying, "Stay about five yards behind me, that way you can see what I'm doing and I don't have to worry about your inadvertently getting into my field of fire. Eyes and ears."

Matt nodded, slipping his ear protection muffs down and adjusting his glasses. Out of habit, Matt reached down and hit his timer as the old man took off at a slow jog, quickly dropping down into the arroyo that formed the creek bottom. His first shot surprised Matt, as he wasn't really looking at the terrain, but realized the old man had never stopped, just acquiring, drawing and firing in one smooth motion then reholstering on the run. Matt looked closely after that and decided all the targets were IDPA[14] targets and some of them were damn well concealed in the brush at ranges from six feet to probably ten yards. Thirty seconds later they came out on a bench by the creek with an old rock building and a metal contraption sitting there.

Suddenly, the old man drew and fired five shots and Matt realized it was a mechanical steel target resetting machine as the six fallen steels dropped down and reappeared upright. Five seconds later, they disappeared and reappeared randomly about ten seconds later.

Matt looked down at his watch, forty-five seconds for the whole run; and now he understood how the old man and Jesse had beaten them at the sniper shoot. They did this all the time, so it was nothing new!

The old man pulled his ears out, turned to Matt and said, "Let's go patch some targets, that sneaky sumbitch put one in the 'y' in that cottonwood and I damn near missed it. Sometimes when Juanita is wanting to screw with us, she'll dress them in t-shirts or camo shirts and it takes forever to find the damn things."

Matt just shook his head saying, "I never saw the first target you shot and I only picked one out the same time you did, the rest I was playing catch-up! And now I see why you call it a calliope!"

Walking back up the trail, the old man patched each target as he came to it, and Matt noted that all but one target was a head shot. Shaking his head, he concluded his thoughts in West Virginia were dead on: this was one old man *not* to mess with!

When they got back to the top, it was Aaron and Jesse's turn. Knowing what was coming, Matt hit his watch as they started, and forty-two seconds later the last of six quick shots sounded. They came back to the picnic table and Aaron was shaking his head. "I'll be damned,

---

[14] International Defensive Pistol Association

that almost looks like one of our training scenarios, but a lot harder. I think I saw three maybe four of those targets! And Jesse hit em all in the head except one!"

Juanita got up and adjusted her ears, turning to Francisco she asked, "You want to watch me shoot?"

Feigning fear, Francisco shook his head. "No, I don't need to be scared any more than I already am."

Juanita stuck her tongue out at him and went down the trail. Forty-five seconds later Matt heard a quick six shots and then a seventh ten seconds later.

Coming back up the trail, Juanita stomped over to Francisco. "*You* are sleeping on the couch you sonnabitch. You *know* I can't see over that damn log... Arghhh... And I wasn't sure on the sixth steel, so I shot it again."

"Matt, Aaron, y'all want to give it a try?" The old man asked.

Aaron shrugged. "Sure, nothing like embarrassing myself here... Not the first time and won't be the last." He got up from the table and walked over to the head of the trail, set his ears and looked at Jesse. "You want to come laugh at me?"

Jesse just smiled and shook her head. "Nope. I'm going to sit here and drink coffee."

Aaron rolled his eyes, hit his watch and started down the trail. Sixty-two seconds later and two additional shots on the steels ended his run. Back up the trail he sat on the bench and said, "Well, one thing's for damn sure, these thigh holsters aren't worth a shi... er... crap for something like this. I tried once to reholster and damn near missed the second target. The rest of the damn time I just carried the pistol."

Matt got up without a word, set his ears, slapped his watch and went down the trail. Fifty-eight seconds later his last shot sounded. A couple of minutes later he was back at the top. "Yeah, Aaron's right, but when you add in the other crap we're carrying, a hip rig just doesn't work either." Poking at Aaron he said, "At least *I* didn't miss any of the steels."

Everybody laughed and the old man stood up, handed the thermos of coffee to Francisco and said, "We'll walk down and pick up targets, meet you at the bottom."

Francisco nodded and took off on the ATV, as the others walked down the trail. The old man and Jesse pulled down the targets as they worked their way down the arroyo. At the bottom they walked to the old rock building and the old man collected the targets and put them in the inside.

Aaron and Matt both stuck their heads in and realized this must have been a pump house at one time. Noticing them behind him, the old man turned. "This was maybe the first building on the site, we're not really sure, but it's been shot at more than once. It was turned into a pump house sometime after the old house up the arroyo was built, and until the 60s this was where they got water from.

The creek is part of an artesian spring, and some of the only reliable water within fifteen or twenty miles. I think that is why this was the original homestead section, and one of the quickest ways to prove it up, was to build a place to live, that qualified back in the day. I can remember as a little kid, there was still a pump in the kitchen of the old house, and you could pump water up from the creek directly into the kitchen."

Walking out and shutting the door, he went over to a covered bench sitting behind the house. "Okay, let's shoot these poodle shooters and call it a day. Matt, Aaron, there are steels out there at 100, 200 and 300 yards. Jesse, why don't you and Aaron start off. I think you guys are familiar with these things."

Aaron walked over to the bench and checking safe, picked up the AR-15 that was laying there. It was configured almost identically to the one he'd carried in combat, lacking only the combined laser/light combo. Rolling it over, he glanced at the fire/safe and realized there was a third position. "Hey, this is a full auto, this is a damn M-16!"

Jesse, grinning said, "Actually it's an M-16 A2 that has been re-barreled with a sixteen inch upper with ARMS rails, and it's got the MAGPUL tactical butt stocks. Papa has all the original pieces and parts up in the safe for them, but we're authorized them and have been since, what 1998, Papa?"

"Yep," the old man answered. "Ever since the North Hollywood shootout. The decision was made by the sheriff to upgrade our 'inventory' and since we've got the Army close, we were able to get some M-16s off them as permanent loans, and the Army ran all of us deputies through their qualifications course. Actually, most of us deputies carried something heavier than an 870 in our cars anyway, because of the time required for a backup to get here. Hell, I carried an M-1 in the trunk for years! Now shoot!"

Jesse and Aaron proceeded to ding the steels with every shot, and Aaron proved to be the better shot with the M-16, as he had a lot more time on them than Jesse, so he was smiling when they finished the magazine.

Matt and Francisco stepped up to the line, and both ran through a magazine each, Matt suddenly realized Francisco was shooting three-round bursts, and every round was impacting the steels. There was apparently more to Francisco that met the eye, because that skill and accuracy was not something that one just picked up.

Stepping away, and watching the old man and

Juanita shoot, Matt asked, "Francisco, you've done that before I take it?"

Nodding Francisco answered, "I was trained in the Mexican military." Turning away he went to retrieve the gun cases for the rifles as the old man and Juanita finished up. Matt guessed he'd touched a nerve of some type, and vowed not to follow up or ask any more questions.

Walking back up the arroyo, Matt realized that it was true; a family who shoots together stays together, and this family could damn sure shoot!

After the guns were cleaned and placed on the bench in back of the house, Jesse went to her room to get a nap and Aaron decided to do the same. Francisco and Juanita went to church and the old man spent some time doing bills and working on the computer.

Matt sat in the living room, casually flipping through channels on the TV, thinking back over the last six months. At the sniper shoot, when he first saw the old man with that old rifle, he was sure it was going to be a clown act at the sniper shoot. *But meeting Mr. Cronin and talking to him opened my eyes and I'm still amazed at how damn accurate the old man is. And Jesse, God what I wouldn't have given to find somebody like her*, he thought.

14 Riding the Range

The old man came into the living room stretching his back, "Hey, Matt, you want to go for a ride? As in horses? I need to check on the stock up on the North 40."

Matt got up. "Sure, as long as it's not a bucking bronco. I haven't ridden in a few years."

They went out and saddled up, and the old man reminded Matt to carry his pistol. "Better safe than sorry and we do get snakes out here."

While Matt went back to grab his pistol and holster, the old man grabbed two personal radios out of the rack and his MT1200 police radio. When Matt came back, he handed one of the personal radios to him. "We use channel five, but in an emergency come up channel nine and hopefully somebody will hear you."

Mounting up and with Rex trailing alongside, they trotted out of the ranch yard and toward the North 40.

As they rode along in a companionable silence, Matt's thoughts churned. *I'm staying in a house with real history, with folks that actually are good folks, what they call the salt of the earth. I'm pretty sure they are millionaires, probably several times over, but you wouldn't know it to look at either of them. And he's been a Deputy Sheriff for thirty years, when he damn sure didn't have to be, and Jesse is the proverbial girl next door, but I don't think most girls next door shoot as well as she does. I'm glad she and Aaron hit it off, Aaron is truly a good kid; well, good man. And after last night, not to mention their interactions with Francisco and Juanita, it's obvious there is a lot of cross respect between the Hispanic community and the Anglos down here. Sure not the way it's portrayed on TV or in the east coast papers. Sure not what I saw growing up in Virginia and the Carolinas. It's times like this I really miss the folks; at least that damn drunk went to jail for killing them. And I wish I'd had the balls to ask Felicia where she lived and for her phone number.*

About twenty minutes later, the old man stopped and gave Matt a quick rundown on the section and what he was looking for. As hard as it was for Matt to believe, they could only run between fifty and sixty longhorns on that much acreage, but the old man explained it was due to the lack of grass and water he said it took about eight to ten acres to keep one cow healthy.

As they rode along, Matt realized it had been a long time since he'd ridden as his thighs started complaining. But he also realized he was up on a real cow horse, as this horse responded to every command and pressure.

Looking down at the saddle he was riding, he noticed there were plenty of scars on the horn and pommel, which meant it was a roping saddle that had seen some use. He also noticed the old man had a rope or lasso or whatever it was called looped through a thong on his saddle horn, and he had a Winchester in a scabbard under his knee. Shaking his head, he decided he'd better stop daydreaming and pay attention.

Pulling up on a bench above the creek, the old man pointed down toward the creek, "Hear that bell, Matt?"

Matt had wondered what he was hearing, but now understood. "Yep, I thought my hearing was going for a while there."

"That's old Bessie, when we need to move the cows for one reason or another, like moving them to a different pasture, we go dig her out of the brush, and the rest of the cows follow her. Good thing she's pretty even tempered, cause she's a big 'un."

About that time, Matt saw Bessie walking out of the brush and saw how big she was. "My God, how big a spread are those horns?"

The old man laughed. "About six feet the one time I measured them, and she'd go about 2000 pounds on the hoof."

Turning back, the old man raised the horses to a canter, and they were soon back at the corral. Rex, tongue hanging out, trotted over to the water trough and drank for what seemed like five minutes, and the old man cussed. "Dammit, I forget to put him in before he does that, now he's going to be wanting to go outside half the damn night. Well, at least I know where forty-eight of the fifty-two cows are, and I guess Toby and Francisco can go back up in a couple of days and ride the fence to make sure that's not down anywhere."

Matt looked at the old man. "You saw forty-eight cows? Where the hell were they? I don't think I saw over maybe thirty total."

The old man chuckled. "Well, it comes with practice, Matt, and knowing what the cows look like and where they like to hide, makes it easy. And before you ask, a good cowman does know all his beeves; I worked for old man Sheppard when I was a kid, and he knew over 500 head by sight. Now granted if you had Black Angus, you might have a problem, since they're all black, but I never got into them. We had Charolias for a while then went to Brahmans, mainly because they were better able to stand the heat, even if they were a little smaller. When Daddy died, we pretty much sold off all the cows, and it wasn't till about fifteen years ago I started back. Since I'm not raising them so much for beef as for the land use, I picked up some Longhorns since they are the more 'native' cattle for here, and not many folks have or want them. We've got a pretty good set of breeding lines working now, and loan bulls and cows back and forth quite a bit."

The ride back to the house passed quickly, with the old man giving more history of the ranch and surrounding area. After turning the horses loose in the corral and stowing the saddles and other gear, they trooped back to the house.

Pouring himself and Matt glasses of iced tea, they sat at the table and the old man continued, "Actually, there's a guy that makes pretty good money with what he calls the 'Bull Bus.' He's got a pretty nice big Dodge and special air conditioned trailer and he hauls high dollar bulls all over the Southwest for breeders and cowmen."

Matt just shook his head and laughed at that image.

15 On Patrol

While Matt and the old man talked, Jesse and Aaron walked into dispatch and Lisa smiled at them. "Thanks for feeding us yesterday. That was great food! And as an atta boy, you get car 214 and Sector three today!" Turning and pulling the keys down she flipped them to Jesse adding, "Actually the reason you get it is lard ass finally broke the seat back in 203, so it's in the shop, and you need to stop by the sheriff's office before you leave."

Laughing, Jesse caught the keys. "Thanks, this will only be the second time I've ever gotten to drive a unit with less than ninety thousand miles on it that I don't fall in a damn hole in the seat every time I get in it! Anything of interest today?"

Lisa held up a hand, poked around on the dispatch station, and came up with a sheet of paper, "The only things I know that is going on are one DPS unit working I-ten in our Sector two, no BOLOs, no other alerts. We're short-staffed today; Sgt. Holmes is out sick, so it's you to me to the sheriff if anything comes up. Sector two is uncovered, but other than that the usual folks are out and about."

"Thanks, Lisa. We'll do the checks as soon as I find out what the sheriff wants, and we'll be on the road. C'mon, Aaron, let's go see what the boss man wants."

As Jesse and Aaron walked out Aaron asked, "Isn't that a little light on the turnover? In the shows you always see a roll call with somebody reading off all kinds of info to the whole shift and they then get a turnover from the folks they are relieving."

"Well, we're reserves," Jesse answered as they walked down the hall. "And being so low on manpower it's kinda devolved to dispatch to handle things, and the sergeant being out reduces it even more. I wouldn't be surprised if that's why the sheriff is in here, since he normally takes Sunday as his down day and is usually at church."

Knocking on the sheriff's door, they walked in to see the sheriff in blue jeans and a polo shirt with his boots up on the desk and a report sitting on his lap. Pushing his reading glasses up on his head he welcomed them in.

"Hey, Jesse, good to see you remembered you actually were scheduled to come in today; I thought you might get distracted or something. Aaron, are you carrying?"

"Yes sir, is that a problem?"

"Nope, just wanted to know what was available if something came up. I assume you're also shotgun qualified, right?"

"Yessir, both breaching and tactical."

"Okay, with Holmes out anything that comes up, get to dispatch and they'll bump it to me. It's been quiet all day, but you never know. If you need back up, it's going to take a while, so Aaron, if there are any issues, I'd like you to back up Jesse until another unit can get on scene." With that the sheriff magnanimously made the sign of the cross and said, "Bless you my son, you're now a temporary Deputy Sheriff of Pecos County for the next eight hours. Go forth and do nothing! Now y'all get out of here and get on the road."

Jesse grinned. "So does he get a badge now, sheriff?"

Laughing, the sheriff answered, "Oh hell no... But I'll consider this a blanket authorization for you and Matt until you leave. Now *go, dejas, get the hell outta here!*"

Jesse and Aaron went out to the car, grabbed Jesse's bag, rifle and spare equipment and loaded unit 214 up. Jesse ran the comms, lights and safety checks, and put the unit in service.

Aaron kept trying to get comfortable in the right front seat, but the cage and radio, combined with his long legs didn't leave him a lot of room. Looking over at Jesse he asked, "Are you sure this is a good idea? I feel like I'm back in a damn Hummer again. The only difference is this one has *no* armor on it."

Jesse reached over and patted Aaron's hand. "I'm sorry, but at least nobody is shooting at us in this thing, unlike what you had to put up with, and this way at least we get some time to ourselves without fifty questions and people wondering what is going on."

Aaron squeezed Jesse's hand. "Yeah, I guess you're right; but damn I can't get comfortable over here. And I think you were right last night it was better that we didn't try to sneak off… There were way too damn many people around asking questions and watching us!"

Jesse just smiled. "Well, there is always tonight, we'll get back late and I know Papa is always asleep by nine, ten at the latest because he gets up at five. And Francisco and Juanita won't say a damn thing, since they like you."

Aaron grinned. "Hell, I'm more worried about Francisco shooting my ass. He does not look like somebody to mess with, much less the old man! I think Juanita would just cut me up and feed me to the hogs."

Pulling out and heading up 18 to their sector Jesse thought about what she was about to say, and whether she should, but realized she didn't want to hide anything from Aaron. Glancing over, she saw Aaron was automatically checking the right side and scanning just like a deputy would, and suddenly she realized he'd done that for real, with real consequences if he missed something. Thinking of Sector three, she took a quick right onto a farm road and told Aaron, "This is the Southern end of the sector, and unless we get a call we basically roam and check out places and things like the rigs, storage tanks and houses out this way. Then I'll cut back over toward eighteen and go up North and on the other side of eighteen for a while. In a couple of hours we can run back to town and grab something to go and then hit some different sections of the sector."

Pausing, she cleared her throat. "And I want to tell you something about Francisco and Juanita that you need to know, but you *have* to keep to yourself."
Aaron looked sharply at Jesse. "What?"

"Seriously Aaron, this is life or death stuff, literally; but I don't want to hide anything from you. Those aren't their real names. Francisco is a former Federale who was targeted for murder by the cartel back in the day. Papa knew and worked with him when he was with DEA. I was just a little girl, but I remember one night Juanita came to the door covered in blood and crying and begged Papa to help her. Papa got Francisco into the house and called the doc, he patched up Francisco and he lived but if you ever see him with his shirt off, he's got five or six bullet holes in him and a couple of knife wounds. And even worse, they killed both their children."

Aaron just looked at Jesse with a stunned expression. "How did they get here?"

"I don't know, but I think Papa called some people and Francisco and Juanita 'disappeared' for their protection. They've lived and worked here since, and as far as everybody here knows they were 'hired' by Papa to help run the ranch. I know Francisco can out-shoot me, and both of them always have a gun on them. You'll never see it, but I'll guarantee they are carrying and willing to shoot, if it comes to that. I *think* the sheriff may know part of the story, because he was a young deputy that Papa trained a long time ago, but he's never said anything and he's one of the few that Francisco and Juanita seem comfortable around," Jesse said nervously and shook her head.

"Wow, that is a helluva story, and it brings up so many questions, I mean with your Papa alone. After what I saw yesterday, and this morning with us shooting… I mean when I met y'all I didn't think much about it until that whole deal with the coin. Matt kept telling me the old man was not one to cross, but damn how well-connected is he? And some of those things up on the shelf in the library aren't from the US of A." Aaron just stopped, not wanting to go further.

"Aaron, I just don't know. Papa never talks about them, and there are times when he just 'disappears' for a week or two or three. And he deflects any questions I asks, and I guess he always has. Maybe I shouldn't have said anything after all, just forget it please."

Aaron quickly answered, "No I mean it opens up a lot of questions, but at least I know not to step on my…"

Grinning Jesse asked, "Your dick? No please don't step on that!" And blushed along with Aaron.

Settling back and feeling more relaxed now, they continued to chat as Jesse did sweeps through the sector, They chatted about inconsequential things to pass the time as they listened to the radio and took in the countryside.

At the same time, DPS[15] Trooper Michelle Wilson was pulling in behind a van stopped on I-10 changing a tire. She picked up the mic, "Dispatch 171, Eastbound

---

[15] Department of Public Service, Texas version of a State Trooper

Ten out by the test track exit making a courtesy stop on a van with a problem, be outta the car for a few."

"Roger 171, call when you're 10-8."

As Trooper Wilson got out of the car she sighed and stretched in relief and started walking toward the van. As she did so, two Hispanic men came around the back of the van one rolling a tire and the other carrying a jack and lug wrench. Trooper Wilson smiled at them and rested her hand on the butt of her pistol without thinking, since they were both large men and pretty rough-looking.

As she approached, one of the men opened the back door to the van and she noticed what looked like a black curtain covering the back area and hanging almost to the floor. She wasn't sure, but thought he said something; but she didn't catch it. She said, "Buenas Tardes Senors, ¿Cómo está?"

The Hispanic holding the jack and lug wrench merely nodded to her, and the other one stepped to the side of the door and turned to face her suddenly he yelled, "Dispararle!"

Trooper Wilson froze for a second trying to figure out what that word meant and realized 'something' was sticking out of the curtain as a flash bloomed in front of her.

She felt a crushing blow to her chest and that was the last thing she knew as she crumpled to the ground in front of the shooter. The second Hispanic rolled her under the front of her car as the first one quickly threw the tire, jack and lug wrench in the van and slammed the door.

Running to the driver's seat, he jumped in as the other one ducked into the passenger's side. The van pulled away from the shoulder and continued up the road as an argument broke out inside the van. They decided they had to get off I-10, and try to get up to I-20. The passenger pulled out a map with their route and traced the quickest way up to I-20, directing the driver to take the next exit.

Fifteen minutes later, the DPS dispatcher heard a panicked voice come over the radio.

"Help, can anybody hear me? There's a police officer hurt out here."

The dispatcher answered, "Sir, where are you and what is the car number?"

"Umm, we're in the eastbound lane of I-ten and I think we're a couple of miles from someplace called Fort Stockton. I don't know what you mean car number."

"Sir, look on the roof of the car, there is a large number painted there, please tell me what it is, and can you tell me what is wrong with the officer?"

"Uh, there's a, uh... Looks like 171, yeah 171 on top of the car; my wife, hang on."

The Dispatcher hit the alert tone for all units, "All units, 171 Trooper Wilson in trouble, I-ten eastbound by the test track, civilian on scene situation unknown at this time. Standby for update." Turning to another dispatcher she yelled, "Call Pecos County and see if they have anybody close, and get them to respond, and get an ambulance rolling!"

The other dispatcher jumped on the phone immediately and started dialing.

Moments later, Jesse's radio and all others in the Pecos County net went off with an alert tone. "All units, DPS trooper down, I-ten eastbound near the test track, any unit close to there respond. 202, what is your Twenty?"

"Ah, 202 is two miles south on sixty-seven, I'm 10-51 now ETA three minutes."

Jesse immediately reached down and punched the area common frequency on and held up her hand to Aaron.

"Uh, er… My wife says it looks like a female officer and she's rolled underneath the front end of the car, but she doesn't see any blood. She said she can feel what she thinks is a pulse."

"Thank you. Is there anyone else there, or did you see anyone when you pulled up?
And are you in front of or behind the trooper's car?"
"Ahh, in front. How long before somebody gets here, my wife thinks she's not well."

"Sir, it will be at least five to ten minutes," the dispatcher replied. "Please describe what you and your wife are wearing so we'll know who you are when the responding officers arrive."

"My wife says she's bleeding from the mouth, but she's breathing at least for now.
Ahh, I'm wearing blue jeans and a red polo shirt and my wife is in a… uh… flowery print dress."

"Dispatch 202 on common, show me 10-23 at scene, DPS unit, red Honda; one Whiskey Mike, jeans and red shirt. One Whiskey Fox print dress."

The DPS dispatcher went out on common, "Roger 202, advise."

Deputy Hart came out of the car with gun in hand, and told the man and woman to put their hands on the car; as he quickly moved to the front of the car, he kept both of them in sight as he reached down and felt for a pulse on Trooper Wilson.

Straightening, he quickly looked at the Honda and noted it was parked on what appeared to be fresh burnout tracks. "Dispatch, 202 on common, I have a pulse, ETA for Rescue?"

"202 three minutes."

"Roger, securing two individuals at this time. Requesting backup ASAP."

"202, backup enroute, ETA three to five minutes."

Deputy Hart proceeded to handcuff both the man and women over their protest, telling them they needed to sort out the situation before he could release them. He walked them back to his car as another DPS unit arrived along with the ambulance.

The paramedic and EMT eased Trooper Wilson out from under the front of the car on a backboard and slowly rolled her over. She was bleeding from the mouth, but alive.

The paramedic suddenly realized he was looking at her vest through the remains of her shirt and this had been done by one or more gunshots. He yelled at the arriving trooper sergeant they had a shooting situation and they needed to pull her vest off to see if she had any wounds.

The trooper immediately got on the radio to dispatch, putting out that this was now a shooting scene.

The dispatcher went out with an alert on the common channel. "All units, update on scene on Interstate ten, officer down situation is now officer shot. All units be aware armed and dangerous individual or individuals are potentially within response area. Vehicle unknown, direction of travel unknown, number of shooters involved unknown. All units remain alert."

Jesse and Aaron looked at each other grimly, and Aaron asked, "Now, what Jesse? Do you need to take me back and go do something?"

Jesse thought about it. "No, we're far enough off ten, I'm pretty sure they are hauling butt either east or west on ten trying to put as much distance between the scene and them as they can. We'll just continue where we are unless we hear different."

The paramedic had loosened Trooper Wilson's vest and determined that none of the rounds had penetrated the protective shield, but at best she had broken ribs and possibly a collapsed lung. Thankfully, the round had not hit dead center, but she still hadn't recovered consciousness; looking at the blood pressure, respirations, and oxygen saturation, the paramedic decided she needed to go to the hospital now. As they strapped her to the stretcher and loaded up their equipment, the trooper sergeant moved to her side and looked closely at the vest. Taking out his knife, he pried a smashed pellet out of the remnants of the vest.

As the crew placed the trooper in the back of the rig and left code three, lights ablaze and siren going, Deputy Hart walked over to the trooper sergeant. "The Honda is clean, and I think they might be parked on the tracks left by the perp's vehicle. I did locate one spent Remington twelve-gauge shell, and I've got it covered with a cup and my glove on top of it."

The trooper sergeant held the pellet between his gloved fingers. "Twelve gauge?"

"Yep. I haven't looked but is her car configured with a camera that we can run back?"

The sergeant ran back to the car. "Damn, no this is the old system with the VHS, and no replay capability. And I don't have a key or a player."

"I know what the sheriff has and I think that is the same thing we use," Deputy Hart said. "Pop the trunk and let me look at it." Keying his radio, "Dispatch, is the sheriff available, we need a master key and VHS player for the in car video, standby." Looking in the trunk, "Dispatch, it's the same as ours, and we need it ASAP, the trooper was shot point blank by a twelve-gauge."

The sheriff answered himself. "I'll be on scene in ten minutes. Do you need any other assist from us?"

"I've got a crew on the way, but you might have your investigator standby if we need him," the sergeant replied.

16 Shots Fired

While this was going on at the scene on I-10, Jesse turned down a dirt road into the bottoms and told Aaron, "I want to show you where I lived as a little girl, before Daddy and Momma were killed. It's only a mile or so up here, and there is a nice young couple, the Altons, with a little baby girl living there now. She used to work at the bank until she had the baby and now she's staying home with her, but it's hard on them trying to make it on one income. If she's home we can stop and take a quick bathroom break too. I usually stop in and check on her when I get the chance."

Aaron nodded and tried once again to get comfortable. Finally, he propped his right leg up on the dash to give him enough room to fit around the terminal, cabling, shotgun and rack and Jesse's rifle all stuffed in the passenger's side floor well.

Topping the small hill, she stopped for a minute saying, "This was so nice as a little girl. I had lots of room to play and there was a nice fenced back yard for me to play with the puppy. That's what I remember most."

Winding down the road from the hill, she crossed the creek and slowed at the driveway, looking at a white van sitting in the driveway. "Huh. I don't think they bought a van, must be a repair man. Hang on while I give her a call." Dialing the phone and receiving no answer, she was debating what to do when she heard pops and Aaron screaming in pain.

Flooring the cruiser, she only made it about forty

feet until the engine quit and she realized what she was hearing was gunfire. It was hitting the car in the trunk but moving forward as the car slowed to a stop.

She screamed at Aaron, "We've got to get out, open your door and bail, I'm right behind you." As she said it, she realized there was blood all over the ceiling, dash and door frame. Aaron managed to get the door open and roll out onto the ground then fell into the bar ditch with a groan. Jesse was halfway over the center console when she felt a slap on her right hip and pain radiating below her vest. Sliding over and face first out the door, she managed to grab her rifle on the way out of the car. She managed to miss Aaron when she landed in the bar ditch, as the car continued to get peppered with what she now realized was a fully automatic rifle.

Aaron lay in the bottom of the bar ditch holding his right leg, and moaned, "AK, maybe a forty-seven or a seventy-four but its full auto. Heard that before. Got me in the leg, I think it's broke and I'm bleeding pretty good. Find the shooter!"

Jesse looked frantically under the car but couldn't see anything but the roof of the house due to the road being higher than the driveway. Squirming forward, she finally got to a position where she could see the house and front yard, and discovered the gunman was leaning against a post on the porch and firing at the car from there.

She keyed her mike, but didn't hear anything and reached for the radio only to realize her radio had been shot off her hip. Her hand came back bloody, and she felt faint for a second, but realized she couldn't afford to pass out now. Squirming back down the bar ditch, she got Aaron in a half-sitting position and got his belt off with his help. He held his pistol and watched as she threw the belt on as a tourniquet and used a stick to tighten it down.

Looking in the car, she saw her cell phone on the passenger's side floorboard, and reached in and grabbed it. Thankfully it was still working, though bloody. She frantically dialed 911. When the dispatcher answered, she said, "Lisa, we're at the old Tate place, somebody shot at us, disabled the car and radio, and Aaron's been shot. There is a white van parked up by the house, unknown plate and so far as I can tell only one shooter. We need backup out here quick. And Mrs. Alton's possibly there as a hostage."

Aaron had his phone out, trying to call Matt, but it kept going to voicemail; he finally left a message and hung up.

The dispatcher went out on the common tactical frequency with Jesse's information and requested all units back up ASAP, and for someone to find out if Mrs. Alton was with her husband or at home.

At the scene on I-10, everyone froze and the sheriff was the first to react, grabbing the video player out of his car and throwing the key to the sergeant. "See what you can get and put it on common. I think we might have just found our perps. Can you call in for your folks to back us up, and also get a Ranger on the way?"

The sergeant nodded and immediately switched to a private channel on his radio and started barking commands.

Jesse hung up and immediately dialed the old man. "Papa, we're at the old Tate place. Aaron's been shot and we're pinned down in the bar ditch. The car's dead."

In the background she heard the alert tone go off on his radio and Matt start cussing. "And tell Matt Aaron is trying to call him."

The old man went cold. "Jesse can you get away by going down the bar ditch? It'll take me fifteen minutes to get there and I'll come over the ridge from the east.

Where are you in relation to the car?"

"Papa, the shooter is just shooting at the car from the porch, but he's slowed down and I don't think he's going to come up here. Aaron can't move, his leg is broken and shot both. I've put a tourniquet on it and he's sitting here, but we can't make it anywhere."

The old man was opening the safe and grabbing rifles, pulling out both his mongrel and a Barrett MRAD[16] in .338 Lapua, and ammo pouches which he shoved at Matt. "Okay, stay in touch with dispatch and we're on the way. What do you have in the way of weapons?" he asked as they headed for the door.

"I've got my Python, the ninety-four and Aaron has his Glock, but I'm afraid to try to get the shotty in case they are watching the car through a scope. We got out the passenger's door and I hope they think we're dead in the car."

"Okay, hang up and save your battery. We're on the way, but will come in quiet. Stay safe, baby."

In a quiet voice Jesse answered, "Yes, Papa." Hanging up, she put the phone in her vest pocket, and turned to Aaron. "We're going to be here for a while. I know how to get around back without being seen, but first we need to get you away from this damn car. How do you want to do this?"

Aaron considered for a minute and finally said, "Well, I can scoot on my butt if you can hold my leg steady, but it's going to be slow. How far do we need to go?"

Looking both ways, Jesse said, "If we got back that way, it's about ten yards to a kink in the ditch, which might be enough to hide you and the grass is a little higher there."

---

[16] Multi-Role Adaptive Design

Gritting his teeth, Aaron tried to reholster the Glock, but in the end just pushed the pistol into the front of his pants and squirmed around until he was pointed down the ditch, "Okay, let's do this."

Jesse reached under Aaron's leg, placed it on her rifle and picked it up as gently as she could, but realized the only way for her to move was on her knees, and that *hurt*...

Minutes later, they finally got to the bend in the ditch. Aaron's face was bathed in sweat, and he was moaning with every movement, but he never stopped inching back. Looking at Jesse, he realized she was crying and reached over to give her a hug, "Thanks, babe, without you I couldn't have made it. Are you okay?"

Jesse wiped her eyes saying, "If I hadn't asked you to ride along, none of this would have happened, and now I don't know what is going to happen. And my damn hip hurts and I want to shoot that sonofabitch!"

Pulling her down Aaron asked, "What do you mean, your hip hurts? Are you shot?"

Jesse turned so Aaron could see her hip, "No. I think the round hit the radio and I got some shrapnel from it, I don't think I'm actually shot. But I can go down here about another thirty yards and get into the creek, and I can get around behind the house and come up a little arroyo that's back there. That way if they try to get out the back, I can nail their asses."

Checking the house, she didn't see anyone outside and the van hadn't moved. Turning back to Aaron she said, "With you this far away from the car, I don't think they will bother to look for you, and if they do I'm thinking you can take them out with that Glock. I know you can shoot that damn plastic fantastic pretty well."

Aaron managed a smile and replied, "Jesse, do what you've gotta do. I can hang on here, and I can call Matt when they get here and relay to him."

Jesse hugged Aaron and kissed him tenderly. "I love you, Aaron, please be here when I come back."

"I'll be here, and I love you, Jesse, and make damn sure *you* come back."

Chuckling, Jesse picked up her rifle and crawled down the bar ditch until she disappeared from Aaron's sight. Sitting the pistol in his lap, Aaron pulled his phone out of his shirt pocket; as he did so he heard the first sirens as they approached. Dialing Matt, he was surprised when he answered immediately, "Matt, I've moved about ten yards west of the car, still in the ditch on the right side of the road. I've got cover but Jesse is trying to get around behind the house by going down the creek and up what she called an arroyo in the back. I can hear a siren coming now."

"Roger, standby," Matt said. Aaron heard more noise and assumed Matt put the phone on speaker. He heard Matt repeat what Aaron had said to the old man and heard the old man cuss, then say something to Matt. Aaron heard some more unintelligible noises then Matt came back, "Okay, your position has been called in to dispatch, and the sheriff and more units are converging on your location from the west and south. We're coming in from the east and will be there in a couple of minutes. Apparently the sheriff is trying to get somebody to answer the phone, but so far no luck. Put your phone on vibrate and I'll call you when we get on site."

"Okay," Aaron replied then shut the phone off and replaced it in his pocket. He picked up the Glock and craned to see the house; seeing nothing he slumped back into the ditch and tried to get comfortable and ignore the throbbing in the leg.

Jesse was crawling by the house and around to the arroyo when she heard the sirens, and called the old man to update her position, she was surprised to hear Matt answer, but told him where she was and was going. She knew Papa was going to be pissed, but she wanted her pound of flesh out of these assholes, and figured they would run when confronted by more than one car.

The sheriff pulled up to the top of the hill and stopped, not wanting to push the situation until he'd seen what he needed to see and had more than just himself on scene. He tried the Alton's number again, but still no answer. Apparently, dispatch had not been able to get in touch with the phone company to make sure the line was open and he had priority.

Hearing sirens coming, the sheriff looked back down the hill and figured at least two cars were on the way. The first car that pulled in was the Trooper sergeant and the second was Deputy Hart. Turning back to the house he broke out the binoculars but all he could see was the front of the house, the white van, and no movement. He panned over to Car #214. It was shot to shit and he was amazed that Jesse and Aaron got out alive. He looked but couldn't see Aaron, nor could he see Jesse. The trooper walked over. "Well, it looks like that might be our van but I won't know till we see the plates on it. They shot Wilson at point blank range and didn't even bat an eye. They're killers plain and simple and this one may not end well. You got a hostage negotiator on the way?"

The sheriff turned. "I'm it. For better or worse, but hell I can't get them to answer the damn phone!"

On the other side of the ridge the old man stopped the Suburban and motioned to Matt to wait. "Dispatch, this is Cronin, I'm on the east side of the Tate place, if the sheriff isn't on, patch me through to him."

The sheriff answered immediately. "John, we're on top of the hill, can't raise anybody down at the house. Are you in position yet?"

"Nope, we're down below the ridge, I wanted to check in before we got up there. Standby one, we'll call Aaron and see if he's seen anything in the last ten fifteen minutes."

Matt was dialing even as the old man reported in. Aaron answered and said there had been no change, and hung up. Rather than try to call Jesse, the old man sent a text to her that simply said, "Twenty?" A minute later Jesse texted "Arroyo."

"Sheriff, no change on the front from Aaron, and Jesse is in the back in the arroyo that runs up to the back yard. We're going to move up and take position at the top of the ridge."

"Roger, John, let me know when you get in position, I'm still trying to call and get an answer."

The old man got out of the truck and methodically set up his rifle, loading it full and putting five extra rounds in his shirt pocket. He handed Matt the Barrett and a box of ammo, and Matt loaded up also.

Rummaging in his back pack, the old man dropped a spare box of 30-06 and spare box of .338 Lapua in and zipped it shut, "Okay, let's go Matt, we're going to walk up to just before the crest, then move to the right about ten yards. Just follow me."

Matt nodded and they moved stealthily up the back of the ridge, then in to a small bench that overlooked the house, road and part of the back yard. The only vehicle in sight was the white van.

Matt got down in a good shooting position and called off the license plate off to the old man, who then reported it on common. The trooper sergeant came back immediately. "That's our shooters. There are at least three of them, and the sheriff is now on the line with them. Apparently they do have two hostages. Per the sheriff, position and standby."

The old man clicked the mic twice in response.

Matt continued scoping and said, "I wish we had a range finder, I hate having to guess the range even though I can usually get close."

"It's five hundred fifteen yards to the front steps, with the angle it'll shoot five hundred on the nose," the old man said in a dead voice.

Matt looked over and was stunned to see tears streaming from the old man's eyes. "Are you alright?" he asked.

The old man looked at Matt and answered in that same voice. "Not really Matt, you see this exact spot was where I shot my son eighteen years ago. *That* is how I know the exact range, it got measured."

Suddenly the radio squawked, "All units, all units pull back immediately, we've got two minutes before they start shooting hostages."

Matt looked at the old man. "What do we do now?"

Savagely the old man answered, "We stay. They can't see us, and I'm damn sure they have no idea we're here. Get back on the damn gun and spot for me if they come out!"

Suddenly, Matt's phone buzzed. He reached for his phone answered it, and hit speaker, partially covering it with his hand to mute it. "Go ahead, Aaron, where are you?"

Aaron's tinny voice came from the speaker, "I'm in the same place in the ditch, and I can see two of them moving around. It looks like they're grabbed a couple of hostages and coming out to see if the others have left."

The old man looked at Matt. "Get on the scope, this may be the only shot we've got. Just spot and I'll do the shooting."

About that time the radio squawked again, "All units report clear at this time." Then the sheriff came over the radio, "John, if you've got anything, take it full authorization." The old man clicked the mic twice, laid the radio down and eased back into position behind the scope.

Aaron's voice came over the speaker. "Two coming out, one with a lady hostage, one with a baby, both armed; can't tell with what, but I'm assuming AKs since I'm pretty sure that is what took out the car. They're standing on the porch, wait, coming to the front of the porch, looks like they are arguing, the one with the baby is pointing to this car. One with the female hostage is coming off the porch, heading this way. Other one with the baby hostage is just standing there looking around."

The old man said, "No shot on the one on the porch, I can only see his legs."

"Yes, sir, the other one is still coming this way, I can't move, leg's broke, but if he gets all the way up here, I'll get him with the pistol if I can. Standby, first one has stopped woman is not cooperating with him, keeps falling; he's yelling back at the one on the porch."
BOOM.

The old man had taken the shot as the second armed thug had stepped to the front of the porch and he got a clear shot. Riding the recoil, he frantically tried to swing to the first armed thug.
CRACK!!!

Matt had taken the shot with the .338 and the second thug crumpled to the ground.

"Matt, what in hell are you doing? Goddammit, you shouldn't have done that, I…"

Coolly, Matt answered, "I was on him when I saw you settle down for the shot, and when they heard it, the woman dropped. The perp was rotating the rifle to shoot her. I know you're good, but there is no way you could have gotten there before he shot her, so I took it."

The old man said, "Movement behind the house!" Swinging his rifle, as Matt jumped back on the .338, he realized he was staring at Jesse through the scope and quickly pulled off saying, "That's Jesse in the back, coming up from the arroyo."

Matt stayed on Jesse, making sure to not touch the trigger and making no attempt to reload a round. "I'm safe over here. Rifle is up, I can't tell what at, but she shot."

They heard the rattle of an AK overlaid with the crack of Jesse's 30-30. "She is down on one knee, just shot again. She's down in the grass."

Matt and the old man realized Aaron was yelling, "What do you mean she's down, please God don't let her be down!"

The old man picked up the radio. "Sheriff, y'all better come on up and come in hot. And bring a couple of ambulances, I think we're gonna need them. Matt and I are up on the ridge to the East, and I'll stay here and spot; Jesse is down in the back of the house and she shot twice, don't know if or how bad she's hurt, and the other Marine Aaron is in the bar ditch ten yards West of car 214 with a gunshot wound and broke leg. I'm sending Matt down to look after him and it looks like Mrs. Alton is running down the driveway with her daughter and will probably be at the road by the time you get here."

With that, he rolled off the gun and dug in his pocket, handing the keys to Matt. "Go check on Aaron and Jesse, I'll walk down in a minute or two."

Matt took the keys, shook his head and taking one more look got up and ran to the truck as sirens sounded coming from the West. He continued talking to Aaron, telling him Jesse would be okay.

The old man just lay there and let the tears come. All these years later, and he still remembered it like was yesterday, and he replayed it one more time in his head. Nothing he thought of or tried to imagine ever worked, other than having gotten to the house earlier, and he'd never forgiven himself for that fifteen minute delay. *If I'd been on time, maybe Jack would still be here. Why? Why?* He sobbed one more time, then wiped his eyes. And now, Jesse. She couldn't be gone. She just couldn't, not again, not here...

A minute later, after ensuring the safety was on, he scanned the back of the house, and saw Jesse slowly get to her knees. He saw blood on her hip, but nowhere else as she painfully staggered to her feet. Keying the radio he said, "Jesse is up in the back, but looks like she's hurt."

His heart beat wildly with relief. She was hurt, but not dead.

The gaggle of cars in the road and in the driveway now included three department cars, two trooper's cars, and Clay Boone's unmarked Ranger car. He could see the medics working over Aaron, and heard Deputy Hart say he was going to check on Jesse. The others were spreading out and approaching the house with the sheriff leading.

The radio keyed and the sheriff came up. "Dispatch, show this location secured for the hostage situation. Mrs. Alton and her baby are okay, and we have four perps down. Requesting an investigation team be dispatched from Ranger HQ in Austin, per Clay. Sheriff, clear."

With that the old man got up, slung his rifle and started walking down the ridge toward the house. His phone rang, and he shifted his hand and answered to hear Jesse say she was okay and asking about Aaron. "Aaron is getting treated now by Doc Truesdale and Hart is on his way around the house to you so don't shoot him." She told him she'd taken out two and been hit in the chest plate. At that time Hart got to her, she hung up and Hart proceeded to help her around the side of the house. Ten minutes later, the old man got to the front yard, and walked slowly to his Suburban, re-stored the rifle and dropped his backpack in the back.

He turned to look at the scene as Matt walked over. "Aaron's going to live, they're pushing some plasma into him and he and Jesse are on the way to the hospital. It looks like Jesse took a round on an oblique from an AK, and it didn't penetrate the chicken plate, but it hit hard enough that it probably broke some ribs, and knocked the wind out of her for a few minutes. I think she's got some spall in her hip from the radio and whatever else was on her belt that got hit by a round too. From what I understand, that happened before they bailed from the car. She said she loves you and she'll be at the hospital whenever you clear here."

The old man just nodded, not trusting his voice to speak.

17 The Aftermath

The old man just nodded and started walking toward the house. Stopping at the first body, he looked down and turned to Matt. "Good snap-shooting there, Matt. I didn't say it before, but thanks for taking that shot. You're right. I'd have never made it."

He stuck out his hand, and Matt shook it. Walking on, they walked by the van to the front porch and the second body. Looking at it, Matt realized the old man had taken a head shot at 500 yards on a snap shot and made a clean dead center hit. He wondered if he'd have taken it in this situation, and was glad he hadn't had to make that choice. The old man didn't say a word as he walked through the house, out the back and to the two bodies there. Jesse had hit both in the head, and pacing it off they'd been about 110 and 130-yard shots. Matt thought to himself that this old man's genes had bred true.

The old man looked at both bodies, and said, "Looks like she wasn't sure if they were wearing vests so she decided on head shots. Probably not a bad idea, since they were both wearing chest pack ammo carriers, and that ol' 30-30 might or might not have given her a good kill."

Matt couldn't let it lie, and asked, "You said something up there about shooting your son? I saw you pretty upset, and I'm sorry, but I've got to ask…"

The old man rounded on Matt, and then realized he wasn't trying to force him to answer, but simply trying to figure out what had caused the tears. "Well, I was coming over to see if Jack had gotten the old car to start; when I topped the ridge, I saw what looked like a fight in the front yard. I jumped out and grabbed the rifle since it was scoped to try to see what was going on, and 'something' was chewing on Jack. I couldn't see what it was through the dust, just something big and with dark brownish fur. I took a shot and whatever it was picked Jack up about that time. I didn't know until later, but apparently I shot him through the heart. I shot again as Pat, Jack's wife came running out of the house and I know I hit that damn thing good the second shot and it dropped. I jumped in the car and hauled ass down the road, but it still took me five minutes to get down there, and when I did, Pat was dead, too. They'd both been chewed and clawed all to hell... And whatever the hell it was, well, it was gone; we followed some damn big tracks that looked like a wolf, and a blood trail that lasted about 100 yards to the creek behind the house before we lost it. They brought in dogs, but we never did pick up a single damn trace of that beast."

Looking up at the sky, the old man brushed tears from his eyes. "God, I tried... I couldn't... It took the ambulance almost a half hour to get out here, and I had to call Amy and tell her. Couldn't let her see the bodies. Thankfully, Jesse had been at our place and she didn't die here too."

Turning away from Matt, the old man sobbed. "I didn't find out until the autopsy that I'd actually shot Jack through the heart, and I damn near walked out and blew my brains out right there. Marty was the sheriff then, and he and Clay did the investigation and determined from the marks and tracks that Jack had been thrown around all over the place and so had Pat. He never said a word about me doing anything wrong, and Doc Truesdale did the autopsy and said Jack was dead long before I shot him."

Matt just shook his head and said, "Now I understand, and I'm sorry I asked, and what you've said will go no further. Thank you for telling me." With that Matt turned and walked back to the house, leaving the old man to get himself back under control.

The old man turned and walked slowly back to the house, the sheriff met him at the back door. "Thank you, John. You and Jesse turned what could have been a really bad situation into a good ending for the Altons; I owe you for that. You need to come see what's in the van. You're not going to believe it!"

As they walked back through the house the old man noticed an empty AK magazine lying on the floor and out of habit placed a chair over it. "You know we're contaminating a crime scene, right boss?"

"You don't know the half of it," the sheriff replied, "We've got two Ranger investigators and the regional DEA guys flying in now."

Walking out the front door, the old man noticed Clay shooting crime scene pictures and looked more closely at the body and especially the face. "Clay, doesn't this guy look familiar to you?"

Clay looked up. "Huh? Wait a minute. Yeah John, that sumbitch does look familiar. Didn't we pop him about five or six years ago on a drug charge?"

The old man said, "I think so, damned if I don't think so. If we did, what the hell is he doing here?"

"Dunno, I wonder if somebody got him out on a technicality…"

The old man shrugged and walked on out to the van meeting Matt and Deputy Hart there. Looking in the side door he realized they were looking at a serious load of drugs. Quickly counting, he guessed somewhere north of eighty kilos coke, and a suitcase full of money on top of it. Things were about to get interesting, so he grabbed his phone and tried to call Jesse. Getting no answer, he left a message that the scene had just gotten interesting and he'd be here a while. Suddenly, he realized something he'd missed in the house, and headed back that way grabbing Clay on the way in. Sure enough, there was a map lying on the living room table, with a route marked on it and notes in Spanish. Grabbing a pair of rubber gloves out of his back pocket, he had Clay photograph the map in position; then slowly unfolded it, with Clay taking photographs of each step.

"Damn, these guys were heading to Chicago! But look at the route, rather than run up I-twenty to I-thirty, they were going to run ten all the way across to Hammond, Louisiana then run north on I-fifty-five. Twenty eight hours at the speed limit, so I'm betting they were going to do most of the driving at night. We need to check the van and see if they've got any other plates in there, and I'm wondering if this note on Hammond is a motel name or a safe house they were going to use. Shit…"

"What's got your knickers in a wad, John?" Clay asked.

"If these guys are supposed to be in Hammond at a specific time, if we can get this info to the right folks, they might be able to roll up both folks in Hammond and Chicago if we actually knew where. We need to check the bodies for cell phones and pocket trash now. And even worse, this needs to be kept out of the news for at least twenty-four hours."

"Damn, you're right! I don't know if Bucky is coming with the DEA guys, but I can give him a heads up, and you're right, we need to move!"

They both headed out the door and met the sheriff at

the van with the possibilities. Clay handed his camera off to the old man, who quickly took the requisite photographs of the body on the porch as Clay made a call. Hanging up, he said, "Bucky is on the way, about an hour out. And he agrees, we need to move on this."

The old man nodded and he and Clay, with the sheriff and Matt watching quickly searched the body. Finding both a wallet and a cell phone, they were hastily photographed, and the contents of the wallet spread out on the porch. Folded up in the inner liner of the wallet was what they thought might be an address, and the sheriff found a pre-programmed number with a 773 area code. Rather than put it over the air, he quickly called dispatch on his cell and asked the dispatcher to see if there was an address in Chicago that matched the name and numbers and to do a reverse find on the 773 number.

Meanwhile, Clay, the old man and Matt photographed and searched the other bodies. Matt noticed the two bodies in the back had two things in common. "Hey, I'm not the expert here, but these guys were walkers or runners, look at the development on their calves. And they both have on identical pairs of running shoes, and I think they match the guy out by the van too. And all these cell phones look identical too."

Clay sent Matt to check on the physical development of the calves on the body by the van, while he and John went through the things collected from the pockets. Matt reported back that body's calves weren't as well developed as the other two in the back yard. Clay looked at the old man. "Coyotes? And which cartel are they? We're too far west to be Zeta, right?"

Before the old man could answer the sheriff came back. "The dispatcher called back with the news that two possible addresses came back, one on the south side of Chicago, and one west of Chicago. The reverse look up came back as cell phone, but the 773 area code showed south side of Chicago. What do you think?"

Both Clay and the old man said in chorus, "Score!"

"Go with the south side address," the old man added.

Clay said that if they could find something for Louisiana, they would have a twofer, but after going through all the pockets and cell phones, the only other number came back to a cell phone in Hammond, LA so the sheriff and Clay both got on their respective phones to see if they could get the records for that number pulled. Clay asked headquarters in Austin to get a search warrant, figuring that might actually pry the needed info out of the phone company in time to do some good. The sheriff and Clay broke off to interview Mrs. Alton, and after finishing with her, allowed her to return to the house and get clothes for herself, her husband and daughter; he then sent them to the hotel in town for the night to give them a little time to themselves after cautioning them not to tell anyone what had gone on out here.

After calling for additional lighting and both Bucky and the two Rangers arriving from Austin, along with various other LEOs from various agencies, the sheriff asked John to assist in not only documenting the shots he and Matt had taken, but the scene at the house itself. He and Matt also had to give multiple statements, and grabbed a couple of pieces of chicken that had been brought in while they wrote out the last statements. It was almost one in the morning before the old man and Matt could get loose from the scene. As they were leaving, the old man checked with the sheriff and found out that Major Wilson, the Ranger Company E commander had brought the chicken. He and Matt walked over, thanked him and handed him $20. "Thanks for thinking of us and bringing the fried chicken, Major. That was truly appreciated."

"That was good shooting John, but damn this is turning into a royal cluster… Bucky is running around like a chicken with his head cut off trying to put a raid together in Chi-town, but his cell phone died and he didn't bring a charger, so you better get the hell out of here before he comes and snags yours."

Looking over at Matt, he said, "Marine, that was a good catch on those two in back being coyotes, and the shoes matching, we'd probably have gotten to that later, but now we have a better idea of how the drugs got in; they were probably walked across by mules, and met the van somewhere south of ten. Turns out the van was stolen from a delivery service last night and the plates stolen off a van in long term parking at the El Paso airport, so this is looking like it was going to be a drive and dump. All in all, y'all did a damn good job here to keep the hostages alive." He nodded to them and walked back toward the house with the sheriff.

Since the sheriff had agreed to take custody of John's rifles for the ballistics and post mortem, along with the boxed ammo for chain of custody; the old man and Matt got in the truck and headed for the hospital. Matt slumped back in the seat and said, "I don't know about you, but I'm still wired just like coming back from combat. I don't know what to do now, but I'm guessing after I find out Aaron's condition, I'd better call in to Pendleton and let them know the situation."

The old man just grunted and kept driving, so Matt just leaned back and looked out the window. As he did, he realized how dark it got out here; instead of the light pollution he was used to on the east coast, the landscape might as well have been painted deep grey, with occasional black shapes blurring by at the side of the road. The stars were crystal clear, and he realized why they called this big sky country. It did remind him of

Afghanistan though, especially up in the mountains.

Twenty minutes later, they'd arrived at the hospital. The old man found a parking place and they walked in the emergency room entrance. Looking around the old man finally spotted someone he knew, and walked over to the nurse. "Cindy, do you know where they stashed the Marine that was brought in earlier with the gunshot, and where Jesse is?"

Cindy sat down and typed on the computer for a couple of minutes. "He's in twenty-five and Jesse's in twenty-six, down the hall to the left. I hope to hell we don't get anything else tonight, we're slap full! And John Cronin, why are you just now getting here? They were brought in seven hours ago! You should be ashamed!"

Holding up his hands the old man responded, "Cindy, we just left the scene. We were also involved and couldn't just walk out. I've been trying to call Jesse for the last six hours, so go easy on us, okay?"

Somewhat mollified, she harrumphed at them and turned back to the chart she was working on. "You better let me know how they're doing before you leave you old grouch!"

"Yes, ma'am, I will."

Easing down the hall, the old man thought to himself that a bathroom break would be a good idea, and said so to Matt, then ducked into the bathroom. Finishing, he walked out to find Matt pacing like a caged bear. "Matt, are you okay to do this?"

"Ah, hell, I hate hospitals. I hate seeing one of my troops in the hospital and I hate like hell that Aaron is in here. No, I'm not okay, but I'll deal. Let's get this done so I can call it in."

As they walked toward the rooms, a nurse came out of Aaron's room. The old man smiled at her. "Hi, Angelina. I'm glad we caught you. We've just cleared the scene and have no idea what's gone on. Can you give us an update on the Marine and Jesse?"

Angelina looked up and cocked her head. "John, I really need to have the doctor tell you tomorrow morning, but I'm guessing Matt needs to call in, right?"

Startled, Matt looked at her and she smiled. "You don't remember meeting me do you, Matt? But you danced with my sister last night at the barbecue."

Coloring, Matt replied, "I'm sorry, I met so many people last night…"

Angelina turned all business. "Okay, come take a quick look at both of them and I'll give you what I have in the charts." Showing them into Aaron's room she stepped out to go back to the nurses' station. Aaron's right leg was in both suspension and a cast; and an IV was dripping into his arm, but he was asleep, so they left. Next door, Jesse was lying on her left side with the covers pulled all the way up but they could see an IV tube running under the covers.

Matt ducked out as Jesse rolled over at the sound of the door opening, tears in her eyes, "Papa, I killed two people."

The old man replied gently, "You did what you had to do. It was you or them."

"But I killed two people, what does that make me?"

"Hon, it makes you a survivor. You didn't have a choice."

"I see their faces, Papa, every time I close my eyes. I see their faces."

Putting his hand gently on her shoulder, he said, "You will always see those faces Jesse, but you have to remember they were trying to kill you."

Looking up at him she grabbed his hand and asked, "Do you still see faces? Do you have nightmares about the people you've killed, Papa?"

"Yes, I still remember them, most of all I remember the first one I killed. Remember that bullet in the glass bottle on the bookcase?"

Jesse nodded.

"That was the bullet I dug out of my flak vest after I hesitated because that VC looked like a kid. He got the first shot off, and it thankfully hit the chicken plate. When that round hit me, it woke me up to the fact that if I didn't shoot him he was going to kill me; but I still see his face…"

Softly Jesse asked, "Will I have nightmares, Papa?"

"Probably. They will be a reminder that you did what you had to do, and a reason to not want to do it again."

Jesse sighed, and dropped her head back to the pillow. "Thank you, Papa."

Tears in his eyes, the old man walked back to the nurses' station. Angelina reached over and grabbed both charts. "Okay, Jesse first. Shrapnel in the right hip, apparently from her radio being exploded. I guess it's a good thing she's a lefty. That would have been a helluva mess digging pieces of a revolver out of her. This stuff was fairly easy to clean up, nothing too deep. The worse injury is three broken ribs on the right side and a collapsed lung, but her vest saved her life. The round didn't penetrate but she's got a bruise covering most of her right chest."

Laying her chart aside, she picked up Aaron's chart. "Okay, your buddy is not in as bad a shape as we originally thought, although we did have to give him three pints of blood. Apparently, he was shot with a full metal jacket round, it entered just below the distal end of the Gastrocnemius muscle and penetrated completely though the leg, the good news is it missed the Tibidis poster…"

Realizing neither of them had a clue as to what she was saying, she pulled up the leg of her scrubs and demonstrated on herself as she walked them through it again. "Ok, lemme try this again, the round entered here, on the inside of his lower calf, and exited over here. He's got a chunk of meat missing on the outside of the calf, and a broken fibula. That's the little bone in the lower leg, that got fixed and while the doc was in there, he confirmed there was no damage to the artery that runs down to the foot, and both the hamstring and Achilles tendons are okay. Six inches in either direction, it would have been bad. In other words, he'll be fine, but will have to go through PT to recover the strength. Doc Truesdale said it wasn't the first time he'd been shot, and looking at the other injuries, he recovered pretty well. Doc will probably kick them both loose tomorrow, since we're out of beds. If necessary, I can come by and check up on them, unless Juanita... Oh hell, Juanita is probably a better nurse than I am. I don't think either one really needs a hospital bed, but Aaron's leg will need to stay elevated most of the time."

Closing the chart she looked critically at them. "Both of y'all look like shit. Go home, take a drink, and sleep until you wake up. I'll call you if anything changes. John if you've got a charger for Jesse's phone in your truck, bring it in. Her phone's dead and she was in a panic that you were calling her."

The old man grumbled, "I was, and didn't want to try going through the damn switchboard here. I'll be right back." He walked off leaving Matt standing there looking at Angelina. She took pity on him asking, "Would you like to call your command and let them know what is going on? We didn't have a number to make an official notification to."

Matt nodded and asked, "Can I use your phone

here?"

"No problem. Dial eighty-four for an outside line, and make sure to leave us the number you called so we can add it to the approved calls list. Damn bean counters around here are nickel and diming us to death on phones among other things."

Matt sat down, dug his phone out and pulled up the Camp Pendleton Command Duty Officer's number. Hitting his watch, he reported the situation to the CDO and gave the hospital number to him. He also gave the CDO both his and the old man's phone numbers along with the sheriff's office number. He didn't detail the level of involvement they actually had in the situation, just that there had been a situation.

The CDO agreed to log the situation and pass it to their respective commands in the morning. As he finished and looked up, he realized the old man was back and leaning on the counter. "I've reported in to the Pendleton CDO, and he's got us logged in, so for right now we're covered. And I just started crashing, so I'm ready to go. Oh, wait I've got to give the nurse the number and length of time on the call."

Hitting his watch again, he mentally subtracted a minute, then wrote on the message pad the number, command's name and estimated time of the call, "Now I'm ready, sir."

The old man agreed, and after thanking Angelina they left and went home. Once there, Matt took a quick shower and crashed. The last thing he remembered hearing was the old man, Juanita and Francisco discussing how to set the house up for two invalids, and whether to move Matt out to the old house. He drifted off to sleep figuring they'd tell him what to do tomorrow.

18 The Morning After

The next morning the old man, Juanita, Francisco and Toby had already finished with breakfast when Matt rolled in and grabbed a cup of coffee. "Sorry, folks, I guess I needed a little extra down time this morning. Is there by chance anything left?"

Juanita got up and walked to the stove. "You tell me what kind of eggs you want Matt, everything else is in the oven staying warm. We understand."

Sitting down and scratching Rex's ears, Matt nodded and answered, "Eggs over easy please and whatever else is holding would be fine."

Toby nodded to Matt and headed for the back door. As Francisco picked up his and Juanita's plates he said, "I'm going to check the fence line up in the North 40 and I'll take Toby, shouldn't be gone more than a couple of hours with both of us running it." Grabbing a couple of personal radios, he kissed Juanita as he went out the back.

While waiting on the food, Matt decided to ask the old man something that had bugged him since the sniper shoot. "Mr. Cronin, why do you always wear grey? I've never seen you in anything but that, and I thought that deputies had to wear a regular uniform on patrol."

The old man leaned back and moved his coffee cup in circles for a minute then replied, "Matt, I've told you to call me John. Now the reason I wear grey is really three reasons, first and foremost, I'm a cheap bastard. Second, back in Nam I learned a lesson about camouflage from the Degar that stuck with me ever since; that lesson was that grey was one of the most effective camouflage colors out there. Third, technically I'm not a patrol deputy; I'm the department investigator, so I really don't deal with the public that much. Well, actually four reasons, if I have to go in the field as a sniper, which has happened, I don't have to stop and change clothes. All I have to do is take off the badge, grab my boonie hat, and I'm ready to go."

Matt thought about it for a second and asked, "But we've spent millions on camo for different locations and terrain and you're saying grey is actually better? Even better than a Ghillie suit?"

Leaning forward, the old man put both arms on the table and slid the coffee cup around again, "Well, maybe not better than a Ghillie suit, but after you eat, how about I give you a practical demonstration?"

Matt nodded as Juanita slid a heaping plate in front of Matt. His reaction was this was way too much food, but once he got a couple of bites in, he realized he was hungry and cleaned the plate. The old man had picked his plate up and rinsed it, then put it in the dishwasher and was in the process of getting another cup of coffee when his cell rang.

Setting the coffee down, he answered, "Hello?"

Listening for a minute, he said, "Thanks Doc, we'll drop by later this morning and bring them some clean clothes and check on them. I'm thinking probably getting Rescue to transport Aaron would be the better answer."

He listened again, and then hung up. Picking up the coffee, he came back to the table. "Well, Doc wants to keep Aaron another day; he said Jesse could probably come home tonight if he could pry them apart long enough, but the other option is to just push her bed into his room and release them both tomorrow. He's a little concerned about some swelling in Aaron's leg and he had to cut the cast to relieve some pressure this morning.

Matt, I need to go in for a bit, you can either come in with me, or stay here and I'll come back and get you in a couple of hours. Your choice."

Matt leaned back and thought for a minute. "How about I stay here? I don't want to be in your way, and frankly I'd like a little down time, if you don't mind."

The old man nodded. "Understood. I'll call Juanita when I'm heading back, we can grab lunch here and by then it should be visiting hours."

"Okay, that works for me John."

The old man asked Juanita if she needed anything from town, and getting a negative, grabbed his gunbelt, swung it on, put on his hat and headed out the door. Matt went back to his room and dragged out his journal; sitting on the bed, he wrote up the incident from yesterday as he would have had it been a military shoot. He documented everything he could remember, and the approximate times everything occurred. Finishing with that, he sat for a minute, and then decided he needed some fresh air, he stopped by the kitchen, grabbed a mug and some coffee and wandered out the front door. He sat in a rocker on the front porch and sipped the coffee, enjoying the solitude and the breeze gently blowing across the porch.

After a few minutes, Matt started replaying the actions from yesterday in his mind yet again, looking for things that could have gone better. He realized they were damn lucky things went as well as they had, considering he and the old man had never shot together before. Other than Sunday morning, they had never even watched each other shoot. Matt also was thankful for the training he'd received and also his instructor tour at the Weapons Battalion, which had taught him to be quick on the uptake with good shooters. It hit him then that he had crossed the old man's line yesterday in his shot. He was thankful they'd actually had enough offset that there was no possibility of crossing barrels.

He felt a cold, wet nose on his wrist as a furry head under his hand shifted and he realized that he'd been absently petting Rex while he thought. Ruefully, he was reminded that animals truly do have a sense of human emotions and Rex must have decided he needed some companionship. Matt, reached over and ruffled the big Shepherd's ears and Rex rewarded him by putting his paws on the arm of the rocker and giving Matt a lick on the ear. Laughing Matt pushed Rex away, and realized he was now in a much better mood. He got up and walked around the house, just looking at the open space and ended up at the corral, watching the horses. He watched Francisco and Toby come back from the North 40 and just smiled at their obviously expert command of the horses and how easily they rode. He noted that Toby really came out of his shell around the horses, and it was obvious they were his true vocation. As Francisco and Toby were unsaddling Matt heard a vehicle stop in front of the house and a door slam. Looking at his watch he was amazed to realize it was almost noon.

Matt walked back in the house to find Juanita busy at the stove and the old man entering the kitchen with Rex on his heels. Surprisingly the old man was smiling, he nodded to Matt and said, "I've got good news, but we'll wait for Francisco and Toby to come in for lunch so I only have to tell it once."

Matt just shook his head and chuckled. "Now you're sounding like one of my colonels, John."

"Oh, *hell* no, I'd never have made it as an officer, trust me!" the old man replied.

A few minutes later, with everyone at the table, the old man told the story. "Apparently Bucky was able to actually get DEA off their asses, got some surveillance on that address from yesterday, and at 5:30 this morning they hit the house with a DEA team. Six captured, no shots fired, and over twenty kilos of cocaine in there along with about two hundred thousand dollars in cash. It was apparently the local control for the cartel's distribution network in Chicago, and right now they're sitting on the house picking up dealers as they come in to get their drugs. So far they've gotten something over ten dealers!"

Francisco laughed and said something in Spanish to Juanita that caused her to smile, and Toby clapped his hands and said something to the old man in the 'Yard' dialect. Juanita commanded, "Eat, I didn't slave over a stove for cold food to be eaten because you're too busy talking. There is plenty of time for talk later!"

Everyone dug in and the food was soon gone. Matt realized he wasn't going to be getting fed this well in California and sighed. Patting his stomach, he realized that actually wasn't a bad thing, since he hadn't been running and he knew he'd put on a few pounds this weekend.

"One question. Did they find anything out on the Louisiana town where they were going to turn or stop?"

The old man shook his head. "Nope, dry hole on that one, it traced to a no-tell motel in Hammond, but there was a reservation in the name on the credit card the head guy was carrying. It had been made by phone, so nothing there either. The sheriff was finishing his report, pulling the radio logs, and getting the chain of custody lined out for the evidence with Clay when I got in this morning. They did the ballistics checks on my rifles, and I've got them back. I also talked to Jesse, and she's going to stay at the hospital, but wanted us to bring books. She said Aaron is in and out, and she's bored with the TV already.

The old man got up and told Matt, "You wanted to know how effective the color grey is for camouflage, come on, I'll show you."

Matt got up and followed the old man out the back door, remembering he'd actually asked that question this morning. Behind the corral the old man stopped, "Okay, Matt, give me five minutes then start down the trail to the range. I'll be within five yards of the track within the first one hundred feet of the start of the trail. Your job is to find me before I say bang."

Matt nodded and started to hit his watch. "Five minutes!" the old man said as he walked down the trail.

Matt hit his watch and turned toward the corral where Toby was working a horse on a lunge line: walking him in a circle in the corral, then trotting, and back to walking. When the five minutes were up, Matt started his approach to the trail head. About twenty feet in, Matt felt the hair on the back of his neck stand up. Looking and stepping carefully, Matt moved as quietly as possible and fell into a combat crouch without thinking about it. Easing down the trail, he tried to look everywhere and was getting more and more frustrated. The old man *should* be easy to find! About that time, something touched him on the back of the neck and he heard the old man say, "Bang."

Wheeling around Matt said, "Damn!" There stood the old man, a short stick in hand, dressed in those grey pants and a grey shirt. The only difference from earlier, the old man had smeared mud on his face and hands, and he had his old grey boonie hat on.

Frustrated, Matt demanded, "Where the hell were you?"

The old man smiled. "Go back ten yards then turn around, I'll show you."

Grumbling, Matt paced back up the trail, turning around, the old man had disappeared. He heard old man say in a muffled voice, "Okay, start down the trail, look to the left."

Matt started back down the trail, looking left and cataloging, tree, trees, rock, boulder, tree, little arroyo, downed tree over a boulder... And the boulder turned into the old man as he stood up facing him.

"Sonofabitch! I thought that was a damn rock!" Matt exclaimed.

The old man just grinned. "C'mon, time for lesson number two. Now we'll go out in the west field. Then I'll tell you how I do it."

Matt followed the old man back up the trail, turning to look back at the spot again, and shaking his head. At the top of the trail, the old man went around the back side of the corral to the west field, opened the gate and told Matt, "Same thing, give me five minutes, and I'll be within a hundred feet of the gate when you start."

Fuming, Matt hit his watch and turned his back on the old man. But he'd taken a good look at the field and there just wasn't a lot of cover there, and the field was pretty much yellow grass and a few mesquite bushes.

Five minutes passed and Matt calmed down. Turning, he scanned the field trying to place anything different from the last scan, not picking anything up, he started walking the field like he had done many times as an instructor during the sniper course. He was a professional at this, and dammit, he'd already embarrassed himself once this afternoon.

Casting back and forth, he hadn't found the old man by fifty feet in, and he thought, here we go again. *Gonna get my ass handed to me twice in the same day,* he thought. Three steps later he heard "bang" and looked down to see the old man pointing a stick at him from six feet away. Matt just stopped.

Getting up the old man walked over and patted Matt on the shoulder. "Okay, I know you're pissed, but let me both tell you and show you how I beat you. First, although *you* don't realize it, you reverted to type and training. Where are you right now?"

Matt just looked at the old man. "What do you mean, John?"

"Where's the sun?"

"Behind…"

"Right, you automatically set yourself up to search down sun. Which way do the shadows go? Away from you, right? And they tend to elongate the lower the sun, right? All I did was use that bush and that piece of stump to break up my outline and shadow it enough for you to miss me because I wasn't moving. If I'd had on black clothes, you'd have picked me out immediately, same with any camo with the exception maybe of that new MARPAT stuff. Now I did smear mud on my face and hands, but hiding them is easy. And the boonie hat is shapeless and doesn't give you any clues to pick up. Hell, go back and read Western history, there are cases where cowboys hid from Indians by staying in the open on slopes and other places as the Indians rode right by them, because they weren't moving. Same down on the trail, I just found a place to break up the outline and shadows to blend in with. I didn't watch you. I *listened* for you to pass. Folks seem to be able to sense when someone is looking at them. Don't look and it takes that gut feeling away."

Turning back to the house he continued, "In Nam, I watched seven of the Degar tribesmen I worked with, dressed in their washed out black PJs, set up an L-shaped ambush within five yards of a trail pretty much with no cover. Two squads of VC walked through that ambush before we hit the leadership who were at the back of the third squad. I blew the Claymores and we took out all but about four VC within less than three minutes. And I saw them do it more than once. When I got back to the States, I played a bit at Camp McCall, the Special Forces camp and found that these old Dickies are damn near perfect when they're about half washed out."

Reaching the house, the old man yelled over to Francisco, "Francisco, twenty minutes for you and Toby to get cleaned up, then we'll ride in and see Jesse and Aaron."

As they walked in the door, Juanita said, "I heard that, we taking one car or two?"

Cocking his head, the old man thought for a minute. "Let's take two, just in case something comes up and I need to go in. We'll go hit the burger joint out on the highway after we see them and grab some dinner. I'm sure Angelina will want to fill you in and we can pick up anything you'll need for when they come home."

19 Unexpected Twist

After finally deciding it was just easier to bring both Jesse and Aaron home in the ambulance, if for no other reason than keeping Doc Truesdale happy, the old man and Francisco had filled Juanita's shopping list plus picking up beer.

They beat the ambulance to the house by about fifteen minutes, and managed to get everything unloaded and the furniture moved around before it arrived. Juanita had dinner cooking when the ambulance pulled up.

Jesse climbed painfully down, and refused to go in until Aaron's stretcher had been pulled out. She hobbled beside it up the steps and into the house, and then supervised the medics putting Aaron in the bed Matt had formerly occupied. Only after that was done did she finally lay down on her own bed for a rest.

A couple of hours later, after a good home-cooked meal, everyone was sitting around the table reliving the last few days and the humor was coming out over coffee and pie. A ringing phone interrupted the laughter and everyone looked at each other as folks grabbed for their phones only to realize it was the landline ringing. The old man walked over to his desk and picked it up. "Hello?"

Suddenly he sat down and grabbed a pencil and started taking notes. "Okay, thanks. So within twenty-four hours you think? Copied all." Hanging up he turned to the others. "Cell phones off, please. Francisco, can you collect them and put 'em in the front hall please?"

A babble of questions started as everybody was turning their phones off, but the old man just held up his hand. Turning back he pulled out an old wheel book, riffled through it and dialed another number. "William Moore, please, John Cronin calling. Yes, I'll hold." He said into the phone. A couple of minutes went by with dead silence in the room, to the point they could hear the hold music for whoever the old man was on the phone with.

"Yeah, it's me. I've got a danger close issue and need some air support. Me and Jesse, and two Marines on orders to Pendleton, but they haven't checked in yet." After listening for a minute the old man turned to Matt. "Social?"

Matt rattled his off, and Aaron did the same, the old man repeated them back over the phone, and said, "Gunny and Staff Sergeant. Alright, I'll see you when you get here."

Spinning his chair around, the old man started to say what was going on when the phone rang again. Grabbing it, he said, "Hello? Yeah, I know who this is…" He listened for a few minutes, and hung up.

"Okay, it seems we have problem. It appears the Feds are taking the shootings away from the Rangers and are coming after us for either civil rights violation or murder."

Leaning back with a disgusted expression, he continued, "Apparently there is a new U.S. attorney out of Dallas who's out to make his mark, and has the backing of both the DOJ and DHS. It looks like we've got maybe a day to get ready for this, so we're going to go full offense on this. From this point forward, no cell phones on, unless it's an emergency, no calls to anybody discussing anything about what happened, no interviews, zip nada… I've got some help on the way, but for right now we're on lockdown, and Francisco and Juanita I have to include y'all in that too. I'm sorry, but I can't take any chances with somebody listening in when they shouldn't." He pointed up.

"Juanita, having said that, would you please go call Becky on your cell and invite her and Jose for dinner? Tell her dinner is at seven please." As Juanita walked out of the room, the old man turned to Matt. "Do you and Aaron have points of contact at Pendleton? Or whatever the new term is?"

Matt looked at Aaron who nodded. "Yeah, usually we have sponsors from the gaining command, and I know mine. Aaron do you know yours?" Aaron shook his head. "Not personally, but I know him by reputation."

"Okay, we're going to probably need those when Billy gets here, so Matt if you could round those up it would be appreciated."

Matt helped Aaron to his crutches and out to the old house and found his orders. Once he got back in the house, Aaron decided he needed to take a pain pill and get the leg elevated for a while, so Jesse got a glass of water and brought it to him. Matt's first thought was that Jesse was really the one that needed to be in bed, but he realized he wouldn't get anywhere with that. Surprisingly, Jesse came in, didn't say a word and lay down with Aaron, and within five minutes both were asleep hands intertwined. Matt finished copying the information from Aaron's orders and turned the light off on his way out. He gave the old man the information, and decided to go for a walk, just to get some time to think. Matt had never been in a situation like this and wasn't sure what was going to happen.

A couple of hours later, as everyone was sitting down to eat, Rex suddenly bolted for the front door barking. The next thing heard was a booming voice, "I'm gonna sue your dumb asses if this mangy damn dog bites me!"

Laughing, the old man called Rex back and stood up to meet the man that strode through the door. At all of 5'6" tall, with a grey pony tail and dressed in a western shirt, jeans and boots he didn't match the voice that came from him. "Staff Sergeant William H. Moore reporting as ordered Sir! And by God I *told* you one of these days I'd have to bail your ass out! Francisco and Juanita, I've got a nice little ranch that needs a manager; as soon as these two go to prison, you're hired!" Looking at Jesse he said, "Damn girl you look like shit! Which one of these is your boyfriend so I can take him down a notch or two?"

Jesse got up slowly and walked over to him and hugged him. "Uncle Billy, he didn't do it, and I got him shot, so I'm the one that needs to be taken down a notch or two."

The old man and William H. "Billy" Moore shook hands and backslapped one another as Juanita set another place at the table.

Walking to his place, Billy shook hands with the sheriff, Matt and Aaron, and said, "No more talk now, I need to replenish my strength after this arduous day of dealing with the philistines." He sat down and then proceeded to eat as much as Matt did. After dinner and dessert, Billy asked for a cup of coffee and said he'd be right back. Matt and Aaron both looked at the old man and Matt asked, "Is that who I think it is? That big time criminal lawyer from Houston that's on TV all the time?"

Aaron chimed in, "I thought he was bigger, he's just a little shit."

About that time, Billy walked back in with a bulging briefcase. "I heard that callow remark, but from Marines I would expect nothing less than foul language and uncouth behavior as becomes their low IQs."

The old man smiled. "Shaddap and sit down, Billy. Yes, he is a little shit, and a mean one at that. And he's the original guardhouse lawyer come to life. This little shit was once an honest Green Beret, who took a sadly wrong turn and left us working class folks for the halls of academia and money."

Putting his hand over his heart, Billy feigned pain and agony saying, "Sticks and stones, but those damn arrows hurt! You sir I will not defend, but everybody else I will, and you'll pay for them all."

Flopping the briefcase on the table, he asked, "Cells phones off and out of here?" After everyone concurred, he drug out a yellow pad covered in notes, and his personality underwent a significant transformation from happy go lucky to deadly serious and he seemed to assume a much larger stature. "Okay, poking around a bit unofficially, Jose, you're about to lose all of the evidence. John and Jesse, they're going to confiscate all your guns. They are also going after your cell phones, cell phone records, and all radio communications. And, Jose, you're going under the microscope for letting evidence get away so to speak for turning the map, address and cell phone from Perp number one to the DEA."

The sheriff started. "Billy how in hell do you know about that?"

Billy just looked at him. "Now, Jose, you know my sources never reveal themselves."

The sheriff just shook his head. "Okay, so what do I do?"

"Nothing, you turned over all the information to DPS and the Rangers, so it's not your call and there is nothing you can do, but they are going after the fact that the scene was cleared in a quote inordinately short unquote amount of time. I think they're going to accuse the Rangers of a whitewash, even though they brought in a couple of folks from Austin rather than using the local Ranger."

The old man interrupted. "Well, Billy, Clay did that on his own, since he knows all of us and figured he'd be accused of bias, and I sure as hell couldn't investigate my own shooting scene. But he *did* do the initial evidence and photographic collections along with the DPS investigator."

"I know, but you know when the Feds want to screw with you, they'll find a way. Hell, they'd have had that scene locked down for a week!" Turning to Matt and Aaron, Billy said, "Okay, Gunny, can I call you Matt?" Matt nodded. "You will be on the road by zero six hundred in the morning for Pendleton, and Aaron you will be on an air ambulance at zero six hundred from the airport here for Carlsbad, as that is the closest field to Pendleton. It has been determined you are in need of further examination and care." Holding up a hand to forestall the Marines and Jesse's protests, he added, "I talked with the JAG[17] at Pendleton, Colonel Powers and he feels they need to get y'all in house so to speak, so they can cover you when the shit hits the fan. Matt, they may try to come after you for murder one, even though Jose has told everyone you and Aaron both were deputized. I need you guy's socials and full names to pass to the good Colonel. Francisco can you find somebody to drive Aaron's truck to California?"

Francisco nodded and disappeared out the back door. "John, I need a check dated… oh, let's say three weeks ago for $5,000 as a yearly retainer fee, and when the crap hits, say you want a lawyer and Jesse you do the same. Jesse, you are under medical care, so do not allow them to get you by yourself for any reason. Juanita, are you still a qualified home health nurse?" Juanita nodded, and Billy walked over to the kitchen phone. Dialing a number from

---

[17] Judge Advocate General

memory, he waited then spoke, "Doc, Juanita is still qualified, so you released Jesse to her care twenty-four/seven, also the air ambulance will be at the airport at zero five thirty, and I'd appreciate it if you were there." Hanging up, he turned to the old man. "John, refer all calls to me and or the sheriff. Expect to get raided and all your guns taken so I'd move any good ones somewhere else. And by that I mean not to Francisco's house. I'm betting they will search the entire property. Jose?"

The sheriff nodded. "I can take care of them, John, and I have just the place."

Reaching in his brief case, Billy pulled out eight cell phones and handed them around.
"Okay, clean phones, Wally World specials. GPS is disabled. All of 'em are programmed with the other seven numbers plus number ten goes to me. John you get one, Jesse you get two, Francisco three, Juanita four, Jose five, Becky six, Aaron seven, and Matt eight. Keep these but don't use 'em unless you absolutely have to."

Closing his briefcase Billy got up and walked to Jesse, giving her a wordless hug.
Shaking hands with the others, he started walking out the door. "We're gonna be in a battle folks, and I can't predict how it's going to end, but I will do my damnedest to knock this shit down as soon as I can." The old man walked out with Billy and wrote him the check as asked, and with that Billy was gone.

Everybody nodded and picked up their phones and just looked at each other. Then Aaron asked, "Jesse is he *really* your uncle, and is he always like this?"

Jesse leaned back in her chair. "Well, actually he's not, but he's always told me to call him Uncle Billy. He and Papa go back to Vietnam I guess, and apparently were stationed together. I think Papa saved his life or something like that, but I just know he shows up here once in a while and that's the only time I ever see Papa take a drink. I went deer hunting with them once, and I know Uncle Billy can shoot too!"

Reaching for Aaron's hand she added, "I don't want you to go, but if Uncle Billy says it's necessary, we better get you packed."

The old man and Francisco both walked back into the kitchen and Juanita handed them refills on the coffee as they sat back down. Francisco looked at Aaron. "I have a man to drive your truck to California. He will be here at five in the morning. He is my friend and has the identical truck. John, will you buy him a plane ticket home?"

"Of course, I will. You know that. Hell, I'll even buy him a first class ticket! Matt, I think if y'all run together and run hard you can get pretty close tomorrow. Can you get Aaron's truck on base when you get there?"

Matt seemed lost in thought. "Uhhh, sure I can do that, but how in the hell did Mr. Moore pull all this off in what, four, five hours? Hell, I don't even know how to get in touch with the JAG, much less who it is. And I'm not sure leaving here is the right thing to do, is it?"
"If Billy Moore says it is the right thing, then do it," the sheriff answered. "We've got your statements, your phone records, and everything else. Personally, I think he's right, and just maybe out of sight will be out of mind; but if not, the military does not look fondly on outsiders trying to pin anything on their troops."

The old man looked at Matt and Aaron. "I've known Billy since the 60s. He was on my A-Team and his specialty was intel and explosives. He's got connections I don't even want to think about, and I agree with Jose, you guys need to be out of here sooner rather than later. Matt, if I were you, I'd leave the cell phone off tomorrow just in case, and the more I think about it,

I'd look at driving all the way through to Pendleton if you think you can." Turning to the sheriff, he said, "Jose let's go figure out what guns I need to move to you, and get that done now."

Matt, Aaron and Jesse all got up and Jesse handed Aaron his crutches and walked to the back door with him. Matt looked at Aaron and said, "I'll be out there at zero five hundred to get your bag, so pack one to fly with and I'll load whatever you don't want in the truck."

Aaron nodded and shuffled out the back door with Jesse. After hobbling back to the old house and getting into the room, Aaron sat on the bed and asked Jesse, "Is this for real? Isn't he being a little melodramatic? I mean, coming after y'all and charging Matt with murder? This is the USA, not some fucking third world country! I could believe this happening down range, but not here!"

Jesse eased down on the bed next to Aaron. "I know. Sometimes I think it's all a dream, but whoever called Papa didn't think so, and neither does Uncle Billy, so I'm gonna go with the shit hitting the fan. You've got to remember, this is South Texas, and DHS and the Feds have been battling with us for years over the border. Hell, Arizona, too. There isn't any real security outside the crossings, and you can wade the Rio Grande most of the time."

Squirming around to face him she continued, "There are, I think, *four* Rangers for the entire border, and CBP simply can't cover all of it; much less the hundred miles inland that's been decreed as 'border' area. There are thirty-two Texas counties that fall in that area, and there are five main legal crossings in Texas, but there are I think twenty-seven total including worker's crossings. But according to DHS the border is secure… And if you believe that shit, I've got a bridge to sell you…"

Pushing herself up, she pulled Aaron's bag from the

armoire, poking in it she asked, "What's clean and what's dirty in here? And do you want everything here to go?"

Grunting, Aaron pushed himself up, and quickly sorted through the bag, separating the clean from the dirty. Putting his Glock on top, he asked, "Any chance I can get this washed?"

Jesse picked up the load of laundry and the pistol case. "Pistol too?" she asked with a grin.

Aaron chuckled. "Only if it's the cold water cycle, don't want it to shrink! Give it to Matt please, and ask him to store it till I can get there. And please come back, I think we need to talk."

Jesse just nodded and walked out with her arms full, as Aaron flopped back on the bed and wondered how to say what he wanted to say.

A few minutes later, Jesse walked back in and gingerly sat on the side of the bed. "You wanted to talk?"

"Jesse, I don't know how to say this, but I don't want to leave like this. I'd hoped we'd have a few days to figure out where we're going or if we're going... I know you're not going to leave here for any length of time, and I'm going to be all the way out in California and maybe other places west of there. And I love you and want you in my life... "

Jesse put her fingers on Aaron's lips. "Aaron, I love you too, but I don't know what's going to happen now or in the next few days. I wanted to spend time with you too, but between the party, us getting shot and now me possibly being charged with murder, I think we just need to wait and see. I don't think the Marines would like you hooking up with a murderer, much less getting caught up any more than you probably will in this investigation that's coming down."

Lying down next to Aaron she wrapped her arms around him. "Just hold me please, just hold me." She kissed him softly.

Aaron reached cautiously over and held Jesse, feeling her tears on his shoulder. "I'll do whatever you want Jesse. I just don't want to lose you."

At 5:00 AM, Matt knocked on the door and found Aaron sitting on the side of the bed fully dressed with one suitcase and one small bag. Pushing the smaller bag to Matt he said, "If you can take this one with you, I'll haul the suitcase with me. I've got my orders and two uniforms in here, I'll figure out how to check in when I get there. Do you want me to contact the JAG when I get on base?"

Matt handed Aaron the crutches and picked up the two bags. "Yeah, you better, and give him copies of all the paperwork we got from the Sheriff including our statements and the investigation report from the Rangers. I'd rather they be forewarned in case the shit hits the fan. Everybody is waiting for you and Juanita has fixed you a couple of sandwiches to go."

As Matt walked out, Jesse walked in and put her arms around Aaron. "I love you, Aaron, and I'll come see you when I can." Then she stood on tiptoes and kissed him hard.

Aaron almost lost his balance, but kissed her back, trying not to squeeze her ribs. By mutual consent, they broke the embrace and Aaron hobbled out the door with Jesse's hand on his back.

The old man had the F-150 parked right outside the door; and Francisco, Juanita, Toby, Matt and one other man were standing there. Francisco stepped forward. "Aaron, this is Felix, he will be driving your truck to Pendleton for you."

Felix stuck out his hand and Aaron shook it. "Felix the truck's running good, and it's full of gas. I've got XM radio so you can listen to whatever you want. In the center console is a little handheld radio, just plug that in and set it on channel five and you and Matt can talk as needed. Thanks for doing this. I really appreciate it."

Felix replied, "Senor, I will take good care of it, and treat it as if it was mine."

After a round of handshakes, Matt and Felix got in the two pickups and headed out.

20 Planes and Trucks

Aaron, Jesse and the old man got in the Suburban and pulled out of the driveway. Fifteen minutes later they were at the airport. As the old man pulled the Suburban onto the ramp, Aaron whistled softly as he looked at the sleek little Lear jet sitting in front of him. "I've never been in something this nice."

The old man glanced over. "Aaron, this is a one-time good deal, only because we've got no other options. In other words, ain't gonna happen again!"

Aaron smiled ruefully. "Oh, I get it sir, I get it; and I appreciate it. But I know Doc's going to hit me with something and I probably won't remember a damn thing... That'll piss me off! I just hope... Oh my God, who is *that*?" Aaron asked as a huge black man in scrubs came off the airplane.

Jesse jumped out of the back seat and ran to the man yelling, "Baby Cakes!" and jumped into his arms.

Doc Truesdale opened Aaron's door. "Son, that's your nurse for this flight."

"My *nurse*? My God he looks like a defensive lineman for the Red...err... Cowboys!"

Jesse led the big man over to the Suburban. "Aaron, meet Trey; he's going to take care of you! Now Trey, don't you be lying to Aaron about me, remember I know where you live *and* where you work!"

The big man stuck out a hand the size of a small ham saying in a rolling bass voice. "Pleased to meet you, my real name is Jonathan Jerome Jefferson, and I go by Trey. And if you call me Baby Cakes, I'll break you in two. Hi, Mr. Cronin. Good to see you again!"

The old man nodded. "Trey, you're looking good, and good to see you too."

Aaron shook his hand and shook his head at the same time. "Okay, time to get this show on the road," Doc Truesdale broke in.. "Aaron, can you hobble over to the steps with your crutches? Do you think you can you make it to the top of the steps?"

Aaron swung his legs out of the SUV and took his crutches from Jesse. After a couple of seconds, he got his balance and slowly hobbled over to the airplane. After a couple of tries to figure out how to mount the steps, Trey said something in a soft voice and put his hand behind Aaron's back. With the help, Aaron was able to get up the stairs successfully, and picked up the cane that Trey had left sitting at the forward bulkhead on the Lear. Using that, Aaron was able to hobble back to the first seat which was configured in a semi-reclined position, with the table removed and a sling configured in the facing chair.

After Aaron sat down and adjusted the sling to a comfortable position, Trey backed out of the way. Doc came in and did a quick, professional examination then turned to Aaron and Trey, "I'd prefer not to give him any major pain pills to start with, but I'll leave what's needed with you Trey. If he is really hurting you can give him one pill every two hours." After shaking Aaron's hand, Doc went up to talk to the pilots and the old man slipped into the chair across from Aaron.

Slipping a card into Aaron's shirt pocket he said, "Aaron, I'm truly sad you got caught up in the middle of this, but know that we'll do everything we can to keep you clear of the fallout. If you need him, just call Billy on the number that's on that card. He'll take care of you, and it won't cost you anything."

Sticking out his hand, the old man told Aaron,

"You're welcome back anytime, and if you need anything just call."

Aaron returned the handshake. "Sir, I can't thank you enough for everything, and I don't blame y'all for what happened, it's just life. I'm just hoping this all blows over or doesn't happen at all."

The old man nodded and moved so Jesse could kneel by Aaron. "I love you, and you call me when you get there, you hear me!" Hugging him tightly, she let go and got up with Trey's help.

Aaron just nodded as he heard the engines starting. "Love you, Jesse. I'll be back."

Jesse turned and, shoulders slumped, walked off the airplane. As she walked, she thought *I'm a big girl and I'm not going to cry.* She looked back, wondering why the bad stuff always happened to her. She loved Aaron, but now they were both in serious trouble, all because of her rotten luck. Sitting in the truck she put her head in her hands. *I love this man, and now he has to run away, and I'm probably going to be arrested for murder? Where do we go from here? Even if we're not arrested, he's a Marine, and he's going to be going all over the world. I'm here and I'm not sure I can leave. And what happens if I end up going to jail? I don't think the Marines would look fondly on that. Damn you Aaron, you sneaky little shit, you got past my defenses and now...*

Jesse sighed. *I better pull up the big girl panties and get on with this. Get well baby, and know I'll be here or there or where ever you want me to be.* Banging her hands on the steering wheel, she glared around to see if anyone had seen her. Everybody was watching the airplane, so she ran her fingers quickly through her hair, and got back out to watch too. The old man reached out and put his arm around her, pulling her close without saying anything.

Trey closed the doors and Aaron heard the other engine starting. Trey sat on the couch across from Aaron and buckled in as a ding sounded and the airplane started rolling. Takeoff and climb to altitude was quick and effortless in the Lear, and Aaron had to clear his ears a couple of times. Trey kept an eye on him and they chatted about inconsequential things until Aaron could stand it no longer. "Trey, I gotta ask, man to man, Baby Cakes? WTF man?"

Trey shook his head, and a rumble came from his chest that Aaron hoped was a chuckle, "Oh man, see Jesse and I were both at UT, and she was tutoring me in English and Math, and I was tutoring her in Biology. She was also my lab partner in Bio and we were in the lab doing an experiment one day when my phone rang. I asked her to get it and she did and made some smart ass comment."

Aaron laughed. "Yeah, she *is* capable of that isn't she. Biology?"

Trey leaned forward. "Yeah, as smart as that girl is she just didn't get biology, she was over-thinking it. I dumbed it down for her, like she did math for me and it worked. Anyway, she makes this smart ass answer, and the girl on the other end, who I was dating at the time said something to the effect of yo' bitch, you better not be effing my baby cakes, I'll cut you. So Jesse just put the phone to my ear, and I get an earful from this girl, and I'm trying to calm her ass down, finally just told Jesse to hang up, which she did. Then she looks at me and goes *Baby Cakes*, really?"

Aaron snickered. "Well, you're not really what I imagine when I hear that phrase, know what I mean? And since I'm asking, two questions: Did you play ball? And what are you doing here as a nurse?"

Trey leaned back again. "Yeah, I played ball, started

three years at UT, second team All-American twice as a guard. Knee let go the last game of my senior year. They did reconstructive and told me to lose 100 pounds and forget ever playing pro ball. Since I was carrying a 3.6 in pre-med, I finished therapy then came back a semester later and graduated. I was looking at med school, and realized I didn't really know if I wanted to be a doctor or not. With my degree and course work, I was basically one semester from an RN degree, so I did that, and found out I actually like being a nurse and working with people directly. Plus in all honesty, I really don't want another four years of classes and the residency and all that other BS. My specialization is geriatric care; since I'm as big as I am, it's easy to actually help people move and change positions, which is hard for most nurses. Also, if people get argumentative, I can, I can subdue them— I guess that is the best way to put it— until some help can get there." Trey grabbed a couple of cokes out of the little fridge on the starboard side of the airplane. "Coke?"

Aaron nodded and Trey popped the can and handed it to Aaron. Sitting back down and strapping back in Trey continued, "I also do this on the side, as I can pick somebody up and carry them on and off the airplane if I have to. My wife now, not the bitch girlfriend, was a friend of Jesse's and she and Jesse got me through Math and English. She's an accountant at the hospital, so we're doing alright. If I decide later to go back to med school, I know I can get in at UT with no problems."

Leaning forward he looked at Aaron. "Now, it's *my* turn. You serious about Jesse?"

Aaron shifted a little and thought for a minute. "Yeah, I am. Probably for the first time in my life I'm serious about somebody… She's something special. She's like, I dunno, the real girl next door, but not."

Trey just cocked his head, and Aaron continued, "I

mean I first saw her shoot, so that kinda colored my whole view of her. She's pretty, but doesn't care. It's like she's, ah... Comfortable with who she is. Hell, she told me she lived on a little farm in Texas, and I didn't give a rat's ass. She made a couple of trips back east while I was still at Quantico, and we got together there. I was only a sergeant, so it was a cheap date. Know what I mean?"

Trey rumbled again, and Aaron realized that was a laugh. "In other words, she fooled yo' ass, right Aaron?"

Ruefully Aaron answered, "She sure the hell did. I talked to Matt and we almost left for Pendleton the next day. The old man scares the hell outta me, too. He's just one cold sumbitch. I didn't see it at the shoot, but Matt picked up on it right off. Hell, I was too wrapped up in trying to figure out how to snake Jesse to really pay attention!

"Then we get out here, and it's like walking into a museum. I mean, that house is what, 130 years old? Logs? And the guns? Shit... "

Trey smiled. "Yeah, first time I visited was when I'd just started to date my wife, and it was a long weekend. Jesse had invited us down just to get away from Austin. I thought the old man was gonna string me up to a tree, he was that cold; but then I realized that's just him. I mean he tricked my ass good. Jesse wanted to go riding one day, but I knew there wasn't a damn horse on that place that could haul my three-hundred-plus pounds around. When the old man told me he had a horse for me to ride, I didn't believe him."

Shaking his head, he leaned forward in his seat. "Until I walked outside with Jesse and Trish, and there stood a Gahdamn Clydesdale! With a damn saddle on it no less!"

Aaron burst out laughing at that mental picture, and

Trey rumbled right along with him. Trey picked up Aaron's empty coke can and his and crushed one in each hand almost absently before flipping them in the trash can on the bulkhead. "Now you've got to realize I'd never been on a horse before, had no damn way to get in that saddle, so they lead the horse over to the picnic table and I climb up on it to get on the horse."

Reaching over, Trey took Aaron's blood pressure and temp again and noted it in his log. "As we start out, I realize Jesse's got a pistol on; and the old man tells her, 'if he falls off, just shoot him, because we'll never get him back up there, and I'm not driving the front end loader that far unless I have to," he said, shaking his head again in wonder. "It wasn't till Jesse told him to stop it, that I realized he was kidding me. But I'm gonna tell you, I didn't dare fall off that damn horse! Jesse told me later it took him a day to find that horse and a couple of hours each way to go get it. And I had to sign a picture for the owner of me quote riding him unquote."

Trey and Aaron heard the engines spool back and the airplane started descending into Carlsbad. The copilot announced over the speakers, "Okay, guys, we're on the way down. Prep for landing and Trey, please confirm when the patient is ready. We should be on the ground in fifteen, and the Marines are waiting to meet us at the fixed base operator's facility."

Aaron tightened his seat belt and gave Trey a thumb's up sign. Trey crouched, stuck his head in the cockpit, and gave them a thumb's up, returned and strapped himself in. Twelve minutes later, they were taxiing up to the FBO at Carlsbad. Trey opened the door and was met by four Marines, one obviously a doctor, two Captains, and a First Sergeant casually leaning against a dirty green Hummer. A Marine ambulance was backing toward the door, waved on by a Navy Corpsman on the ground. Trey looked at the doctor. "You want to come aboard, or you want him in the ambulance first?"

"Is he mobile enough to get there?" the doc asked.

"With a little help, yeah."

"Okay, bring him off." The doc turned and stopped the ambulance where it was.

Trey looked at Aaron. "Okay, up and at em, they want you in the ambulance, use the canes to get here, and we'll help you down the airstairs and I'll get your bags in a minute."

Aaron got up, maneuvered himself around and with the cane hobbled forward to the door. Leaning into the cockpit, he thanked the pilots and grabbed his crutches and hobbled down the airstairs. The two corpsmen had pulled the stretcher out of the back of the ambulance and when Aaron got on the ground guided it to Aaron and had him sit on it. Strapping him in, they wheeled him back to the ambulance and lifted him into the rear and secured the stretcher in its locks. While the doc was dealing with Trey for the medical files, the first sergeant came over and grabbed Aaron's bag from Trey and carried it to the Hummer. The first captain got in the rescue followed closely by the second one. The first turned to the corpsmen. "Gents, give us a minute of privacy will ya?"

The two corpsmen left immediately and closed the side door behind them; after they were gone, the first captain said to Aaron. "Staff Sergeant Miller, I'm Captain Hurst from the JAG office. You will be taken from here to the hospital for an inprocess, and admittance. Then, when that is finished, you will be placed in a private room with restricted access. At that point, I will come interview you on the events that took place on Sunday."

Aaron started to respond, but the captain held up his hand. "Say nothing now. Hold it until I interview you. I have the incident reports and witness statements you've already given in Texas."

"Yes, sir," Aaron answered.

The captains switched places and the second captain said, "I'm Captain Jones. I'm your company commander at first MSOB[18]. I know this is a strange situation, so until your interview with Captain Hurst, we'll hold off on the official welcome and all that crap. First has your bag, I'm assuming your records are there right?"

"Yes, sir, right on top. That and a couple of uniforms are all I brought with me."

The captain nodded, as the side door opened. The doctor stuck his head in and said, "Alright guys, out. I need to get him to the hospital and get him admitted. Y'all know where we're going to be and he's in room 120."

Stepping back, the doctor motioned to the two corpsmen to load up, and the two captains climbed out of the ambulance to be replaced by the doc. As the ambulance left, the two captains climbed into the Hummer and followed.

Trey and the two pilots watched the little procession leave and headed for the FBO office to hit the restroom, grab a snack and gas the Lear for the return trip to Texas.

Trey's last thought on Aaron was that maybe, just maybe, Jesse had met her match with this one. He vowed to check up on her more regularly.
***

Arriving at the Camp Pendleton hospital, Aaron was taken directly into an examination room by the doc, who quickly cut the scrubs bottoms off, then removed the cast and bandages. Poking and prying at Aaron's leg, he asked all the normal questions, stopping occasionally to

---

[18] Marine Special Operations Battalion

refer to the treatment record Doc Truesdale had sent along.

Finally satisfied, he told Aaron, "Okay, this looks pretty good for three days in, but I want to get an IV into you with some additional antibiotics and a sleep aide, and I'm going to rebandage this with a soft cast and admit you for now. I don't want you walking on this, so if you have to piss, either use the bedpan or ring for a nurse, I don't want you trying to do it yourself, understand?"

Aaron nodded, and the doc turned to the two corpsmen after he'd finished the rebandage, "Okay, haul his ass to 120, no need to screw up anymore sheets or a gurney. Tell the charge nurse I'll be along but nothing by IV until after his interview. Understood?"

With a chorus of "Yes, sirs," they pushed Aaron out of the room. The doctor took Aaron's record and the additional treatment record and went over to admissions to get young Staff Sergeant Miller, Aaron one each entered into the Big Green Machine's system.

As soon as the corpsmen had deposited Aaron in his room, the two captains and the first sergeant came in. The captains took chairs and the first sergeant leaned against the door. Captain Hurst reviewed with Aaron what had gone down on Sunday, asked numerous questions. By the time he was done, Aaron felt like he'd been put through the ringer.

Aaron finally got to ask a question on of his own about what was going to happen next, and was stunned to hear that the JAG didn't have any idea. He said, "Well, I got a call from Colonel Powers, and he told me last night to come meet the airplane and get you in the hospital immediately and get a statement. Everything else was up in the air, including whatever the hell I'm supposed to get a statement about."

The two captains left, and the first sergeant finally

came over and introduced himself saying, "Miller, I'm Sergeant Brill, you got yourself in a world of shit haven't you sergeant? You get shot and never get a round off in return? What the fuck were you doing?"

Aaron looked up at the First. "I never got the chance to shoot, I was in a damn four-foot deep ditch trying not to bleed to death and giving intel to the two that took out the first two bad guys. And, honestly, I have no fucking clue as to what's going on here. Yesterday afternoon, I was being taken care of by my girlfriend, and looking forward to recovering there for a few more days. Her grandfather gets a phone call from somewhere, a lawyer shows up, and the next damn thing I know, I'm on a fucking Lear Jet, and here I sit. The only good thing out of this is the lady and her baby are safe, and four bad guys are worm food. Other than that, I don't know shit, Sarge, so what now?"

Sergeant Brill flipped a chair around and sat straddling it. "Well the first thing we do is keep whoever is trying to fuck you over away from you. I'll take care of getting you signed into the Batt. Where's your vehicle and household goods?"

"My truck's being driven out from Texas and it will probably be here tomorrow if I know Matt. As far as the household goods, your guess is as good as mine. Matt and I were going to get a place, but I don't know what's going to happen now."

Brill nodded. "Would Matt be Gunny Carter by chance?"

Aaron shrugged. "Yeah First Sergeant, we were in 2MEF together; got orders to Weapons Battalion together and both ended up here at the same time. We rented an apartment together at Quantico, and figured to do the same again."

There was a knock at the door. "Okay, lemme go

handle this shit, and see what the good Captain has up his sleeve. I'll check back with you tomorrow, or send the clerk over with the stuff you need to sign. And don't think I'm this easy when you get to the company. I'm just goin' easy until this situation gets unfucked."

"Trust me First Sergeant, I never thought anything different." Aaron said.

With that, the first sergeant left, the nurse came in and hooked up the IV, and shortly thereafter, after a quick call to Jesse, Aaron was sound asleep.

21 The Raid

US Attorney's Office Dallas

In his new corner office, Al Deal, the new US Attorney for the North West Division of Texas leaned forward in his chair and continued to take notes as the speaker phone rattled on, "No sir, actually that shooting down in Pecos County is not in my jurisdic…"

His contact and rabbi at the Department of Justice overrode him, "I don't give a shit, we haven't been able to jack that attorney out of Southwest Division yet, so he won't even look at this stuff. I didn't put you down there to sit on your ass and wait for cases to fall into your fucking lap, if I say it's in your jurisdiction then it will be!"

"But Mr. Rodman, I…"

"Shut up and get hot on this. You've had two days, and you haven't gotten a damn thing done yet. Hell, we even pushed your tame little security team down there to get these cops and keep those yahoos down there off the backs of the minorities and especially the Hispanics. That was the deal, they got us elected, we get the pressure off them and their illegals."

"I'm working on this, but the judges…"

"Deal, don't give me problems, just get it done before this leaks and they find out what's fixing to land on their asses. That was the agreement, remember?"

"Yes sir." And Deal realized he was talking to a dial tone, his rabbi had hung up on him.

Punching the intercom, he asked the secretary to send in Myers, and he dialed another judge's number on the list.

When he got no answer, he slammed the phone back in the cradle and looked at Federal Security Officer Myers. "Goddamn judges, I can't get one to sign the search warrant and the arrest warrants both. Nothing yesterday afternoon and now this one won't either. And every damn one wants more information than I'm willing to put in the paperwork. Did your team get all the evidence from Austin yesterday?"

"Yes sir," Myers replied. "But not without some hassles. They wanted to know why all of a sudden this was becoming a federal case, when they say it's an open and shut good shoot. And it appears there are issues with the chain of custody on at least a couple of items that there seem to only be photos of, with no actual evidentiary material."

Scoffing, Deal swiveled around in his chair. "Good shoot, my ass: four dead Hispanics, after a *two* minute hostage negotiation? Sounds more like vigilante justice to me, and remember that's what we've been sent down here to uncover and prosecute. This administration got voted in on the backs of the minorities, and we've got to step up enforcement against these rogue cops, just like we did in New York City."

Myers smiled. "Yes, sir, we did put a few away, didn't we? Do you want me to sit around here or start mobilizing my team for a take down on this bunch in Pecos County?"

Deal tapped the table with the end of his pen. "Lemme make one more call, and I'll decide."
Turning to his phone list, he flipped through till he found the number he was looking for. He put the phone on speaker, signaling Myers, for quiet.

A female answered, "Judge Gillory's office, may I help you?"

Deal went with his best lawyer voice. "Yes, ma'am,

this is US Attorney Deal here in Dallas, I need to speak with the judge immediately if possible, I have two federal warrants I need signed out as soon as possible."

"If you will fax them over to 2145125555, I can have the judge review them and get back with you," the woman replied.

"Ma'am, these are time sensitive," he urged. " I need to get them done today. I will have them there in five minutes, and will call back in ten, please have the judge available to take my call then." Gently replacing the phone in the cradle, Deal then pounded on the desk. When he was in New York he'd never been treated this way. "God damn bitch, how dare she!"

Myers, used to his boss's outbursts, ignored the show of emotion and picked up the stack of warrant paperwork. "What's that fax number?"

Deal threw the piece of paper at Myers, and slumped back in his chair as Myers went out to the fax machine. Coming back in, he said, "Done, and I just realized we get to take down a couple of Marines, this might be fun!"

He looked at his watch. "Yeah, I think this is one of those hunt club deals; you know, Texas has a lot of them. What if this one is people instead of animals?"

Glancing at his watch again, he hit redial on the speaker phone as Myers resumed his seat. The same female answered. "Judge Gillory's office, may I help you?"

Deal again with his best lawyer voice. "Yes, ma'am, this is US Attorney Deal here in Dallas, I faxed the two warrants, and now I need to speak with the judge."

"One moment please."

"Judge Gillory, to whom am I speaking?"

Deal unceremoniously replied, "Judge this is US Attorney Deal in the Dallas office. I just sent over two warrants I'd like to get approved immediately before the possible perpetrators can scatter or destroy evidence."

"Well, I'm not sure I can do this with this little information" Gillory said.

"Can you expand the reasons and justification a bit?"

"Well, Judge, I understand you're new to the federal bench, but at the federal level we try to limit disclosure of sensitive material or possibly classified material," Deal answered. "'That's why there is not a lot of detail, because this involves officers of the law, and we don't want word getting back to them immediately from any leaks."

"Well, I'm not sure about this, especially arresting both police officers and Marines. I'll sign it but I'm not going to sign off on arresting them. I'll put in here remand to custody, that way the Marines will have control of their personnel. And I'd really like to see more detail on this."

Deal's face turned red, but he maintained voice control. "If that's what you want Judge that would be fine. When can we... I expect to have those back in hand?"

"Give me about thirty minutes," Gillory replied. "I want to check on the federal statutes before I sign them."

"Thank you, Judge. I'll await your pleasure." Viciously punching the speaker phone off, Deal turned to Myers. "Get your takedown team heading for the airport, use the chopper to fly to El Paso, and I'll have DHS task CPB[19] to supply you with vehicles out of Fort Bliss. And make sure your team wears the Federal Police patches, no TSA or DHS on this one. Oh yeah, and there might be a female involved so make sure you've got one on your takedown."

Myers stood up, "Okay, black shirts and brown

---

[19] Customs and Border Patrol

pants, Police, dyke one each, got it. If we take the helo, that's going to be about three hours down there, and then an hour and a half drive back to this Pecos County. Can't we get the King Air or something a little faster?"

Deal rounded on him. "No, dammit, if I request the King Air, that has to go through channels here, with the helo, I can get that tasked by DHS and direct support from CBP also through them. Do you really think this bunch of dinosaurs here would authorize this raid?"

Shrugging, Myers moved toward the door. "Probably not. Do you want a call when we take them down?"

"You know better than that— do it the usual way."

"Okay, I'll see you tomorrow morning then."

After Myers left the office, Deal paced until he heard the fax machine start humming. Slipping out of his office, he confirmed the papers were from Judge Gillory, and spat when he saw the judge had in fact crossed out arrest and written in "remand to custody" in the margin with his initials. Deal hunted through the directory on the fax machine and finally found the flight operations detachment at Love Field's fax number. Writing a quick cover page, he sent the fax and returned to his office. Pulling out his personal address book, he dialed a number in his cell. "Yes, Pat Shover in operations, please."

After a minute, Shover came on the line and Deal asked him if he still could add an operation to the schedule. When Shover said he could, Deal said, "Okay, I need a Blackhawk, Love Field to Ft. Bliss in an hour or less. Tac team deployment and retrieval after the op, and I need two vehicles at Ft. Bliss with full tanks of gas for the Tac team to use."

"Give me thirty minutes to confirm the tasking on the Blackhawk, but it's going to take a while to get CPB to provide vehicles," Shover said. "What's the timeframe on them?"

"Three hours, and they'll probably need them for five or six hours. Anybody gives you any shit, this is by direction from the front office, so if there was a problem, bump it up."

"I'll get it done," Shover assured him. "Off the books as usual?"

"Yep". Deal decided he'd done a good morning's worth of work, so he awarded himself an early lunch and left the building.

Myers was already pissed when the team finally got to Ft. Bliss, and Spears didn't help his frame of mind when she hauled ass into the hangar to piss. Damn woman should have thought of that before they left, Myers didn't like her to start with. She'd been a stuck up lezzie bitch when he was just looking for a little fun, and sneering at him ever since. But hell, Deal said bring a woman, and Spears qualified, more or less. After sorting out the team between the two vehicles, he put Spears in the other vehicle and made her accountable for all the weapons. Just a little extra work, but maybe she'd screw it up, and he could get rid of her.

Finally, they piled into the trucks, and as they pulled out he realized they wouldn't get to where ever the hell this address was until almost 7 PM, which meant a dusk takedown and maybe a dinner time takedown which would be even easier as everybody would be in one place. He smiled at the thought, and punching up lights and siren hauled it for the main gate; piss on the Army, he thought, they can't do crap to us for speeding, since we're *their* bosses!

***

The old man leaned back in his chair, patting at his belly. "Juanita you've outdone yourself again, between the tacos, the Chili Colorado, the guacamole, and the pintos with jalapenos, I know I'm going to pay for this in the morning, but damn that was good!"

A murmur of agreement sounded around the table, and Ronni Boone got up with a groan. "But, John, I brought dessert, and it's a homemade apple pie, you've got to try some!"

Clay looked over at Jesse. "Girl, I'll bet you'll eat some with a little Blue Bell on top wouldn't you?"

Jesse smiled. "Mr. Boone, you know damn well I'm a sucker for Blue Bell, and Ronni's pies are to die for, of course I'm going to eat some, weight be damned!"

That brought a laugh around the room as Juanita and Francisco started helping Ronni dish up the pie and ice cream. Suddenly, Rex bolted for the door, barking his warning bark. The old man and Clay both reacted, getting up and moving toward the front door as they heard multiple car doors slamming. The old man looked at Jesse, "Text the sheriff that the raid is going down." Jesse nodded a pulled out her phone, typing quickly.

The old man nodded to Clay who stopped and took a position in the doorway to the kitchen as the old man went to the front door. Stepping to one side, he looked out and saw seven people running for position with one stomping up to the front door in full tac gear with an M-16 at the ready.

In fact, Myers had decided he wanted to lead this takedown, since he was hoping for a promotion, and this would look good on the reviews. He'd deployed the team for a standard perimeter takedown rather than the normal stack, figuring this would be perfect as he smelled food and assumed they were probably all sitting down to dinner in the kitchen or in front of the TV.

The old man flashed a hand sign for eight enemy back to Clay, and grabbed Rex's collar and told him to sit.

Rex sat, but continued to rumble in his chest as the old man slid just out of sight through the screen door. The old man looked back at Clay, who nodded knowing what the old man wanted.

As Myers started banging on the door, Clay slid back into the kitchen and the old man stepped directly into the door way, surprising the man who took an involuntary step back.

Rex growled quietly again as the old man asked, "Who are you and what do you want?"

The man stepped back up, but pointed the rifle down at Rex, and waving his hand with the search warrants said, "Myers, Federal Police with a search warrant. Open the door!"

The old man didn't move. "Not so fast, bud. Let me see that search warrant."

"Open the damn door, old man!" Myers yelled.

To which Rex responded with a growl that backed Myers up two steps and he dropped the search warrant and arrest warrant as he grabbed his gun to shoot.

Very quietly the old man said, "Son, you shoot my dog, I'm gonna shoot you. This dog is not threatening you at all, but it's obvious he doesn't like you worth a damn. Now either hand me that search warrant or get the hell off my property. One or the other, but make it quick!"

Myers heard the others call in position, and Bronson say there were multiple buildings behind the house. All the others called ready to take the house in his earpiece, but he suddenly realized if he gave that order, he was probably going to be a dead man.

Spears came around the corner of the house and looked at the situation then whispered into her boom mike, "Appears to be a standoff at the front door. I'm going to slide along the wall and see what's going on.

Everybody just hold position."

As she moved along the porch, the old man felt Rex shift subtly beneath his hand and heard the boards squeak, "You tell whoever is trying to sneak up the porch to step out, or this is going to go rodeo right now!"

Myers decided as soon as Spears stepped out, he was going to yell the go word, and hope this old bastard shot Spears. As she stepped forward into the light and the old man's sight and Myers got ready to yell, the Tac team heard a scared voice come over the net. "There's somebody out here in the dark, Bronson's down and there's a big knife at my throat! Please don't do anything stupid!"

The old man directed Spears. "You! Pick up that search warrant and hand it here; your boy Myers doesn't seem capable of doing that." Spears had trouble hiding a smile, but did as directed, and the old man opened the door enough to take the search warrant and arrest warrant both.

As the old man glanced at it, Myers slid behind Spears and barked, "Tell whoever is holding my folks out back to let them go and maybe they won't go to prison for assaulting a federal officer."

The old man glanced up at Myers, then resumed reading. "Hey, Clay, come get a load of this one!"

Clay walked through the doorway from the kitchen and across to where the old man was standing. He handed him the papers, and they both took a step of separation.

Now, both Spears and Myers had three things to watch, two old men and one growling German Shepherd. Clay flipped through the second document, and pulled out his cell.

Myers yelled, "No phone calls old man!" But Clay ignored him. Dialing he waited and then said, "Hey

Major, Boone here, you know anything about a federal raid tonight? No? Well if you're in the area, you might want to drop by Cronin's place, 'cause there's one in progress here right now." He listened for a minute, and then hung up.

Turning to the old man Clay said, "John it appears they want to arrest you, Jesse and both Marines for murder. And they want all your guns, too... And this is a fed warrant, not a state one. Oh yeah, and the major will be here in ten... I say we invite them in, and everybody get comfy while we wait on the major."

The old man turned to Clay. "Well, this is your jurisdiction, if that's what you want, that's what we'll do." With that, he told Rex to heel, opened the door and invited Myers and Spears in.

As they came through the door, Myers was steaming. He'd totally lost control of the situation and Spears had seen it all. Should have shot the damn dog to begin with, he thought.

Spears looked closely at the two old men and realized both of them had badges on, and guns that she hadn't seen because of the backlighting. At that point, her knees got weak when she realized how close they'd come to a gun battle that she wasn't sure they would have won.

Myers demanded, "You better let my men go, and right fucking NOW!" The old man sauntered through the kitchen and Myers could see him leaning out the back door. He said something loudly, but Myers couldn't understand whatever gobbldegook the old bastard was speaking. Whatever it was, he sounded amused, and that just pissed Myers off further.

The old man turned to Myers. "Now you tell your folks to come in the back nice and polite, cause if they don't I'm not going to be responsible for what happens out there."

Myers spoke softly into his boom mike, and the rest of the team started trickling in the back door.

Spears looked around the kitchen and realized there were three women and one Hispanic male all sitting calmly at the table eating ice cream and pie. A chill ran down her back as she realized they not only weren't frightened, they purely did not care that there was a Tac team in the house. She'd never seen this level of calm during a raid, and she started to wonder what they'd gotten themselves into.

McClintock came in abashed with a stain in his crotch helping an obviously woozy Bronson. The older Hispanic woman pointed the two of them at two worn wooden chairs by the door with a sniff of disdain. Then she turned to the room and asked, "Would anyone like coffee or iced tea, or some pie or ice cream?"

The old man looked at Myers stopping any response. "I'm John Cronin, this is my grand-daughter Jesse Cronin, and we are the only two on this warrant who are present. Neither I nor my grand-daughter knows the present whereabouts of either of these other individuals. Since I'm assuming this is in relation to the shoot out on Sunday, this search warrant is invalid since it does not correctly reflect the weapons used which are what you are here to collect."

He threw the warrants on the counter and picked up his coffee cup and took a sip. Jesse nodded, and gave the old man a thumb's up hidden by the table. He grinned for a second, and turned back to Myers.

"No, we're going to take all your guns, every damn one of them," Myers sneered.
"We don't know how many of them have been used in other murders, so we're going to take them all."

The old man just cocked his head. "Really? You

really want every gun?"

Myers raised his chin and glared at the old man, and John noticed the slight fat roll of an impending double chin poking out from underneath the man's chin strap. "Yes, that's why it was written the way it was," Myers responded superciliously.

Shaking his head, the old man walked out of the kitchen. "I'm going to the bathroom, you want to come watch?"

Myers turned red, but didn't rise to the bait. The old man went into the little bathroom in the hall, took a leak and turned on the water. He quickly took out his phone, typed a quick text to Billy Moore, washed his hands, and felt his phone vibrate. He saw "K, OTW" on the screen. He smiled, put the phone back in its holster and returned to the kitchen.

Spears walked over to the older Hispanic lady. "Ma'am may I have some pie please?"

"Certainly," Juanita replied. "My name is Juanita. Would you like ice cream with that?"

"Please, Juanita." Myers glared daggers at both of them but Spears just shrugged. *What the hell, it smelled good, and this whole op was blown. Might as well get something out of it*, she thought, as she made a mental note to request transfer the hell out of Texas. *This was definitely not like New York.*

Everyone heard a siren coming closer, then shutting off and a door slamming. Rex never moved, staying at Jesse's side and totally focused on Myers. A knock on the door followed shortly and the old man walked to the living room. "Come on in, major, we're all in the kitchen."

A second siren was now heard in the distance as the Major stepped into the house and shook the old man's hand. "John, I called the sheriff. I figure he didn't get notified either, so that should be him. I'll just wait until he gets here."

"Thanks for coming, major. Can I offer you some pie and ice cream?"

Major Wilson burst out laughing. "God, John, you are one ballsy SOB!" At that point, the sheriff came up on the porch, and the old man told him to come on in.

The three of them walked into the kitchen, which was now almost full and presented almost a surreal scene, between the women and Francisco sitting quietly at the table drinking coffee, a Tac team standing nervously around the room and Ranger Clay Boone leaning against the sink, sipping a cup of coffee.

Major Wilson glared around. "Who's in charge here?"

Myers tried to reassert himself. "I am," he said. "This is a federal search warrant. Who the hell are you?"

Pulling his jacket back, Major Wilson reached for his credentials and said quietly, "Son, watch your mouth. For your information, I'm Ranger Wilson, and I'm the senior man in Company E Texas Rangers, which means you're in *my* jurisdiction without *my* knowledge, running some kind of raid, and *that is not done.* Now, let me see all of your credentials."

Myers reared back, "I don't have to show you shit, I'm a federal officer, and…"

Wilson's .45 was pressed between Myers' eyes, and he said in a very quiet voice, "Either show me creds or go to jail for impersonating an officer of the law, and if you reach for *anything* other than your credentials I will spread your brains all over Mr. Cronin's kitchen and apologize later. Do you understand me?"

Spears looked on in amazement, hardly believing that old man got a pistol out that quickly, and looking around, realized the other Ranger, Cronin and his granddaughter were all smiling and none of them had anything in their hands. The hair on the back of her neck started standing up, and she very carefully reached for her badge and ID and pulled them out of her vest and handed them to Ranger Boone.

He nodded with a smile and motioned with his head, and she collected all of the other IDs and brought them back to him. Myers finally reached in his vest and pulled out his ID and Wilson removed it from his fingers without ever moving the .45.

Clay motioned with his head, and Spears walked over and took Myers ID and brought it back to Ranger Boone.

Clay shuffled through the IDs and said, "Major, that's Myers, Rodney, agent, DHS, one each. No rank given."

Wilson re holstered his pistol and glared at Myers. "Now what in the hell are you doing in my jurisdiction without notice?"

Clay handed his boss the two search warrants, and the major read rapidly through them. Handing them to the sheriff, he considered Myers. "What is this all about? This looks more like a damn fishing expedition than a real warrant, and it doesn't specify which guns you're going to take."

At that point, the old man broke in, "Major, he says *all* of them to see how many have been used in murders."

Major Wilson smiled at Myers. "Do you realize what you're getting into son? Do you have any idea how many guns are in this house?"

Myers spat back, "Oh maybe twenty, maybe thirty; and who knows how many murders we can clear with them. Based on..."

Wilson quietly asked, "Based on what?"

Limply Myers said, "Based on what's been going on

down here with rogue cops."

Wilson just shook his head. "John, two questions: what is the oldest gun you have, and do you know how many guns you have?"

"Major, the oldest one is an 1851 Navy, and at last count one hundred seventy eight."

"John, how many are fireable of that number?"

"All of them are, major. All of them, and we have ammo for each of them."

"Ah… Papa," Jesse interrupted. "Did you count the Glock 19 I bought last week?"

The old man turned and smiled. "Thanks, Jesse. Major, make that one hundred seventy nine guns. And before you ask, I'd say we have something in the neighborhood of eighty thousand rounds of cased ammo in the powder house, and probably eight, ten pounds of powder, and fifteen thousand primers, and probably six thousand bullets and cases. If you really want exact numbers, I can go get my book. Oh yeah, and two cases of TNT, and a couple of hundred feet of primacord, and two boxes of detonators."

Smiling gently, Major Wilson said, "No John, that's close enough. So Mr. Myers, just how far back are you intending to go looking for murders?"

Myers just stared at the old man, his mind not processing the sense of what he'd just said.

"Mr. Myers, did you bring enough evidence bags for one hundred seventy nine guns? And enough transport for them? I only see two vehicles out there; I don't think you could even get all the guns in two vehicles, could you? And how many evidence sheets did you bring? Enough to document each gun, and all its ammo? I don't think so. Tell you what you're going to do, if this is about the shoot on Sunday, you may collect those weapons and no others under this search warrant.

Clay, you got a camera handy?"

Clay pushed off from the sink. "Yes, sir, boss. Ronni would you hand me the little camera in your purse?"

Ronni reached in her purse, pulled out a compact Sony and handed it to Clay.

"Clay, lay these IDs out and take pictures of them, then take pictures of each of these *agents*. You, Spears, you seem to have a little sense, you may inventory and collect the weapons used in the shoot on Sunday. And, Clay, make sure you have pictures of all three weapons before they're bagged, don't want them damaged now do we?"

Myers spluttered, "No, you can't take our pictures, that's illegal and besides, that…"

Slumping, he just glared at Clay as he took his picture. When he'd finished, Clay walked over to the old man. "Okay, John, which safe are the guns in?"

The old man looked at Jesse. "Where's your ninety-four?" Jesse pointed to the office, so the old man led Clay and Spears into the office.

Opening the antique bank safe, the old man stood back and said, "Agent Spears the three weapons you want are the scoped Winchester 94 in the third rack from the left, the scoped Winchester Model 70 in the next to the last rack on the right, and the Barrett MRAD in the last rack on the right. Those are the three weapons used. Would you remove them from the safe and place them on the table for Ranger Boone to photograph them please?"

Spears just stood there for a moment, staring at the safe. It was more like a vault than safe, and she'd never seen this many guns in any place other than their own armory, even her dad didn't have this many. She once again vowed to herself to get the hell out of this state, sooner rather than later. Gingerly she removed each rifle in silence, laid them out, documented them, bagged them and handed the old man the bottom copy as a receipt.

She couldn't help glancing at the other rifles, and noted two M-16s sitting in the safe, along with some kind of monster rifle with two barrels a couple of rows in; turning to the old man, she asked, "Sir, what is that monster sitting two rows back? The one with two barrels?"

The old man chuckled. "Miss, that is a Holland and Holland 500 nitro express double rifle. It shoots a 570 grain bullet at 2100 feet per second and almost 6000 foot pounds of energy at the muzzle. That particular gun is seventy years old and well used, so it's only worth about seventy thousand dollars. Somewhere around here is the original leather case for it."

Reaching on the top shelf, he took down two rounds almost four inches long and a half inch in diameter. "These are what it shoots."

Spears just looked at them wide-eyed, as he put the rounds back. He noticed her looking down at the M-16s and said, "Yes, those are M-16s and yes they are full auto. They are my and my grand-daughter's duty rifles issued by the sheriff. Would you like me to call him in here to verify that?"

Glancing at Clay, who was grinning at her, she looked back at the old man. "Uh… No sir. That's fine."

"Okay, are we done here?" She nodded and Clay picked up two rifles and walked out, leaving the third for Sparks. She picked it up and followed the old man back into the kitchen.

It was apparent that Major Wilson had been holding court in the kitchen, as Francisco, Juanita and Jesse were having a hard time concealing grins. When Sparks walked in with the last rifle, the Major turned to Myers again. "Okay, here are the rifles, since this arrest warrant says remand to custody, and since you're in *my* jurisdiction, I will take custody of these fine people and that finishes this off. Now all of you get your asses out of my jurisdiction and if I or any of my troopers see you here again without a courtesy call, you *will* be arrested. Do you understand?"

Myers turned an interesting shade of purple, but nodded and stomped out of the house, closely followed by the rest of the Tac team. Doors slammed and the two SUVs quickly departed the driveway.

22 Now What

Major Wilson pulled out a chair and sat down. "Juanita, can I get a piece of that pie I smell and maybe some ice cream on top if you have it?"

Juanita took another bowl out of the cabinet as the old man went to the back door and called out in the Degar dialect. Toby came in the back door smiling, wearing a large Bowie knife on his belt.

Chattering happily to the old man in Degar, he told him how he'd smacked one of the bad people in the back of the head and used his handcuffs and tie wraps to bind him up; he'd then snuck up on the second one and put the knife to his throat because he'd moved before Toby could hit him.

The old man relayed the tale to the amusement of all, and Toby got a reward of pie and ice cream with the major.

The old man pulled out his cell and called Billy, but didn't get an answer, so he assumed he was still en route. He sent a quick text to call the house and grabbed a cup of coffee and sat too, "Major, how's your daughter doing? I know Angelina said she was in another room in the hospital, but I didn't have a chance to stop by and see her."

"She's doing pretty well considering she took a full blast of twelve- gauge at point blank range," Major Wilson answered. "Thankfully, she had her level three vest on, and it absorbed the pellets, but she's got five broken ribs, a punctured and collapsed right lung, and a knot on her head the size of a golf ball. Doc says he's going to keep her for a few days, but they got the lung to re-inflate yesterday, and her vision wasn't too blurry today, so things are looking up. Thanks for asking, by the way."

Shifting in his chair, the Major said, "Okay, the real question is what in the hell am I going to do with you and Jesse since I now have you in custody? Jose, I can't ask you to put two of your deputies in your own jail, and..."

The house phone rang. The old man answered and listened for a couple of minutes, then turned to the room. "Well, major, Billy Moore had just landed, and he said he's got Judge Cotton coming in, that we should meet him at the courthouse, so maybe he has an answer." Looking over at the sheriff he asked, "Jose, do you trust me to drive myself and Jesse into town, or do you want to haul us in?"

Clay couldn't help himself, and started laughing, which started everybody laughing in a final release of the tension. The sheriff finally said, "John, if I can't trust you now, because of this put up BS, I don't need to be the sheriff; but it's really the major's call."

Major Wilson looked at Clay. "I ought to make you haul them in for laughing, but I guess we'd better go see what your high dollar lawyer has up his sleeve. Drive yourselves for all I care, I know you're not going anywhere!"

Ronni begged off on riding along as she said, "Yet, another damn courtroom. I'll stay here and catch up on all the dirt with Juanita."

Clay ended up riding with the major, while the sheriff took the lead with the old man and Jesse in the Suburban and the major bringing you the rear in his Crown Vic.

Arriving at the court house, they found a blue-jeaned

Billy Moore pacing outside the side door and talking a mile a minute on his cell phone. His beat up briefcase leaned against the door as a reminder for him to pick it up on the way in. When everyone came up the sidewalk, Billy looked around. "Where are the Feds? Are they somewhere behind or are they buried in the South 40, John?"

The old man laughed but all the others grimaced, and the major said, "Mr. Moore, that's not funny."

"You must be Major Wilson, Company E, right?" Billy replied. "I hope your daughter is recovering, and Major, I've known John for *way* too many years. In fact, in a few cases I helped John bury the bodies, so that wasn't actually a rhetorical question…"

The old man laughed, and Jesse looked at them both with a strange expression. Shaking his head in amazement, the major said, "I can't believe you just said that to three officers of the law, much less while these two are under arrest for murder! Sounds like I need to arrest your ass, too, Mr. Moore!"

Billy stuck out his hands and said, "Oh *please* do!" Then he dropped into a serious mien, "Judge Cotton is waiting on us in chambers, and he's already pissed so let's not keep him waiting, if you don't mind."

The old man said, "Dare I ask?"

Billy just shook his head and opened the door for everyone. As they trooped down the hall, Billy gave the old man a careful/slow handsign and pointed ahead. The old man nodded and gave him a thumb's up.

They filed into the Judge's chambers, and took seats facing the desk. Judge Cotton looked over his glasses and stubbed his cigar in an ashtray already overflowing with cigar butts.

Glaring at all of them, he started in. "Miz Jesse, you close your ears for a minute, I need to cuss these assholes out." Pointing at the major he added, "Hack, what the hell is going on, and where are these gahdam papers? And Jose and Clay, what the hell is going on in this county that you're not telling me?"

The major handed over both the warrants and the Judge proceeded to read them with assorted snuffs, coughs and mumbles under his breath. Finally he looked up and asked, "Was *anybody* in this damn county aware that this shit was going on?"

A chorus of no's and shaking of heads followed, with Major Wilson starting to vent, but the Judge held up his hand to stop him: "So you're telling me you had no idea, no advanced notice, nothing? Correct?"

"Nothing."

"No."

"No idea, thought it was being handled in Austin."

The judge looked over at Billy Moore. "Billy, I notice you haven't asked to see the warrants, so I'm going to assume you somehow got your hands on them, and no I'm not asking... I don't want to know or have to hold you in contempt. I see that Gumby Gillory was the turkey they got to sign this one out, but I've never heard of this guy Deal. Anybody else ever heard of him?"

Another round of head shakes, and Jesse finally spoke up. "Judge Cotton, none of those *officers* were Texans either, they were all from up North."

Nodding, he looked down at the warrants again. "John, I don't think they meant for you to be taken into custody here, I think they meant to haul you back to Dallas and dump you in a federal holding tank. The way this warrant is written is screwy, to put it mildly, and I don't know of another judge who'd sign something like this without a lot more detail." Glancing at Billy, he continued. "Since there is no requirement or request for bail, I'm assuming you are requesting a bail hearing for your clients, correct Mr. Moore?"

Billy stood up and began pacing. "Judge, this is all happening three days after this whole incident occurred, after both the sheriff and the Rangers from Austin have deemed it a good shoot and from what I hear, there is pretty good evidence that these guys were not only drug runners, they were going to Chicago to set up a distribution center. The leader seems to have been a known drug runner and lieutenant in the Cartel. They tried to murder the major's daughter without a single reason other than her uniform. The official report is not even released yet, and here we have a federal warrant out of a *different jurisdiction* for weapons and arrest of four people for murder? This would be nol prossed by any competent prosecutor with two brain cells to rub together based on evidence at the scene, but now we have a new regime, er… administration and it appears they are coming after people who are fighting the drug industry under color of racial profiling. Everybody in this room except you and I were at that scene, either as participants or investigators, so I'll throw my clients on the mercy of the Court and request bail an…"

Judge Cotton stopped Billy with a glare. "Okay, enough already. Sheriff, your recommendation?"

"Judge, hell, I authorized them to shoot," Sheriff Rodriguez replied. "I'll sign their bond myself."

The Judge turned to Clay. "You?"

"Far as I'm concerned, Jesse shot in self-defense, they'd already shot her and Aaron before the first round was returned. We found fifty-two cases for 7.62 by 39 in the front yard and thirty-two in the backyard. All John and the Marine Matt did were take shots to save the hostage's lives. This is pure BS."

"Major?"

"RoR[20] em, I can't think of many people in this area

that are less of a risk than these two."

Judge Cotton turned to the old man and Jesse. "Based on the recommendations of knowledgeable law enforcement officials, and pursuant to the laws of Texas and Pecos County, you two are released on recognizance. And, Billy, you better hope I win at poker tonight, or the next time I see you I'll have your guts for garters. Now all of you get the hell outta my office."

Jesse, in a low voice said, "Thank you, Judge. I don't understand what's happening here."

He turned to her and said gently, "Mizz Jesse, I think they are going to try to steamroll y'all, but they don't understand who they are dealing with. Not just with you two, but with Billy. You're gonna be alright. You got good people around you."

She nodded and followed the others back to the parking lot.

---

[20] Release on Recognizance

23 Heads Up

Jesse bolted from the Suburban as soon as they pulled in the yard, running in and grabbing the clean phone from her nightstand. She quickly searched through and hit the pre-programmed number for Aaron, but got no answer. Frustrated, she then tried Matt's number with the same results. She was debating whether to try Aaron or Matt's regular phones, when she remembered Francisco's friend was driving Aaron's truck. Going into the kitchen, she asked Francisco, "Can you please call Felix, and find out where they are and tell Matt to turn on the other phone? We need to let them know what's happened here."

Francisco agreed, and quickly got Felix on the line, in round about Spanish, he determined they were at least two hours from Pendleton, and told Felix to get on the radio to Matt to turn on the other phone and for Matt to call Jesse.

Ten anxious minutes went by until Jesse's phone rang, and as she snatched it up, she realized she didn't really know how to tell Matt what had happened without giving too much away. Thankfully, Matt was on the ball. "You wanted me to call, am I to assume you had visitors?"

"Uh, yes, we did, pretty much as expected."

"Just y'all or all of us expected to be there?"

"All of us."

"Did they know we're on vacation?"

"Ah... No they didn't."

"Do they know where we're camping?"

"I don't think so, but I'm not sure."

"Okay, I think we'll be at the campground in another couple of hours. I'll let the other campers know to expect guests, probably tomorrow."

Jesse smiled finally. "I think that would be a good idea!"

"Okay, bye now," Matt replied. "Phone will stay on as long as we need it."

"Okay, bye."

Meanwhile, in the loaned SUVs, Myers and the rest of the FPS team continued their drive back to Ft. Bliss and their ride back to Dallas. Myers fumed in the first SUV about how to spin what had happened, and realized he was pretty much screwed. He'd kicked Spears and Bronson and McClintock to the other SUV while he, Thompson and Warren rode in relative comfort and plotted a way to blame the others.

In the second SUV, Spears rode behind Hearn who was driving and shared the back seat with McClintock and Bronson. Thankfully, Bronson was in the middle, but she still had the window cracked to keep from smelling McClintock's piss stained trousers. Bronson was complaining about his headache, and Turner finally turned to Spears. "Okay, what in the hell went on out front? We were ready to take the place, I thought, until you called us off."

Spears laid out what she'd seen, and what she'd noticed after they got in the house, and more importantly, what was sitting in the gun safe. She also told the others she was going to request a transfer tomorrow, and going on vacation for a while because she was damn sure they all almost died tonight. McClintock chimed in that he still didn't know how many were outside, and nobody had ever come in. Bronson still had no idea what happened to him, but between him and McClintock they managed to confuse the time line enough to think there were at least two or possibly more people out in the dark with them.

When the tac team finally got back to Ft. Bliss, they went quietly to the ramp, climbed on the helo and flew back to Dallas in total silence.
***

Back at the house, Jesse was feeling much better about what had happened, she wondered where everyone went. Then heard the TV volume go up; turning and going into the living room she realized everybody had congregated in front of the TV as the 10PM news broadcast from the Houston station came on, and she also noticed Billy Moore sitting in the corner with the phone to his ear nodding. "We've got it on now. Thanks, yeah we'll check both channels."

The breaking news roller came across the screen, and the male news anchor derisively known as "Big Hair" came on in his usual ZOMG, the world is ending voice. "Breaking out of Dallas, but impacting our listening area, two Deputy Sheriffs in Pecos County and two Marines are in custody tonight suspected of murder in the deaths of four Hispanics in rural Pecos County on Sunday. According to the US Attorney's office in Dallas, numerous questions surrounding the shootings have forced the US Attorney's office to take these people into custody. They are Captain John Cronin and Deputy Jesse Cronin, father and son; and two Marines whose connection with the Cronins is not known at this time. The Marines are a Gunnery Sergeant and Staff Sergeant, current duty stations unknown. We are expecting a press conference tomorrow morning in Dallas and our reporter will report from there live!"

Billy quickly switched to the El Paso channel, and caught the female anchor known as "Little Hair" breathlessly exclaimed, "Cronin and Deputy Jesse

Cronin, father and son; and two Marines whose connection with the Cronins is not known at this time. The Marines are a Gunnery Sergeant and Staff Sergeant, current duty stations unknown. Miguel Ramirez will be reporting live from Dallas in the morning with more details, and we have called the Pecos County Sheriff's office, but there was no response as of press time."

Turning the volume down, Billy snorted. "Well, we know which playbook those two are using, and both of them have a hard on for any LEOs caught doing anything. I'm going to go call the sheriff and hope he caught the broadcast. He better be ready for the shit to hit the fan tomorrow morning."

"Why do they both dislike LEOs so much Billy?" Jesse asked. "That doesn't make a lot of sense."

Billy laughed. "Well, Big Hair no longer has a driver's license, since his multiple drunken driving arrests, so he now has a paid driver, which is coming out of his salary from the station, and Little Hair has her license suspended for multiple speeding tickets and she's on a restricted home to work only license. Of course both of them blame law enforcement, not their own bad habits."

Turning to the old man, he asked, "John can I use your office for a while, I need to get things set up for tomorrow morning when the US Attorney or his minions come a callin' to try to transfer you to federal custody. And I'd recommend y'all all go to bed; from here on out, this is all my baby."

The old man nodded. "Billy, you are free to use anything you need, you know where the bed is, the bathroom is, and breakfast is at 5 AM. And going to bed does seem like the best approach. And thanks. We all appreciate what you're doing for us."

Billy grinned. "Oh, you haven't seen the bill yet,

John."

The old man shook his head and shooed everybody out.
***

In California, Matt and Felix were an hour out of Pendleton when Matt decided to take a break, trade in some coffee and get a refill. They'd cut off from I-10 onto I-15, figuring if there were any BOLOs out for them they would probably be on I-10 and I-5 primarily, especially if DHS and or CPB were involved, they patrolled I-5 much more religiously than I-15 for some reason. Seeing a pay phone, Matt got $3 in change and called the Command Duty Officer's office, after identifying himself, the CDO[21] personally came on the line and told Matt they were waiting for him to come directly in and Colonel Nelson had a driver standing by to take Felix to a local hotel for the night and to San Diego for the flight back to Midland tomorrow morning.

Matt replied, "Sir, we'll be there in an hour, is Staff Sergeant Miller on base yet?"
The CDO informed him that he was and was being taken care of; he also reiterated for Matt not to go by his leased apartment but to come directly to base and the quicker the better.

Matt hung up and briefed Felix on what he'd been told. Felix agreed and they got back on the road. An hour and ten minutes later they rolled up to the main gate at Camp Pendleton and were immediately waved through. Matt was handed a map and told to report directly to the CDO and Felix was to follow him with no deviations. Arriving at the headquarters building, Matt and Felix parked in front of the building and walked up to the main doors. They were met by a staff sergeant, who escorted

---

[21] Command Duty Officer

them to the head, then to the CDO's office. The Captain, who was standing the duty, met them at the door and welcomed Matt and Felix into the office and pointed to seats. Matt and Felix after almost seventeen hours on the road elected to stand, to the amusement of the CDO. Finally, the CDO got down to business.

"Gunny, here's the skinny, I don't know what you've done, but it's rattled cages all the way to the big man in the corner office, so here's the drill. You will be considered as reporting aboard as of now, on staff as of now, and you will report to the Transient Quarters immediately after leaving here. You will not talk to anyone, pass go or collect $200. Understood?"

"Yes, sir," Matt replied. "Wilco. I do have weapons that need to be secured at the Armory Sir."

Pointing at Felix, the CDO said, "Sir, many thanks for your assistance in moving SSGT Miller's vehicle from Texas to here, and after you follow the Gunny over to the Transient Quarters, SSGT Almond here will take you to the Holiday Inn outside the gate; he will also pick you up in the morning at 0600 and transport you to the San Diego airport. Do you need any funds tonight or in the morning?"

"No sir," Felix replied. "I have money and Senor John gave me enough money for food and hotel and I have the reservation number for my flight back to Texas tomorrow. I would like to know of Senor Aaron's condition so that I may pass that back to the people at home who are concerned about him, if I may."

The CDO thought for a second, and then dialed the hospital. He got the floor nurse, spoke for a minute, listened for a bit and then hung up. "Sir, you may tell those who need to know that SSGT Miller is resting comfortably, and there are no complications that either the nurse or the doctors are aware of, and he is expected to make a full recovery."

Felix nodded. "Thank you, sir."

The CDO looked at Matt. "After you secure your weapons, you will return directly to the Transient Quarters. Tomorrow morning after you grab a bite to eat, again speaking to no one, you will report back here to Colonel Pearson the JAG at oh eight hundred. Clear?"

"Yes, sir," Matt replied.

Making a shooing motion, the CDO said, "Okay, duty done, y'all get out of here. Almond, you know what to do."

Amid the "Yes, sirs," everyone departed with Almond leading them to the Transient Quarters. Parking in the back, Felix unloaded his bag, and walked over to Matt.

Matt shook Felix's hand. "Felix, I owe you a debt of thanks for driving Aaron's truck out here, especially pushing through, I know this has been one helluva trip and both Aaron and I owe you a big one!"

Felix nodded. "Thank you for allowing me to help you my friend. I wish you and Aaron only the best. Please come back and see us if you can, you know you will be welcome." With that, Felix turned and walked to the duty van, hopped in and SSGT Almond drove him to the Holiday Inn.

Matt made a quick run to the Armory, checked in both his guns and Aarons and drove back to quarters. Unloaded his bag from the truck and making sure he had both sets of keys, humped the bag up to the back door of the quarters. Checking in, he got his room and after a quick shower, crashed.

24 Lawyer Up

The old man walked into the kitchen and saw Billy sitting at the table with the house phone to his ear, and an empty cup of coffee at his elbow. The table was half covered with yellow sheets of paper with notes all over them. Pouring himself a cup, he held up the pot. Billy nodded and the old man brought the coffee pot over and refilled Billy's cup. Billy scribbled a few more notes saying, "Okay be at the sheriff's office at zero eight hundred, prepared to go live. Thanks Willie!"

Hanging up and banging on the table, Billy started laughing. "Oh, we're gonna have some fun this morning!"

Juanita and Francisco had come in without either of them noticing. "What kind of fun Senor Billy? And I hope you're going to clean up that mess before I serve breakfast?" Juanita asked.

Bill, still chuckling, started picking up papers. "Oh, you'll have to wait and see. I've got Little Hair set up with a live press conference with Jose at zero eight hundred, and Willie's bringing an independent crew that's going to feed live to Fox. John, I need you and Jesse to stay here and not answer the phone unless I call on a clean phone. Juanita, Francisco, if you answer you have no idea where either of them are, got it?"

Juanita cocked her head. "Yes, Senor Billy, but… Oh, I get it…" Francisco just smiled and nodded. Juanita turned briskly to the fridge. "Bacon, eggs, hash browns and biscuits work for everybody?"

Everybody nodded, and Billy racked and stacked his

papers. "I'm going to go take a shower, back in a few."

Jesse hobbled into the kitchen, looking back at Billy. "Gah, he looks worse than I feel, and that's pretty damn bad."

The old man said, "Well, I think Billy was up all night, and I'm dreading this phone bill, but it's his ballgame, so I'm not going to complain… Yet…"

Twenty minutes later, Billy, now freshly shaved and showered, came back in an old robe saying, "John, don't know whose this is, but I didn't want to mess up my suit, and can I borrow a vehicle?" He dug into the breakfast Juanita set in front of him.

"Sure, you can take the Suburban, since I'm stuck here. Do we get a hint of what you're going to pull?"

Billy just shook his head, and the old man rolled his eyes. After breakfast, everyone picked up their dishes, and trooped in to rinse them while Juanita loaded the dishwasher. Billy went in and unplugged his charger and put the phone in his briefcase. He disappeared into the bedroom and came back out a few minutes later dressed in a suit.

The old man whistled. "Damn Billy, you clean up pretty good."

Billy preened. "Unlike you, I actually pay attention to style, and I am not afraid to dress in the latest fashion; unlike you, still wearing Dickie's like some poor working shlub…"

The old man grinned and flipped the keys to Billy. "We'll be here, I'm assuming you'll be back some time this morning, right?"

"Yep, like I said, turn the TV on the El Paso channel at zero eight hundred." With that Billy was out the door. Jesse hobbled back to her room and with Juanita's help cleaned up and came back into the living room.
***

Meanwhile, in Dallas, Myers was standing outside Deal's office when he came in. "Alright, what in the hell went on last night? I checked with detention and nobody's there! And where are all the guns, there were only three checked in!"

Myers, pacing in front of the desk, started laying out the story he'd concocted with the two other agents last night, but was interrupted by a knock on the door. Deal yelled, "I'm busy, come back in an hour." Whoever was knocking then left. Myers finished his description of the failure, basically laying blame on Spears for dereliction of duty, and admitted that the Rangers had buffaloed him on the arrest, due to the wording of the warrant.

Deal swung around holding out his hand. "Okay, gimme the warrants back. I'll get them fixed and get another judge to sign them."

Myers said, "Uh, I would, but the damn old Ranger kept them. He wouldn't give 'em back."

"What! You let a warrant get out, and now you can bet both the Rangers and that damn sheriff have them. Shit, who knows who has seen them by now? At least Gillory's signature is on them. Dammit…"

***

At the ranch, the old man was sitting in the office working on the books when Jesse realized it was almost 8 AM. "Papa, it's almost time."

The old man grumbled and came into the living room, as Juanita, Francisco and Toby came in from the kitchen. Turning on the TV, he set the channel and slumped back in the rocker. The others arranged themselves around the various chairs and watched as the roller came up with the breaking news caption and dissolved into Little Hair standing in front of the Sheriff's Office. In her usual breathless voice she said, "We are here this morning in Fort Stockton for a press conference by the Pecos County Sheriff in response to our report from last evening. The sheriff has promised this reporter an exclusive after the press conference, and here he is now."

The old man flipped over to Fox News, and sure enough it was also carrying the interview, but from a slightly different angle. He switched back as the camera panned over to a podium set up in front of what appeared to be a car covered in a car cover and focused on the podium as the sheriff walked out in his dress uniform. Suddenly the old man leaned forward in the rocker, slapping the arm. "Oh, you sneaky sumbitch! This is going to be a public beatdown!"

Jesse looked at him, but snapped back to the TV when they sheriff came on. "Good Morning. I am Jose Rodriguez, I am the Sheriff of Pecos County, Texas. As you may have heard last night, two of my deputies were remanded to custody to be charged with murder in the deaths of four Hispanic males at a remote ranch here in the county. First, let me say I take this as a personal insult, not only to me as the sheriff, but also to the men and women of this department, and to Pecos County itself."

Looking down and then back up he continued, "When I was a young man growing up here, we didn't have TV. We couldn't afford it, but we had a radio. I used to listen to a newsman named Paul Harvey who used to do stories in parts, and the last segment was what he called the 'rest of the story.'"

He paused to take a sip of water. "I'd like to tell you the rest of this particular story you heard the beginning of last night. The first part of the rest of the story is a young female State Trooper who cannot be here this morning, because she is still in the hospital in serious but stable condition after being shot at less than six feet with a twelve gauge shotgun by one of these so- called innocent men. Luckily she had her vest on, and that is what saved her life, but she was seriously injured." He walked over to the white van with the camera panning to follow, and the old man realized it was the actual van, leaning back the old man smiled and chuckled softly.

Opening the back doors of the van, the sheriff walked back six feet away. "The young trooper was shot from *this* range by one of these four who poked the shotgun through that curtain and did their damnest to kill her. Why? Because their leader, Ricardo Garcia, yelled out to shoot her. We have that on tape, and the video from the patrol unit showing the shooting taking place; both of which have been distributed to your station."

Walking back to the podium, he put both hands on the podium and looked directly into the camera. "Ricardo Garcia is a well-known name to law enforcement down on the border. He's a lieutenant in the cartel. He's been convicted twice on drug charges, and was wanted on both sides of the border for at least twelve homicides. That's the first part of the rest of the story."

Taking another sip of water, he nodded at the cameras. "Here's the second part of the rest of the story: it was almost thirty minutes before we were able to access the camera information and during that time, Garcia and his accomplices had gotten off I-ten and were moving North through the county. They happened on a ranch in a remote location and decided to hole up there. One of our deputies, whom I won't name; since that was supposedly our agreement with all the stations down here about not naming deputies involved in shootouts with the drug cartels, was on patrol with a young Marine doing a ride along. They approached this remote ranch, noted a strange vehicle in the driveway, and slowed to check it out."

Nodding to the deputies, the sheriff turned back to the camera and continued, as the two deputies pulled the cover off car #214, and even Little Hair inadvertently reacted to the damage along with most of the bystanders.

"This was what happened. There were fifty-eight rounds that were fired on full automatic at this vehicle at an approximate range of seventy-five yards, and forty-two rounds impacted the vehicle. If you zoom in on the driver's side door and window, you can see that window is shot out and there are five rounds that penetrated that door. Now if you zoom in on the window, you' will notice a brown stain covering the passenger's side of the car. That is the blood from both the Marine and the Deputy being shot without provocation. Again, we know from the hostage that Ricardo Garcia told one Jesus Ramirez to quote go blow the cops away unquote. Jesus Ramirez is another cartel member, a part of Garcia's crew as they are called, and he is an escaped murderer from a prison in Mexico City. His body count was thirty-two deaths he claimed credit for. The deputy got off a call that they were under fire about the time we realized what vehicle these four were driving."

Pausing, the sheriff looked directly at the camera, "I was one of the multiple responders from four departments, including DPS, Rangers, DEA and of course our deputies. I am a certified negotiator, and attempted to establish contact with the four, but they refused to answer the phone until we had multiple units on scene. We were over three-hundred yards away, to prevent any possible reaction, but when Ricardo Garcia answered the phone, he gave us one minute to –as he said, disappear before he started shooting hostages— That tape has also been provided to you. Unknown to Garcia, we had managed to get two deputies one of whom was accompanied by another Marine on a ride along into position to observe the house; as the scene commander I had authorized the two deputies to take a shot if they got one in order to save the hostages. When Garcia came out with the baby as a hostage, and sent Ramirez with the female hostage toward the police car with direction to make sure they were dead, the deputies took the shots that resulted in the two Hispanic men being shot and killed."

Jose, looking out over the crowd that had gathered, took another sip of water. "Oh and one more thing, the last two more men who came out the back door were firing their AKs on full automatic, they were taken out by the first deputy, who is now receiving care for not only for being shot in the hip, but also multiple broken ribs from being hit in the vest by at least two rounds from an AK. There were forty-seven rounds fired in the back of the house as those two made a run for the creek."

The sheriff walked over to the van again camera following, pulling the curtain aside, he gestured inside, "This is what those quote innocent unquote men were hauling. One hundred kilos of cocaine and almost two million dollars in cash."

Even Little Hair gasped at that as both cameramen turned the cameras and zoomed in on the cocaine and money lying in the back of the van and now in plain sight.

Stalking back to the podium, he added, "As a result of the material found in the van, additional arrests were made in Chicago which effectively shut down what was planned to be the end of the distribution chain for this and follow-on shipments of cocaine. Due to the fact that this was an officer involved shooting, and Texas Rangers were on scene, I requested they bring in a team to conduct the investigation. Major Wilson from Company E determined since they had also been represented on scene, brought in investigators from Company F, which is the Ranger Headquarters Company in Austin. The Rangers from Austin conducted the investigation, took all statements and based on *evidence at the scene*, determined the officers were correct in the shots they took to preserve the lives of the hostages. *That* is the rest of the story. I will now take questions."

The old man applauded the TV set, saying, "Outstanding, Jose, thank you!" All the others agreed.

Little Hair stepped into the shot with a mike in hand and asked, "But, sheriff, what you've said here this morning contradicts what the US Attorney released last night, how do you explain that?"

"Ma'am, I can only tell you what happened, I don't know what the US Attorney in Dallas, which by the way is *not* the US Attorney with jurisdiction here, used to base the arrest warrants on, so you'd have to ask him."

"Well, where are these deputies, and those two Marines? Why aren't they out here to defend themselves?"

"Ma'am, I have no idea where the Marines are, as they left yesterday morning for their bases. As far as the deputies, one as I said is under nursing care for injuries, but they were both arrested. But their lawyer is here and I'm sure he'll be happy to provide a statement."

Billy Moore stalked to the podium as Jose stepped away. Little Hair looked confused and started to turn away, but Billy said, "Just a minute. I have a statement concerning the deputies I've been asked to defend. First, by publically naming the deputies, Mr. Deal has painted a target on both these fine officers, I guess the only suspects he identifies are law officers, which kinda makes me wonder who's side he's on. This incident was fully investigated by the Texas Rangers from Austin, so I'd suggest you also ask them what they presented to the US

Attorney."

Pausing for effect Billy continued, "And while you're at it, ask the US Attorney why he decided to arrest these deputies with a DHS tactical team of eight personnel at 1900 last night with no notice to either the Sheriff's department here, DPS, the US Attorney for this division of Texas, or notification to or request for assistance from the Texas Ranger Company for this area. By the way, normally the US Attorneys works with the US Marshals to arrest suspects and normally the also notify at least DPS and the Rangers."

Little Hair, a bit off base, asked, "Well, why did they shoot so quickly, and why did they shoot to kill, if they're such good shots, why not just wound them?"

Billy, ever the showman, shook his head as if Little Hair was the proverbial dummy in the class. "Well, Missy, these drug runners had already started it, by shooting up this car we're standing in front of. Dontcha think that just might color the responding officer's response? And the threat to kill the hostages? What would you have them do, try to wound the perpetrators so they could then kill the hostages before the officers could respond? You do know, don't you, the two hostages were a young mother and her baby, right?"

Little Hair said, "But the US Attorney must have had *some* reason?"

Billy nodded. "Well, apparently Mr. Deal- ironic name isn't it? Oh was I not supposed to say his name? Well, he was a low level DOJ civil rights lawyer in the New York office until two months ago. He seemed to do a lot of cases against law enforcement for civil rights violations but in six years he only had _one_— count 'em one— conviction all the rest seemed to have been settled out of court. And he had his own little tactical team from DHS that worked with him on arrests up there in New

York. And now he comes down here and jumps jurisdictions? I have to wonder where *he* is getting his instructions from, don't you?

Little Hair started to interrupt, but Billy continued, "Now in this administration all of a sudden he's pushed up to a full US Attorney and moves to Texas, and although he's supposedly now divorced from the DHS organization, mysteriously this tactical team also shows up in Texas, and based on what happened last night, apparently takes orders directly from Mr. Deal. See it's like this: it seems there was a DHS helicopter laid on, and this tactical response team in full combat gear was already on their way to the airport before this search warrant and arrest warrant were ever signed. Don't you find that a bit strange? I know that I do."

Looking at the camera, he added, "You know, I think you need to go talk to some folks, starting with this Mr. Deal, oops sorry, and maybe the Texas Rangers and a few others."

Little Hair, looking dazed merely said, "Thank you and that's it from Fort Stockton, now back to you in the studio Larry."

Three different newspaper reporters could be seen swarming Billy as the camera shut down.

25 JAG

At 0730 Matt was standing at parade rest in his service dress greens outside the Judge Advocate General's office in the headquarters building. Not knowing what to expect, he'd just driven through McDonalds for breakfast, rather than chancing the galley and running into somebody he wasn't supposed to talk to. He'd heard the phone inside ring a couple of times, but there was nothing he could do; so he stood patiently by. At 0745 a sharp corporal came down the hallway, looked at Matt and said, "Gunny Carter, right?"

"Yes, corporal, that's me."

"Good, the colonel wants to see you ASAP, and he'll be here in fifteen. I've got just enough time to get the coffee on. Need a cup?"

"Corporal, you should know *no* gunny will ever turn down a cup of coffee! Lead the way, and by the way, your phone's been ringing since 0735."

The corporal shrugged. "Probably the head shed, they seem to forget we're three hours behind them, which actually pays off when they do the Friday dump. At least I get three hours to work on it, instead of thirty minutes like those poor SOBs at Quantico."

Matt chuckled. "Heard that. Been there doing that until two weeks ago."

The corporal made herself busy fixing coffee and even dug out a guest cup for Matt, pouring it just before the colonel came through the door. Matt started to come to attention, but he was waved down as the colonel nodded, helped himself to a cup of coffee and disappeared through an inner door without a word. Matt could only think of Ichabod Crane as the colonel disappeared.

Ten minutes later, the corporal's phone rang. She listened, hung up and motioned to Matt. Going to the door, she knocked, opened it and said, "Colonel Carson, Gunnery Sergeant Matthew Carter is here for his interview."

Matt marched in and came to attention in front of the colonel's desk. "Gunnery Sergeant Carter reporting as ordered, sir!"

The colonel stood up. "At ease gunny, I'm Bill Carson, and for my sins I'm the HQ JAG for Pendleton." Coming around the desk, he shook Matt's hand and steered him over to the small conference table sitting to the side of the office. "More coffee?" he asked.

"No sir, I'm fine. Sir, do you know how Staff Sergeant Miller is doing?"

Carson motioned for Matt to sit, and took the chair across from him, "As of 1700 yesterday, he was resting comfortably, and the doc says he'll fully recover. We're keeping him under wraps and in the hospital, and I didn't want you to see him before I had a chance to interview you. It's not that I don't trust you, but I want an impartial interview without his having given you a heads up. Matter of fact, I had Captain Hurst interview him day before yesterday after he arrived, so I've asked the captain not to sit in today, so that we can do an internal comparison here. Now, we'll do this informally, but I will be taking notes."

Picking up a stack of flimsies from the side of the table, he sorted through them, pulled out a stack, and slid them across to Matt. After doing so, he picked up a yellow pad, took a pen from his uniform and quickly wrote the basics across the top of a fresh sheet.

"Now, gunny, do you recognize that stack of

paperwork I just gave you?"

"Yes, sir, this is my interview given to Ranger Clay Boone and another Ranger at the scene on Sunday evening," Matt replied.

"Okay, now let's start with your departure from Quantico and go from there."

Matt recounted the trip and had gotten up to the point of arriving and the Tate place when the corporal knocked on the door and stuck her head in. "Colonel, there's a US Attorney on the line from Texas, and he's pretty insistent. Do you want to take it, or have him call back?"

"Texas, huh?" Looking at Matt he said, "Something tells me this is about you. Stay here, but be quiet. Understood?"

"Yes, sir."

Carson got up and walked behind his desk. Nodding to the corporal, he said, "Okay, conference it in here, but stay on the line and take notes please."

Seconds later the phone rang. "MCB Pendleton, Judge Advocate General's office, Colonel Carson speaking, this is not a secure line, subject to monitoring. May I help you?"

Listening for a minute he said, "Deal, and your first name and initials please? Uh huh, phone number?"

Scribbling notes on the pad he listened again. "Well, I need more information that that Mr. Deal, we have at any given time in excess of two thousand Marines here, and I'm sure there are a lot of Carters and Millers. And, no, I don't know them all."

Listening again, he sat, looking thoughtful. "Well, I need their socials and also their reporting commands if you have them. No, I'm not sure either of them are here; no I don't have ready access to something like that."

A minute later, Carson smiled like a shark and

pumped his fist. "Tell you what, why don't you fax me those pieces of paper, since they seem to have what I need on them. My fax is 4425551212."

After another minute, he added, "No, Mr. Deal, simply put, that is not good enough. I need both the warrants and whatever those documents were that you read the information from. Simple, fax that to me, and I'll get with S-1[22] and see if we can find them."

The colonel paused, listening. "No, Mr. Deal, if they are here they will be confined in accordance with UCMJ procedures pending further official documentation from you. Again my fax is 4445551212. Thank you."

Hanging up, Carson walked back to the conference table. "Okay, that was about you and Miller. That asshole wants you arrested and turned over to federal custody, preferably today. Ain't gonna happen. Why don't you take a break and get some coffee and hit the head, I need about a half hour here."

Matt got up. "Yes, sir, when I get back I'll wait in the outer office?"

Distracted, Carson mumbled, "Fine." As he wrote more notes on the yellow pad.

As Matt left, he noted the Corporal pulling pages off the fax machine. Shrugging, he wandered down the hall, hit the head, and went in search of some coffee.

The corporal came in with the faxes, handed them to the colonel. "Here you are sir. These are redacted all to hell, unlike what we got the other day."

Glancing over them, he said, "Okay, take these and the statements we got on Tuesday and send those to the US Attorney's office in San Diego, attention to Ken Carson. You've got the number, right?"

Gathering up the papers she said, "Yes, sir. Got it in

---

[22] Adjutant and Administration

speed dial!"

Grinning, the colonel added, "Time to stir the pot, corporal. Time to stir the pot!"

Carson got another cup of coffee and returned to his office, dialing the phone he waited for an answer. "Hey Marjory, this is the good looking Carson. Is the ugly one there?"

Laughing, he said, "Well, those papers on the fax are for him, and I do need to talk to him most skosh."

Glancing back over his notes, he waited and popped his pen on the desk. Finally the phone transferred. "Hey, Ken, Bill here. Got a strange one this morning. You ever hear of a US Attorney out of Dallas named Deal? Sort of an asshole?"

Hearing a negative, he continued, "No, I got a call in the blind this morning, wanting me to arrest these two Marines and turn them over to y'all."

Listening he said, "Okay, see what you can find out and give me a call back, will ya?" I gotta go talk to S-1 and see if they even exist here. K, Say hi to Carol for me."

Thirty minutes later, Matt returned to the JAG office and was immediately ushered back into the colonel's office. They resumed the questioning and walked through the entire shooting and aftermath, including how Aaron was flown out of Texas, and how he and Felix had driven straight through from Texas. As they were wrapping up, the corporal stuck her head in, "Colonel your cousin is on the line."

Carson went back to his desk and motioned Matt over. "Be quiet. I'm going to put this on speaker, I think you might be interested to hear what he has to say."

Matt nodded and moved to the front of the desk and the colonel hit speaker and answered, "What you got Ken?"

"Well, it looks like Deal, Alfred Michael one each is one of the new kids this administration is pushing down our throats. And oh by the way, I've been told I can retire in three months, or be demoted, since there are at least a couple of new attorneys coming here. Anyway, he's the new Northern District of Texas US Attorney, and apparently came over from Justice. Not much known about him, but I'm going to tell you both that warrant and the redaction he did stinks. And I don't understand why he didn't come through this office to have us make the initial contact. Looking at the statements from both those Marines, I don't see anything that points to a murder charge, much less anything else; unless it's a medal for doing good!"

The colonel looked at Matt. "So, Ken, what would you suggest I do if these Marines do turn out to be aboard the base?"

"Honestly, I'd keep them there and not admit a damn thing," Ken said. "But I gotta ask, if you only got the redacted paperwork from Texas, where did that set of statements come from?"

The colonel looked up at the ceiling, "Well, Ken, I got a heads up and received a complete copy of the investigation, witness statements, and the memo from the Texas Rangers in Austin clearing not only this Marine but both the deputies, calling it a good shoot. I was told it was quote just in case unquote something like this came up."

"Where in Texas did this take place?" Ken asked.

"Just outside Fort Stockton, why?"

"Well, Marjory just came in and turned my TV on and there is a replay of a interview on Fox, er… press conference with a Sheriff Rodriguez in Pecos County."

The colonel looked at Matt, who gave him a thumb's up.

"Well, Ken I don't have a TV so fill me…"

Ken interrupted, "Aw shit, that damn Moore is defending the deputies, which explains how you got the info."

Looking at Matt, who nodded again, the colonel asked, "Moore? Which Moore?"

"That damn Billy Moore," Ken said. "Deal's stepped in it big time."

Staring at Matt, the colonel looked surprised. "Billy Moore the big time Texas lawyer? Why would he be defending two deputies in South Texas?"

"I dunno," Ken said. "But I need to get off here and make some phone calls. If I were you, I'd lay low and if you find those Marines, keep 'em close. Gotta go." And he hung up.

The colonel thoughtfully hung up the phone. "Gunny, did you know that Billy Moore is involved in this?"

Matt unconsciously came to attention. "Yes, sir, Mr. Moore came out to the house Tuesday night and told us what was going on. He's the one that got Aaron flown out here, and told me to get out of town."

Almost to himself the colonel asked, "How the hell does a deputy sheriff get Billy Moore doing things for him?"

"Colonel, I may be out of school here, but Mr. Cronin and Mr. Moore were in Fifth Special Forces together; and have stayed in touch. And Mr. Cronin is more than just a deputy sheriff; he's also rich and owns over three thousand acres of oil wells and cattle. He paid for Aaron's Lear jet without even batting an eye."

Carson threw up his hands. "Any more good news there, gunny?"

Matt came fully to attention, "Well, sir, Staff Sergeant Miller's dating his granddaughter and sole heir.

She's the one that Aaron was riding with when he was shot, and she's the one that took down the two perps in the back."

"Jesse is a *she*?" Carson said in amusement.

"Yes, sir," Matt replied.

"Damn… Okay, we're done here, go see your cohort in crime and then get checked on base. I'll route a routine request to S-1 for info on y'all. I'd recommend you continue to live in the TQ until this is sorted out, and we'll figure out something with your landlord. Dismissed."

"Yes sir, thank you sir." Matt did a picture perfect about face and departed.

As Matt was driving over to the hospital, he reflected on the past couple of hours. He just hoped Aaron had been as open and up front as he had. Pulling into the hospital, he realized he had no idea where Aaron's room was and whether or not he could even see him. Distracted, he parked in the lot and trudged toward the front entrance. He heard someone yell "Gunny," but figured they wouldn't be yelling for him, until he heard "Carter."

Stopping, he turned and saw First Sergeant Brill jogging toward him. "Damn, man, are you deaf or what?" Brill stuck out his hand. "Welcome to the real Marine Corps, Matt. 'Bout time you came out west and earned your living for a change."

Matt smiled. "Brillo, how the hell are ya? Long time no see. What? Ten years at least!"

"Yeah, at least, and if you're gonna start that shit, its back to Casper for you, asshole."

They both laughed as they walked to the front entrance, "What are you doing here Matt? Looking for Miller?"

"Yeah," Matt said. "How did you know that?"

"Well, I'm his First, and I was on the way to check on him. He's been going batshit since they've got him isolated, and he's already tired of the TV channels and wanting out of here. I understand y'all are going to be renting an apartment out in town."

"Yeah, already got one, but I've been told to stay on base until a little situation gets worked out."

Brill laughed. "Yeah, heard all about that. Come on, I'll take you back to Miller's room. Is he a pretty good kid?"

Matt filled Brill in on Aaron's career to this point, and Brill cleared Matt with the nurse at the nurse's station. As they walked into the room, Aaron was pushing the remains of a breakfast tray away from the bed and trying, against doctors orders, to get himself up and out of bed so he could go to the head.

Matt got him up on his feet, then shook hands and watched Aaron hobble on his crutches to the head. Coming back, Aaron fiddled with the bed until it was more like a recliner and they filled each other in on the details of each of their trips and their respective interviews with the JAGs. Brill interrupted a couple of times, just to clarify various facts in his own mind.

Brill dropped Aaron's check-in sheet on the tray and said he had work to do. Shaking hands with Matt, he headed out. The nurse came by and allowed Matt to push Aaron to the cafeteria where they had a typical hospital lunch. Aaron begged Matt to sneak him some McDonalds later to which Matt laughed and said he'd see what he could do. Matt had to go start his check-in at First Marine Division, so he left, promising to return later.

Matt headed back to HQ and S-1 to pick up his paperwork; he spent the rest of the day going from place to place, back to the hospital for an in-processing physical, back to HQ, then housing, over to see the Gunner and get the keys for the range facilities, and he finally got back to the transient quarters at 1700.

Looking disgustedly at the check-in sheet, he realized he was only about half done, and he knew he had a least a full day of inventories at the range, plus meeting his new troops to do. He dug his new base sticker and placement diagram out of his uniform pocket and remembered he had a scraper in the toolbox in the truck, so he decided to change and get the new sticker on. He hadn't realized until the security person handed him an E-7 gunnery sergeant sticker along with the base sticker that Pendleton used those.

Taking a chance, he dialed the clean phone and the old man answered, Matt filled him in on the events of the day, and updated him on Aaron's condition. The old man told Matt that Jesse was talking to Aaron now, and Aaron was bitching about the food. Matt laughed and remembered he was supposed to get Aaron a Big Mac.

Changing out of his uniform, he grabbed the stickers and a day pack and headed out the door. Scraping the old sticker and placing the new ones, he figured that was good enough. He drove through McDonalds and grabbed a couple of burgers and fries, eating his on the way to the hospital. In the parking lot, he shoved the other one and fries in the day pack and headed into the hospital.

26 No He Didn't

US Attorney Ken Carson was in a quandary, so he paged Marjory. "Marj, would you come in please?"

Thirty seconds later, Marjory was sitting in front of his desk. "What's up boss?"

Flapping the stack of faxed pages, he said, "Marj, I, well, *we* have a problem. This whole thing with the Marines and these two deputies down in Texas stinks to high heaven, and having to deal with Billy Moore in the middle of it has the makings of a large settlement, or worse. What also concerns me is this Deal in Dallas didn't even go through us, or the Marshals here; he tried to end run all of us. Marj, ahhh, can you pulse your network and see if there are any good folks left at either Office of Professional Responsibility or Public Integrity that I can dump this pile of crap on? And can you get Willie Stanton over at FBI on the phone? I need to get some more ammo before I take this up the chain."

Marjory nodded, flipped her steno pad closed and asked, "You want SAC Stanton first or afterward?"

"First, I need to go see him, and that's a damn hour drive up there."

Marjory left and a minute later his phone rang. "Carson."

"Ken, this is Willie, what's up?"

"Willie, I got a steaming pile of shit dumped in my lap this morning and I need to pick your brain. Can I come see you?"

Willie laughed. "Actually I'm heading into town now, and I've got a meeting at ten with the Coasties over that smuggling op they took down last week. How about Perry's Café there by Old Town? I haven't had any good pancakes in a long time!"

Ken groaned. "You're killing my diet. See you there." Picking up his briefcase he put the faxes in it, locked it and headed out the door. "Marj, I'm meeting Willie at Perry's back in about an hour." She nodded as she continued to listen on the phone.

Pulling up in the parking lot at Perry's, Carson saw Stanton's unmarked sitting off toward the back of the lot. Pulling in next to him, he grabbed his briefcase off the seat, and they walked into the restaurant together. The waitress recognized them and showed them to a table in the back where they would have some privacy.

After ordering, Carson pulled out the faxed pages and pushed them across the table. "Willie, do you know anything about this? This sounds like something the FBI would be in the middle of, or DEA, or hell maybe even CBP."

Quickly scanning the flimsies, SAC Stanton alternately nodded and shook his head. He went back to Matt's testimony and re-read it carefully. He finished just as the food was delivered, and handed the flimsies back to Carson.

"Ken, this isn't one of ours, or anybody else that I'm aware of. Sounds to me like a stumble on that could have gone the other way in a hurry. I don't see a damn thing here that would even make me want to look at any of them for murder, much less anything at all. They did what they needed to, extracted the hostages safely and didn't lose any of the good guys, or girls in this case."

Nodding around a mouthful of pancakes, Carson agreed. Taking a sip of coffee he said, "Yeah, Willie, that's the way I read this too. But a bigger concern, at least to me, is that I got these third hand from the

Marines, and still haven't heard jack shit from Dallas, *and* apparently this Deal character wanted to have DHS pick up the Marines rather than Marshals. I don't like that one bit. And the local sheriff down there did a presser this morning that pretty much corroborates the story here, including shot up police car, a hundred keys of coke and two million in cash. And they name the perps as being cartel connected."

"Ken… Dammit, hang on a second," Stanton said, as he took out his phone and called one of his agents. "Taylor, what was the name of that expert from Texas that came out and taught the class on smuggling vehicles and boats?"

Listening for a minute he said sharply, "You sure? You're damn sure about that? Okay, thanks, Taylor." Hanging up he looked at Carson. "Well, here's ya one more turd to pile on to that mess. I'm betting that Deputy John Cronin listed in these documents is a DEA and FBI, and hell, probably CIA asset; he's an expert of smuggling both people and drugs, and he comes out and teaches classes on how to recognize possible vehicles for search, and then how to search them. If he's the one I think he is, he's a National Academy grad and gets invited back to teach on a regular basis."

Carson leaned back. "Shit that means I need to get back and make some calls quickly. We damn sure don't need any more egg on our faces right now." Getting up he threw $10 on the table and picked up his briefcase. "Willie, I owe you one. You might have just saved our collective butts here."

Stanton nodded, and as Carson walked out he took out his phone again and called FBI HQ, getting transferred to the National Academy, he asked for the SAC there, and passed along what he'd just found out. He leisurely finished breakfast, tipped the waitress, and walked out of the restaurant whistling.

Carson walked back into his office. "Any luck, Marj? Please tell me there is somebody left that cares back east, 'cause this just got a lot worse."

Marjory looked down at her pad. "Well, everybody down to the deputy directors are all new, but Valdez is still the GC[23], and Makepeace is still the PEP[24] lead. According to the secretaries, those are the only old guys that haven't been replaced yet. Do you know either of them?"

"Yeah, I met Valdez at the quarterly meeting last year, just before he moved up to General Council, but I don't know Makepeace. Who does he report to?"

Marjory consulted her notes again. "As the planning, evaluation and performance guy, he reports to the Chief of Staff, so he's higher in the food chain than he GC. Valdez? Since you at least know him?"

Heading toward his office, he said, "Yeah, Valdez first, if he's not there Makepeace. Thanks Marj, you saved my ass again!"

Marjory smiled. "Oh, I'll add it to the list boss."

Carson barely made it to his desk before the phone rang. "Mr. Valdez is on the line sir."

Leaving the phone on speaker, he waited for the connection. "Mr. Valdez, this is Ken Carson, I'm the Attorney for the San Diego district and I've got a situation I need to bring to your attention. I remember you from the quarterly, and frankly, I don't know who else to take this to."

"Yes, I remember you, Ken," Valdez said. "And you've done a lot of good work down there, so if you're calling me, I've got to assume this is pretty serious."

---

[23] General Counsel
[24] Planning, Evaluation, and Performance

Carson went on to detail what he knew, how he'd found it out, and his fears about the possible repercussions in their relationship with not only the Marines but the Navy. Twice Marjory came in and picked up documents and faxed them to DC, so apparently the secretarial mafia was at work simultaneously with them.

After a half hour, GC Valdez said, "Ken, I agree that this needs to be looked into sooner rather than later, but right now I have to go see the deputy director, and right now. I'm going to push this to OPR and make some calls myself. Are you going to be in the rest of the day?"

"Yes sir, other than lunch, I'll be here till at least six PM. Other than the normal meetings I don't have anything on the schedule for today."

"Thanks," Valdez said. "I'll get back to you." He hung up and Carson leaned back in his chair, ruminating on whether or not he'd done the right thing. Marjory brought him a cup of coffee, saying, "Well, in for a penny, in for a pound boss?"

Carson sighed. "Yeah, I guess that's about it Marj. Can you get Colonel Carson on the horn?"

As Marjory headed back to her desk, he got up and followed, going by her desk he said, "Gimme a minute, all of a sudden I need a bathroom break."

Nodding in sympathy, Marjory reviewed her notes, and called the secretary at the FBI office, "Helen, my boss just pushed this whole Texas shooting mess up the chain, and also passed along what he'd gotten from your boss at breakfast. You might want to clue him in, in case he gets any calls."

Helen thanked her and told Marjory she would. They chatted about kids, pets and useless husbands until Carson came back. Hanging up, Marjory called Pendleton and after chatting for a minute with the corporal, found out that Colonel Carson was in meetings for the next hour.

At 1:00 PM, Marjory called back and the corporal got Colonel Carson on the line as Marjory transferred the call to Ken.

Ken punched the speaker. "Hey, cuz. I bumped this up to the front office in DC, and here's a piece you may not know. That Deputy John Cronin is apparently a DEA and FBI, and maybe a CIA asset; he teaches classes on smuggling both people and drugs, to a lot of law enforcement types."

"Yeah," Colonel Carson replied. "I poked some folks back east and apparently he's also taught some of our special ops folks about VBSS too."

"VBSS?"

"Err… It's a program called Visit, Boarding, Search and Seizure. It's what our Navy and Marine folks and Coasties do to go aboard both friendly and un-friendly vessels at sea. The more I'm finding out the less I think any of this shit is even remotely possible."

"Huh? That's a new one on me. Ah, hang on Marjory is waving a note under my nose."

Ken muted the phone, took the note from Marjory and whistled. "Damn, *that* was quick!"

Turning the mute off, he said, "Well, Bill, this is an interesting twist, per the Chief of Staff for US Attorneys in DC, we are directed not, repeat not, to attempt to apprehend anyone on this warrant and are to consider them cancelled, null and void. So I guess that lets your folks off the hook. I hope it's not going to cause them any problems with their commands."

"Nah," Bill said. "Hell, I haven't even briefed it out to the COS here, much less up to the General. I'm sure the word will filter out, rumors will abound, but it'll all go away in a month or so. Bottom line: no harm, no foul."

They made small talk for a couple of minutes, then hung up after agreeing to get together for dinner in the near future.

27 Recovery

Camp Pendleton Hospital-

Matt burst into Aaron's room without even thinking and casually glanced at the woman sitting there. "Hey bud, we're officially off the hook, all charges dropped, and good to go."

"Outstanding!" Aaron said. "Do you know if Jesse knows?"

"No idea, but I wanted to make damn sure you knew ASAP!" Aaron grabbed his phone off the tray and dialed and Matt finally looked at the woman, realizing she was smiling at him.

"Felicia?"

Felicia laughed. "Yes, Matt. It is I. Angelina wanted me to come check on Aaron and let her know how he was doing. Since I'm not far from here, I decided to drop by today. And I'm glad to hear you are—how you say—off the hook?"

Smiling broadly, Matt said, "Oh yes, I'm glad to be off the hook! And you're not far from here are you? I never got the chance to see you again and didn't know how to get in touch with you."

"I wasn't sure you wanted to," Felicia said. "I thought you were afraid you would break me." Grinning, she looked at Aaron. "Tell Jesse to call my sister and fill her in."

Aaron nodded and continued to listen to Jesse.
***

While Jesse was on the phone with Aaron, the old man talked to Billy Moore and the sheriff on a conference call.

"You and Jesse are officially off the hook. The warrant's been cancelled and I've got one of my associates in Dallas going by to pick up your guns tomorrow. I got a call from the Deputy AG about this, and he apologized and hopes we won't sue. I told him we'd take that under advisement, considering your and Jesse's names have been put out there for every druggie in the Southwest to take a shot at."

The old man grunted an acknowledgement, and the sheriff said, "Billy, I don't have enough personnel to cover any real threat for any length of time, and I don't know that even the additional manpower would help."

"Billy, Jose, don't worry about it," the old man said. " People will make their try and die on the doorstep. After we kill enough of them, they'll stop trying. Plain and simple."

"At least make sure they're on your property, John," Jose said.

And Billy chimed in, "Or get extra diesel for the backhoe— just saying John."

***

At the hospital, Matt and Felicia had walked down to get coffee and give Aaron some privacy. They got coffee and sat in a back corner of the cafeteria; Matt just looked at Felicia. "I'm sorry about what happened in Texas, I didn't mean to leave without talking to you."

Felicia laid a hand on Matt's arm. "I understand. You had to go right then and there. I too wanted to see you again, but did not want to seem forward. I live down in Escondido. It is what we could afford, and a nice little house. My job with the Border Patrol is out of Santee, East of El Cajon. I'm how you say, jack of all traces?"

Matt smiled. "It's jack of all trades Felicia, so you do a little bit of everything? Is that what you mean?"

She sighed. "Yes, everything but change oil in the

trucks and if they could figure out a way, I'd be doing that too. I am supposed to be translator, but when I'm not, I do what needs to be done."

Felicia looked at her watch. "I need to go. I have to get to sleep early because I leave for work at six in the morning."

Screwing up his courage, Matt took a step toward her. "Felicia can I get your number and call you later?"

Felicia smiled. "Of course, Matt."

They exchanged numbers and Matt walked Felicia to her little Toyota and he felt like walking on air going back into the hospital. Back in Aaron's room, he asked, "Any idea how much longer they will keep you here?"

"I think they were talking about putting on a hard cast tomorrow, then kicking me out. The nurse was saying four to six weeks in the hard cast then rehab, but I don't think it will take that long. I start PT day after tomorrow after the cast sets."

"Okay, I'm still in the TQ, at least for tonight. I'll go check on the apartment when I leave here. Jesse doing okay?"

Aaron shrugged. "She's happy this bullshit is over, but I think her hip is bothering her more than she's letting on. And I think she's going to work and sitting crooked and it's making her back and ribs hurt worse! Damn stubborn woman!"

Matt laughed. "Pot calling the kettle black there, Aaron. I remember you pulling the same shit after Fallujah."

Aaron cocked his head. "So, what's with you and Felicia? Y'all were gone a long time."

"Well, we wanted to give you some privacy, so we got coffee and talked, and I've got her number so maybe I'll give her a call," Matt said. "Okay, I'm outta here, I'll go see what shape the place is in, and at least unload the trucks." Matt stood. "Also, I'll call shipping and see if they can set up a delivery for tomorrow afternoon. You can probably supervise if nothing else."

Aaron nodded, planning the grief he would give Matt later, as Matt left.

Back in Texas, Jesse mulled over what she needed or wanted to do. "Papa, I'm trying to go back to work, but between the hip and the ribs, I'm hurting and it's to the point I can't sleep worth a damn at night either."

"Well, they told you to stay out until you felt like it," the old man said. "So, I'd call them tomorrow and say you're going to be out at least another week. And if I were you, I'd go see Doc Truesdale tomorrow. And I damn sure don't want you back in the patrol car for at least a month. I've already cleared that with Jose, and you're off the schedule until at least the first of November."

Jesse sighed. "Papa, that's just part of it. I'm having some nightmares too, and I don't know how to deal with them, I keep… Well, I keep seeing those two coming at me, and I can't fire… Or the gun doesn't work or something."

The old man got up and walked to the couch, sitting beside Jesse and putting his arm around her shoulder. She slumped gratefully into his arms.

"Hon, those will be with you forever. They'll fade eventually, but sometimes things will bring 'em back. You know you did the right thing, and God knows what would have happened if you hadn't shot. Well, actually you probably wouldn't be sitting here… Remember, a nightmare can't hurt you, it's not real. Wake up, drink a glass of water, get up and move around. And stop worrying about them, the more you worry…" He held up his hand as Jesse looked up in frustration. "It sounds impossible, but it's not. Just put the damn things out of your mind. You used to listen to the radio at night, do that again. You're not going to get over them tomorrow, but I promise you they will go away."

Feeling her sigh in his arms, he continued, "Jesse, you're under a lot of stress, between trying to get well, worrying about Aaron, and your job, all those things contribute. I know Doc gave you some sleeping pills. I want you to take one tonight. Okay?"

"Okay, Papa," Jesse said. "I'll try. I'm like you, though. I *hate* pills and not being aware of what's going on. And you're right I do worry about Aaron, he's a long way away and in a hospital with nurses…"

The old man burst out laughing, "Jesse you have *nothing* to worry about, trust me, you've never seen military nurses, I have. They ain't like the ones you see on TV."

Over the next month, both Jesse and Aaron mended, and talked almost every night. Aaron usually bitched about either the paperwork of being a squad leader, or the PT, or the professional training he was doing. All this stuff was required, but he admitted he'd rather be in the field, and actually *doing* things with his troops.

Matt and Felicia cautiously established a friendship, and saw each other a couple of times a month. Matt's job at the base range depended on which phase of training was going on, with day and night shoots occurring sporadically, and he also found out he was responsible for Reserve unit training, but he got a handle on it.

Jesse's hip finally healed and she was able to get back to work, and slowly started working out and jogging again, but her situational awareness was much higher now, and she never went anywhere without her pistol close. She met Trooper Wilson, and the two of them hit it off, and started getting together weekly to work out and talk.

The old man was quiet and watchful, and he and the sheriff continued to pulse all their contacts to see if there was any word on the street about a hit. Thanksgiving came and went with nothing popping, although both Aaron and Matt were stuck with the duty and had to stay in California, much to Jesse's disappointment.

Jesse had finally gotten fully back in shape and was back patrolling to make up her hours to get the forty hour per month average she needed, but she also realized she needed to see Aaron, and scratch another itch.

Saturday morning she called him and woke him up. "Hey you, grumpy! You trying to sleep in again?"

Aaron mumbled, "Normal people do sleep in on the weekends you know. What damn time is it anyway?"

"Oh it's nine here," Jesse said. "I'm getting ready to head out on a ride, but I wanted to know if you're going to be around in two weeks."

Aaron was suddenly wide awake. "Why?"

"Cause I want to come see your dumb ass!" Jesse said. "It's been almost three months and I want to look you in the face, and hold you in my arms, okay?"

"Jesse, I want that too," Aaron said. "But dammit we're going in the field Monday. I know we're supposed to be back, lemme see, twelve days from now, so that..."

"That would be Thursday, so I'll fly in Wednesday night and get Matt to let me in, okay?"

"Uh, sure..."

"Well gee, you just sound *so* enthusiastic!" Jesse said. "Seriously, if it's a problem, I won't come."

Aaron jumped. "No, dammit Jesse, I'm half awake and I want to see you. I'll help pay the ticket and figure out how to get you here. You going to fly into San Diego?"

"Nope, Papa won't let me, because of the druggies, I can fly in to Los Angeles, it's cheaper anyway. I'll get a rental and drive down, and plan to be there around six in the evening. And if Matt's not around, I'll call Felicia and we'll go do a girls night out!"

Aaron groaned. "Oh God, not a girl's night out! You'll be grumpy as hell and … and…"

Laughing, Jesse said, "Oh shut up, you've never seen me after a girl's night out, so I don't want to hear it! I'm going riding then I'll come back and make the reservations. Do you still want to come here for Christmas?"

Aaron sobered. "Yeah, if y'all don't mind. There's not much for me at home between my brother and sister, I'm pretty much the baby killer in the family and they've managed to turn the folks against me."

Jesse heard the pain in Aaron's voice, but knew she couldn't do anything. "Okay, do you know if Matt wants to come too?"

"I don't know," Aaron said. "I think it depends on what Felicia is going to do. Matt doesn't say much, but I think they're getting pretty serious."

Jesse laughed. "So who is chasing who?"

28 On The Range

Matt came awake suddenly, and couldn't figure out why. Then, he heard another soft scraping sound. Getting up quietly, he grabbed his Glock and moved down the hall toward the noise, as the light in the kitchen came on. Coming around the corner of the hall, he broke out laughing as he saw a sleep-tousled Jesse trying to reach the coffee can up on the top shelf.

Rounding on the laughter, Jesse spat, "You asshole! Get over here and get the damn coffee down. I hate you tall sumbitches... Anybody with any common sense has the coffee *near* the damn coffeepot."

This caused Matt to laugh even harder as he came into the kitchen and laid his Glock on the counter, making sure it was pointed in the safe direction. He pulled the coffee can down. "Sorry, Jesse, neither Aaron or I has any problems with it, didn't think about you; damn, why are you getting up at four AM!"

Defensively Jesse shot back, "Hey, this is sleeping in for me. I'm normally up at oh dark thirty at home, and that would have been an hour and a half ago! And I was trying to be quiet since I knew you needed your beauty sleep, so there." She stuck her tongue out at Matt.

Matt chuckled. "You should have just banged stuff around, that's how Aaron and I both do it, so we both sleep right through that. Well, now that I'm up, are you going to fix the coffee or play with it?"

Sticking out her tongue again, Jesse loaded the coffeepot and started hunting through the fridge for breakfast things. Not finding anything to make, she turned back to Matt. "Gah, don't you have *anything* edible in this place, all I see is junk food and protein bars, which by the way do not need to be refrigerated! Can I borrow the keys to Aaron's truck? I'm up and now I'm hungry."

Matt pointed at the coffeepot. "Coffee, shower, clothes and I'll take you to breakfast. I needed to go in early this morning anyway, as we've got a test shoot today on the Barrett MRADs we got in Friday. The colonel wants everything set up by zero nine hundred for the scout snipers to come over and test fire them."

Jesse pulled the coffeepot out, stuck a cup under the drip, poured Matt a cup and handed it to him. Pulling her cup half way out, she topped it off and deftly switched the pot back under the drip and took off for the bathroom without a word.

Twenty minutes later, Jesse came out of the bedroom dressed in a dark top, jeans and boots; she twisted her hair into a pony tail, threw a wrap on it and twirled her cap on her hand. Matt was sitting at the kitchen table waiting in his Utility uniform and Jesse said, "I thought we were going to breakfast?"

"We are," Matt said. "We'll go to this greasy spoon I know that won't say anything about me being in utilities. You got everything you need?"

Laughing Jesse responded, "Watch, wallet, ovaries, and glasses, I'm good to go."

Matt just shook his head. "Never should have told you that damn joke. C'mon, let's go."

After a quick breakfast, Matt drove on to Pendleton and out to the range facility on the far side of the runways. Pulling in, he looked at the building and said, "I thought I turned the damn lights off before I left on Friday. Damn, I'm getting old."

Going up to the door, he unlocked it and stepped in,

hearing a high pitched whine, he stopped dead. He pushed Jesse back out the door, and put his finger to his lips for quiet, and moved quietly through the building toward the armory in the back. Sticking his head around the door far enough to look in, Jesse was able to see him relax and shake his head.

As the whine stopped, Matt bellowed, "Toad, what the fuck are you doing in my range house?"

From the other room Jesse heard, "Gahdamn, you bout scared the shit outta me you asshole, and I almost screwed up this sear!"

Matt went through the door and Jesse figuring it was safe, followed to be greeted by Matt picking up a short heavyset Marine in a bear hug and simultaneously cussing him for all he was worth. Jesse tried to stifle it, but she burst out laughing at the sight, causing Matt to drop the other Marine and Jesse to note he was *really* short for a Marine.

Turning, Matt said, "Sorry 'bout the language Jesse, but this useless piece of sh... asshole, ah hell, corporal.."

To which the little Marine said indignantly, "Sergeant, dammit!"

Laughing, Matt finally said, "Sergeant Toad Moretti, best damn armorer in the Marines and worst damn Marine you ever saw, may I present Jesse Cronin, and before you even think about it, she's Aaron's girlfriend."

The little Marine turned and faced Jesse, stuck out his hand and in a broad New Yawk accent said, "Pleased to meetcha miss. Don't believe a word this big bast... er..."

Snickering Jesse asked, "Asshole?"

Toad smiled. "Yeah, dat works... Asshole says about me. It's all lies and fabrications, and made up."

Jesse realized Toad really was about as ugly as a mud fence, with a big Roman nose, and beetling brows, needing a shave; and even though he couldn't be more than 5'6" he looked to be as strong as an ox. Looking at the table she saw at least two rifles in pieces and what looked like a couple of trigger assemblies literally torn apart on the table. Matt glanced at the table and did a double take. "Dammit, Toad, what are you doing?"

Abashed Toad replied, "Well, I was moving my spares in before I checked in last night, and saw the Plan Of the Day said you were test shooting today, so I dug around until I found the guns, and I noticed none of my guns were here, so I was fixing one up for you, and I decided to check out this Beret MRAD, whatever the hell it is, and it needed a little trigger work, and I was smoothing up…"

Matt interrupted. "You were what?"

Toad replied airily, "Oh, I'm on orders as the armorer here, so I figured I'd get here early, and get the spares put up."

"Spares?" Jesse asked.

Both Toad and Matt started to answer, but Toad deferred to Matt.

"Well, Jesse, it's like this: each armory is allocated a specific number of guns, spare parts, equipment and things like that. But every armorer I know has quote spares unquote, in other words things he can't or won't do without. All these guys have a system so when they know they're going to get inspected, the spares are shipped to an armorer that just finished his inspection, and after the inspection they're shipped back. Also good armorers screw up a weapon or two, too much lube or something similar so the inspectors can find it and knock 'em down from superior to excellent. What happens then is the booze comes out and they sit around drinking and BS'ing for the rest of the inspection. In other words, they've got a racket going that the Corps hasn't broken since 1776."

Jesse smiled at the description as Toad had turned back to the bench and continued to work, his hands seeming to move of their own accord, and never reaching for the wrong piece. Literally in minutes, both rifles were re-assembled and he ran a rag over both while replacing the MRAD in its case and the M40A5 sniper rifle back in the rack.

Turning back to Toad, Matt said, "Go clean up, get some chow and be back by zero seven thirty, the colonel will be here at zero eight hundred, and we need to sight in both rifles for the test, in addition to setting up the range."

"Aye, Aye your gunnieness," Toad replied with a smile as he hurried out the door.

While Toad was gone, Matt, with Jesse observing, set up two sets of lanes, one with steel targets at 400, 600, 800, and 1000 yards, alternating between lanes, and another set of lanes with targets at 100 and 300 yards.

When Jesse asked, Matt explained they would first sight in the rifles, to ensure accurate scopes and then once the snipers showed up, each would sight in on the targets, then move to the steels and shoot them at the various ranges. Each sniper would fill out an evaluation of the rifle, scope, ease of use and their impressions of the rifle.

Matt said, "I taught a class last week using Barrett's training documents on the MRAD and we broke down one rifle in class for the snipers to look at and fondle."

"Fondle?" Jesse asked with a smile.

Matt hesitated. "Well, play with the rifle, you know…"

Jesse just laughed as Matt turned to start laying things out.

By 7:45 AM, Toad had returned, obviously cleaned up and fed, but already starting to look like he'd slept in his utilities, they sat and sipped coffee, each wrapped in their own thoughts for a few minutes, until zero eight hundred when Colonel Ortega arrived and Matt called, "Attention on deck!"

Matt and Toad popped to attention when the colonel strode in, and Jesse got up from the chair she was sitting in. Matt reported all was in readiness, and the colonel looked at Jesse with a question look, and then he turned to Toad, "Moretti, disappear for fifteen."

Toad barked, "Yes, sir, colonel!" And disappeared out the front door.

Turning back to Matt he asked, "Gunny?"

"Sir, this is Ms. Jesse Cronin," Matt replied. "She's here as my guest because I didn't want to leave her sitting in the apartment. She's Staff Sergeant Miller's girlfriend and he's still in the field. They were supposed to be back yesterday, but apparently got hung up."

Jesse, not knowing what else to do, nodded and stuck out her hand.

Colonel Ortega shook hands with her. "Miller, First SOBs? That Miller? He's your roommate, right?"

"Yes sir, that Miller. And I hope I'm not causing a problem."

Relaxing, Colonel Ortega walked over to the coffeepot and poured himself a cup. "Gunny, it's not a problem for me, and pleased to meet you, miss. Now the real reason I kicked Toad out was I want to know if you can handle him, gunny. He made sergeant again for the third time, and I'd like to see him keep it, if you know what I mean. He's not actually due for another two days, but knowing him, he's doing his armorer shit behind my back yet again. Sorry, miss."

Jesse smiled. "No problem, colonel, I've been around Matt and Aaron long enough to know they can't form a complete sentence without cussing!"

The colonel just looked at her for a second, and then

broke into a wide grin, transforming his whole personality.

"No problem, sir," Matt said. "I'll work his ass in the damn ground, and keep him if not on the straight and narrow, at least close enough for government work. We've been through this before. I need to go sight in the rifles before the shooters show up, so if you'll pardon me, I'll go get this done and I'll make Toad go put up pasters on the targets."

The colonel nodded and Matt picked up both rifles and a spotting scope and disappeared out the front door yelling for Toad. The colonel sat behind Matt's desk and looked at Jesse, "Miss, are you the one that was in the shootout with young Miller and gunny?"

Jesse took a moment to walk over a refill her coffee before answering. "Yes, sir, that was me, and I'm truly sorry for all the problems it caused Matt and Aaron with the warrants and all."

Ortega waved her comment off saying, "That wasn't an issue, but I have to say the way it got handled did leave some egg on that assh...er Attorney's face, so I'm happy for that. First SOBs don't actually come under my command, but I know their CO pretty well, and Staff Sergeant Miller has come back pretty well from his injury, but seems to be strangely reticent about saying anything about it or you. You're a mystery woman around here, which is unusual for Marines. Hell, they talk worse than a bunch of old ladies in the damn nursing home, hence the curiosity."

Both of them cocked their heads as they heard the rifle fire three times in slow sequence, then Jesse sat in front of the colonel and rehashed the story from beginning to end for him. He shook his head in amazement. "That is one helluva story, miss, and no wonder Miller doesn't talk about it; much less about you

267

or your family. Just out of curiosity have *you* ever shot a Barrett?"

Jesse laughed. "Yes, sir, I've got about four hundred rounds through our MRAD."

"*Your* MRAD? Four hundred rounds? Damn, what's the longest shot you've made if you don't mind my asking?"

Jesse answered, "Well, technically it's Papa's MRAD, but I train on all the rifles too, and my longest good hit was sixteen hundred yards; I tried a couple at eighteen hundred but the wind got me on those, so I quit."

Matt and Toad came back through the door at that moment, with Toad carrying both rifles and heading for the bench to give them a quick cleaning. The colonel smiled at Jesse and turned to Matt. "I think we have a situation where we might have some fun with folks, gunny. Are you up to it?"

Matt looked from the colonel to Jesse. "What kind of fun, sir? And is this fun gonna come back and bite me in the ass?"

Ortega laughed. "Oh, probably, but it'll be worth it. This lady told me the rest of the story you and Miller refused to tell us, and I find out she's probably more familiar with the Barrett than we are. Now here's what I want to do…"

Amidst chuckles, outright laughter and snickers, a plan was put together: at zero nine hundred, a major, a captain and twelve shooters showed up at the range.

Jesse stayed inside and out of sight as Matt set up the parameters for the shooting, handing out evaluation forms and started cycling the snipers through the weapons.

The colonel, major and captain sat behind the line and observed. Just before they finished, a truck showed up and a Marine Gunner stepped out. Putting on eyes and ears, he walked over, casually saluted the officers present and stood watching the shooters.

Turning to Matt he asked, "Any problems? Guns working okay? Any ammo issues?"

"Not a one, Gunner Price," Matt replied. "These are pretty good rifles, if I do say so. And it seems like the troops like 'em, even if they are tending to shoot a tad high because the bullet drop is about half of the M40A5."

Gunner Price looked at Matt. "Half?"

"Yep, 413 inches at 1000 for the M40A5, vice 201 inches at 1000 for the MRAD. Guys are having a hard time actually holding correctly unless they reset the scope between shots."

While Matt had the gunner distracted, the colonel motioned to the range shack for Jesse to come out. She stuck ear protection in, and putting on her shooting glasses, sauntered out to the line. She didn't say a word, just stood at the back of the group, but was quickly noticed by the snipers that had completed their evals and were standing around.

Finally, the last two completed their rounds and Matt jumped down on the gun that Toad had worked on, taking a couple of shots on the target to make sure the scope was on.

Matt introduced Jesse to everyone, not saying anything about whom she was dating, and she asked in a bored voice if they were done yet. Matt looked at the colonel. "Sir, would it be alright if she shoots a round or two since she's been sitting out here all morning?"

The colonel looked around. "Well, do you think she's safe and knows the rules, Gunny?"

"Yes, sir, I've been shooting with her a couple of times."

"Objections anybody? Hearing none, let her put a couple down range if she wants to."

Matt made a production of getting Jesse set up on the

rifle, to the snickers of the snipers who realized she was going to try to shoot a bolt gun with the wrong hand. Bets started being made among the snipers and Matt heard at least one say, "She'll shoot one round and come off the gun crying." Another was betting $20 she wouldn't even hit the target. The colonel and the Gunner were quietly talking as Matt got up from "positioning" Jesse on the gun.

Giving the commands, Matt took the range hot, as one of the snipers strolled over to the spotting scope.

Jesse shrugged and settled in, causing the sniper to take a second look and ask quietly, "Which target?"

Jesse said, "Closest to distant in order. Target."

The sniper quietly said, "Send it."

Jesse fired, worked the bolt cross handed, fired and worked the bolt four times with four hits in under twenty seconds. Getting up she turned to Matt with a smile. "Gee, that was fun, and easy too! Can I do some more?"

The colonel was laughing, Gunner Price was not looking happy, and most of the snipers were standing slack-jawed, with the exception of the one who had been on the spotting scope, who leaned over to Jesse. "You're a damn ringer aren't you? And you know those were four head shots, right?"

Jesse smiled, and said quietly, "Yep."

One of the sore losers amongst the snipers called out, "Yeah, maybe she can do that here, but I doubt she could do that in the real world like we do!"

The colonel stepped up beside Jesse. "Gents, let me tell you two things: first *never* underestimate anyone, here or on the battlefield. Second, yes this lady can shoot, both here and in real life. I may be breaking a confidence, but I think this is important." Glancing at Jesse, she shrugged and he continued. "She has two kills under fire by full auto AKs from less than two hundred yards, and she was in the open when they took her under fire. Oh, by the way, those kills were with a Winchester 94. This is Deputy Jesse Cronin, from Pecos County Texas, and they are fighting a war every day down there with the drug runners and smugglers."

Grumbling, the snipers and their Platoon leader got in the truck and left, while the Gunner walked over and shook her hand, "Good shooting, miss, and I should have known better… You're Miller's girlfriend, right?"

When Jesse nodded, he smiled. "Sumbitch better tell me *all* the damn story next time. I don't like losing, much less to the colonel."

Ortega came over a laid a hand on the gunner's shoulder. "Gunner, it's all about intel and this time I had the intel!"

The gunner looked around and spotted Sgt Moretti, "Moretti, you better have a gun ready for me by Friday, or your ass is mine!"

Turning, the gunner left without another word.

Moretti looked glumly after the gunner. "Oh man. this is NOT gonna be fun, 'cause I'm going to have to break into the spares."

Jesse looked at him. "Why, and would somebody explain what a gunner is?"

Toad scuffed the ground. "Well, see it's like this: officially, the Marines dropped the 1911 back twenty plus years ago, but the gunner, he likes 1911s and that's all he carries. I don't even think the Gen'ral has the balls to tell him to carry an M-9."

Matt and Colonel Ortega laughingly agreed, prompting Jesse to ask, "But isn't he just a warrant officer? Colonel, aren't you his boss?"

Ortega answered, "Well, it's like this, the Gunner Price is an odd bird, he's got 24-25 years in the Marines, been a gunner or warrant officer for ten years. He took over a company in Fallujah when the leadership went down with the screaming… Montezuma's revenge, and fought them for three days before anybody higher found out. He's an advisor to the Battalion commander, and he trained the battalion commander when he was a First Looie, and knew the general when he was a captain, and honestly, he's probably better versed in combat operations than I am. So no, I'm not about to call him down… "

Jesse laughed. "Now, I understand."

Her phone rang, and as she answered it, a big smile spread across her face. "Aaron's back and heading for the apartment. Matt can you run me out there?"

Matt nodded as Jesse headed for the truck. The colonel just laughed. "True love, ain't it grand?"

29 Together Again

Matt dropped Jesse off and headed back to the range with a smile on his face. Jesse walked up to the apartment door and stood there in indecision, knock or use Matt's key? Aaron solved the problem by opening the door and picking Jesse up in his arms, kissing her softly. Jesse laughed. "Uh, Aaron, can we go inside please? *You* may be an exhibitionist, but this girl isn't."

Aaron laughed and carried Jesse back into the apartment and kissed her again. "Is this better?"

"Okay, much better, but close the door!"

Aaron stepped away to close the door and Jesse got a look at his shoulder and back. "Aaron, what happened? Reaching up and lightly touching his shoulder, she traced the bruise that went half way down his back.

Rotating his shoulder and grimacing he said, "Well, we do play rough some times. Actually, the squad was supposed to be evac'ing me as a casualty and the sumbitches slipped on the rocks and dropped my ass."

Jesse snickered, then leaned over and kissed his shoulder. "I'll kiss it and make it all better."

Aaron laughed and suddenly stopped and sniffed. "You've been shooting! What the hell? Did Matt sneak you on the range?"

"Umm, not exactly… I'll tell you after I get a shower."

Lying in bed after they'd made love, Aaron poked Jesse. "Okay, now give with the story!"

Jesse rolled into Aaron's arms and proceeded to tell him what had happened. Aaron vacillated between laughter and horror and what they'd pulled off, and fear when he found out they'd played the trick on the gunner. "Oh damn, y'all are gonna get me killed, the gunner *does not* take stuff like that lying down."

Jesse poked him back. "Hey, if you'd been here on time, this wouldn't have happened because we'd have been occupied this morning and I wouldn't have gone in with Matt, so this is actually *your* fault!"

Poking turned into wrestling, which lead to a natural conclusion until Jesse started snickering then laughing, causing Aaron to stop what he was doing. "What? What's so funny?"

Jesse said, "Oh don't stop, I'm just thinking about Eileen, my old roommate, and thin apartment walls."

"Huh?" Aaron said.

"Well, let's just say Eileen was rather *vocal*, to put it mildly. Actually it sounded like a cat fight with all the yowling and screaming when she was getting laid. I used to just turn the TV up loud so I didn't have to listen to it, and one day the neighbor actually asked why we were letting the cats fight at night. I didn't have the heart to tell her we didn't have any cats…"

Aaron rolled over and started laughing, which totally destroyed their mood for maybe a minute.

Matt came in at 6 PM and yelled through the door, "Y'all want to go to dinner?"

Aaron looked at Jesse who nodded. "Sure, thirty minutes?"

"That will work," Matt said. "I told Felicia I'd pick her up at seven-thirty."

A half hour later they met in the living room, and Matt caught a glimpse of Jesse's badge on her belt. "You carrying?"

Jesse nodded, "Of course, under Federal Law HR 218 I'm allowed to carry anywhere in the US. I'm not about to be unarmed this close to the border, especially not with the amount of crap with the cartels going on out here. And frankly, both Papa and I are worried about being targeted for killing since our names were put out there by that asshole US Attorney and the media. Thankfully, y'all didn't get named on the TV broadcast, but I still think y'all should pursue getting carry permits out here."

Matt and Aaron both shrugged, and seemed to blow it off, which kicked Jesse into high gear. "No, both of you listen to me! This isn't a game or a joke, these people play for keeps. There have been over thirty thousand murders in Mexico tied directly to the cartels, and probably two to three hundred in the States, but no one but LEOs are seeing the big picture because DHS and DOJ are hiding that info. There have been hits in Phoenix, McAllen, San Diego and of course Brian Terry and other Border Patrol folks."

Poking Aaron in the chest she continued, "You don't want to lose, and I'm betting if you went to your lawyer, or JAG or whatever the hell he's called, he could help! So do it!"

Matt and Aaron mumbled assent and somewhat mollified, Jesse stomped out the door to the trucks. Matt decided to take his, that way he didn't have to try to scrunch up in the back, and also didn't have to try to give Aaron directions to Felicia's house.

Picking up Felicia promptly at 7:30 PM, a discussion ensued as to where to eat, and Felicia finally convinced them to try a new, to her, Mexican restaurant she'd heard about from one of her co-workers.

They finally found it on a side street in Carlsbad. Both Matt and Aaron were a little worried about the condition of the neighborhood, but Felicia seemed perfectly comfortable and chatted merrily with Jesse about home and Angelina and how the kids were doing. The food turned out to be excellent, and Matt and Aaron finally relaxed a little bit, even though the two of them and Jesse were the only non-Hispanics in the place.

Jesse and Felicia decided to go to the ladies room, since there was a bit of a drive back to Escondido. Unbeknownst to them, four Guatemalan 'cowboys' had come in and begun harassing the female waitresses; as Jesse and Felicia exited the rest room, one of the cowboys pulled one of the waitresses down the hall, but stopped when he saw Felicia and Jesse.

Letting go of the waitress, who quickly scrambled back toward the dining area, he yelled, "Amigos, I found two pretty putas back here, and one of them is a gringo!"

Looking between the two of them, he advanced slowly while another cowboy stepped in behind him. Felicia told him in Spanish they were not putas and their men were waiting in the dining room, but the cowboy just laughed and grabbed at Jesse.

She used a judo move to put him on the ground and control him with the wrist. He yelped, which caused his partner to rush Jesse as he pulled a knife. Jesse maintained control of the cowboy and drew her Python, which stopped the second cowboy cold, but as Felicia attempted to move out of the way, he grabbed her and put his knife to her throat.

It was a classic standoff until Jesse saw Matt and Aaron filling the hallway. She spit at the cowboy in Spanish that it was a mistake to bring a knife to a gunfight, and she was going to shoot him between the eyes, which caused him to crouch behind Felicia and gave Matt the opportunity to come over his back, grab his wrist and twist him away from Felicia. Matt squeezed the wrist until the cowboy let go of the knife, then continued to squeeze until there was a crack and the cowboy screamed in pain as his wrist bones were broken.

Jesse took the opportunity to put the first cowboy on the ground his stomach and told Aaron to get her cuffs out of her purse. She handcuffed the first cowboy and went over to the second one, now slumped against the wall and cradling his wrist. She pulled the Python back out and tapped him none too gently between the eyes. When he looked up, all he saw was the end of the barrel and loaded cylinders while Jesse told him quietly in Spanish what she would do to him if she or Felicia ever saw him again. The cowboy's bladder let go at that point, much to everyone's disgust.

The owner yelled down the hall that the police were on the way, as sirens were heard in the distance. Matt had his arm around Felicia and Aaron had turned and was facing the dining area, his Benchmade knife in hand and partially hidden behind his leg. Over his shoulder he said, "Looks like the other two split, and we've got a lot of interested observers out here, but nobody's making a move to help."

A couple of minutes later, two Carlsbad PD officers came through the door, and Aaron yelled, "Hey guys, back here!"

The older officer led, and when Matt and Aaron moved aside, whistled. "Well, what do we have here? And whose handcuffs are those?"

Jesse had her credentials in her hand, and proffered them saying, "Mine, and I'd like them back please; I don't have any spares with me."

The younger officer looked at them in disgust. "You better not be carrying a weapon. That's illegal since you're not a California certified law enforcement. And what gave you the right to handcuff him, and who broke this one's wrist?"

Jesse started to reply, but Matt over rode her. "I

broke this asshole's wrist because he had a knife to this lady's neck. Should I have let him cut her throat?"

His tone backed the young officer up, and he put his hand on his sidearm, until the older officer said, "Alright, everybody calm down. Miss Cronin, you want to walk me through what went down?"

Jesse gave him a rundown on the events as they occurred, while the officer sent the younger one to interview the owner, wait staff and patrons who were willing to talk.

The older officer did a quick search of the two and came up with four packets of cocaine. He turned to her and said, "Looks like you got us some drug runners, and it's too bad the other two got away, they probably had drugs in the car."

Jesse shook her head, "Dammit, I *do not* need anymore drug runners causing me problems, why do you say they are drug runners?"

The officer looked at her, "Well, the hats… Some of the gangs use tennis shoes as identifiers, but the Guats seem to like fancy cowboy hats like these, and it's usually the first thing they buy with their money. And they usually get a packet or two of coke as a bonus."

The officer turned to Felicia corroborated Jesse's description of the events, and when the officer flashed his light on her neck, saw a thin line of blood. He nodded and radioed for an ambulance and a backup to meet the perp at the hospital to arrest him after treatment. He pulled out a pocket camera and photographed the scene, including Felicia's bloody neck before allowing her to clean up. He also noted the round abrasion on the second cowboy's forehead and asked, "What made that?"

Jesse pulled her jacket aside, and showed the holstered Python. The officer whistled again, saying, "Glad you didn't shoot him, I'd have hated to take that pistol for evidence!"

The officers asked the four of them to fill out witness statements, and they were ushered to a table near the kitchen. As they were filling out the statements, the owner came over with water and more iced tea, and presented each of them with flan, compliments of the house. They were finally allowed to leave after a detective had finally showed up and looked at the pictures, read their statements and listened to the description of events. He assured them their information would be held in strict confidence, since these two would be deported immediately for the illegal drugs.

Jesse got the older officer off to the side, asking, "Hey, what is it with your partner and his comment about my carrying? Under HR 218, I'm allowed and that is federal, not a state thing."

The officer said, "He's a newbie, and here lately it seems all the California training is pushing limiting guns for everybody. Hell, in some jurisdictions in this damn state, they're trying to prevent local cops from carrying off duty! Don't worry about him. I'll jack his ass up in private."

Jesse finally got her cuffs back, and she and Felicia visited the ladies room once again, but this time Matt and Aaron were standing in the hallway when they came out.

It was after midnight when they finally dropped Felicia off, and she and Matt stood in an embrace for minutes at her front door before Matt finally came back to the truck. Finally back at the apartment, Aaron and Jesse crawled into bed, and Jesse started shaking. Aaron put his arms around her and held her, "Adrenalin dump?"

"Yeah, not as bad as at the Tait place, but damn..."

"Hey, nothing wrong that," Aaron said. "I did it after every mission, especially when we were in the shit. I used to shake like a raccoon shitting peach pits."

Jesse laughed at that mental picture and snuggled closer. Soon, they were both asleep. And hour later Jesse woke up out a horrific nightmare about the two she'd killed in Texas, sweating and crying. She and Aaron stayed awake for almost two hours while he talked to her and comforted her. He also reminded her she had not shot anybody last night, so she wasn't a crazy woman and he wasn't worried about her shooting him in her sleep. They finally got back to sleep about four in the morning, but Jesse was still having mood swings all day. Aaron cued Matt and they just let Jesse sort out herself without their interference.
***

Three days before Christmas, after flying out of Los Angles at Jesse's insistence, they landed at Midland, to be met by Francisco rather than the old man. Francisco loaded the bags in the back of the Suburban and flipped the keys to Jesse. "You drive. I hate this pig dog of a truck!"

Jesse caught the keys, laughing. "Francisco you're just spoiled, you like your little truck and Juanita's car, and anything bigger makes you nervous, unless it's the tractor, then you're in hog heaven. And where is Papa by the way? He forget and go on patrol today?"

Francisco hung his head. "No, Senora. He's down in Laredo with Bucky and some of the new patrol officers to try to stem the Christmas rush on drugs. You know they like him to come down and teach the new kids, he's got a sixth sense, I swear he can…"

Francisco stopped and walked to the back door, getting in behind Jesse he continued, "He promises to be home tonight, and said you will know where to put everybody. Juanita wanted to know what you want for supper and gave me a shopping list if you want some of that strange California food."

Matt and Aaron both laughed at that, earning a sharp glance from Jesse. "I figured we'd eat what Juanita is cooking, and I don't think she's ever asked me that."

"She said that wasn't for you, but for your guests."

That got everybody laughing and they proceeded home with Matt and Aaron telling stories about Pendleton and their respective jobs, and Francisco filling them in on the goings on at home since Jesse had been gone.

When they got home, the old man was there, and they once again detailed the incident in California for him. Even after he pressed on the issue, Jesse and Matt both assured him there was no possibility the Carlsbad PD had given out their names to anyone connected with the incident.

Christmas Eve passed quietly, with Jesse and Juanita going out at the last minute when they realized they were out of pie crusts for the Christmas pies. Aaron took that opportunity to go talk to the old man, knocking on the door to the office, he said, "Mr. Cronin, er, John can I talk to you for a minute?"

The old man turned around. "Sure, come on in Aaron. What's on your mind?"

Aaron stammered, "S-s-sir I'd like to ask your permission to ask Jesse to… Well to marry me."

The old man leaned forward. "Aaron, are you serious about this? Given all that's happened and y'all being separated like you are?"

"Yes, sir. I've been thinking about it for the last three months, and when Jesse went down in the back, I thought she'd been shot and killed and I thought my heart was gonna stop. I didn't want things to end that way, and I realized how much I really missed her and love her since I left for Pendleton."

The old man leaned back. "Well, I only see one problem, Aaron."

Looking crestfallen Aaron said, "What is that sir?"

The old man banged his hands down on the arms of the chair, causing Aaron to jump, "That damn Ford you're driving. You cannot be a member of this family and drive one of them! Anyway, the one you have to convince is Jesse, not me!"

Aaron just stared at the old man for a minute, then smiled ear to ear. "If that is the only issue, I can fix that next week sir! I'm hoping to ask Jesse tomorrow if that is okay with you."

"Aaron, I don't care when you ask her, that is between you and her."

Aaron stuck out his hand and he and the old man shook hands, and Aaron floated out of the room. A half hour later, Francisco walked in with the feed and vet bills, and the old man said, "You owe me twenty, he asked me today, and he's going to pop the question to Jesse tomorrow."

Francisco smiling ear to ear dug a $20 out of his jeans. "Gladly will I pay you, John. Juanita and all the women will be very happy with this, and they will start planning the wedding as soon as Juanita tells them!"

Christmas morning dawned clear and cold, and snowflakes started dusting down about 7 AM. In honor of Christmas, the decision had been made to delay breakfast until 7:30 AM and let everybody sleep in, but everyone started gathering in the living room about 7:15 AM. The old man was up, dressed and a cup of coffee in hand, along with Juanita and Francisco when Jesse finally came out of her room in sweat pants and a sweat shirt. Matt came in fully dressed and finally Aaron came through the back door, followed by Toby.

Presents were handed out with everybody oohing and aahing over the various gifts. The old man gave Matt, Aaron, and Toby CRKT M-16 knives, and Toby especially was ecstatic over the gift. Francisco got a new pocket watch, and Juanita a new set of kitchen knives for their house. Jesse got a new pair of Ostrich Lucchese boots in Havana leather color, and the old man got a new gun belt and holster from Rowe's Leather for his barbecue 1911. Matt and Aaron exchanged gifts, and both laughed when they realized they'd bought each other the same thing, spare magazines for their Glocks. Aaron had given Jesse a pair of filigreed earrings, but he surprised her by kneeling in all the wrapping paper, and holding out a small box, "Jesse, I love you. Will you marry me?"

Jesse put both hands to her face, and started crying. Aaron's face fell, and he started to get up when Jesse grabbed him and pulled him to her, "Yes, yes, *yes*!" Then she pushed him away and ran crying from the room.

All the men looked on in amazement, as Juanita got up and went to Jesse. Aaron looked around. "What in the hell?"

The old man just shook his head. "Women..."

In chorus, all the other men said, "Amen."

During and after breakfast, Matt was nervous as a cat on a tin roof, until his phone rang. It was Felicia inviting him to her family's house. After the old man drew him a map and loaned him the Suburban, he was all smiles. Taking another package from his room, he bolted out the door.

Jesse alternated between sitting with Aaron and whispered conversations with Juanita, along with phone calls for the rest of the day. Toby disappeared into the bunk house right after breakfast, and didn't show back up until dinner. Matt was nowhere to be seen, so they ate without him. Toby shyly handed both Jesse and Aaron gifts wrapped in the left over paper from the morning, and said something to the old man in Degar, which he translated.

"These are good luck charms Toby carved for you on this day. In his culture, you would now be married, so this is to him, your wedding present." Aaron shook hands with Toby and thanked him, and Jesse gave him a hug and a kiss, making Toby blush.

Bucky came by late Christmas afternoon and dropped off a bottle of 18-year-old Macallan Scotch for the old man. As they sat in the office he quietly said, "So far it doesn't look like any of the cartel folks made the connection between you and Jesse and the four runners you took out. Ironically, the initial reports may actually have helped on that because of the quote innocent unquote statement. They all think it was because of the Chicago end, but Jose is back on their target list, because of the presser he did. We haven't chased this all the way to ground yet, but it looks like this was one of the Zeta offshoot channels that is trying to expand itself. Right now, all of the info we've got says the cartels are containing their killings within their chains south of the border, but I'd still be careful if I were y'all."

"Well, I guess that's good news in a way." The old man continued, "Jesse, Aaron, Matt and Felicia had a run in with some Guat cowboys in California earlier this week, but I don't think that will make any waves, because it wasn't related to them hauling drugs."

Jesse wandered in and Bucky got the rest of the story from her, and then begged off, saying he had to get home. With a round of Merry Christmases he was out the door shortly afterward.

About 9 PM, Matt finally returned, and kept trying to turn away from folks. Finally, Jesse saw the side of his face, and said, "Oh my God, Matt, who gave you the black eye? Did you get in a fight?"

Matt turned beet red mumbling, "No, it's not what

you think."

Juanita came over and grabbed Matt's face. "Let me see. What the hell happened?"

Matt sighed. "Well you know little Pedro?" He asked, holding his hand about knee level. "He wanted to play and I got down on the floor with him, and he was playing and kicked me with his new cowboy boots! And I need to ask a question, what does Oso Blanco mean? All the kids kept calling me that."

Juanita doubled over laughing, and then went to the fridge, and pulled out a piece of liver. She cut it in half and brought it to Matt. "Put this over your eye, maybe it will take a little of the swelling down, and maybe you won't have too much of a black eye."

Aaron chortled. "Oh man, wait till the guys at the base hear this! Matt got his ass kicked by the littlest Mexican!"

That caused everybody to start laughing, and only Rex heard a car door slam. Rex ambled to the door and barked once, and the old man went to answer it. He came back with Felicia in tow, and everyone burst out laughing again at the sight of her, causing Felicia to literally stop in her tracks. She looked at Matt, with the liver on his eye, and got a devilish gleam in her eye. "So what story did you tell them, Matthew?"

Matt grumbled. "The truth— that Pedro kicked my ass."

Felicia laughed and said, "Oh my God, my whole family is so embarrassed, I bring a guest over, and he gets beaten up; they are all afraid you will be mad at them."

Matt smiled. "No, I'm not mad, but I *do* want to know what *Oso Blanco* means. None of the kids would tell me."

Felicia laughed again and said, "Oh, they are calling you the White Bear! I think it's because you are so big and were playing with them and growling like a bear."

Somewhat mollified, Matt reached out and Felicia came and sat on his lap, casually putting her arm around Matt's neck. "I just wanted to make sure you were okay, and ask Jesse if what I heard is true?"

Jesse nodded and Felicia jumped up and drug Jesse down the hall to talk.

The next few days flew by, and Jesse ended up driving Matt and Aaron back to Midland to catch flights back to Los Angeles. She and Aaron embraced and planned for the next visit, with Aaron wanting Jesse to come back out in late January, when he would have a few days off prior to the MSOB deploying for further training.

Jesse pulled into the parking lot and watched until Matt and Aaron's airplane took off before somberly driving back home. Jesse realized she was truly happy, and spent the ride home figuring out whom to invite, who the bridesmaids would be, and reminded herself to get with Juanita to plan the wedding dinner.

30 Thailand Here We Come

The house phone rang, but the old man ignored it, concentrating on getting the end of the month accounting done. Jesse yelled from the kitchen, "Papa, it's for you, Joe somebody!"
The old man sighed and punched the speaker on the phone, "Cronin."

A scratchy voice came back. "John, this is Cho, I need your help, if possible."

Turning to concentrate and grabbing his wheel book the old man said, "Hey, Joe, I haven't heard from you in quite a while, what have you got?"

"People smuggling and corruption I believe, we've got a lead again on a possible smuggling operation that I believe ties into the 666 heroin you've been seeing coming in through Mexico, but every time we investigate, it doesn't seem to pan out. I'm afraid if I go through channels to officially ask for you, it will tip off whoever is running the operation and getting information from inside the government."

The old man grunted. "Not fun, Joe, but how can I help?"

"John, I have a copy of your paper, and one of my officers attended your seminar earlier this year, so I think I need your consultation to look at what we are doing and see if you find things we are missing in our investigation," Cho responded.

"Well, if I come without approval, I won't be able to help. So what would I be doing?"

"No, John, if you come here for a vacation say, then

I can hire you as consultant, pay you a fee, and give you official status with the Central Bureau. That would be most effective for me, I can bury paperwork for weeks before anyone outside my team is aware you are here and working. This is short lead time. Next week expecting ship to call at Laem Chabang for twenty-four hours. It is Chinese ocean going freighter, and believe they are paying off Port Authority, but it carries legal cargo too."

Scratching a note '3rd week Feb' on a notepad and circling it, the old man said, "Joe, let me see if I can get off on this short a notice, and I'll get back with you by tomorrow. Is there a good number?"

Cho rattled off a long string of numbers that was the international code for his phone, and asked that the old man call him at the same time tomorrow.

Looking at his watch, the old man decided to make a couple of calls before going on shift, and see what the situation was. First calling the SAC at the National Academy, he determined there weren't any issues with official support to Thailand and got the code word for requesting a meet with the onsite FBI agent at the American Embassy in Bangkok. Next he called Bucky to see if he was aware of any situations with the international drug shippers, and nothing turned up other than a shortage of heroin after the latest bust in Los Angeles. His last call was to the sheriff asking for a meet at lunch.

He turned to the filing cabinet against the back wall and pulled out his shipboard smuggling folder and threw it in his gear bag, figuring he'd have time to review it during patrol.

Telling Juanita he was leaving, he loaded up and hit the road. The morning was quiet so he was able to review the folder and get some possible ideas of ways to support Joe. At noon he met the sheriff at Bienvenidos and found him at the back table as usual. Quickly ordering the taco plate and iced tea, he turned to the sheriff. "Jose, would you mind if I take a little vacation next week? I got a call from Cho over in Thailand and he needs my help on a smuggling situation over there."

"Hell, as soon as I get the request from state, I'll sign it and you don't have to take vacation John," Jose said.

"Well, Jose, that's the rub, there isn't going to *be* a request. Cho is afraid there are conspirators inside the government, possibly inside the agency, so he doesn't want to submit one. The last two times he's asked for help have been a clean miss. This time he seems to have good intel, and wants to bring me in as a hired gun so to speak. That way I'll have at least *some* status if not *official* status."

The sheriff leaned back in his chair and stared at the ceiling for a minute. "John, I'm not going to tell you no. I know you don't need this job, but this request just raises the hairs on the back of my neck. Something doesn't sound right!"

"I know," the old man said. "But I've already made a few calls, and there aren't any indications that either the FBI or DEA are aware of that indicates the Thai's are going off the reservation. And I've known Cho for over twenty years, and worked with him before. Remember?"

Jose chuckled. "Oh yeah, that butt ugly damn elephant I still have to move around every time I go on the back patio, and Betsy refuses to hide it... Seriously, if you go as a tourist, that means no weapon John, and I'm not too comfortable with you being over there without one."

"Jose, I'm not going to be doing anything but sitting in an office in all probability or at worst case, I'll go down to the pier and look at a boat while it's tied to the pier with half the Central Bureau at my back."

Shaking his head, the sheriff said, "Okay, I'll take you off the schedule next week and all I'll say is be careful."

Nodding, the old man agreed and they dug into the food. After lunch, the rest of the day passed quickly, and the old man pulled back into the house at a little after 6 PM. After going online and making reservations with American to get there, he looked at hotels and realized the only one recognized was the Hilton Millennium in Klongson, wincing as the made the reservation, he decided he'd better get enough consulting fee out of Cho to at least cover the airfare and hotel, if nothing else.

The combination of the two was damn near $10,000! But, he admitted to himself, he was just too damn old to spend twenty plus hours sitting in coach, much less deal with the lack of sleep. At least business class had better seats and the booze was free.

After dinner he finished up the books, and called Jesse into the office. "Okay, I'm going to be out of pocket next week, little trip to Thailand. The sheriff has given me time off, and I'll be leaving Sunday and should be home next Saturday or Sunday.

Since you're already running things, I don't have to tell you what to do, other than you'll have to actually get up and let Rex out."

Jesse just looked at the old man, "Work related?"

He shrugged. "Kinda, sorta…"

"In other words, don't ask 'cause you're not going to tell me."

"Jesse, it's not that, it's just that… Well, I don't want you caught up in the middle of this if it goes south."

"Papa, I'm a big girl now, and a deputy too, and I'm running the books and the ranch pretty much, so I'd think you would be able to trust me."

"Hon, it's not about trust. It's about a world I hope

to God you never have to get into. It's not pretty, nor is it real healthy for either side. You don't need any more nightmares."

Jesse turned and stomped out of the room and the old man turned back to the computer. It wasn't like he didn't trust her, he just didn't want to inflict the horrors on her that he'd seen and still had nightmares about. Or another set of nightmares... Smiling to himself, he thought, *hell a few more and they'll be taking a number to haunt my ass*.

He drug out his wheel book and wrote a note to buy a couple of bottles of Blanton's and thought about what kind of clothes to pack; checking the weather, it looked like low 90's for next week and probably rain, hell it seemed like it rained every day there.

Since this was an unofficial trip, no uniforms were needed, but maybe a couple of pairs of Dickie's wouldn't be out of line. Polo shirts, slacks, and comfortable shoes. Try to look anything but American, so maybe those slacks and shirts he'd brought back from Italy would work.

At 6 AM the next morning he called Cho back and told him he would come. Relaying his arrival time and hotel in generic terms and figuring Cho would pick up on the references. The rest of the week went smoothly, except for Jesse ignoring him. His research complete on the known heroin routes and players in Mexico, and the sketchy details he was able to get on the trans-pacific shipments were all filed on the laptop along with a list of questions for Cho. Saturday night he packed a suitcase, had Francisco drive him to Midland; he caught a flight up to DFW and stayed at the Hyatt at the airport until his flight on Sunday morning.

The Dallas to Los Angeles flight wasn't bad, at least he got fed in first class, but then he had to hang around

LAX waiting on the Cathay Pacific flight to Hong Kong. Boarding was finally called, and he boarded in business class to find a clean airplane, young and attentive flight attendants, and juice, tea, or coffee offered in a real glass or a real cup, rather than the usual plastic ware one got on a US airline.

Twelve hours later, the plane landed at Hong Kong and the old man realized that even with the upgrade he was stiff as a board, and tired as hell. It might be 7 PM Hong Kong time, but to his body it was 6 AM, and he decided to walk around and find something to eat, and maybe some coffee.

He finally ran across a Starbucks, and realized he had nothing but greenbacks, so he used the credit card with the smallest limit and hoped to hell they didn't scam him for the balance on the card. Sitting at one of the small tables, he tried to figure out how much he'd just paid for a lousy cup of burned coffee and an overpriced piece of supposedly lemon cake.

The cake reminded him of the days in the Army with what they used to jokingly call the dessert driers in the chow halls. They might have looked pretty and allowed the soldier to pick his own dessert, but damn they were *always* dry as a damn bone...

Two and a half hours later, it was back aboard another Cathay Pacific flight, and with two more hours of flying, finally touched down at Suvarnabhumi Airport on the outskirts of Bangkok. His bag was one of the last bags to show up and he picked a line for customs, which was, as usual, the wrong damn line.

He cleared customs after having to pay an import fee on the Blanton's, and wondered why the Thai's seemed to like doing things backward. Most countries you cleared immigration or passport control *then* cleared customs; but no, not here.

Another line and the old man was mentally mooing as he was herded along through the ropes. Clearing passport control, he stepped outside and inhaled the miasma of Southeast Asia- smoke, rotting jungle, people and shit.

Shaking his head, he looked around and noticed a group of what appeared to be chauffeurs waiting to pick up incoming passengers even after midnight. As he started for the taxi line, he casually glanced at them and realized one said Cronin-083.

He stopped and looked at his watch while he tried to figure out what was going on, then looked at the chauffeur more closely. He realized it was actually the young Thai he'd met last year at the National Academy seminar.

Walking over, he played dumb and said, "I'm Cronin. I assume you have a car ready?"

Bowing, Som said, "Sawasdee krup, please come this way Mr. Cronin. May I take your bag?"

As Som grabbed the bag and began walking out, the old man said, "Thank you. I assume you have the directions to the hotel, correct?"

"Yes, sir, the hotel arranged everything, as requested."

They walked to the chauffeured car park and Som placed the bag in the trunk of the black Mercedes along with the old man's briefcase. Looking casually around, and seeing they were not being watched, he said, "When I open the door, please to get in quickly."

The old man nodded and let Som lead him around to the passenger's side door. When Som opened it, the old man slid in quickly, and as the door shut, he realized there was someone in the back seat with him. He started to react, but a voice said, "Please don't hit me again John, I still remember the last time!"

The old man relaxed. "Dammit Joe, you almost got nailed for that."

Cho shifted in the seat and said, "Oh, I know, but I had to take a chance on doing it this way for now. I'm just glad you picked up on Som's sign and remembered our class number, and he didn't have to go chase you down. It's almost an hour to the hotel, and we know this car is clean, so it will give me a chance to brief you and tell you what I would like you to help with."

"Okay, so I'm here," John said. "Now what the hell is going on, Joe?"

Cho turned on a reading light as they pulled out of the parking area, picked his briefcase up off the floor, opened it and said, "First your passport John, I need to add a stamp that will tell the police to not trouble you."

Handing over his passport the old man said, "I hope I'm not going to have to rely on that."

"No, this is just one piece," Cho replied. "I assume you have your credentials, right?"

Carefully marking over the passport stamp, he pulled a small stapler out and stapled a folded page into the passport, then handed it back.

Reaching into the briefcase again, he took out a multipage document and handed it to the old man. "Here is your consulting contract, and your check. Just sign on the last page and you'll be official. And put this in with your credentials, this is your official paperwork that shows you're working with us."

The old man flipped quickly through the document and figured in for a penny, in for a pound as he signed it. Looking at the check he was startled. "Damn, this is for twenty thousand dollars!"

"Well, your plane ticket was almost nine thousand, and your hotel will be another two thousand, and five hundred for food, and one hundred an hour for your time, so there it is. I know you're not cheap John, and I really *need* the help on this one," Cho said.

The old man shook his head in amazement. "Damn, okay, you've got my attention now!"

Sticking the check in his pocket, he returned the signed contract and sat back.

Cho proceeded to outline the case as he knew it, the girls who would go missing from NEP[25] and Soi Cowboy which he explained was where the sex trade had moved when Patpong Road changed. Occasionally, a body would show up, but mostly the girls would just disappear into thin air. The snatches always seemed to take place within a week of certain ships that were known to have ties to the drug trade pulled into Laem Chabang.

They had been close a couple of times, but never seemed to find either the girls or prove there was anything being smuggled aboard the ships. That was what had keyed Cho, between last Tuesday and last Thursday twenty-two girls went missing, and not a single lead existed. All of them were either Laotian, Cambodian, Vietnamese or Thai orphans; in other words, no families were going to be complaining. They had also picked up indicators that a large shipment of heroin had left Afghanistan was thought to be moving east through the Golden Triangle for shipment to either Mexico or the States. Cho had decided that he would not go outside the Central Investigations Bureau on this one; as he felt there were spies in both the police and port authority.

Forty minutes later, Cho finished briefing the old man, and as the car turned onto Nakhon Road, told Som to pull over at a bus stop. Shaking the old man's hand, he said, "Get some sleep. Look around a bit tomorrow, and plan on going to work tomorrow night. Someone will

---

[25] Nana Entertainment Plaza

give you instructions at the Lantern in the hotel at six PM tomorrow night."

He slipped quickly from the car and Som continued on to the hotel, pulling up in front, he played the perfect chauffeur, obsequious and hoping for a good tip. The old man realized he still hadn't changed any money and vowed to do that immediately if not sooner.

Som handed both bags out and pulled a third small briefcase from the back, "Sir, please don't forget your computer."

The old man stopped, started to reply and just nodded and took the bag. Making a production of it, he gave Som a $20 bill as a tip and thanked him. He stacked the bags and carrying the second briefcase walked to reception.

After checking in, he changed $200 into Baht and was rewarded with a wad of multicolored bills, and figured it was play money time again. He let the bellhop lead him to his room, tipped him what he thought was the equivalent of $5 and hauled his bag onto the king sized bed.

He went back and locked the door, and then went to the small briefcase Som had given him. Opening it he found an Ed Brown Kobra .45, three magazines and fifty rounds of Speer Gold Dot ammo, along with a Don Hume holster and dual magazine carrier.

Safety checking the pistol he grabbed a pen off the nightstand and function checked the pistol also. He figured the trigger pull was right at four pounds, and the way it shot the pen out of the barrel, the firing pin was good.

The old man smiled as he loaded the pistol, put it in the holster cocked and locked and placed it on the nightstand. Pulling out his phone, he realized he'd forgotten to let Jesse know he made it, so he quickly texted her, then decided to take a shower and see if he could sleep.

Amazing himself, he soon drifted off even with an eleven hour difference in the local time and his body clock.

31 The Hunt Is On

The old man woke up at 8 AM when the sunlight hit him in the face. Blearily looking at his watch, he couldn't remember if he'd reset it the night before or not. He rolled over and looked at the bedside clock; it said 8:05, so he reset his watch to that time, hoping it was correct. As he tried to set up, he groaned as both hip and shoulder decided to let him know they hurt. Rolling his shoulders finally got a little relief, and he decided a long hot shower was definitely required this morning. He performed the morning ablutions, and went looking for breakfast. He hit Lantern, grabbed coffee and a roll, and called it good. Checking his phone, he realized Jesse still hadn't acknowledged his text, so he sent another that he was up and going to work. Based on the instructions he'd received from his FBI contact, he went online and found the American Embassy, but it was too far to walk, being over on Wireless Road, so he went back down and got a taxi from the queue outside the hotel. Twenty minutes later, he paid the driver and knew he was going to need more play money.

Approaching the Marine corporal on guard, he told him he needed to see Mr. John S. Bach. He was directed to wait, the Marine made a quick call and about ten minutes later, a young man from the embassy approached him. "You're the gentleman requesting to see Mr. Bach, is that correct?"

"Yes sir, I am," the old man said.

"Passport and creds please."

The old man handed over the passport with his

credentials underneath and the young man looked at the passport, and then quickly scanned the credentials. Noting the CIB note that Cho had supplied, he quickly handed the credentials back and turned to the guard. "Buzz us through please. He's cleared."

The young man turned and walked toward the side of the building, entered a side door, and led the old man downstairs. At a secure door, he turned to the old man. "Cellphone? If you've got one, turn it off and put it in one of the slots. No other electronics, right?"

The old man pulled out his cell, turned it off and stuffed it in a slot. "Okay, I'm clean."

Opening the cypher lock, he led the old man into the secure space, flipped on a flashing blue beacon in the ceiling and yelling out, "Uncleared in the space."

He directed the old man into a conference room just inside the door, told him to wait and closed the door on his way out. The old man heard a click and figured he was locked in, so he sat down facing the door and waited. About five minutes later, the door clicked again, and an older man walked in saying, "You Cronin? I'm Wallace Hearns, for my sins I'm the Legat here and boss of this bunch of misfits and malcontents."

The old man got up and stuck out his hand, they shook and he said, "Yeah, John Cronin out of Texas. I need to give y'all a heads up on what I'm over here for, since this is kinda off the books, at least as far as the Thai government is concerned."

"If it's CIB it is either drugs or trafficking in persons, right? Sit, sit... Need a cup of coffee?"

Sitting back down, the old man said, "Sure love one, black if you've got it."

Hearns left, but didn't close the door. A couple of minutes later, he was back with two Styrofoam cups of coffee and three other people, including one that looked

Thai or maybe Vietnamese.

They all took seats and Hearns made the introductions. "Phillips, Torrence and Phan; all FBI agents and working all the smuggling angles. So what you got? I got a heads up from Milty that you would probably reach out to us while you were here."

The old man repeated what he'd been told by Cho last night, and what he suspected his part was going to be.

"Interesting," Hearns said. "We'd heard rumors about another snatch and grab the other night, and some nibbles about the possibility of a heroin shipment, but this is the first confirmation we've gotten of it. Also, FYI we're right in the middle of a major US and Thai training exercise, Cobra Gold, which is driving us nuts. Buncha damn Marines and Navy in country, and I don't have enough folks to cover all the places and crap going on."

"Any possibility there is any interaction there?" The old man asked. "Or are these totally disassociated events?"

Hearns leaned back in the chair and sighed. "Well, there is always some low level stuff anytime there is a big military exercise in country. Normally it's a few guys running bus loads of hookers into the field, and maybe some Thai-Stick low grade grass. We don't usually get heroin moved to the military, as they don't tend to use at a level that would make it worth the risk. Same with the kidnapped girls: too much risk and very little reward. Usually these are older bar hooks out of Bangkok, who are looking at an easier chance for money, since there is less competition. Phan, you got anything to add?"

Agent Phan leaned forward. "Not really, but a major move of heroin right now is a bit unusual. I know the last shipment got nailed in an LA warehouse, so maybe this is a rush job to fill that gap. If so, I'm betting it will go via South America, then Mexico before it gets into the States via the southern border.

The old man filled them in on the last bust they'd had in Laredo, and the fact that it was a mixed load of cocaine and heroin, which was highly unusual. Normally, each drug was shipped separately.

A few more questions back and forth, and the three agents left. Hearns asked, "You carrying John? Or do you need a weapon?"

"I'm carrying, but it's a loaner from CIB, you need the serial on it?"

"Yeah, that and a number for you, cell if you have it. That way if something comes down I can reach out to you."

"Okay," the old man said. "Ed Brown Kobra, serial number is 2434, and my cell is a Texas cell that supposedly works here. 2145551212."

Hearns copied the info down and said, "You okay for mags and ammo? Oh wait, that's a .45 isn't it?"

"Yeah, but I'm good on both. Three mags and a box of Gold Dots."

Hearns slid a card across the table. "Okay, here's my official card, and my direct cell is on the back. I can't offer backup, but if you need comms, we can get you in and get you connected if you need it. CIB seems to be pretty clean, but a lot of the other government organizations seem to be holey as hell; Colonel Wattanapanit seems to have a good head on his shoulders, and he works with us on occasion."

The old man laughed. "Yeah, Joe was my roommate at NA, so I've known him for a while. We did an op a couple of years ago that ended up getting a big bust in LA, both drugs and money. I think that's why he called me and believe it or not, I'm actually getting paid for this gig!"

Hearns laughed. "Cash the check quick! Anything

else? If not let's get you out of here, and I can get back to the daily cat herding."

The old man laughed and allowed Hearns to escort him out the door. He picked up his phone and the same young man walked him out of the embassy. He caught a taxi back to the Hilton, mulling over what he'd heard and not heard this morning, and what impact the military exercise might be having on Joe's operations.

Heeding Cho's warning about working all night, the old man took a nap and got back up at 5 PM. He decided since he was going to be working, it was Dickie's, rather than tourist clothes. Going out the door, he realized it was raining, so he picked up his black rain jacket; heading downstairs at 6 PM, he went to Lantern as directed and had a salad and tea. Finishing dinner, he waited to be met; instead the waiter slid him an envelope folded under his check. Stuffing the envelope in his pocket, he paid the bill and wandered out of the restaurant. He found a quiet corner of the lobby and quickly looked at the paper inside. It was directions to walk a block to the bus stop, be there at 7:15 PM, and cab number 233 would pull to the curb and pick him up. He would know the driver. Looking at his watch, he shoved the paper and envelope in his pocket and headed out of the hotel. The rain was actually refreshing, and he enjoyed the short walk. Standing just past the bus stop, he checked his watch and looked up to see a taxi pulling in. It was number 233, and Som was driving again. "Good evening, Sam," he said, getting in. "I'm sorry you're getting stuck dragging me all over Bangkok, but I guess that's what you get for working for Joe, right?"

Som nodded and smiled as he pulled away. "Yes, Captain Cronin, we who drive are serving too, but I'm out of the office, so no complaint here."

Twenty minutes later, the car went through a fence

into a gated compound which the old man figured must be one of CIB's safe houses. Som parked the taxi and led him into the foyer of the house, then into what must have been the living room. Now it was more like a command center, with phones, blackboards, computers on tables and radios and ten people milling around and working.

The old man went over to Cho and shook his hand, motioning to the corner of the room. "I need to let you know I checked in with the Legat today, just to let them know I was here. SAC Hearns took the number of the Kobra and now I'm good with them if anything comes up. He's got a young agent named Pham there, and I don't know his background, but Hearns seems to think a lot of him."

"Thank you for being honest," Cho said. "And, yes, we know Pham; he's actually Vietnamese, but he's fluent in Viet, Thai and I think Cambodian languages and a few dialects. He's worked with us a couple of times. He is a virulent anti-communist and hell on drugs. But now, let me brief you. Things have accelerated a bit."

Cho stepped to one of the larger displays. "Here is a photo of Laem Chabang taken two hours ago. It appears our target ship has pulled in twenty-four hours early, and it is now offloading its scheduled cargo. We believe they will have completed the offload by now, and will start onloading sometime in the morning. I have an agent watching the ship, but he cannot access the port, so he's using long range IR system. He's reported the lights on that pier went out about a half hour ago, and two trucks pulled up to the gangplank, but they appear to be onloading provisions or small boxes only. He has not seen any sign of additional persons going aboard, and it appears nothing other than, how you say, CONEX[26]

---

[26] CONtainer EXpress intermodal freight transport container

boxes have come off. He has not seen them remove the hatches or access internal storage on the ship. I have a helicopter loaned to us by the Navy, and we will leave for Sattahip at oh three hundred. Sam will pick you up at the hotel at oh two hundred, and bring you to the airport."

The old man shrugged. "Well, I'm not sure until I can see it up close, but it looks like an older class of ship, with both holds and racks to carry what looks like a two high stack of CONEX vans. Looking at the picture, it looks like it can carry a maximum of what, twenty-four vans, eight to a section over the three holds. Now the big question is, whether or not there is access to the holds… No wait, there has to be access for them to run their safety checks and bilge checks."

Shaking his head, he said, "I need eyes on Joe, sorry."

"No problem," Cho said. "We can go aboard tomorrow morning after we get to Sattahip."

"Okay. Uh, one thing, do you know where I can get a backpack? All I brought was a briefcase, and if we're going to fly, I'd rather have a backpack for my stuff. And I guess I better go get some sleep?"

Cho turned to Som and they held a short conversation in Thai; he turned back to the old man, "Sam will stop on the way back and get you a cheap backpack; and yes, you should go sleep. I need you awake for tomorrow."

The old man thought it was a bit of a dig, until he realized Cho was smiling, so he nodded and turned to Som. "I'm ready when you are."

Som made a quick stop at one of the bazaars along the street, coming back with a cheap copy of a North Face backpack, and waved off any payment. He dropped the old man off at the hotel, and promised to be back at 2 AM. The old man went up to his room, moved a number of items from his briefcase and suitcase to the backpack and laid down to get a couple of hours of sleep.

Waking up at one, he took a quick shower, and dressed in his normal grey Dickie's. Belting on the Kobra, and the spare mag pouches he checked that they seated well and the pistol came smoothly to hand. Satisfied, he looked out the window, and sure enough, it was raining again. Grumbling to himself, he grabbed the rain jacket and slipped it on, covering the pistol and pouches. After a quick check of the room, he was out the door.

Som was sitting in the Mercedes when the old man came out of the lobby and he quickly pulled forward and jumped out of the car to open the back door. The old man got in and settled back. "Sam, I'm trying to do the math here. If we fly to Sattahip, how do we then get to Laem Chabang? And what time do we get there? Why not just fly directly into Laem Chabang?"

Som glanced in the rear view mirror. "Sir, the issue is alerting those at Laem Chabang we are coming, which would happen if we land there. The Navy is concerned enough that we are loaned one of their helicopters, and they will provide transportation for us from the base to Laem Chabang, which will take about an hour from my understanding. We should be there about sunrise."

The old man grumbled, and sat further back, trying to nap for a few minutes, figuring this was going to turn into one of those days. Seemingly minutes later, he felt Som brake the car and realized they were in front of a small hangar. Som got out, opened the old man's door, and then opened the trunk. Pulling out the old man's backpack, he handed it to him, pulled another much fuller backpack out of the trunk and locked the car. The old man looked at him in surprise. "Oh yes sir, I too am going on this raid. I will lead the team at the pier."

The old man nodded and looked at Som with a new perspective, as they walked through the hangar. They found five other young officers and Cho standing in front of what looked like a US helicopter. Cho smiled. "John, good morning! Are you ready to go flying?"

The old man laughed. "You're crazy; but I must be crazier to go along with your little scheme here, but let's do this. And where the hell did y'all steal a US chopper?"

As they walked out to the helicopter, Cho said, "Oh, we bought ten of these from the USA. That helps for compatibility between our Navies and Marines."

That reminded the old man about his earlier question. "Joe, what is this I hear about a big exercise, Joint Cobra or something like that? How much of that could be tied in to this?"

Cho looked puzzled for a second. "Oh, you mean Cobra Gold? It is a joint US and Thai Navy exercise. We don't have much to do, as most of that is taking place in the country side, very few are in town until next week, and then we will ramp up all officers to cover all the bars and sex areas. We do not believe this is connected at all, but the kidnappers may think we are too busy to worry about them right now."

They climbed aboard the helicopter and the old man leaned over and yelled, "God, this brings back memories, shitty canvas seats, noisy as hell, and stinks of hydraulic fluid and jet fuel! And are you *sure* those pilots are old enough to fly this thing? They both look about sixteen!"

Cho laughed. "John, these are two very experienced pilots, they routinely land this chopper as you call it on ships on sea. They are very good!"

The old man nodded and stuffed the foam earplugs the crew chief handed him and leaned back trying to get as comfortable as he could. The helicopter took off and an hour later after bumping and bouncing through the night and rain, landed on a long runway and taxied for what seemed like a half an hour. It finally came to a stop on a small ramp and they climbed gratefully off the helicopter; as they did, the old man looked around with a puzzled expression. "Joe, where are we? This place looks familiar."

"This is Utapao International," Cho said. "It used to be the Royal Thai Air Base Utapao, and America flew many bombers and tankers from here during the Vietnam war, along with a small Navy Detachment that operated from this area. We are about an hour from Laem Chabang, so we need to load and go."

The old man shook his head. "I think I flew out of or through here back then."

The team, along with Cho and the old man loaded up in the van and Som once again played chauffeur. At Pattaya they got caught up in a traffic jam, and finally Cho told Som to put the beacon on the roof and get them through it. Som did so until they got to the intersection of Hwy's 3 and 7, where they found two buses had hit and one was rolled over blocking Hwy 3 from side to side. They finally managed to back track and get on a small side street, weaving through neighborhoods and finally back on Hwy 3 a mile or so north of the intersection, but that took almost forty minutes.

Cho kept dialing a phone number without success, finally at almost six, they reached the main gate for the port. Standing forlornly on the side of the road was the man Cho had been trying to call, who waved them down.

Som stopped the van and Cho hopped out; Cho stood talking to the dispirited man for about five minutes then slid the door open and the man got in the van. Cho turned to Som, rattled of a comment in Thai, then turned to John, "We head back to Sattahip, the ship is gone. They loaded sixteen CONEX boxes and got underway a half hour ago. We run with lights now, we have no time to waste."

32 The Chase

Cho spent most of the ride back to Sattahip on the phone, making multiple calls to a variety of people some seemingly with positive results, others not, if the old man was reading the body language right. They finally arrived back at the ramp and the helicopter started engines as soon as they rolled up. Cho rushed everyone onboard the helicopter and made one last call, screaming into his phone to be heard over the noise, then leaned over to the old man.

"We are going to a Navy ship, they are closing the coast to pick us up and we will board the ship at sea. The weather is not good, but we have a track on the Chinese ship, it is making for the international waters."

The old man just nodded and stuffed more ear plugs in his ears, thinking this was *not* part of the plan, but what the hell, it wasn't the first time he'd been on a boat. An hour later, when they finally broke into a clearing in the weather, he looked out the window and noted this was a pretty good sized ship. He wasn't sick, but he'd been damn close a few times as they'd dodged weather and finally had to fly through what he guessed was a thunderstorm. He knew he'd never been in a bumpier ride, and now acknowledged that the kids flying the helo were as good as Cho had said they were.

As they came in to land, the crew chief opened the hatch all the way and started leaning out as the helo rocked around; the old man was scared they were going to hit the superstructure, then they landed hard on what turned out to be a very small helicopter pad on the back of the boat, ship, whatever.

Ducking under the still spinning blades he followed Cho forward into the superstructure. They were directed to what the old man guessed was the wardroom due to the number of officers standing there. Cho and an officer with three bars and a circle on his shoulder boards stood talking quietly off to the side of the wardroom as tea and coffee was passed to the rest of the arrivals.

After about five minutes, Cho waved the old man over. "Captain Wattanapanit, this is Captain John Cronin, of the US police forces. He is expert on smugglers and smuggling. He is assisting us in this investigation and graciously agreed to come along to provide his expertise."

The captain and the old man shook hands, and the captain asked, "Captain Cronin, are you familiar with the term VBSS?"

"Yes sir," the old man said. "Many years ago I did that, and I have also discussed this capability extensively with a variety of both US and foreign personnel."

Captain Wattanapanit nodded. "That is good, as the ship we are chasing now is staying in the weather front to try to hide. We will board with the team I have onboard for training under the current exercise. I would like for you to attend the briefing and provide any comments you feel are necessary."

The old man nodded and stepped away from the two men and asked for a cup of coffee. He noted there were multiple conversations going on and noticed Som off in another corner talking to a small officer in what looked like the old Army forest BDUs. The old man decided to work himself over that way, since he noticed what appeared to be a beret rolled up in the man's cargo pant pocket.

As he moved closer he saw a tab on the right sleeve that confirmed this officer was a Thai Seal. He grinned to himself, thinking things were about to get interesting for the ship they were going after. Som noticed him and introduced him to Lieutenant Kai, confirming he was the platoon leader for a Thai Underwater Demolition and Assault Unit, better known as Thai Seals and a platoon was aboard as part of the Cobra Gold Exercise doing practice VBSS boardings.

The old man saw the captain pick up a phone on the sideboard, and within minutes he felt the ship turn and increase speed. Cho came over and told them, "We will go to crews mess, there we will brief the target and decide how to take the ship. The captain and I don't believe we can fly to the ship, so we must board from RHIBs[27]. Lieutenant Kai, you will be in charge, if possible I and Sam and John here would like to accompany your boarding party." LT Kai and Cho had a rapid exchange in Thai; finally LT Kai nodded and led them out of the wardroom.

Weaving through the passageways they went down ladders and decks to the crews' mess where the rest of the platoon was assembled. The old man went to the steam line and picked up a coffee cup and started to fill it, as he did so he heard a voice behind him. "Mr. Cronin… John?"

Turning around, he came face to face with Aaron. "What the hell are you doing here, Aaron?"

Aaron looked at him. "Well, I could ask you the same question, sir. I'm out here with two others from my squad on the Cobra Gold exercise; we're doing cross training with the Thai Seals. We've been practicing VBSS boarding against different participants in the exercise, and they are doing counter boarding operations."

---

[27] Rigid Hull Inflatable Boat

The old man shook his head. "Well, this is not going to be an exercise, Aaron, this one is real, and there is a possibility of both drugs and people involved in this one."

Aaron nodded. "Okay, these guys are good, and we've integrated pretty well with them."

LT Kai called, "Attention on deck!" As the captain came into the crew's mess. "Seats," he said. "Gentlemen, we are one hour from intercept of the target vessel. They are remaining inside the weather front and running at about 12 knots for international waters. We will make bridge to bridge notification of a boarding action; if they refuse to stop, we will fire across their bow and at that time assume an opposed boarding status. Lieutenant Kai will be the boarding action commander. I will now turn over the briefing to him."

LT Kai briefed the standard boarding procedures and determined that two RHIBS would be used with a primary team and secondary team. He directed that Cho, Som and the old man would be with the secondary team, and would not board until the primary team had secured the vessel. He also moved the Marines to the secondary team to provide security for the additional members of the team. After a short Q&A, the briefing broke up into smaller discussions.

Shortly afterward, the ship began rolling more and as they went back up the myriad of ladders, they began to hear rain hitting the sides and decks of the ship. The old man asked the wardroom steward for some clear plastic wrap and wrapped up what looked like a hair dryer to try to keep it dry. Som looked on curiously. "Sir, may I ask, what is that?"

The old man held up the now wrapped device. "Sam, this is a thermal gun. It detects heat and registers a temperature. Not sure if it will work, but I'm going to haul it along, anyway." Storing it back in his backpack, and wrapping his cell phone up the same way, he stuck the cell in an inside pocket and zipped up the backpack. He hoped to hell neither would get too wet and fail to function. He guessed he'd see how well the Kobra stood up to saltwater and rain and resigned himself to a cold, wet ride.

Thirty minutes later, wearing a tactical vest that was one size too small with a chicken plate inserted and trying not to take deep breaths, he gingerly climbed into the RHIB sitting on the blocks. The other RHIB was loaded and swung out as the ship maneuvered close aboard the Chinese ship. The old man reached under his rain jacket and touched the butt of the pistol to ensure it was still in the holster. Even though the vest was small, it came down behind the butt of the pistol and felt uncomfortably like it was trying to push the gun out of the holster.

He now understood why Matt and Aaron had the thigh rigs, but that wasn't an option here and now. Suddenly, the ship turned and a spate of Thai came over the ship loudhailer. Cho leaned back. "Well, they are refusing to stop, claiming international waters, but what they don't realize is that part of the Gulf of Thailand is in fact enclosed by our country and therefore is considered territorial waters out past the twelve nautical mile limit from shore. The captain has decreed this will be an opposed boarding, therefore the Seals are allowed to fire if threatened."

The old man turned and saw Aaron and the other Marines locking and loading their M-4s and checking their M-9s as the word filtered back. The tension started ramping up as the ship turned to launch the RHIBs on the lee side and as soon as the first RHIB was in the water, it powered away toward the Chinese ship. The deck crew swarmed over their RHIB, attaching the lifting lines and giving the quick disconnect lanyards to the coxswain and one of the Seals in the front of the boat.

With a jerk and swing, their RHIB was over the side and dropping quickly toward the water as the coxswain started the dual outboards. As soon as it touched the water, he yelled a command and the Seal yanked the disconnects. They flipped the lines away and spun away under full power.

Through the rain he could barely make out the Chinese ship, but as they got closer, he could see the first Seals swarming up what looked like a rope ladder from the starboard stern of the ship. As soon as the first RHIB was emptied, Cho barked an order to the coxswain, and they went in under the ladder, and started up. Aaron insisted on going ahead of the old man, and had one of his squad bring up the rear. Cho bounded up the ladder like a twenty year old, which pissed the old man off to no end as he grimly climbed the slick ladder hoping to hell he wouldn't slip off and die in the water.

Finally aboard, and surrounded by the Marines, Cho and the old man went forward and up toward the bridge as the Seals fanned out to inspect the ship. On the bridge, Aaron broke off two of the squad to assist the search team and Cho began questioning the ship's captain. The old man just stood back and watched the rest of the bridge team. He kept getting drawn back to one man with two stripes that just didn't fit somehow, and noted that individual was constantly watching the captain and the captain would occasionally cut his eyes toward this man.

Cho finally got disgusted with the captain and turned the questioning over to Som, and the old man nodded in the direction of the front of the bridge. Cho came over. "This is not productive. He says they have done nothing illegal and we are pirates attacking them in international waters, and he refuses to give authorization to search. I told him we will search, but right now nothing unusual is being reported."

Turning and looking out the forward windows the old man said, "Joe, I think we have a Goomba over there in the corner with the two stripes. He's... Something's not right about him, and he doesn't seem like a subordinate to the captain at all. I'm not doing any good up here, so I'm going to go prowl and see what I can find if that's alright with you."

Cho nodded and LT Kai detailed one of his Seals to accompany the old man and Aaron. The old man asked the Seal where the galley was, and the Seal led them there. The old man poked around in the galley, looking at the prep area and looking in the various cold lockers. Coming out he said to Aaron, "Way too much food aboard for this small a crew. And did you see the size of that pan the cook was cleaning? I've never seen a Wok that big! And the dishes were piled pretty high, I quick counted thirty plates, and I don't think the crew is that big." As they cleared the galley, he turned to the Seal. "Can you ask LT Kai the ship's compliment and I guess if you would lead us to the forward hold please."

The young Seal nodded, keyed his mic and asked a question, got an answer and turned to the old man. "LT Kai say fifteen on manifest. He say number one hold open now."

The old man looked thoughtful, as the Seal led them back up to the main deck and out onto it, then forward to the forward hold where one hatch had been slid partially back. Looking down, the old man surveyed the hold, and noted it was lightly loaded, which made sense considering one didn't want a lot of weight on the nose of the ship. He climbed down the ladder attached to the aft bulkhead and walked forward among the single level of crates. Aaron talked with the Seal petty officer and came back. "Nothing. All these are marked Hong Kong and all of them are originating in India. No indication of any tampering either."

The old man grunted an acknowledgement. . "What's the last frame in this hold? We'll need that as we work back." As he was waiting for Aaron to come back, he looked up and saw another ladder that disappeared under the deck on the far side of the hold. Pulling out his Surefire flashlight, he shined it up toward that corner and observed what appeared to be a dogged hatch at the main deck level.

Aaron returned. "Frame 59 is the last marking I see, and that's on the one about a foot from the bulkhead. And there is no through bulkhead hatch."

The old man nodded, and started climbing. Back in the rain, he looked at the number two hold and decided there was no way to get under the CONEX vans to pull a hatch cover. As he walked around the back side of the vans he looked left and right, and counted eight stacked two high on the left, and eight in two rows of a single stacks. Continuing across the beam of the ship, he looked aft and counted another set of eight vans there stacked two high. Looking at the Seal petty officer he asked, "Has anyone searched this hold yet?"

To which the petty officer responded, "No sir, we are not sure how to enter."

Turning to Aaron, he said, "Check that Ventilation funnel there and see if there is a hatch at the deck level please." To the Seal he asked, "Would you ask Lieutenant Kai to send a ship's bosun down here please?"

The old man turned back to see Aaron and another Marine boosting one of the Seals up and holding on to him as he slid into the funnel. He was pulled back out and said, "Yes, dogged hatch at deck, maybe funnel turns on and off."

Aaron and another Marine tried twisting the funnel

first one way, then the other, suddenly it broke loose and turned 90 degrees to the right and they were able to lift it free. At that point a bosun accompanied by another Seal approached and lapsed into voluble Chinese accompanied by hand waving and an attempt to put the funnel back on. When one of the Seals translated, it was basically dangerous cargo, do not enter. Which simply meant the old man was *definitely* going in there now.

They got the hatch undogged, and open, did a quick air check and told the bosun to turn on the hold lighting. He said it didn't work and he that he was not responsible for anything in the hold. The old man leaned over the coming and shined his light down, seeing various blue and green tractors lining the floor of the hold. He smelled a strangely familiar odor, but couldn't place it. Moving out of the way, the Seals slid easily down the ladder and fanned out in the hold.

A niggling thought kept floating around in the hind brain, but the old man just couldn't drag it out. Finally, he decided to take a closer look, and climbed carefully down the now rain slick ladder to the floor of the hold.

"Aaron, do me a favor and find out what that forward bulkhead number is, will you please?"

Flashing his light over the hold he saw all the tractors were Indo tractors, in two different sizes. He asked one of the Seals to confirm the onload and destination for them, and the Seal came back they had been loaded on in Mumbai, and were destined for Hong Kong which was the next port of call. The old man thanked him and continued to quarter the hold, as he got to the front bulkhead, he noted the only thing in the hold that wasn't a tractor was a wooden crate about 5x5 by four feet high. It was centered against the front bulkhead and secured with heavy strapping both to the bulkhead and the deck plates. The old man kept sniffing and suddenly it hit him: red lead! *That* was what he smelled! Yelling to Aaron, he said, "Aaron, check for any places where there is fresh paint. That smell is red-lead anticorrosion paint!"

Aaron and the Seals all searched, but to no avail. Finally the old man got down on the floor and looked under the crate. By squirming around he was finally able to see something protruding from the deck of the hold that showed bright red paint, and got slowly to his feet. "Gents, I think this may be what we're looking for, there is another hatch under this crate. Let's see if we can move it."

After unstrapping it, the combined strength of the Seals and Marines couldn't budge it, so the old man requested LT Kai or Cho's permission to open the crate and remove enough items to allow them to move it. Concurrence came quickly, but they had to wait for bolt cutters and a set of wrenches to take the top off. As the old man studied it, he saw flakes of rust had been knocked off the bolt heads. He told the Seals what he wanted and started the long climb back to the deck.

Climbing back to the deck he asked Cho to come meet him, and Cho, Som and LT Kai appeared shortly thereafter. In the lee and out of some of the rain, he explained what he'd seen and what he expected to find. LT Kai went to observe, and told the leading petty officer to use the same method to access the third hold and report back. That hold was also stacked with tractors, but the lights were on and vent fans working. The old man turned to Cho. "Is Captain Wattanapanit a relative? Or was that just sheer luck that you both happen to have the same name?"

Cho shrugged. "He's a second cousin, and doing pretty damn well for himself and the family."

LT Kai reported by radio they had the top off the

crate and it appeared to be filled with heads for tractors, but they looked rusted. He also reported they could not see the bottom of the crate and were starting to take the heads out, but they were very heavy.

The old man and Cho looked at each other and both shrugged.

33 Bingo

Cho and the old man stood in the lee of the bridge and chatted quietly as they waited for LT Kai to report one way or the other after the crate was emptied. Aaron and his Marines were wandering through the CONEX stacks when the young Corporal came up with a bedraggled kitten. He brought it over to where Cho and the old man were standing, and the old man looked at it with distaste.

"Where did you find that thing?"

"It was over by one of the CONEXs meowing and scratching at the door. Dunno why, but it'd be dead if it was out here too long. Must have gotten out when we were opening hatches and passageway doors."

Suddenly, the old man straightened up and reached for his backpack. "Son, show me exactly where you found that cat!"

Everyone looked at the old man strangely, but the corporal led them back to the second of four CONEXs in the second stack. The old man took out his thermal gun and pointed it at every one of the eight CONEXs he could get to in the two rows. Then he went back to the one where the cat was now meowing again. He put the heat gun almost against the metal, then walked to both adjacent CONEXs and repeated the actions. Shaking his head, he walked back to the second CONEX and looked closely at the customs tag, then said, "Cho, get somebody up here with bolt cutters, we might have a bingo here."

Cho looked at the old man. "John what's gotten in to you? This is one of what, sixtee…"

"Joe, this is one of twenty-four! How many did your guy say were loaded this morning?"

"Sixteen."

"So where did the other eight come from?"

Cho just looked at him, and then gave a quick order into the radio. The old man walked back to the end of the stack, and looked up at the bridge windows. He noticed the two-striper staring back at him and walked back to Cho. "Did you ever do anything with that two-striper on the bridge?"

"No," Cho said. "He's just the third mate, and the captain had him on the bridge for training."

"Something about him bothers me, I can't put my finger on it..." the old man said.

One of the Seals came trotting up with the bolt cutters and the old man walked over to the CONEX. "I think this may be where your kidnapped women are, note this Customs label has been tampered with. Let's pop this lock and see what we have, shall we?"

Just as the Seal popped the lock, LT Kai's excited voice came over the radio in Thai, but the old man continued to release the dogs and with a grunt of effort, pulled the locking bar up and swung the door open.

The misma of unwashed bodies, and stale food hit him in the face as he stared at a group of totally silent naked women. Cho stopped talking into the radio and dropped the radio to his side and stared. Suddenly they heard a shot fired, then another from the starboard side. Aaron and his corporal turned and advanced weapons up and ready to fire as Cho followed.

A small boy tried to bolt from the van as the old man heard an AK firing on full auto and heard the rounds impact the door from the starboard side. The old man reached down and grabbed the boy to push him back in the CONEX. He felt a stinging sensation in his right side

321

and upper leg as he pitched the boy back to the women. He saw Cho, Aaron and his corporal turn and return fire past him, so he slammed the door and popped the locking bar back down, then turned and ran for the Port side.

Sliding past Aaron, he leaned back against the CONEX and slid down to a sitting position. Aaron backed around the edge of the CONEX as the corporal and Seal ran to the last rack of CONEX boxes before the bridge. Aaron knelt and said. "You okay? And what the fuck is going on? Who the hell did we just shoot? That dude wasn't one of ours!"

The old man just shook his head to try to clear the ringing. As he did, he caught movement out of the corner of his eye, grabbed Aaron by the front of the vest and yanked him down as he shot past Aaron and put two in the x-ring between the eyes of a surprised Asian in black pajamas with an AK in his hand.

Aaron had landed on his side, and suddenly he fired a three round burst from his M-4 down the lane between the CONEX vans. "Shit, there was another one. I've got this side. Can you cover your side?"

"I've got this side forward, but I can't cover aft," the old man said.

Aaron keyed his radio, and told the corporal to cover aft on the Port side, and have the Seal cover aft on the starboard side. Seals started popping out of the hatches from the second and third holds, and started taking turns providing overwatch and covering fire while others moved forward. More firing erupted forward on both the Port and Starboard sides, both AKs and M-16s then dropped off to silence. LT Kai called all clear over the radio, with a body count of eight killed.

The old man went to stand up and winced in pain, causing Aaron to offer him a hand. Looking down, Aaron saw blood on the deck. "We need to get you checked.

You're bleeding." He called for a medic and the two of them helped the old man into the crew lounge at the base of the bridge rather than try to deal with the wound on the open deck. One of the Seals came in and poked and prodded the old man, eliciting a wince of pain when he moved his hands down over his hip. He told the old man to drop his pants, and when he did, the medic snickered. He told the old man to lay face down on the table and the old man finally realized the pain was actually in his right butt cheek. Aaron and the corporal both stood with weapons at the ready, pointed at the front and rear entry doors, until Cho lead twenty-two naked women and one small boy holding the kitten into the lounge. The old man looked over and sighed, this just wasn't his day.

The women were raiding the snacks and everything in the fridge, until the small boy came over to stare at the old man. As the old man was lying on the table he was just about at the boy's eye height. The boy solemnly held out his cat toward the old man, who finally said, "No thank you son, I think he's yours. And you can thank that cat for us finding you."

The little boy clutched the cat possessively and turned to look over his shoulder. One of the women said something rapidly in Thai, and the little boy turned and smiled at the old man before running back to the woman.

The medic finished with him, and gave him a shot in the butt that hurt almost as badly as the gunshot. He helped the old man get his pants back up and his belt fastened tight enough to hold his pants and gun up. The old man tried to get up but between the pain in the butt and the sudden dizziness, he decided to just stay where he was. He felt the ship heeling and he assumed they were turning back toward Laem Chabang. He wondered how long it would take to get there.

The medic had apparently set up shop in the lounge

as he treated two of the Seals for minor wounds, one shot in the arm and one shot in the leg. The next thing the old man knew, the Chinese two striper was shoved into a chair next to the table with blood all over his white shirt and a rude bandage on his right shoulder. Cho came over and there was a rapid exchange in some language the old man didn't recognize, but Cho was laughing when it ended, and the Chinese was just pissed.

Aaron came over and crouched down. "Thanks for saving my butt out there, Mr. Cronin, can't tell you how much I appreciate it."

"Hey, I did it for *both* of us," the old man said. "If I'd let you get shot, I would never hear the end of it from Jesse!

"Well I won't tell her if you won't…" Aaron said and grinned.

The old man laughed. "I don't think that is going to work when I show back up with a gunshot wound in the butt. My God, all the years in combat, and I come over here on a quiet operation and I get shot in the butt. I'm never going to live this down!"

"If you hadn't grabbed that little boy, he'd probably be dead right now, so I think that was a pretty good trade," Aaron said, as he patted him on the shoulder and walked over to the group of Seals standing around LT Kai.

Cho, LT Kai and Som stood with the group, until Cho pulled the LT aside. After about five minutes, Cho came over and kneeled next to the old man, "We're going to be flown directly to Bangkok from here, but due to your injury, the decision has been made to lift us onboard the helicopter rather than try to do two boat transfers. As soon as LT Kai's injured are returned to the Navy ship, they will come back for us. We are on our way back to Laem Chabang with the ship and crew under arrest for smuggling."

The old man shrugged. "I'm just along for the ride at this point, so I'm going where I'm told. Bangkok works for me though and you're gonna owe me for a new pair of pants dammit."

Cho chuckled. "Add it to the bill John, add it to the bill."

A few minutes later, a helicopter could be heard hovering overhead and the two injured Seals left. Another ten minutes and the helicopter was back. Aaron and the Corporal came in with a Stokes Rescue Litter and eased the old man into it face down, with his backpack under his head for a pillow. After strapping him in, Aaron crouched. "Mr. Cronin, we're going back to the patrol boat and continue our ops, but when you get home tell Jesse I love her and I'll see her in a couple of months when we get off this deployment."

The old man nodded as best he could. "Will do, Aaron, and thanks to you and your corporal for saving my life too. This has been one helluva day!"

Aaron and the Corporal carried the litter out to a cable hanging from the helicopter and fastened it into place. The next thing the old man knew, he was rising into the air and downdraft and spinning under the helicopter. He noted the Navy ship was close aboard the Chinese ship and that was about it. He felt someone grab the litter and with stops and starts, he was pulled into the helo by the crewchief and Som. They slid him crossways in the helo and the crewchief slammed the hatch shut.

That was the last thing the old man remembered until the helo landed and he was pulled out of the helo by men and women in white uniforms. The next time he woke up he was in a hospital bed with an IV running into his arm and a dry mouth. He also realized he was on his back and his butt was cold, which made absolutely no sense. He tried to say something but nothing came out, so he tried to reach for what looked like a glass of water. His movement woke Som and he reached over poured a little water into the glass, put a straw in it and held it where the old man could sip it. The old man croaked, "Thanks, where in the hell am I?"

"Sir, we brought you directly to Bumrungrad, it's the international hospital here in Bangkok. They have a landing pad on the roof and the colonel felt it was necessary as you seemed to be unconscious for most of the trip. Our doctor came and checked on you and cussed us for not putting an IV with er… the clear liquid that starts with a p…"

"Plasma?"

"Yes, sir, either that or blood into you prior to leaving. Apparently you had lost a good bit of blood."

"Thanks, Sam. I guess that makes sense. Where's Joe? And did you get stuck as my baby-sitter yet again?"

Som smiled. "Sir, I do not mind. It has been very educational. The colonel is awaiting me to call him and let him know you are conscious."

"Tell him I'm conscious, pissed off and hungry. What time is it, better yet, what day is it?"

"Oh, it is Wednesday, sir," Som said. "It's about 9:00 PM. You have been out for almost thirty-six hours; I will ask for some food to be sent up."

The old man nodded. "Thanks, I appreciate it."

Som stepped out the door and a doctor came through immediately after. The old man could only stare, as the doctor looked like the living embodiment of Buddha. He was short and just about round, with a totally bald head and a beatific smile. "Mr. Cronin, I am glad to see you back among the living. We had to put some blood back in you and took the precaution of rechecking the injury and adding some antibiotics to your IV. You should be free to go tomorrow."

The old man shifted. "Thanks, doc, but I gotta ask, why is my butt cold and I'm not feeling any pressure on it, but I'm lying on my back?

The doctor laughed, "Oh, you are in a special bed, which has a cut section that allows us to rotate patients with bedsores, it just so happens it also works in your case, and the reason your behind is cold, is that you only have on a gown and there is no sheet or gown between you and the air."

The doctor left and the old man dozed for a little while, until he smelled what he thought smelled remarkably like a Big Mac. Opening his eyes, he was confronted with the sight of a smiling Cho, SAC Hearns and Som, all standing at the foot of his bed. In Hearns' hand was a familiar bag, and sure enough it contained a Big Mac and an order of fries.

34 Homeward Bound

As the old man wolfed down the Big Mac, a Marine lieutenant-colonel stepped into the room, nodding to Hearns and the others.
"Well, John," Cho said. "We almost screwed up with you, but at least we got you here in plenty of time and it looks like you will recover with no lasting damage other than a dimple in your cheek."

Hearns laughed at that, and the others chuckled, and the old man responded, "Joe, if you ever repeat that *joke* to anybody that knows me, I will hunt you down like the dog that you are! But I do have a question: I never did hear what Lieutenant Kai found, I remember something over the radio, but we got a tad busy about then."

Cho walked to the door, opened it and looked up and down the hall before returning to the bedside. "John, you were right, there was a hatch there, and it did go into the bilge. One of the Seals found a storage compartment under the water and when he popped it open, out floated one hundred twenty kilos of high grade Afghan heroin, sealed in half kilo sticks with rubber coating that fit perfectly through the gas tank openings on those tractors. And those women were able to give us information on who their captors were as an added bonus. We now know who in Port Security was in on the deals. One of the women was sent to pleasure him the night before they were loaded aboard and she was able to pick his photo out of a photo lineup."

The old man whistled at that, and Hearns chimed in, "Bout twenty four million in street value, and looks like it was destined for China and points east including Zeta in Mexico, and tied directly to a couple of Tongs operating out of Hong Kong and the west coast that do both drugs and human trafficking. Some of those tractors were supposed to eventually end up in Acapulco after a couple of transshipments, so we've got a pretty good look into their methods, but they don't know it, at least for now."

"For public release," Cho said, "this is going to only be about the recovery of the kidnapped women and we will be able to hold the ship and crew for quite a while. These trials take time, especially when we want them to." Then he smiled, and it wasn't a pretty smile.

Hearns turned to the Marine. "This is Colonel Betts, he's on the DAO[28] staff here, and is the primary liaison for the Cobra Gold exercise, and he's got a few questions."

The lieutenant-colonel looked around and said, "First, I'd like to stay out of any classified areas, although I'm sure everyone here is cleared, but this isn't exactly a secure space. The reason I'm here is the colonel with MSOBs is a bit concerned that his Marines got in a shooting situation without his knowing about it, or approving it. Secondly, all we officially have is what Staff Sergeant Miller put in his daily summary that was routed from the Thai Naval vessel, which is decidedly brief."

The old man and Cho looked at each other and Cho took the lead, explaining the entire situation and the way they came to be on the ship and decisions that were made. The old man said, "Colonel Betts, I just want to make sure it gets documented that Staff Sergeant Miller and the corporal with him saved my butt by taking out one of the guards that had me pinned down and they directly

---

[28] Defense Attache Office

contributed to the saving of those women's lives."

Betts nodded, and after a few more queries seemed satisfied that he had the whole story. Cho said, "John what we have is a problem of how to get you home. I know you have a ticket on Cathay Pacific, but I'm not sure you can sit, much less sit for that long a trip. We are looking at options now, but they may require you staying here possibly up to a week until you can safely travel."

Betts and Hearns had a whispered conversation and Lieutenant-Colonel Betts said, "We might have an option to get you to Pendleton, but it won't be quite as glamorous as Cathay Pacific and the flight attendants are nowhere near as good looking."

Cho looked at the lieutenant-colonel. "How sir would you do that, if I may ask? The only option we could come up with is an air ambulance configuration but those do not exist within any reasonable costs."

"Well sir," Betts replied, "it just so happens we have a dedicated lift leaving tomorrow evening out of Utapao. It's a C-17 direct to Pendleton and as of about two hours ago there were two open stretchers in the package. It's taking Marines that have been injured in the exercise back to the states for treatment. This happens every year, so we've got two packages programmed on the birds whenever they come through between now and the end of the exercise."

"Colonel, I appreciate that, but I'm a civilian, not retired military, so how could you possibly get me on that?" the old man said.

"John," Hearns replied, "we can make you official as a govie supporting an international cooperation agreement in the law enforcement side that was injured in the performance of his official duties. That should take care of that."

Lieutenant-Colonel Betts smiled. "I can go convince

the green beanie in the corner office to go along with that, and he can go fight with the Air Force, he owes them a couple anyway."

Everyone was nodding in agreement and the old man said, "Tell him this old green beanie appreciates it. I was Fifth SF back in Nam."

Betts and Hearns looked at him with a new appreciation, and both nodded. Cho agreed and said he would get the old man's things from the hotel and bring them to the hospital, and lay on a helicopter to fly him to Utapao. After a few more minutes of conversation, everyone except Cho and Som left, and Cho turned to the old man. "John, about your pistol…"

The old man said, "Joe, that's your pistol I was just borrowing it, and there is no way in hell I can take it back with me, especially on an Air Force airplane. They'd shit little green apples!"

Cho laughed, and Som looked at them until Cho explained the joke in Thai; then Som burst out laughing, "John, I was going to ask if we could keep it, since it is evidence of the firefight and important piece of documentation when matched with the bullets from the Chinese guard. By the way, that was very good shooting!"

The old man shrugged. "Honestly, I don't even remember shooting, much less how many rounds I fired. That was pure old hind brain running the meat sack; and if there was a conscious thought, it was long after it was all over. I can only remember thinking those women were way too quiet, and I would have been screaming my head off."

"That reminds me, *how* did you know they were there? I know you had that little what…" Cho said.

"Oh, the temperature gun, it registers in tenths of a degree, and of the eight vans I checked," the old man said. "That van was almost four degrees warmer than any others, and that included the two adjacent to it. That's a trick I use for looking for Coyotes smuggling. Humans generate heat, and multiple humans generate a lot of heat compared to inert materials. It's really simple, and it works about eighty percent of the time. The other way is weight. Look for the odd weight either too light or too heavy compared to the rest of the cargo; but that wasn't an option here."

Cho and Som both nodded in appreciation. "Thank you, we will add that to our techniques also John."

At that point, the doctor came back in and chided Cho and Som in Thai and shooed them out like a couple of naughty children. Checking the old man's vitals, he asked, "Have you exercised yourself today?"

"Uh, say what, doc?"

"Have you voided bladder or bowel today?"

The old man shook his head, but suddenly realized he *really* needed to piss; "Uh, how do I do this Doc, I know there is a hole in the bed, but..."

The doc laughed. "I help you up, you go piss like a man, standing up!" With that he picked the old man up like a baby and set him on his feet. Holding his arm, he reached for the crutches at the head of the bed. "They should be about right, please to take yourself to the bathroom."

The old man hobbled to the bathroom, dragging the IV stand behind him and pissed for what seemed like minutes, then hobbled back to the bed. After a couple of tries, he figured out how to get back in bed, and did so with the doctor looking on approvingly. "Bladder only?"

"Yeah, doc. But I needed that."

"You no void bowel by tomorrow, we do it for you," the doc warned.

The old man nodded grimly as he laid back. The

next thing he knew, the sun was shining in the window and Som was asleep in the chair. In the corner he could see his bags, neatly packed and stacked on top of each other. He leaned over and groaned as the pain hit his butt, which woke Som with a start, "Are you alright sir?"

"Sam, other than my butt, I'm fine, but I gotta go, and damn if I can figure how to get up."

Grumbling, the old man got up with the nurse's help and managed to lay back down after she flattened the bed out. The bandage was changed, and not gently, something cold and astringent that burned like hell was wiped on his butt, and a running commentary in Thai including laughter punctuated the entire evolution. When they were finished, he was stood up, and the nurses took his gown, gave him a sponge bath, again with much laughter and the old man caught Som blushing a couple of times, but there was nothing he could do. At his direction Som opened his bag and pulled out pants and a shirt that he didn't care if they got ruined, and the nurses helped him dress.

As he was hobbling around, he thought to himself: *damn, how am I going to get home from Pendleton? And how am I going to get... Shit...* Fumbling in the night table, he dug out his phone and called Billy Moore, who picked up on the first ring. "Billy, I need a favor, can you get the Lear with Trey onboard to meet me at Pendleton tomorrow afternoon?"

Billy of course wanted to know why, and the old man answered testily, "Well because I got shot, okay? And if they can't get into Pendleton, oh hell, no make it Carlsbad, I'll get a ride over there, Okay? I'll explain the next time I see you."

Billy laughed and said he would handle it, and the old man decided to text Jesse rather than calling her. He basically sent that he would be home late tomorrow evening and he would call when he got in. Minimal details were a good thing sometimes!

Cho came in with Hearns and the confirmed everything was on track, and chatted for a few minutes until it was time to take the old man to the roof for the ride back to Utapao. Cho shook hands saying, "John I'm truly sorry you got shot, but I cannot express either my or my government's appreciation for what you've done to help us. I owe you one my friend."

"No biggie," the old man said. "I'm just glad we got those women back, and the drugs were just a bonus as far as I was concerned."

Cho nodded, and Hearns said, "We've logged your participation and it's been pushed back to Hoover, and the Deputy, so I don't expect to hear any ramifications. This one goes down as an atta boy."

The old man shook his hand. "Well, it didn't quite go as planned, and I'm going to hold you to keeping those Marines out of trouble. And I'm not planning on coming back anytime soon! I lived through two sets of exciting times, and I sure as hell don't want a third!"

The old man went to shake hands with Som, only to have him say he was accompanying the old man to Utapao. The old man replied, "Ah, Sam, babysitting to the end, or making damn sure I get on the airplane?"

Som grinned and everyone else laughed; but he didn't answer.

The nurses efficiently strapped the old man face down on a small stretcher and briskly maneuvered him to the roof, where what appeared to be the same SH-60 and pilots awaited. One more round of handshakes, and he was loaded aboard, strapped down. An hour later they landed at Utapao and taxied to the same remote ramp, now seemingly half filled by a grey USAF C-17. The crew chief and Som got the stretcher off the helicopter and the old man demanded they let him off the stretcher and hand him the crutches. Shrugging they complied, and the old man hobbled over to the aft ramp of the C-17 with Som carrying his bags. A pretty young USAF Sergeant met him at the ramp, asked his name and checked him off the manifest. She whistled, and a male loadmaster came over and took his bags aboard, so the old man turned to Som, "Sam thanks for everything, and I hope to hell you get some down time after this. I know babysitting is not fun, but I truly appreciated the assistance, and I hope Joe takes care of you for this!"

Som laughed. "Sir, the pleasure was mine, this was truly a learning experience!"

The old man said, "Yeah, in how *not* to do things!"

Som shook his hand and trotted back to the helo that had now restarted its engines. As he climbed aboard, he turned and waved one more time before the hatch was closed. The old man looked around and was trying to decide what to do, when he saw Lieutenant-Colonel Betts and a green beret standing near the small building at the side of the ramp. Looking at the Sergeant, he asked, "How long before we launch?"

"At least an hour," she replied. "We're waiting for the Marines and their lift is a half hour out."

That made the decision for the old man and he hobbled over to the building. As he got there, a second Marine came around the corner from the parking lot, and the old man saw that he was a full bird colonel, he also realized the Green Beret was a full bird too. Lieutenant-Colonel Betts came to attention and saluted the Marine Colonel, and all three turned to the old man. Lieutenant-Colonel Betts introduced him to Colonel Wojokowski, the Defense Attache; and then to Colonel Able, the battalion commander for the Marines in the exercise. Colonel Able was frowning and started to say something when Colonel Wojokowski said, "Just call me Wojo, and Betts tells me you're one of us."

The old man dug out his coin, and handed it to the colonel, "Let me guess, colonel, Tenth Group?"

He laughed as he handed the coin back. "The name gave it away, right sir?"

Colonel Able looked on curiously, so the old man handed him the coin. "Well, that and the tenth flash and bout half way round the world from your AOE, so it was pretty easy. I'm glad to see nothing's changed in the Army." Wojo laughed and nodded at that.

Colonel Able handed the coin back and asked, "Were you in Nam?"

"Yeah, three times," the old man said. "Once, a year with the Yards, sitting on the trail. Sixty three to sixty five."

"So you were in the shit then?"

The old man nodded. "Yep, neck deep a coupla times. Colonel I want you to know your Marines did a helluva job of bailing my tired old ass out on this little op they got drug into."

Colonel Able nodded. "That is something I'd like to get a little more info about, if you don't mind."

Colonel Wojokowski nodded. "Me too."

The old man's bland recital of the operation had both of the colonels glancing at one another more than once, and both read between the lines that this was an old warrior. They both asked a few questions, and decided it had been a win for the good guys.

The old man decided to start for the airplane and the three officers walked with him, as they got to the airplane, a CH-47 taxied down and turned into the ramp area. Colonel Able said, "This must be my sick, lame and lazy ones." This generated smiles around, knowing that he was joking to cover his worry over his men.

The young loadmaster pointed the old man to the top of the ramp and he hobbled up slowly to be met by an older female nurse with colonel's insignia on her collar. "Where do you think *you* are going mister?"

The old man politely responded, "I'm one of your patients for the ride to Pendleton, and I just need to sit down if you don't mind."

To which she said, "No you're not buster, we don't haul civilians, this aircraft is reserved for military only, specifically Marines, so turn your butt around and get off here."

The old man whistled loud enough to catch the young loadmaster's attention and motioned for her to come where they were standing. She trotted over and asked, "Yes, sir?"

"Would you please show the colonel the manifest with my name on it, she doesn't seem to believe me," the old man said.

A young Lieutenant nurse stopped in front of the old man. "Sir, are you our last patient?"

Chuckling, the old man replied, "Well, there seems to be some discussion of that right now."

Shaking her head, she added, "Well, in any case, you need to get over here and sit, because you look like crap. Now come with me." She led him over to the last stretcher on the bottom tier, and he lay gratefully on his side. She got him a bottle of water, and quickly took his vitals.

Both colonels came strolling back down the cargo area, and Wojo mimed scoring one, which got a smile from the old man. Colonel Able asked, "Is there anything you need?"

The old man almost said no, then remembered he was going to Pendleton. "Yes sir, is there a way to get a message to Gunnery Sergeant Matt Carter at Pendleton?

I'm going to need a ride to Carlsbad airport and he's the only one I can think of."

Able nodded. "Carter that runs the range at Pendleton, that Gunny Carter?"

The old man nodded, and Colonel Able snapped his fingers. "Cronin, wait a minute, is your daughter the one that fucked with my snipers?"

The old man chuckled. "Actually my granddaughter, and I think there was a Colonel Ortega involved in that, from what I heard."

"No problem," the colonel said. "I'll get a message to him to meet you. Travel safe Mr. Cronin, and enjoy the flight, I don't think we'll have, or you'll have a problem with the Dragon Lady as you called her."

He shook hands and moved off to talk to each of his Marines. Colonel Wojokowski squatted by the stretcher. "I told that old bag that if you weren't on the airplane, it wasn't leaving. Period. She started squalling like a stuck pig, until I called the poor captain that's the aircraft commander down and told him the same thing. He told her he would be happy to get the command post on the horn and let *her* explain why they were still sitting here. Well, I need to go raise some more hate and discontent, so you travel safe, and thanks for makin' us look good! DOL sir, DOL."

The old man stuck out his hand. "Thanks, colonel and DOL, even if I'm no longer active."

The colonels left, the aft ramps closed, and the C-17 taxied out and lumbered into the air. Six hours later, they landed in Guam for gas and food; two more pilots came aboard, and they started the next leg, seven more hours and they landed at Hickam Air Force Base in Hawaii, cleared customs and immigration, and everyone but the patients got off. An hour later, refueled, re-crewed, and with yet more box lunches, they departed for California;

five hours later, they touched down at Pendleton.

35 The Reception

As they taxied in, the nurses and medics started prepping the stretchers for transport, and the loadmaster cracked the aft ramp, letting in a blast of cold air. That woke the old man up, and he wondered where his bags had gotten to; waving down a passing medic, he asked him to send over the loadmaster.

"Sergeant, I have a suitcase and briefcase somewhere on this airplane, and I'd really like to get my jacket out of the bag if you can find it."

The loadmaster smiled. "Yes, sir, I was told where they were, and I'll get it for you right now, before things get busy."

The old man managed to get most of the way up, and was able to sit leaning on the healthy cheek as the loadmaster returned with his bags. The old man slipped the jacket on, and finally got his crutches unstrapped from the stretcher. The airplane finally stopped and the engines wound down as the loadmaster finished opening the aft ramp and dropping it to the ground. The old man looked out to see a line of ambulances advancing on the airplane and idly counted them, then counted again and wondered if one of them was for him. He saw a group of Marines come up the aft ramp and reached down for his bags, trying to figure out how he was going to do this.

He looked up to see Matt standing in front of him grinning. "Shot in the ass?"

"Ah, gahdammit, I am gonna shoot somebody for that. Hello, Matt and thanks for meeting me."

Matt laughed. "Well, from what I've heard, you

should consider yourself lucky that was all that got shot. Felicia is here too, apparently Angelina called her to come check on you."

The old man rolled his eyes. "No damn privacy as soon as the women get involved! Do you know if there is an airplane at Carlsbad for me?"

Matt nodded. "Big black guy named Trey? He's standing with Felicia right now; they wouldn't let them on the ramp."

"Okay, so how is this going to go down?"

"Well, I talked to the corpsman, you're going in the last ambulance, he'll stop by Operations and pick up Trey and Felicia and I'll go get my truck and follow y'all to Carlsbad."

"Oh shit. That means every damn woman in town is going to know what happened, and Jesse and Juanita are going to give me a ration of shit as soon as I get home. I should have stayed in Thailand."

Matt shrugged. "Well, all I'm gonna say is I'm glad you're not coming back in a box."

The old man nodded, and the medics told Matt to move he was in the way. They quickly and efficiently pushed the old man back down on the stretcher and carried it quickly to the last ambulance. Matt picked up the bags and followed them, putting the bags in the side door and reminded the corpsman to stop at Ops for Trey and Felicia. The corpsman nodded and Matt trotted toward the parking lot to get his truck.

The corpsman drove slowly off the ramp and stopped for Trey and Felicia to hop in. Trey was all business. "Dammit John, did you forget to duck again?" As he quickly took the old man's vitals, poked in various places, and grabbed his lower legs and pulled his socks down and held both legs in his hands.

"Dammit, Trey, your hands are cold! What the hell are

you doing?"

"Checking for distal pulse and temperature. Were you really shot in the ass?"

Felicia giggled when she heard that saying, "Oh, Mr. Cronin, I'm sorry to laugh. I know it's not funny but…"

The old man snorted. "Hell, Felicia, it seems like everybody and their damn brother knows, so yes, I got shot in the ass. There! You two happy now?"

Trey rumbled his usual laugh. "John, it's not like you're going to be able to hide it, and I told Jesse to go pick you up a rubber donut at the pharmacy. You're going to need one when you get home, so shut up. Now details; where, how, how long before treatment? What do you remember about the hospital treatment? Did they give you any paperwork? Or am I totally going to have to guess here?"

"Pick one," the old man said. "First you tell me to shut up, then you ask twenty damn questions. Check the briefcase, there's an envelope in there that's probably the treatment stuff. I hope you read Thai."

Trey let go his legs, pulled the socks back up and rifled through the briefcase until he found the folder. Meanwhile, Felicia sat on the side of the stretcher and grabbed the old man's hand, "One thing is for sure, it didn't help your temper as usual. I don't see how Juanita and Jesse put up with an old grouch like you." But she said it with a smile.

"You know Doc Truesdale and Angelina will be meeting you to take you to the hospital and she wants me to call her with any requirements."

The old man rolled his eyes and said, "Damn women, y'all just won't leave a man alone will you?"

Felicia chirped, "Of course not, without us you would still be grunting and digging in the dirt for your food."

Trey rumbled and the old man finally laughed. "Okay, I give, I give."

Trey poured through the medical records, and whistled. "*Three* pints of blood? Damn, John, you almost bled out, and I'm amazed they let you out of the hospital this soon! What the hell, was there any on scene treatment?"

The old man said, "Yeah field medicine by a Thai Seal with me bent over a table in a lounge on a Chinese ship with twenty-two naked women watching and my ass hanging out for everybody to see."

Felicia's laughter pealed out and Trey rumbled again. "Sure, John, like I believe that."

The old man shrugged. "Okay, think what you want, since you don't want to hear the truth. About a half hour later, we were hoisted off and flown to Bangkok, I'm guessing an hour or so total there. They landed on the roof and I woke up the next night. I was out for quite a while. As far as my being here now, it was the easiest way to get me out of Thailand. Otherwise, I'd probably still be there waiting for my ass to heal enough to be able to sit in an airline seat. "

Trey shook his head. "Damn Thai doctors chicken scratch is almost as bad as ours. Who was your doctor there?"

"Don't know his name, but he looked like a Buddha statue. Don't think he ever said his name."

Trey sniffed. "Well I don't see any blood seeping through your pants, your vitals are okay, and you need a bath. But I think you can last another three hours, so I'm going to rig a drip and get some more antibiotics in you between here and Fort Stockton."

The ambulance slowed and bumped onto the ramp at Carlsbad. Trey hopped out and directed the ambulance to back up near the airstair and had it stop.

Matt came through the FBO office carrying the old man's bags, and gave them to the co-pilot as Trey helped the old man down from the ambulance. The Corpsman made a quick pass through the back, and at a nod from Trey, and a quiet comment from Matt, pulled away to return to Pendleton. Trey picked up the old man, much to his embarrassment and carried him up the airstair and gently set him on the entry to the Lear. Holding him up with one hand, he reached back and pulled two canes from the cubby and gave them to the old man. "Okay, ease yourself back there and lay on your stomach, I need to make sure you aren't putting any pressure on the wound, and we'll get this show on the road."

Felicia came onboard, and bent to gently kiss the old man on the cheek. "You get well, Senor Cronin. I want to see you at the wedding in three months."

She backed out and Matt said, "I'm not going to kiss you, but I *do* want to hear the rest of the story. I need to be able to give Aaron a ration when he gets back."

The old man nodded, and Matt backed out as well. Trey closed the airstair, and strapped the old man in after he started an IV as the airplane taxied out.

The old man was slept out after the flight from Utapao, so Trey finally got the story out of the old man, and marveled at the dispassionate, clinical descriptions the old man used. Trey wondered yet again what the old man had done in Vietnam and other places. He shuddered, thinking to himself, *this is one man I never want mad at me or my family.*

Trey checked the old man's vitals again and decided to change the subject. "John, I am gonna be so damn glad when this wedding is done. Beverly is on the phone every damn night either with Jesse or Juanita or who the hell knows. Jesse's asked her to be a bridesmaid, and she's over the moon; but how many damn phone calls and emails and texts does it take?"

The old man said, "Trey, best thing to do is keep your hands and feet clear and just let them go. If you try to do anything, you're gonna bring the wrath of every damn one of them down on you and all of us. They're worse than a damn den of baby rattlers and twice as deadly right now."

"Dammit John," Trey grumbled. "I was hoping you'd give me some advice based on your long years of experience."

"Trey, my only advice is go on vacation until the wedding day; trust me, you won't even be missed!"

The PA came on and the co-pilot said they were descending into Fort Stockton and would be on the ground in ten minutes.

As they taxied in, the pilot came on the PA. "Looks like quite the reception committee out there. Bout the only thing missing is a fire truck."

The old man pounded his head gently on the seat. "Dammit, I *knew* I should have stayed in Bangkok."

Trey just rumbled and released the strap so the old man could start getting up to get off the airplane.

After the old man got to a sitting position and the airplane came to a stop, the old man said, "Trey you *will not* carry me off this damn airplane. I will go down the airstair on my own. If I fall I fall, but you will not carry me, do you understand?"

Trey looked solemnly at the old man. "John, I won't embarrass you, but at least let me get on the ground first in case you fall, alright?"

"Alright, give me the damn canes and put my crutches where I can get them at the door."

Trey nodded and helped the old man up, then moved the crutches to the door, and climbed off the airplane. The old man got to the door and almost went back to the couch. Jesse was standing anxiously at the bottom of the airstair holding Trey's arm; arrayed behind them were Doc Truesdale, Angelina, the sheriff, Billy Moore, Clay, Major Wilson, and Bucky.

The old man managed the stairs and Jesse reached out, but didn't touch him. "Papa?"

"Jesse, I'm alright, I only got shot in the ass, not in the head."

She hugged him gently and started crying; he tried to hug her and ended up dropping the crutch. Trey slid in and supported him and he held her.

Doc Truesdale finally stepped in. "Jesse, stop that shit, I need to get this old fart to the hospital so I can see how bad those damn Thai witch doctors screwed him up."

Jesse snuffed and laughed. "Okay, Doc."

There was a babble of voices as everybody crowded around and asked how he was doing, what happened, and Doc finally yelled, "Enough dammit! Get the hell outta the way so I can get John to the hospital. Y'all can come visit him in four that is F-O- U- R hours."

Trey, Doc Truesdale and Angelina got the old man over to the ambulance and on the stretcher. Trey and the medic loaded him in, and Doc Truesdale and Angelina got in with him. The ambulance left for the hospital and everyone crowded around Trey, who could only say the old man had made the trip well, and he didn't know anything about what had happened other than what was in the medical records, which he couldn't discuss because of HIPAA.

Trey climbed back on the Lear and left for Dallas, and everybody else adjourned to the Sheriff's Department. Jose broke out more coffee cups and everybody talked about how the old man had looked until the conversation trailed off. Jesse called Matt to let him know the old man was home and told Matt she'd call with an update after she talked to him.

Finally, everyone could stand it no longer, and they piled into their respective cars and descended on the hospital. Angelina met them at the nurses' station and said, "Five minutes and then it's two at a time, okay? And you get ten minutes and the next two can go in."

It was almost comical as the men tried to decide who would get to go in first with Jesse; Billy finally prevailed, being as how he was the lawyer and all. His justification was he had to "warn" his client about all these law enforcement types that were going to try to get him to admit to something.

Jesse and Billy went in as Doc came out, and Billy broke out laughing as he saw the old man lying on his stomach with a tent over his butt.

"Fuck you, Billy. It ain't polite to laugh at the injured," growled the old man.

"Hmmm," Billy said. "I seem to remember you laughing your ass off at me when I got shot at Dak To and you had to feed me because both arms were in casts. So I'm gonna laugh!"

"Papa, are you okay?" Jesse asked.

The old man said, "I'll be fine, and Aaron is okay too."

Jesse stuttered, "Wha... Aaron... How..."

"Well, I ran into him while I was there, and he's doing fine and looking forward to seeing you soon."

Jesse just sat, totally confused. Billy said, "John, seriously be very careful what you say. I don't want to have to bail your ass out again."

The old man tried to roll his shoulders, but just looked over at Billy. "It's all taken care of, Billy. Fibbies are involved, I'm cleared on the shooting I did, and we took down a Chinese smuggling operation that they've missed for two years. Twenty-four million in heroin, some of it headed here to the Zetas, and twenty-two women rescued. Trust me, this one is all good."

Now it was Billy's turn to goggle at the old man. Jesse reached over and grabbed his hand, "Papa, we *are* going to talk."

Angelina came in and said, "Okay you're done, out, out!"

As Jesse and Billy left, she whispered to Jesse, "Stick around." Jesse nodded.

Jose and Bucky came in next, and Bucky said, "John, I got the prelim report from Hearns via my DEA guy there; that info on the heroin routes is going to pay off for us. You done good! And I've shown it to Jose, Clay and Hank Wilson, but I'm not letting any copies out. Glad that Marine that's gonna marry Jesse didn't take one."

"Bucky," the old man said, "you don't know how close he came, and he saved my butt by taking out the Chinese guard that shot me in the ass before he could get something more important. But I'm just hoping my name doesn't get put out there again… dammit"

"John," Jose said. "I'm going to consider this a line-of-duty injury, so we'll cover all the medical expenses and any rehab you need. You take whatever time off you need, okay?"

"Thanks Jose, but I can cover…"

"Stop that shit, John. Just stop it."

Angelina came in and ran them out, and escorted the two Rangers in. Clay deferred to the major, who said, "Damn fine work again John, and I'm truly sorry you took one in the ass, but from what I read, you saved that little boy, so that should count for something."

The old man just nodded, and Clay said, "John, I found it really interesting that these guys are using damn near the same routines we're seeing here. How do you account for that?"

The old man huffed, "Well, whether we like it or not, it *is* a global business. They are passing what works around the world, and you gotta remember, the Chinese are the original smugglers. This Tong out of Hong Kong is tied to LA, Chicago, Panama, Mexico, New York and who the hell knows where else. And they are using legit businesses as cover, which I don't think we've seen here yet, at least not to the levels they do it. And they had some folks pretty high in the Thai Government, Police and Port Authority involved."

Clay said he and Ronni would come by tomorrow, and they left after congratulating the old man again.

Everybody had left when Angelina called Jesse back to the nurses' station, and told her to go back in.

She sat with the old man as he told her about running into Aaron and parts of the story, leaving out how close he'd come to getting shot in the back. He dropped off to sleep and Jesse pulled the sheet up, gently kissed him on the cheek and left the room.

The next morning Francisco, Juanita and Ronni all showed up at 0800, much to a grumbling Doc Truesdale's displeasure. He made them wait until he'd finished rounds, and then told them ten minutes each.

The next morning Jose, Jesse and Clay all showed up and Doc threw up his hands. "Dammit this is not a revolving door; I'm going to kick his ass loose this afternoon so I can get some peace and quiet around here!" Jesse picked the old man up at 1600 and drove him home, helped him into the house and turned his care over to Juanita. Rex, knowing something wasn't right, stayed close by the old man, but never bumped him or jumped up like he normally did. Francisco and Toby kept things running smoothly and Juanita kept him fed and medicated until he was able to get up and around.

36 Winding Down

The old man slowly recovered his strength as he healed, and vowed *never* to get shot in the ass again. He now truly understood the literal meaning of pain in the ass. He was working on his second rubber donut after Rex ate the first one, thinking it was a play toy. And he'd moved to using the laptop standing at the kitchen counter to do his email and ranch business, much to Juanita's displeasure. She complained that he was always underfoot, and drinking way too much coffee, and that he was even grumpier than normal.

Sleep had been an issue for a while, too. Every time he rolled over, he woke himself up. But slowly he got back in the swing of things, and finally one morning looked at Francisco across the breakfast table.

"Francisco, I think we need to go check the cows up in the North 40 and see if we can move some of them off the creek and down one pasture to the south. I didn't like what I saw from the road yesterday, it looks like they're eating the grass all the way down to the roots, and that's not good for spring grasses."

Francisco nodded. "Okay, John, I'll get Toby to saddle up Buttercup for you, can't take any chances with your butt can we?"

Jesse laughed and Juanita coughed to cover her laughter, as Toby said, "Okay Mr. John, Buttercup, she will be ready."

The old man just glared at Francisco and muttered under his breath, but didn't countermand him.

Jesse looked at him. "Papa, be careful, you're not as

young as you used to be, and I'm tired of putting up with your grouchiness. And I need those figures on the fuel for last year, and depreciation on equipment and hardware for taxes, that crap is all due in two weeks."

The old man said, "Okay, fine, I'll be careful, and you'll have all that stuff tonight. And talk about grouch—you're not exactly miss sweetness and light around here either!"

Toby, sensing an argument brewing, bolted saying, "I go get horses ready." And was out the door.

"Alright you two, stop it," Juanita said. "I won't have any of this at the damn breakfast table, and yes, John, you have been a grouchy old asshole the last couple of weeks. Now get the hell out of my kitchen and take your grouch out on the cows."

Meekly, the old man said, "Yes, ma'am."

The old man and Francisco rinsed their dishes and headed out the door, realizing they were in trouble. Rex showed his loyalty following the old man out. Jesse and Juanita said "men" at the exact same time, and both started laughing.

Jesse said, "Juanita, I don't know what in the hell I was thinking with the May wedding, and my having to do taxes both here and at work. I'm so damn frazzled I don't know up from down, and having to put in my forty hours a month of patrol is now burning the candle at both ends and in the middle."

Juanita smiled. "Welcome to growing up, Jesse. It doesn't get any better when you have to deal with a husband in addition to your own life. You have a life too, and it's going to be an adjustment to have to start balancing those things."

"Juanita, why didn't you go back to work?" Jesse asked. "I know you're a certified RN, and I would think you could have made a heck of a lot more that the pittance Papa gives you here."

Juanita said gently, "Jesse there are reasons, those are not for you to know; but I will tell you that I could not ask for better than what we have here. John has done more for us than you will ever know until after we are gone. I will not speak of this again, understood?"

"Yes ma'am," Jesse said. " Well, I guess I better trot my tired ass off to the office. If I get in early maybe, just maybe, I can get some work done before the BS starts."

"Okay," Juanita said. "Just remember Saturday morning we're having another meeting on the wedding and Padre will be here along with your preacher."

Jesse nodded and headed for the door and work.

Juanita decided to bake a blackberry cobbler for dessert as a peace offering for both John and Jesse, and started making a list for a trip to the store.

The old man, Francisco and Toby mounted up and trotted up the trail to the North 40, bantering back and forth and with Francisco trying to teach Toby Spanish. Considering that Toby barely spoke English, and his native tongue was Degar, it was quite a challenge, but Francisco truly liked the little Montagnard and was truly in awe at his ability with the horses.

Toby was up on a horse he called Diablo, blacker than the ace of spades and twice as mean, but in Toby's hands he was as docile as Buttercup. Old man Johannsen had given Diablo to John, because he was afraid the horse would kill somebody, and he just wanted to be rid of him. As far as they could determine Diablo was a cross between a Mustang stallion and a pure bred Arab that bred truer to the Mustang than Arab line.

That reminded the old man he owed Toby another bonus for the last horse he'd broken to halter. He drug out his wheel book and wrote himself a note.

Once they got up to the North 40, they started hazing

cattle out of the bottoms, and true to form the old bell cow trotted to the fore and then moseyed south almost as if she knew what the old man wanted.

They noted three cows and three heifers that were about to calve and decided to drive them on down to the corral at the house to save time and trouble later. The old man thought about all the things that needed to be done and groaned, there were sure as hell going to be some long nights coming.

It seemed like the damn cows just loved to calve in the middle of the night, and they'd either drop every other night or half one night, half the next. He made a mental note to check with the Vet on his availability for the next couple of weeks, and also to call the extension program at the University to come out and record the ear tags, birth dates, sex, markings and tag numbers. He and Francisco discussed whether or not to castrate any bulls and that precipitated the ongoing argument over Dystocia scores and Body Condition Scores.

The old man thought all three of the cows were sevens, and the three heifers were sixes, but as usual Francisco was one number lower. Finally, the old man said, "Okay Francisco, you win, better get out the calf jack and lube that sucker up. And there is a new Dillon dynamometer in the barn, so you might as well test pull and see if it's going to work."

"Already found it," Francisco replied. "I ordered a new case of lube, we were down to one bottle, and that was two years old. I also found some skinning gloves that go to the shoulder, so I ordered a case of them."

The old man nodded. "Francisco I'm just being a pain in the ass, sorry. I guess this last one shook me more than I thought. Between that and Jesse getting married, I'm about as bad as a damn cat in a room full of rocking chairs."

Francisco laughed. "John, I understand. Even though Jesse is not mine, I worry as if she was. We know she is the light of your life, and all of us will do anything to protect her."

They drove the cows and heifers into the corral and the old man stepped gingerly down from the saddle, rubbing his thighs he groaned, "Damn. Now it's the butt *and* the thighs!"

Toby and Francisco both laughed, and Toby took the horses to cool down and put the tack back in the tack room.

Francisco headed for the barn to start prepping for the calving and the old man reluctantly returned to the house. Taking the computer from the kitchen counter, he retreated to the office and sat gingerly on his donut in the rocker.

Rex whined and wanted to be petted, so the old man took a couple of minutes with him, and realized he felt better for it.

He decided he'd had enough of sitting on his ass; and it was time for the pity party to be over. He called the sheriff, telling him to put the old man back on the schedule and he'd be out and about tomorrow.

He also called Bucky and told him if he needed an instructor, he'd be glad to assist starting the following week.

Looking at the time, he buckled down and got all the tax paperwork ready for Jesse. He found everything except for one damn receipt, so he called the company and spent twenty frustrating minutes trying to get a receipt either emailed or faxed.

When he hung up he still didn't know if he was going to get one or not. He finally finished everything and started to sit back when Rex took off like a shot, he looked at the clock again and realized it was almost 6

PM.

The slam of a car door told him Jesse was home and he walked into the kitchen as Rex bounded in ahead of Jesse and he almost ended up in a heap. Grumbling at Rex he said, "Traitor, I walk you, feed you and as soon as she shows up it's like I don't exist."

Rex just cocked his head, and took off down the hall after Jesse.

After everyone sat down for supper, the old man said a prayer, then added, "Okay, y'all are right. I've been an asshole. I'm going back on patrol tomorrow and the pity party is over. Jesse, everything you need is on the desk except one receipt from Morgans, and I don't know if we'll get it or not."

Jesse got up, came around the table and hugged him, "Thanks, Papa, now get out there and kick some ass!" Everybody laughed, and he said, "Jesse, that might have to wait a day or so; but I'll get to it."

After dinner Juanita brought out the blackberry cobbler, and ice cream to everyone's enjoyment, and all was right with the world.

Epilog

The old man was hiding in his office as the house filled with what he'd come to think of as the coven, while they plotted the wedding. Francisco and Toby had deserted him, going over to Ellington's early to help them with some fence repairs, and Juanita had told him he had to stay, "just in case."

Grumpily, he flipped through the TV channels as he worked on emails and the ranch books; he shouldn't have taken the day off, dammit. He had the MT1200 police radio on low in its charger, just keeping an ear out for any action in the county.

Finally, in desperation he called Bucky, "Hey Bucky, John Cronin; hate to bother you but I need to you bail me out."

Bucky said, "What? What the hell have you done now John?"

"Bucky, this damn house is full of women day in and day out planning for this damn wedding, and I swear they've turned into a coven of witches. One of 'em hissed at me a while ago when I went in to get a cup of coffee. You got any training classes coming up you need help with?"

"Matter of fact," Bucky answered, "I'm doing a Laredo class starting tomorrow afternoon, on Bridge four. I could use your expertise, since Charlie is off this weekend."

"Oh, bless you, my son! That will get me out of here early tomorrow, and if I milk it right, I won't have to be back here before Sunday night; two whole days of freedom!"

Bucky laughed. "You want me to officially request you through Jose?"

The old man said, "Yeah, otherwise Jesse will blame me and Juanita will probably call Jose to check. She's acting more like my wife than Francisco's wife lately."

"Well, she did have to step up when Amy died, and she pretty much *is* Jesse's surrogate mama," Bucky said.

"Oh, I know, but damn, it's like they are chaining me to the house, and giving me all kind of crap to do; like I don't have anything else to do or worry about or..."

Suddenly the alert tone sounded on the radio, followed by the dispatcher calling Car 4, which was his call. He gratefully snatched the radio. "Dispatch, car four; go with your traffic."

"Car four, 10-25, 10-43 Car two eleven with a signal seven; first dirt road south of sixty-seven and Old Alpine to the right."

The old man thought for a couple of seconds. "10-4 ETA thirty minutes."

The old man said to Bucky, "Bucky, I gotta run, got a dead body down toward the Brewster County line."

"Okay, lemme know if I need to push somebody that direction." Bucky said and hung up.

The old man flipped his gun belt off the hat rack, put it on, grabbed his hat and radio and headed for the door. As he was walking out, Jesse called, "Papa, where are you going?"

"Got a signal seven down south of ten. Don't know when I'll be back."

Yep, life was getting back to normal, he thought as he put his cowboy hat on and headed out the door grinning.

ABOUT THE AUTHOR

JL Curtis was born in Louisiana in 1951 and was raised in the Ark-La-Tex area. He began his education with guns at age eight with a SAA and a Grandfather that had carried one for 'work'. He began competitive shooting in the 1970s, an interest he still pursues time permitting. He is a retired Naval Flight Officer, having spent 22 years serving his country, an NRA instructor, and currently works as a engineer in the defense industry. He lives in Northern Virginia, this is his first novel.

Made in the USA
San Bernardino, CA
12 March 2014